DEEP PLANT

JACK BETHEL

aBM

Published by:
A Book's Mind
PO Box 272847
Fort Collins, CO 80527

ISBN: 978-1-949563-71-9
Printed in the United States of America

CHAPTER 1

1923
MOSCOW

A glance at the calendar confirmed what he already knew: December 1st—soon an already-late frosty blanket would sweep south to envelop all the Russias. Comrade Felix stopped his thoughts there. "We are not Russia anymore: *The Union of Soviet Socialist Republics.* History will not be kind to the name," he thought. Too ponderous. Too long. One gets lost from the beginning of the name to the end. But then, maybe it is appropriate, given the distance from Saint Petersburg in Europe to Vladivostok on the Pacific. "Eleven time zones—a brute of a country to govern." He shook his head of this thought, "Too easily distracted these days."

It had been a glorious last six years. Vladimir Ilyich Lenin had orchestrated the Bolshevik Revolution, toppling the Tsar and had recently led the new USSR to victory over the counter-revolutionary White Army. He sipped his tea, gazing at the clouds gathering overhead: Mother Nature's velvet fist. The coming snows would seal the country into an icy cocoon, locked away from the world, for another winter. Come the spring thaw in six months, will the nation be any different? Do Russians ever really learn anything during the special time in our snowy strait jacket? Comrade Felix was certain the paralyzing cold was at the heart of the Russian soul. Music, art, and literature all reflected this tortured self-identity. He agreed with what Dostoevsky wrote:

...the most basic, most rudimentary spiritual need of the Russian people is the need for suffering, ever-present and unquenchable, everywhere and in everything.

Exhaling a mouthful of smoke, he sadly shook his head. "Even our great revolution has gone off-track." The promise of Marxism was slowly being subordinated to the realities of consolidating power. An opportunity to alter history's landscape came but once a century, or longer. As the luster and hope of the Revolution faded, the people shrugged their shoulders resignedly, preparing to settle in under a new brand of Tsars. But these were thoughts for another day.

Comrade Felix had just been summoned to Gorki. Since the General Secretary's first stroke in 1922, Vladimir Ilyich had been spending ever-greater amounts of time away from the Kremlin in the comforts of his dacha, which was formerly the Governor General's Palace, but appropriated—seized, in reality—by the Bolsheviks after the Soviets moved the capital to Moscow in 1918. The palace now served Lenin. Other than a small house staff, Lenin had the Palace to himself. Now, virtually entombed in the prison his body had become since his last stroke in April of 1923, he spent most days being attended to by his doctor, the cook, and nurse as he was drinking tea, smoking, and having reports read to him by his chambermaid.

A workaholic like Lenin himself, Felix Dzershinsky had crushed all opposition to the Bolsheviks while laying the foundation for the twentieth century's first world-class secret police organization. *Iron Felix*, as his enemies secretly called him, was at the apex of his power. The leader of the Cheka, he and Lenin had recently reorganized the secret police into the new GPU, State Political Directorate.

But just a year previous, Lenin had been rethinking some of the state security apparatus. In October of 1922, the Civil War had finally been won, the Whites defeated. Power now was firmly in Bolshevik hands. In light of recent health setbacks and sensing his increasingly fragile mortality, Lenin was more open to restraining his secret thug force. While Felix continued to support a strong central role for the GPU, he was prepared to yield before Lenin.

But slowly.

"Maybe the old man will die before he can gut what we've built. The counter-revolutionaries and the West can't be trusted. Someday, we need to be able to strike the Americans before they even see it coming."

* * * *

1958
MOSCOW

Since assuming the leadership of the newly formed Committee for State Security—the KGB—earlier in the year, Ivan Serov had strengthened his position through an adroit balance of suppressing possible successors within the agency while cultivating favor with the ruling elite. Currently, he enjoyed the favor of Comrade Khrushchev.

Unlike his predecessor thirty years before, Ivan Serov had been forced to rise to power through more subtle methods. While Comrade Felix had been successful through sheer dedication, to brutally eliminating all threats to the Central Committee and the Communist Party, Comrade Serov had needed to employ methods that were more cunning. Surviving Stalin's Great Purge of the 1930s, Serov, on orders from Stalin, personally executed two leaders: first Tukhachevsky and then one of his predecessors, Nikolai Yezkhov. Hurting people was both a necessity and an art form for Serov. Working in close proximity to Stalin and his stooge, Lavrentiy Beria, *the Butcher*—as Serov came to be known—claimed to have the ability to "break every bone in a man's body without killing him."

But like his predecessors, the Butcher was equally dedicated—*obsessed* was too strong a word, but only barely—to devising a way to strike at the heart of America, bringing the arrogant, entitled beast to its knees. However, the KGB might at last have the dagger they needed after years of research by Soviet doctors whose expertise was in techniques of thought control and brainwashing. "A stupid term," thought Ivan. Later in the day, he would be reporting his findings to the Politburo; Comrade Khrushchev was certain to make him a Hero of the Soviet Union. This would change the world.

CHAPTER 2

1964
NEW YORK

Elena rolled out of bed with a headache. Her husband, Alexander Foronopov, was an early riser; he was already downstairs making breakfast, which was fine with her. Food preparation—and its attendant focus on style, presentation, and balance—did not appeal to her. Soon, he'd depart for work. In truth, Elena did not enjoy mornings; it reminded her the daily struggle was never too far away. Work and death. The two constants. Family was her only pleasure, and even there she had little control. Someday, they would see how much she'd done for them.

She and Alex had emigrated from the Union of Soviet Socialist Republics in 1937. Quickly, they shed their old-world trappings, assimilating into the surrounding New York bedrock. Alexander shortened his name to Alex and found work at Fordham University as a janitor. Elena had suggested Americanizing *Foronopov* by melding it to *Fordham* and coming up with Ford.

Formerly a government employee in Moscow, she'd applied for numerous government jobs, but with little success. Most agencies, departments, or bureaus saw USSR on her résumé and moved on to the next applicant. Finally, success came when she landed a job as an assistant on the crime desk at the *New York Times*. She had come to love the job, the excitement. Some criminals displayed passion welded to arrogance, while others exhibited desperation born of rejected love. Crime was life. Today, she was the assistant editor on the desk. This afforded her free time out of the office in pursuit of her personal obsession: cold cases.

But this morning, she labored to get going. She'd been working on a new project that had kept her up late into the night. Now she was paying the price. Fortunately, there were no kids left in the house to mind. Because of Alex's position at Fordham, both their boys, John and Michael could attend tuition-free. Their older boy, John, had graduated a year previously and was now working on a graduate degree at Saint John's. The baby, Michael, was still at home, but left early in the morning for classes.

"Myshka, are you ready for breakfast?" Alex called from the kitchen.

Elena rubbed her head. "No," she responded, "just leave it, and I'll eat soon."

"Okay. Will you be by later?"

Entering the kitchen, she grimaced, "Not today."

"Good enough. See you tonight." Alex leaned down to plant a small kiss on his wife's head and then withdrew out the door.

At the screen door, Elena prompted, "Remember, Michael is bringing his girlfriend by."

Alex waved his acknowledgment as he strode down the sidewalk.

CHAPTER 3

1964
NEW YORK

Arriving at his office, just off Columbus Circle, Doctor Maxim Merinov stopped dead in his tracks. Leaning against the door, a newspaper. *The signal.* He knelt as if retying a misbehaving shoelace and subtly looked about. Satisfied he was unobserved, he stood, gathered his *New York Post* newspaper leaning against the door, and entered the Center for Right Being. In his office, he lifted the phone to dial a number. After a single ring, he hung up. Raising his hand, he counted as the second hand on his Universal Genève Vintage Medico Compax precisely ticked thirty times. Redialing the previous number, he let it ring twice before hanging up.

Sitting, he opened his appointment book. Noting a morning meeting at eleven, he picked up the phone once more. He dialed.

"Anderson residence. May I help you?" a voice said.

"Mrs. Anderson? It's Doctor Merinov."

"Doctor, how are you—oh you're not calling to cancel are you?"

"Dreadfully sorry, Mrs. Anderson, but something has come up and I must reschedule. Please do not be too upset with me."

"Oh Doctor, never. When would be good for you?"

Merinov flipped pages in his organizer. "Would next Tuesday be good? Same time?"

He heard the sound of shoes walking across a floor and pages turning, "That would be fine, Doctor."

Merinov added a dash of oil to his voice. "Most excellent, Mrs. Anderson, and again, sorry for the inconvenience."

"Next Tuesday then. Have a good day, Doctor."

Replacing the receiver, Merinov stepped to a filing cabinet and collected files for the remaining patients he would see that day.

CHAPTER 4

1964
NEW YORK

Coming out of the subway station at Forty-Second and Bryant Park, Elena guardedly examined a signpost while casually surveying the vicinity. Strolling into Bryant Park, she paused to reach into her purse. Taking out a pack of Pall Malls, she lit one and again scanned her surroundings. Coming to a statue, she stopped, feigning interest in it. Once more, she took inventory of the landscape. A couple of puffs, she dropped the butt and entered the adjacent New York Public Library. She paused at the reference desk, taking a small pencil and a scrap of paper before stepping into the crime section. Down the rows she went, stopping at a section on police history. Selecting a book entitled *Police Methods of the 1800s*, she skimmed its contents—stopping at page 120. Removing the paper and pencil from her bag, she scrawled the tiny letters FH in the center of the page. Replacing the book, she printed the number 120 onto the scrap of paper, before putting it back into her satchel.

Making her way to fiction, she found the book she was looking for on the bottom shelf. Drawing something from her coat pocket, she knelt as if reaching for the book. But instead, she took the item from her hand and wedged it into a small, unseen crevice on the shelf right above the book she pretended to be examining. Standing, she brushed her fingers over a couple of titles before leaving.

Outside, she once more lit a cigarette, coldly ignoring a man's outstretched lighter, courteously proffered to her. After a moment, she started away. At the base of the library steps, she dropped the balled-up scrap of paper into a wastebasket and withdrew back into the streets.

A few minutes later, Doctor Merinov, newspaper in hand, strolled to the library steps. At the basket, he stopped to separate the paper. He dropped two sections into the container before feigning interest in a discarded piece. Reaching into the garbage can, he recovered the desired section and the balled-up scrap, hiding it in the paper. Casually, he continued up the steps into the library.

Inside, he made his way to a reading cubicle. A last check of the immediate area assured him he was alone and he separated the balled scrap from the folds of the newspaper. Reading the number, he put the note into his pocket and continued examining the periodical. After a few minutes, he stood and deliberately stretched while gazing about. Tossing the paper into the refuse bin, he started toward the library's crime section. He perused the titles before lifting *Police Methods of the 1800s* off the shelf.

After another glance, he opened the book to page 120. Reviewing the page, his eyes came to rest on the letters FH. He replaced the book and headed for the fiction shelves. Searching the titles, he came one entitled *Fallen Heroes*. Kneeling, Doctor Merinov also bypassed the actual book to probe the recesses in the shelf above it. His fingers found pay dirt and he drew out the tissue-wrapped item, putting it into his pocket without looking at it. Once outside, the medical man summoned a cab.

"Where to bub?" the cabbie asked.

"Penn Station."

From the cab, Doctor Merinov entered the terminal and headed into the nearest men's room. In a stall, he reached into his pocket, fishing out the item recovered at the library. Unwrapping it revealed a locker key. Noting the number, he replaced the key, stepped out, washed his hands, and departed. Going to a row of bins, he glanced about before shuffling to number 668. Opening the locker, he took out a folder. Without examining it, he strolled quickly away.

Back at the office, he brought the folder to his desk. He studied it for a moment before flipping it open and commencing reading.

Before leaving that night, he took a potted plant off a table in his lobby and put it near the front door.

CHAPTER 5

1964
NEW YORK

At her desk, Elena unlocked a drawer and removed a file labeled OPEN INVESTIGATIONS. In it were numerous sheets, each detailed NYPD crimes—mostly murders—that were no longer being actively worked. Often, a case became *cold* after the initial police investigation had failed to produce a suspect, motive, witness, or generally could not give the district attorney's office enough *best evidence* to proceed to trial. The file moved into the hands of a group of investigating officers who would continue to probe the most promising initial leads. But, often as not, the files remained open for years.

Since coming to the *Times*, Elena had scored a number of triumphs in resolving open cases. Her most successful had been the Zacharias double murder. Entertainment lawyer Benjamin Zacharias, and his wife Mitzi, lived an over-the-top life: apartment in the city, house on Long Island. From the outside looking in, they enjoyed a Promethean lifestyle: parties worthy of Mount Olympus, magazine-cover nightlife, summers in Maine, and winters in the Bahamas. But Mitzi, who was already famed for her spending, wanted more.

She discreetly began an affair with her husband's partner, Roman Hansen. Together, the two of them planned the murder of her husband. On the killing night, however, plans changed. When Roman killed Benjamin, Mitzi used the same gun to shoot Roman. As police arrived, they'd found a distraught wife holding her dead husband in the library of the Zachariases's Long Island home.

Her story to authorities said she'd come home from her social club to find Roman had murdered her husband. The reason was insurance. It would have been paid out to Roman—who would have in turn paid Mitzi for Benjamin's half of their lucrative business practice, which was expected to grow over the next few years.

Mitzi freely admitted she was having an affair with Roman, but claimed to know nothing about his plan to murder her husband. When she'd come home to find Benjamin bleeding on the floor—with Roman calmly drinking a glass of Scotch, Mitzi had "gone crazy," picking up the gun from the desk and shooting Roman.

While the case seemed closed, something about the pictures of Mitzi in the paper bugged Elena. Later, over dinner, she told Alex the grieving widow looked *too pleased* about something—as if cheating on a test without being caught. While interviewing one of the investigating officers, Elena learned that Roman belonged to a Connecticut gun club, which only buttressed the police argument that Roman had been planning Benjamin's murder. At the time, it seemed like lazy police work.

One day, Elena visited the club Roman was touted as having belonged to: The Long Island Rainbow Fish and Hunt Club. The manager was no help whatsoever, but the range master remembered seeing Roman at the club on numerous occasions. "Case closed," she first thought, but, as she packed her things to leave, he added that Roman couldn't hit the side of a barn with a gun even if he was standing right in front of it. Seems Roman spent most of his time in the club lounge with a woman while his son Porter was on the range for hours at a time. Squinting, Elena brusquely thanked the man and left.

Elena got the *Times* to spring for a private investigator to follow Mitzi. Initially, nothing turned up and her editors crowed that she'd really been mistaken about the case. Grudgingly conceding, Elena happened to read in the society column that Mitzi was going on an extended stay at the family compound in Maine. Playing a hunch, Elena slogged up to Winter Harbor on the coast of Maine to keep tabs on the grieving widow. Within the week, she bagged her biggest trophy.

It was with grim satisfaction that she'd walked into her boss's office and dropped an envelope on his desk. Opening it, he was stunned to find pictures of Mitzi and Porter, half-naked, kissing by the pool overlooking the Atlantic Ocean below. It appeared—while in the middle of her affair with Roman—Mitzi had taken a shining to his son and added Porter to her stable. It did not take long before both were in jail, claiming the other had masterminded the double murders and the DA had had little trouble securing convictions, sending both Mitzi and Porter to the electric chair.

After this, it had become easier to justify the time, energy, and resources to pursue things she perceived had both a human and newsworthy angle to them. It was satisfying work; there was nothing more exhilarating than resolving a supposedly unsolvable case. It did not happen often, but when she finally cracked a case and presented her findings to law enforcement, Elena would derive an extraordinary rush of righteousness.

It was odd, but bringing a coward—who probably thought they'd gotten away with a perfect crime—to justice appealed to her sense of equality. Elena Ford had developed a small, but loyal group of devotees at the NYPD. Each November, they'd take up a collection to purchase a turkey and all the fixings, a pumpkin pie, and a bottle of Scotch; then they would deliver it to the Ford home on the Monday of Thanksgiving week.

But this work also tied in with Elena's perception of history and destiny. Throughout time, the strong were always taking advantage of the weak or small. Those who could not defend themselves. Someday, through work like hers, the world would be a much better place.

CHAPTER 6

1964
NEW YORK

Elena found it ironic to step off the ferry into the shadow of the Statue of Liberty. "Someday," she thought, "it will be a genuine emblem of freedom." In dark sunglasses and head bonnet, she wore a coat to ward off New York Harbor's biting wind. Stopping to consult a guidebook, she made her way around the base coming to a stop where she could view the entire island unfettered. Taking a Kodak Brownie from her handbag, she snapped pictures.

After a moment, a man stepped up gesturing first to the statue and then to her, Elena nodded. He took the camera and stepped back to aim. While looking through the viewfinder, he scanned the surroundings. Finished, he handed Elena the Brownie.

"We're clear," Doctor Merinov said. Nodding good-naturedly, he started away when Elena stopped him.

Opening her tourist guide, she pointed to a random page. Merinov played along. Graciously, he took the book and pointed in the general direction of downtown, across the water, and occasionally nodded his head.

"I got the file. This is genuinely amazing stuff. Does the Center have an estimate of when we'll have access to the technology?" the stranger asked while pretending to laugh.

Elena played along with the acting. "Unknown."

"Do I need to come in for a briefing? I'm not due to visit home for another four months."

"Not yet. I'll keep you posted."

Without waiting for a reply, Elena took the book and walked away. This new project would transform the balance of power between the USSR and America. Tersely, she glanced up at the silent statue. “Soon.”

CHAPTER 7

1964
NEW YORK

At home, Elena prepared pierogi for dinner. Tonight her son Michael, who was a junior at Fordham, would be bringing his girlfriend for dinner. Their older son, John, had graduated the previous year and was now in law school at the City College of New York. Always more driven, John would not only find a great, high-paying job, but the right girl to decorate that life. It had not been the same for Elena. Work had always held more interest than Alex, who was very loving but dim.

Michael moved slower, taking more notice of people, things, and events. In many ways, he was like his father. No drama, no spark. Steady. But, he'd always admired Elena's work and it did not surprise Elena, when two years later—after graduating college—Michael would go into law enforcement.

His choice in girls was likewise determined. Sophia. She was not Russkaya, but in America, everyone married whomever. Hardly a great beauty, Sophia was nonetheless attractive; she was blessed with a warm, genuinely caring attitude. She and Michael had met the previous spring at a football game and they'd become inseparable. Of course, Alex liked the young lady, but Elena would have preferred Michael wait to get serious about a girl.

At the table, Michael and Sophia were discussing the coming presidential election between President Lyndon B. Johnson and his Republican challenger, Senator Barry Goldwater.

"Michael, Johnson is not up to the challenge of the Soviets. They own half of Europe, the Chinese are starting to flex their muscles in

Vietnam, and Castro is tightening his grip on Cuba. Goldwater will stand up to those bastards," Elena said as she passed the butter.

"But mom, LBJ can continue some of Kennedy's policies," her son replied.

"Michael, I think your mom is right about LBJ's foreign policy. I'm not sure he knows what he's doing," Sophia quietly added, pushing her peas around the plate.

Michael looked between his mom and Sophia before looking at his father, who smiled sheepishly, indicating he was on his own in this one. "A-Bomb Barry is not the right guy for the White House, I mean—"

"Don't use that language in my home," Elena said. "He's a United States Senator and you will treat him with respect. Is that clear?"

Later, washing the dishes in the kitchen, Michael took a wet dish from Sophia. "You know your parents love this country; they just want the best for it and you and John," Sophia said as she stacked the dry plate.

"I know. It's just that she is a bit ... extreme sometimes. I can't always figure her out. And Dad—well he's always deferred to Mom."

Michael shut the water off and turned to hug Sophia. "I'm glad I met you. Thanks for a great dinner."

"Your mother made everything."

"Yes, but the best part was having you here. Thanks."

CHAPTER 8

1969
NEW YORK

Michael exited the car coming to the passenger side as the front door to his parent's home flew open. Elena poured down the steps of a charming brownstone to help Sophia. Michael moved to the trunk and commenced unloading a warehouse of supplies. Recognizing his grandmother, the baby in Sophia's arms broke into a broad smile. Elena took the child, lifting him up in joy.

"*Nicholas Ford*...sounds like a senator, yes?" his grandmother gushed.

Alex and John Ford descended to help Michael.

"Mom has Nic's future already lined out," John smirked.

"Just like yours?"

"Doubt it. I think she's still mad I didn't become a lawyer." John mimicked their mother, "John, tell me again what an MBA is. I never heard of this before I came to America. They teach you how to be in business—I tell you how to be in business. Charge a lot of money and make your workers stay late on Christmas Eve. What do you need an MBA for?"

The brothers shared a communal laugh as they watched Elena, Sophia, and baby going up the steps into the house.

"Probably too late for your son; Mom's got him in her clutches now," John added. They started lugging things up the walkway. "So you're a full officer now—off probation?"

"That was a year ago," Michael grunted.

"Sorry. What a' they got you doing?"

"Routine stuff. Patrol. Walking a beat. Meeting the neighbors. I'm over in Brooklyn—Sheepshead, Brighton actually. More crime than downtown, but also just getting used to police routine more than anything. So what about you—Mom *was* a little upset when you left law school."

"Interning at Goldman. I love the hum of the exchanges, the rhythm of commerce, business, moving numbers around. Mom would never understand."

"Rhythm of commerce—sounds like a rock group." Michael shook his head slowly. "What about girls, dating anyone? You know Mom will corner me later, 'Why isn't your brother finding a nice girl?' Anyone I should know about? You know I'm a cop; I can find stuff out."

John laughed. "Mom's a better investigator than you are and she's found out nothing." The hurt look on his little brother's face made him put up his hands. "Just kidding. There is someone. Westchester—her family is from Westchester."

"Ooohhh," Michael drew out his response to emphasize the address. "Mister Big Shot now. Have they had you out to the country club for brunch and a round yet?" Michael joked good-naturedly.

"No not ... what are you talking about? We don't even play golf," John fired back.

Michael disappeared through the front door, calling back, "Not yet."

CHAPTER 9

1969
NEW YORK

At his desk, Merinov tried to make sense of the research treatise he was reading. It was after ten at night, normally his best time to work, but tonight the paper's techno-jargon was gibberish to his foggy brain. This one was probably a dry hole like all the others he'd read. Thinking back over past research, his mind drifted. He put the document down and closed his eyes for a moment.

* * * *

Born in Moscow in 1920, Merinov's family had left Russia for Switzerland when he was five. His parents had not approved of the anti-intellectual boorishness of the Bolsheviks. It affronted their appreciation and respect for order. His father and mother were both accountants and quickly found employment within the quiet fabric of Swiss banking. Reared within the meticulous detail of Alpine culture, Merinov had developed a penchant for both knowledge and secrecy.

He'd come to America in 1950 to pursue post-graduate studies at the University of Indiana. After a masters, Merinov made his way to the big time at Columbia where he received his doctorate. It was also at this time that Merinov, like an unsuspecting bug, had fallen into the KGB's spiderweb. Being homosexual, even in a progressive city like New York, still required a degree of circumspection. One night at a club, he'd let his guard down and gone home with a stranger. Days later, a woman came to his office. Coldly, she placed an envelope on his desk and waited for him to open it. Certain it contained a snake or something equivalent, he slowly picked it up. The woman never took her eyes from him as he pulled out pictures of him with the man he'd met at the club.

"Doctor Merinov, you are doing great work. Your doctoral thesis on hypnosis and thought suggestion was very intriguing. We'd like to help you further your studies," the woman said, her Russian accent almost undetectable.

"Then why threaten me with these?" Merinov said, tossing the photos across the desk.

"Threaten? Oh Doctor, you're too dramatic. We aim to *protect* you."

His options seemed limited. While there was growing acceptance of homosexuals in America, Merinov was uncertain he'd survive a review of his visa if his orientation became public. In addition, there was the equally troubling consideration of how his parents would react when they found out. Finally, and probably the most important—he did not want to lose his practice; he wanted to stay in New York, which was by far the most exciting place he'd ever lived.

Then there was the research. In the prime of his career, Merinov was gaining recognition in the field of hypnosis and its impact on addiction, behavior modification, and thought control. Someday someone would discover a way to actually implant a thought into someone's mind—and like one's own DNA, it would become part of the person's personality. Total mind control. Research was taking place everywhere and he was discouraged now he'd miss out on the great breakthrough that would ultimately secure someone the Nobel Prize.

Regretfully, he'd gone to work for the KGB ... mostly as a freelancer. His role fell to things like interviewing other potential spies to see if they were hiding anything or interviewing Soviet diplomats assigned to the United Nations to determine if they were considering defecting.

Slowly and casually, his handler—the woman running him—began using him to experiment with people employed by the US government and already working for the Soviets. The goal of these experiments was to influence, persuade, or condition them to seek out and steal highly classified material, beyond what they were currently providing, but would require above-average risk of being exposed.

* * * *

Merinov opened his eyes, returning his attention to the article. It was a paper from East Germany about the advances in hypnosis and thought suggestion. Experiments conducted by the Nazis in World War II, which were continued by the Office of Strategic Services—the OSS, which was the forerunner of the CIA—indicated a combination of electroshock therapy combined with drugs like LSD, mescaline, and peyote had produced a surprising array of outcomes.

Certain test subjects had been conditioned to take up smoking, where prior to the experiment, they'd never touched a cigarette. Others who'd never tasted foods like liver and onions, haggis or octopus, had been brainwashed into a love for these extreme dishes. A number of female subjects had been induced to have sex with total strangers, without hesitation. Still more had been convinced they needed to rise at a certain time each day. But it was a small group of subjects, three really, who'd shown a willingness to hurt someone—in reality someone in a picture—but none of these experiments were ever carried out.

The report's summary indicated that ultimately, none of the research subjects had permanently retained the implanted thoughts or behaviors. Merinov understood this, but he was trying to wade into the technical part of the report to see if there were reasons or forgotten clues he could use. For years, he'd been researching the holy grail of psychology. Could he actually *brainwash*—a term he deplored—a human being to do something totally foreign to their personality, temperament, ethics, or deepest-held beliefs? Could a person cause another human to do something they would not normally be expected to do? Could that mean the individual human could be controlled?

During the Korean War, the Chinese attempted a number of times to alter the thoughts or actions of American POWs. They tried a multitude of techniques to form compliance, persuasion, and re-education. Ultimately, the Chinese were able to brainwash some twenty-one American servicemen, most of whom did nothing more than refuse to come back to the US after the war. Out of the thousands of American prisoners held worldwide by communist countries, one could argue that brainwashing was not very effective.

The CIA also tried. After World War II, the newly created CIA experimented with mind control. Operation Bluebird. Then Chatter. Artichoke. MKDELTA. MKULTRA—all projects utilizing drugs, hypnosis, electroshock, and other things in attempts to get a subject to follow instructions or carry out a certain activity. Besides the Americans and Chinese, certainly the Soviets, the North Koreans, Vietnamese, Cubans, British, and probably the Israelis, were working to crack the code.

The new training and conditioning techniques Doctor Merinov learned from the KGB were both awkward and promising. They might be able to program people, but they came with some side effects that disturbed him. Anger. Nightmares. Headaches. Merinov had hoped the KGB would have worked up some improvements, but he was still waiting.

Over the years, Merinov's focus had shifted from coercive methods to more cooperative. What could make someone more conducive to a foreign thought or behavior without employing the harshness of drugs or shock? Could someone's brain be altered to be more receptive to an alien thought? Of all places, there was new work from the great American advertising machine crosstown on Madison Avenue; they were using subliminal messaging that was showing promise. He'd also been hearing rumors out of the USSR about light therapies that sounded like science fiction. But ultimately, Merinov thought a potential subject not only needed the implanted thought or action-to-be-accomplished, but also would need an overwhelming amount of trust in the person conditioning them.

Slowly, he put the paper down, turning to stare out the window of his office into the emotionless night.

CHAPTER 10

1969
NEW YORK

"Merinov," Elena coldly said, displeased to even have to speak with a man she considered spineless, while continuing to stare at the Statue of Liberty.

While he knew she could see him coming, it still unsettled him when she addressed him without looking at him. "Elena."

"How is the training coming?" Elena asked, her head buried again in a guidebook.

Gesturing to the Statue of Liberty, Merinov replied, "Interesting choice of words." But Elena's stern glance made clear she'd little interest in his opinions. "Good, a bit challenging, especially with some of the advancements they've made, but I'm getting comfortable with it."

They stood awkwardly for a moment before Elena probed. "Why the meeting?"

Rubbing his hands nervously, he finally said, "Look, I think what we are doing could change the world, but should we be doing something like this? I mean this is—"

"You're paid very well to do what you're told; am I not correct?"

"Yes, but still it's ..."

It took everything she had not to slap the man in the face to strengthen his resolve. "It's what we do. Now, get a hold of yourself." She waited for him to gather himself. "How are the current batch of subjects?"

"Struggling."

Elena looked in her guidebook. After a long silence, she squinted at the New York skyline. "Why?"

"Same as last time."

Elena examined her gloved hands gripping the book as she thought, "Stiff and cold these days. I'm getting too old for this." Then she spoke aloud, "You said the advancements—"

Merinov interjected, "I know. They're getting better. But the human mind can't be forced or manipulated to do things against its own inherent, or learned, ethical hierarchy."

"What does this mean?"

Sensing he was moving to a stronger position, the doctor said, "People, even criminals, have a learned moral code. Good and bad. Transcendent and evil. Right and wrong. What we're trying to do is rewrite ... actually *override* the code. Making progress, but it's like two steps forward, one-and-a-half back." He paused, lost in some distant constellation.

Elena detected something. "What?"

Realizing his face had flushed him into the open, he shook his head, the thought too dreadful to voice.

Elena squinted, menace lurking in the soft features of her face.

"Okay," he hesitated, certain his next words would damn his soul. "What if you started with a baby?"

It took a moment. Then Elena smiled. "Of course—it's so simple." She put a hand on the stranger's arm as if meeting him for the first time. "How soon can the therapy be reconfigured?"

Ashen, the man lurched back, "Are you insane? What kind of person would ask this?"

A dismissive chill descended as Elena shoved her tourist guide into her purse. "Make the necessary adjustments. I'll contact the Center for new direction and candidates." Starting for the ferry, she paused, her laser-beam glare reducing the man to rubble. "And don't contact me again unless it's an emergency. Are we clear?" She did not tarry for an answer.

CHAPTER 11

1969
NEW YORK

At his front door, Alex paused to identify the sounds coming from inside his house. Normally, he could distinguish voices, but he noticed as he was getting into his fifties, he was struggling to hear the full audio spectrum. This had led to him increasing the TV volume to levels Elena could not tolerate. But today, he thought the sounds were almost ... *muffled*. Inserting his key into the lock, he opened the door to find Elena and another woman seated in the living room. Both women looked up, startled.

"I'm not stumbling into a Comintern meeting am I?" Alex joked.

With what Alex could only identify as a look of relief, Elena stood. "Don't be absurd, honey. Galina and I were just making plans."

"Plans?"

"For Sara—you remember."

Alex scowled. "I thought her birthday was last month," he noted.

"It was. We're just planning on what she's wearing to the dance next week," Elena replied.

* * * *

The Dements, Galina and her husband Fyodor, had left Russia for London in 1950, coming to America in 1952. Since then, they had been regular parts of the Ford household.

Their daughter, Sara, had arrived in 1955—and while there was an age gap between her and the Ford boys, they still thought of her, if not like a sister, then a cousin. Galina had instilled in her daughter a deep love of culture, especially Russian, as well as impeccable manners and respect for her elders.

* * * *

Bewildered by how women invested so much into social events, Alex just smiled as he passed through into the kitchen. Just before bedtime, as he was taking the trash out, he reflected: "Elena normally hates any reference to the Party—even in joking. And she *never* calls me honey ... " But after a pause, he shrugged, wanting to get back into the warmth of their house.

CHAPTER 12

1972
NEW YORK

It was a nice, crisp afternoon, typical of a New York autumn. Not yet cold but pleasant. On the back patio of Elena and Alex's home, Michael, Sophia, and John reclined comfortably on cushioned lawn chairs as Nicholas scatted about.

"Watch the baby while I go use the powder room, okay honey?" Sophia said to Michael.

But the child had a mind of his own and off he went after the cat as Michael and John watched, amused.

Michael took a sip of his beer. "So how is married life?"

"Fabulous. Danielle is a dream, man."

"Cool."

John looked sideways at his little brother. "It always sounds weird hearing you try to use street talk, man."

Gesturing to himself in mock indignation, Michael shot back, "Me? How about you ... *maaan*. Big trader at the New York Stock Exchange and all?"

Exiting the house with a tray of cold cuts, Elena snipped at them. "You boys be nice. Stop talking garbage. Your son and nephew are watching." Both men turned to look at Nicholas who was eying the cat atop the backyard wall. After a moment, the tabby decided it had had enough toddler time for the day and disappeared over the wall, leaving Nicholas alone. Suddenly the three-year-old plopped down in a snit, beginning to cry. Michael and John turned back to Elena who huffily disappeared back into the kitchen.

"So, has Mom started in on you guys yet?"

John replied, "Sort of ... a little maybe, but D and I—we want to travel a little, have some fun. You know? When you and Sophia decided to have Nic, I mean, you were ready, right?"

"Yeah," Michael nodded gently. "We were. Mom pushed, but we knew what we wanted."

"Exactly. So I think we're gonna ... we'll see when the time is right."

"You mean when Mom thinks it's right?" Michael jokingly said.

"Ha ha. So, what are you doing these days? Patrol still?"

"Yeah, which is okay with me, I like the field. Can still help people better face to face than sitting in a prowl car, you know?"

Nodding thoughtfully, John asked, "Where now?" Michael eyed his brother. John put his hands up defensively. "Okay, you told me, but I forgot. Brooklyn right?"

"Mostly, but spending more time down at Brighton lately."

Eyebrows raised, John mused, "Huh. Wouldn't think much crime there."

"Not yet. But—and Mom would find this amusing—used to be older Russkaya, but now there's an uptick of Ukrainians, Kazaks, Uzbeks, and other mid-Asian settling there. So far, it's quiet. Still, I imagine they'll be stepping on each other's toes soon enough."

Thoughtfully, John nodded but said nothing.

Danielle poked her head out the screen door, "Lunch boys." Both men stood to head into the house, "—and don't forget Nicholas."

Sheepishly, they turned to find the tot asleep on his side.

As they retrieved the child, John quietly said, "Just be careful, okay?"

CHAPTER 13

1972
MOSCOW

Like most people she knew, Elena was reluctant to visit hospitals. The rooms were overcrowded by depression, disease, and regret—while death lurked just beyond the doorway. Anyone other than him, she would not have made the trip. She was directed to a room, but the patient was away receiving treatment. Finding a seat in the lobby, Elena rubbed her tired eyes before drifting off.

* * * *

In 1934, as the Revolution was consolidating under Stalin, twenty-two-year-old Elena had been sent by a teacher from the Heroes of the Red Order school for a job interview. Her instructor, Dama Sirova Kurakin, held Elena in high regard. The instructor knew a man at a government agency who was looking for an administrative assistant—the term *secretary* being decidedly too bourgeois and un-proletarian. It was an innocuous position—routine matters: typing, maintaining the calendar, and filing.

The teacher, however, was also familiar with the agency's less-public structure, and was sure Elena would be a good fit. She was an excellent student; Kurakin also perceived in the younger woman a steely resolve to do ... *whatever* needed to be done to get ahead. Kurakin had firsthand knowledge of the job requirements.

After Lenin's death, there had been a power vacuum atop the Soviet leadership. For a while, a troika—comprising Joseph Stalin, Lev Kamenev, and Grigory Zinoviev—had attempted to guide the ship of state. This only proved to be an obstruction to Stalin, whose ultimate goal was complete control of the country. Slowly and ruthlessly, he eliminated his co-leaders, as well as his competitors, for Lenin's legacy. A thug at heart, Stalin's best, and only, tool was the often-changing secret police.

Before his death, Lenin had reformulated the Cheka into the GPU, State Political Directorate, then into the OGPU, Joint State Political Directorate and most recently into the NKVD, People's Commissariat for Internal Affairs.

Prior to her teaching duties, Kurakin worked at GPU as a field agent. Her boss had been a man who answered to Felix Dzerzhinsky himself. Born to privilege in Saint Petersburg in 1892, Valentin Orlov was descended from a wealthy shipping family that traced their lineage to the earliest days of the old boyars who'd ruled Muscovy before the rise of the Tsars. It was surprising when a young Orlov, early on, embraced Marxism and the Bolsheviks. A quick student of human nature, he recognized Lenin's ascendant star.

The rising leader likewise saw something in young Orlov and commended him to his new director of state security, Dzerzhinsky. A good administrator, Orlov rapidly proved to be even better at something not taught in any school: *terror*. The Cheka, the ruthless Felix had built, needed people capable of discharging the most odious of tasks, including torture, rape, and murder. Orlov excelled at directing his agents to infiltrate opposition groups, hunt down subversives, betray confidential sources, and when necessary, execute enemies of the people.

On a trip to Archangel, Valentin had chanced upon a remarkable find. Sirova Kurakin, a secondary school teacher of all things, had been assigned by the local soviet council to guide Orlov as he commenced a roundup of authorities known to be sympathetic to the Whites—who were in a fierce civil war with the Reds for control of the country. Orlov had rapidly been impressed with the young educator. It was not her local knowledge or intelligence, but her ruthlessness. Coldly, she'd directed Orlov to the homes of Orthodox priests, a hospital administrator, the police chief, and even the head of her own school. Most were never heard from again.

Later, as they lay in bed together, he'd asked what made her inform on so many of her fellow citizens.

"Revenge," came the chilling, monotone response.

Blood vendettas would provide more service to the Revolution than even that of dedication to the cause of the Proletariat. Kurakin followed Orlov to Moscow where she continued her labors for the Cheka. But in time, she'd exacted as much blood from old enemies as she could while the new ones offered no personal satisfaction. She eventually left the secret police, and Orlov, returning to education in the Moscow suburbs.

But she and Orlov had maintained civil relations and occasionally dined together.

"This one is excellent," she'd said as he refilled her glass with vodka. "Just don't try to sleep with her, okay?"

Feigned hurt colored Valentin's response. "Sirova, why would you say that?"

"Because you and I both know that your last two assistants got their jobs for their willingness to compromise their morals in the name of the Revolution, *da*?"

Valentin sniffed.

It was what Kurakin suspected, but never personally witnessed, that got Elena the job. "Elena is not some plaything. Respect her and she will serve you well."

And she had. Newly married, Elena Foronopov had not allowed Orlov or the Revolution to seduce her. But where Sirova Kurakin had tired of the blood, Elena had been willing to go farther than her predecessor. Orlov marveled at his protégé's compartmentalization. After breakfast with her husband, Elena had arrived at GPU headquarters where, in icy calm, she observed forced confessions and torture. She even accompanied Orlov on trains carrying prisoners to forced internal exile in Siberia.

She seemed impervious to the pain of others, and yet she always stopped—wherever they were—to feed feral cats. Over the years, on the instances Valentin had dined at the Foronopov home, he'd been borderline astonished to observe his assistant carrying out domestic tasks, never offering a hint of what she did for a living. Orlov was almost afraid to see how Elena kept her house and husband in perfect order. It was with little hesitation, when there came an overseas opening in the Soviet intelligence directorate, Valentin knew whom to turn to.

In New York, the NKVD had an extensive network of operatives. The NKVD station chief, or rezidentura, was a garrulously loud man. Employed as a back-set designer for a number of New York theater companies, Kristoff Chernenko enjoyed blocks of downtime between shows for espionage. For years, he'd been good at running operatives at government agencies, manufacturers, and colleges. Information had flowed back to Moscow.

But he was also a man with a big lifestyle. He liked being on the town. Assimilating into a western lifestyle, as part of his cover, had eroded his focus. Exacerbating things were his increasing, long bouts of drinking. Field activity required good organizational skills, married to discipline—both of which Kristoff struggled with.

He started getting sloppy. Kristoff became aware that one of his sources was under FBI surveillance. While not a complete deterrent to running an op, it did require more caution and planning when setting up and carrying out exchanges. Chernenko did neither and it blew up in his face.

The surveilled agent was a research chemist for a munitions company in New Jersey that was developing a new secret bomb for the army. When he had new information for the Soviets, he'd call a number and ask for Mr. Green. The person answering would tell the caller, "Very sorry, but you have the wrong number." The person taking the call then alerted Chernenko, who'd put his operatives into motion.

The dead drop was a particular bench in Central Park. Information would often be secreted in a tiny metal cylinder. At the designated bench, the spy, after a thorough scan of the area, would take the small metallic vial and wedge it into a fissure on the underside of the wooden seat. Soon after this, the spy would depart. After some time, another person—a woman pushing a stroller—would approach the bench.

Sitting down to take a "breather," she would reach into the stroller, affecting as if tending to a baby. Removing a blanket, she'd lay it on the bench next to her. While gently rocking the buggy back and forth, she'd slide her free hand beneath the blanket and retrieve the stashed container. Eventually, she'd put the blanket, with cylinder wrapped inside, into the buggy; she would then stand and depart. The woman was a *cutout*. She neither knew the informant nor Chernenko, and if caught, could plausibly deny whom she was employed by ... she was just paid to pick up a parcel. At home, she'd package the cylinder and mail it to a PO box where another cutout would retrieve it. Finally, the second cutout would stash the canister on the underside of a pay phone in Times Square where Chernenko would recover it.

Unknown to Chernenko, the woman—curious after a recent drop—had mailed the capsule as normal, but the next day had camped out at the post office to see who came to the PO box. On this day, the second cutout was out of town on a family matter. Chernenko impatiently opted to compromise the normal protocol ... one designed to protect everyone in the chain ... and pick up the package himself. After observing Chernenko arrive at the post office, open the PO box, and take the pouch, the woman followed him back to the theater district where he entered an alleyway near the Saint James Theater. She'd seen Chernenko's distinctive moustache and *puffy* haircut.

A short time later, the FBI sprung its trap. Chernenko's New Jersey operative made his normal deposit, but when the female cutout came to the bench with her buggy, something seemed off to her. Initially, she reached for the cylinder, but suddenly thought better of it and sought to re-insert it into its hiding place. She stood to depart when suddenly waves of suited men burst from the surrounding bushes. The woman halfheartedly challenged the G-men.

"What did I do? I'm just sitting here!" she barked.

"Ma'am you're under arrest for—"

"For what—I've done nothing ... " but angrily shaking her head, she clammed up.

After a thorough pat down and search of the pram, the inspecting agent turned to the agent in charge, "Nothing."

Just then, a soft *thud* came from under the bench. Stooping, the agent in charge stood, a sinister smile on his face. The spy's eyes widened in shock as the man opened his gloved hand, revealing a tiny gunmetal cylinder. "For treason against the United States of America."

Initially reticent, the Soviet agent opened up about her seemingly harmless part in the dead-drop chain. But hard men, trained to recognize even a whiff of fear, sensed she was holding back. A couple of days in a dark room, with no sunlight, and little sleep, food, or water changed her perspective. Soon the FBI was in Midtown Manhattan looking for a puffy-haired man with a distinct moustache.

By its nature, a blown drop results in data, an operative, or both captured by the Americans. Spies and their handlers prepare for these exigencies in varying degrees of retreat. These might be avoiding all contact with the blown operative, terminating PO boxes or other drop locations, and even leaving the country.

Once Chernenko became aware of the missing data drop, he retreated to his apartment, certain the FBI was still monitoring the bench. He was able, under the cover of a busy day, to send a completely unknown operative to the park and confirm the cylinder was gone. Chernenko called in sick. He shaved his hair and moustache and took refuge in a Soviet safe house.

Meanwhile, his absence from the theater district only confirmed his identity and the FBI soon issued an APB for Chernenko. Within a week, Kristoff Chernenko was in Moscow ruefully briefing the NKVD and Elena on his network, protocols, drops, safe houses, and his operatives's habits, behaviors, strengths, and weaknesses.

Elena came home that night and told Alex, who thought his wife worked for a government import-export agency, that she'd been fired from her job. Angry and hurt, Elena asked him how he would feel about leaving the country. Initially, he was shocked, but after thinking it over, he declared his support. Having lost most of their relatives to deprivation, the First World War, and then the Russian Civil War, the Fornopovs had neither strong loyalties nor real family left in Russia. With little fuss, they quietly left their motherland.

Blending in with groups of Jews, dissidents, and White émigrés, Elena and Alex arrived in New York in the summer of 1937. With immigrant fervor, they commenced a rapid melding into the fabric of the Russian community. But with little interest in actually becoming an American, Elena looked for "cover work," while Alex, with the help of the local NKVD apparatus, secured a job with the New York City Department of Sanitation.

Valentin Orlov remained Elena's superior for most of the next thirty years...through the Stalin purges, World War II, the onset of the Cold War, Stalin's death, the liquidation of Beria, the rise and fall of Nikita Khruschev, and then during most of the sixties. Through the decades, Elena Ford had been one of his most valuable assets. It was to her that he first indicated the development of the great plan—one so audacious as to change the course of history.

It traced its origins to the dawn of the revolution. It was more than manipulation, influence, or even brainwashing. It was total control. Pioneered in the fifties, the technique had been honed in the sixties, but had reached deployment status in the seventies. Ever subject to refinement, the program's components underwent periodic updates necessitating trips to Europe where Elena would meet with Orlov for briefings. Still, the best candidates had not panned out. The programming, as that whimpering ninny Merinov had indicated, had not been completely assimilated by any of the subjects they'd tested it on.

* * * *

All this faded from her mind as there came a tap on the shoulder.

"The director can see you now," the nurse said.

Elena gathered her things and girded herself. A deep breath and she stepped into Orlov's hospital room.

CHAPTER 14

1972
MOSCOW

Stepping from her taxi into Lubyanka Square, Elena eyed the Neo-Baroque building that belied its grim purpose: home to the Soviet secret police since the Revolution, the joke was that it was the tallest building in Moscow because one could see Siberia from its basement.

As she entered the building, Elena paused to acknowledge the foreboding, dark statue that both honored the founder of Soviet espionage and guarded Lubyanka Square against tainted influences. After having her ID verified, she was directed to Orlov's office on the fifth floor—ironically, overlooking the Children's Store in the next building. The desk was immaculate, devoid of any personal touches as well as clutter. In the center of the desk sat a flat folder. Inside, it held a single piece of paper, which read: SEE ERICH VON GRUPP IN A.

She looked up as she tiredly rubbed her eyes. One thing that irritated her about her boss was, Orlov loved the idea that using initials somehow shrouded things in secrecy. It wasn't too hard a reach to determine Grupp was in *archives* deep in the bowels of the building.

Returning to the lobby, she was again asked for her ID before being directed to a special, off-the-lobby elevator to archives in the basement. As the doors parted, she could see an armed uniformed guard behind a desk. Stiffly gesturing to a logbook, Elena signed it. With a frosty formality, the guard gestured to a subordinate who escorted her deep into a labyrinth of file cabinets, cubicles, and nooks buried along the walls. In a niche behind a shelf of musty books, the guard nodded to a man, his back to them, bent over a map on a desk.

Elena knocked gently on his office door. Startled, the man jumped, spinning to face her.

"*Ach du lieber*!"

Elena squinted silently. Removing a white glove, she proffered her right hand. "Elena Ford."

Lost in thought, the man suddenly smiled. "Ya, Valentin's girl."

Letting the remark slide, she put her bag and gloves down. "As you know, Orlov is dying. He briefed me at the hospital that you would be taking on the handling of my network and—"

"Ya," Grupp stopped, "he briefed me also." Uncertain if his accent was registering, he added, "You know I am Stasi?"

"Orlov said you were the best he knew at spy craft and managing an intelligence apparatus."

Grupp noted the microscopic tint of condescension in her voice. He smiled broadly. "I am honored. Likevise, he vas most profusive in his consideration of your abilities."

Elena gave a slight dip of her head.

The man gestured back and forth between them. "You know East Germany and the USSR are allies in the global fight for the liberation of the proletariat."

"Certainly, Comrade Colonel."

The German turned to a small, yet massive steel cabinet behind him, thinking, "Orlov said she was hard." Removing a key from his vest pocket, he unlocked it. Opening the ponderous door, he removed a file and put it on his desk. "What can you tell me about this?"

Turning the folder over, she read the two letters: PS. She looked up into Grupp's stony, yet hopeful, eyes. "What do you want to know?"

"Everything that is happening in America. Then I will brief you with the latest technical updates."

CHAPTER 15

1976
NEW YORK

Elena studied the baby boy in her arms. He stared back with his piercing-green eyes. "You will change history." Reluctantly, she gave the child up as his mother collected him before moving to the sofa where she stuck a bottle in his mouth. Elena did not approve of substitutions for a mother's natural feeding but said nothing.

Coming in with two cans of beer, John Ford sat next to his wife, who gratefully took one. Trailing them were Michael, Sophia, and Nicholas.

"Time for another feeding honey?" John jokingly said.

"Him and me both," replied Danielle as she took a sip of beer.

John looked up to find Nicholas studying the baby. "You want to hold him big man?" John asked.

Nicholas shook his head uncertainly. "Nic, you won't break him. It's okay honey," said Sophia.

Finally, the boy took a seat between John and Danielle, who gently placed the baby in Nic's hands. "There. You're doing great, sweetheart."

A smile broke upon the older boy's face as he fed his cousin.

"So, did you guys decide on the baptism date?" asked Michael.

"The tenth ... only date Saint Nicholas had open," John replied as Nic looked up at the mention of his name, "Not you Nic, the Cathedral."

Elena beamed with pride. "My grandsons—Nicholas and now ... Christopher Alexander Ford. I'm so proud." Standing, Elena headed for the kitchen. "Sophia and Danielle can you join me?"

The men watched them depart. Turning to Michael, John asked, "What you working on these days?"

"Same old, Brighton, organized crime, gangs, hook—" Michael shot a glance at Nic who seemed impervious to the conversational drift. "Girls, gambling, but narcotics now. Trade is up over the last five years."

John pursed his lips but said nothing.

Nic looked up. "Dad could I be a cop someday?"

Eyebrows raised in mock surprise, Michael threw his head back, laughing in patriarchal pride, "Absolutely!"

From the kitchen came the unmistakable voice of their mother. "You boys hold it down in there."

Michael and John exchanged glances before smirking some more. Finally, the moment subsided.

"How do you think she is?"

John replied, "Good—I guess. Still a shock Dad is gone. So fast, it seemed."

"Pretty awful." After a second, Michael quietly asked, "She's been on a few more of those long ... trips—*research* she calls it."

Eying a nearby picture of their father, John nodded absently.

"For the paper. She says it's organized-crime stuff here and she's checking sources in Europe or Asia."

"Yeah ... so?" John cautiously replied. "Keeps her busy. I think it's good."

Nodding silently, Michael rubbed his forehead while looking out the window.

CHAPTER 16

1976
NEW YORK

“It’s a shame Alex could not be here today. I know Sara would be so honored,” Galina Dement said, greeting the Fords on the steps at Saint Nicholas Cathedral.

“Ah Galina, I am honored you remembered him.” Elena turned as her clan mounted the steps. In succession, John and Danielle, then Michael and Sophia gave Galina a hug.

“How’s Uncle Fred?”

Galina huffed, “*Uf’a* these American nicknames—Fyodor is in with Sara, preparing. Man would trip over his shoelaces if you didn’t tell him how to get down the aisle.”

“Where’s the groom?” John asked, “Everhill, right?”

Smilingly pridefully, Galina said, “Stephen Everhill. He’s in back with his groomsmen.”

* * * *

At the wheel of his Chevy Impala, Michael made the turn up the drive to the country club where the reception would be held. “Wonder what they’re going to do after they get back from the honeymoon?”

Sophia replied, “I’m sure Sara will want a career … besides having kids. Women are out in the workforce in bigger numbers now.”

From the back, John slyly commented, “Winged Foot—money is good.”

Seated next to Danielle, Elena *tsk’d* in disapproval. “You two, always with the money. Stephen is fortunate to be marrying Sara. Strong values and character like her mother. She will be a good wife and mother.”

In the front seat, Michael and Sophia exchanged glances. "What?" Looking into the rearview mirror, he wilted under his mother's glaring rebuke. Michael feigned hurt ignorance. "What did I do? John made the comment."

"You disapprove of somethееng," Elena said, her Russian accent rearing its head when she was riled up.

"Mom, look I didn't mean anything. But you're always dismissive of money and wealth. Besides, I don't know Sara or her family that well—you do remember I'm twelve years older than her?"

"Rubbish. The Dements have been in our home for years. Sara is like a cousin to you. Now, you two behave."

Looking out the rear window at the golf course, John opined, "I like Sara and ... what's his—Stephen." He looked across the back seat into the distrustful eyes of his mother. "Really, I do. It'll be nice to get to know them."

Squinting, Elena said nothing and directed her gaze back out the window.

CHAPTER 17

1980
NEW YORK

"It's good to make a nice living isn't it?" Galina asked.

A beautiful afternoon in the shade of a large elm in Central Park had done nothing to soften Elena's frosty disdain. "Absolutely. But not at the expense of," she gestured to children playing on the swings, jungle gym, sandbox, and other apparatuses, "enjoying your kids."

Thoughtfully, Galina folded her hands in her lap while staring vacantly toward the playground. Eventually she said, "Thank you for taking the kids to the doctor for the checkups. I know Stephen and Sara are very grateful."

Elena gently brushed Galina's arm. "You're most welcome. I can't believe how big Mallory has gotten—how old is she now?"

Beaming, Galina said, "Three. Looks just like Sara, doesn't she?"

Nodding sagely, Elena just smiled. "How are Sara and Stephen doing?"

"Wonderful. How about yours?"

"Michael is now a captain working in the organized-crime department. Sophia takes care of Nic, who is eleven. John is working in something to do with mergers at Goldman Sachs. Danielle works for ArtBistro in Soho—"

"I heard of that, sort of avant-garde—yes?"

Tilting her head dismissively, Elena replied, "Seems a waste of her talent. None of my kids listen to me."

Galina studied her friend. "So serious." Just then, she reached out a hand to Elena's arm, "Look."

Near the sandbox, Chris was holding Mallory's hand; he removed a splinter and gently kissed the finger. A moment later, both dashed away toward the swings.

Gushing, Galina said, "They are so good together."

Elena smiled broadly while thinking, "They are good. They'll make their families proud."

CHAPTER 18

1985
SAINT PETERSBURG

It had always been easy for Slaga Dmitriev. After failing out of secondary school, at the age of seventeen, he'd gone into the army. The bosses had determined he was particularly good at hurting people, and he found himself in the Spetsnaz: USSR Special Forces. A tour in Afghanistan had transformed him—hardened him—forging his personal code of conduct. He'd learned both what men and he were capable of doing. He discovered there was a fine line between what men *had* to do to others and what they *wanted* to do to others. Probably the greatest thing he'd learned ... what *he* was willing to do to get what he wanted. Very few human beings will ever learn this, and even if they find it, even fewer will actually do it.

His unit was tasked with reconnoitering targets before the main army units would attack. Often, the group would range far behind enemy lines in pursuit of information, weaknesses in enemy fortifications, and vulnerability of supply lines, while also discovering where elimination of local or regional leadership was needed. Information extraction was something Slaga excelled at. But he also underwent a metamorphosis while in Afghanistan.

The volcano of cruelty slumbering within him was never far from erupting. As people gave up information, in the mistaken belief that it would save their lives—and when the end game had arrived—he was surprised to find himself work to return a person's dignity to them before killing them. Often, he would offer the victims a cigarette or some sop that would calm his quarry while he sought to rebuild a bridge back to humanity for their souls. At the chosen moment,

Slaga would smile gently and a subordinate would shoot the victim from behind.

In the end, there was still death, but Slaga thought his actions differentiated himself from his peers—many of whom took great delight in not just torturing victims, but exposing them to a final degradation of blunt force: to watch as men raped and brutalized his family before shooting each of them.

Toward the end of his second tour in Afghanistan, another thought came to him. *Information* was the most valuable asset on earth and Slaga was good at getting it. What if he could make people do things for him?

Upon his return to Moscow, Slaga's skills and distinguished service were rewarded with the ultimate assignment: Alpha Group—the most elite and secret service of the Spetsnaz—similar in nature to the American Delta Force or Britain's Special Air Service, SAS. Until his assignment, Slaga had heard only whispers of the unit's existence.

The company made one-hundred-mile marches across the Ryn Desert in full-dress uniform while carrying eighty-pound packs. In bivouac, men were held down on their backs as lit cinder blocks were positioned on their stomachs and drill sergeants wielded sledgehammers to break the flaming masses.

The challenge that most intrigued Slaga—that he maybe even fantasized over—was the Oymyakon Break. An eastern Siberian town named Oymyakon was supposedly the coldest place in Russia. In 1924, scientists recorded a temperature of minus ninety-six degrees Fahrenheit in the town on the Indigirka River. Besides the record cold, the town was part of Stalin's Death Ring.

During the Great Terror of the 1930s, some political prisoners were tortured or shot. Perhaps the worst sentence was to be sent to the Oymyakon forced-labor camp. Often, the labor to build roads, buildings, railroads, and other infrastructure linking Siberia to the rest of Russia was the only thing to keep prisoners alive. The cold was so cold—it was ironically called *hellish*.

Alpha Group had perfected a new brand of torture. Taking would-be members to Oymyakon where they were forced to stand outside for one hour in sub-zero temperatures with nothing on but boots and underwear.

Surviving this attempt to break a recruit opened the doors to a new world: a world of high stress, high demand, and high expectations. It was also one of ultimate privilege and respect. It provided better food, pay, and health care, along with paid vacations anywhere in Europe. Women—and sometimes men—often high-party functionaries or members of government, or even married members of the party, sought out the Alpha members like ancient Romans pursued gladiators for nights of abandon.

It was here, in Oymyakon, that Slaga first learned of mind and brain control: how to manage one's thoughts to withstand staggering cold and desert heat straight from the surface of the sun. Master one's thoughts, master the world. It was at Alpha that new whispers came: telling a story of complete brainwashing, a plot born decades earlier at the hands of Dzershinsky with the blessing of Lenin himself. It would strike at the very heart of the USSR's greatest enemy: America. *Whispers*, however, was all it ever turned out to be. Old-wives nonsense that weaklings rolled out to aggrandize a collapsing empire.

Slaga loved every moment of his ten years in Alpha. Until, he didn't. Fairly prescient most of his life, Slaga had seen the disintegration of the Soviet Union before most. Prior to the Wall coming down in 1989, he'd already begun the surreptitious movement of his assets to Swiss bank accounts in Zurich. As the USSR disintegrated, Slaga recognized the opportunity to be made in the black-market sale of Spetsnaz training and the employment of increasingly idle commandos.

Rwanda. Djibouti. Croatia. Bosnia and Herzegovina. Sierra Leone. Somalia. Afghanistan—this time to help one tribal chieftain defeat another, and vice versa. After a while, the conflicts all looked the same. Fabulous pay, same black hearts, same meaningless outcome.

One day, while Slaga was home in Saint Petersburg, an old comrade who'd gone into business for himself—if the Russian mafia qualified as a business—invited Slaga to lunch. The two men met at Koryushka, right on the river, overlooking downtown. His friend regaled Slaga with tales of wealth and business opportunity to be had.

"*Da.* You'll be wealthy beyond the Tsars!" the man said.

"Tino, I am already wealthy," Slaga replied.

The man leaned back thoughtfully in his chair while crossing his arms, eyes drifting to the Winter Palace across the river. "Do you ever think about *control*?"

Slaga's ears perked up. "Control?"

"Control." Tino pointed at the Palace, "The Tsar had control, and then the Bolsheviks ripped it from him."

"*Da* ... took it, then murdered him."

"Exactly."

Slaga nodded before turning his eyes to Tino. "So?" He knocked back a slug of vodka. "What can be done?"

"I'll tell you."

Suspiciously, Slaga eyed his friend. "Tell."

"America."

"America? America what?"

"Do you know what the rule of law is?" Without waiting to know Slaga's ignorance, Tino continued. "Rule of law means that the musors cannot just decide to arrest or screw with you. They're subject to laws that restrict what and when they can get into your business. *Control.*" He let this percolate before continuing. "You should come to America. I'll make you my number two."

After lunch, the man dropped a wad of rubles on the table and strolled off. "Think about it."

Slaga nodded again while draining his vodka, his mind twirled the idea: "America. *And* control."

CHAPTER 19

1985
NEW YORK

Doctor Merinov arrived at the Center for Right Being to find the door unlocked. Unsettled, he entered his office only to find Elena Ford with a stranger, seated in his lobby.

"Elena, if I'd known you—"

"Doctor, please meet Stephan Grigor. *Doctor* Stephan Grigor."

His eyes darted from one to the other and back in a vain search for safe harbor. He looked from the indifferent expression on Grigor's face into the sneering dismissal in Elena's eyes.

"Why?" he asked.

As if she hadn't heard him, she said, "You will bring Doctor Grigor into your practice, introduce him to your patients as a new partner, and indoctrinate him in all your ongoing projects ... *all* of them."

"I'm still a young man—I don't need a partner."

Deliberately, Elena removed the white glove from her right hand, and with a speed that blinded both men, slapped Merinov across the face. "Doctor, this is not an offer. You are retiring for medical reasons. Doctor Grigor studied in Europe at the same schools as you and would be a natural successor." Elena paused, little noting the tears welling in Merinov's face. "Am I clear?"

Racing through the short list of options, Merinov finally nodded in concession.

Squinting, Elena replaced her glove and then departed without a word.

The new psychiatrist icily studied Merinov. A tall man, Grigor's cold-blooded temperament and polar-blue eyes conveyed neither sympathy nor understanding. Merinov could have been a bug under a microscope.

While his resentment of the newcomer and anger at Elena only grew, he was helpless to find a way out. His appeals to Elena fell on the rocks of her scorn and indifference.

In the office, the two doctors developed a relationship of forced pleasantry. Merinov, knowing his time was limited, did as little as he could to help Grigor, employing a passive-aggressive cold war with his replacement. For his part, Grigor, recognizing Merinov's effeminate reserve, quietly went about asserting his dominance over him, looking for opportunities to emasculate him.

To Merinov's growing alarm, Grigor proved a quick study. With patients, he displayed a gentle bedside manner—that, wedded to his Russian background and accent, were easily embraced by the clinic's well-heeled patients, who associated things European with knowledge and sophistication. He was most appreciated by many of the female patients, who were drawn by a magnetic, animal persona. Soon, he was shouldering half the caseload. Still, many days Grigor wandered past the hallway with the door whose sign read LIGHT LAB, wondering what must lie behind.

Being forced to groom his successor, Merinov continued to put off Grigor's inquiries, replying, "Soon." Slowly, Grigor fell into the rhythm of the day and the practice, pushing the hidden room to the back of his thoughts.

Finally one day, after another brutal denial by Elena that ended with the threat of veiled harm, Merinov appeared at Grigor's office doorway.

"Come with me," he said. In response to Grigor's raised eyebrows, Merinov added, "It's time."

Wordlessly, Merinov led Grigor to the Light Lab. Unlocking the door, Merinov stepped into a dark room. Hesitantly, the young doctor followed.

Suddenly the lights flashed on and Grigor blinked, searching for his bearings. Shielding his eyes, he slowly lowered his hands, gasping in astonishment. Thick panels in soothing pastels of soft purple, light blue, and savory green adorned the walls. The floor was covered in shag carpet. Grigor imagined the room to be completely sound proof.

A device hung from the ceiling, and in stark contrast to the comfort of the room, it appeared sinister. Surmising it was some sort of periscope—Doctor Grigor inspected the long, black metal tube, which was approximately six feet in length. It descended from above, and at the end was an elbow joint. Protruding from the joint was another piece telescoping out. On it hung a black, neoprene mask that a patient would place over his or her head. What was most striking were the crystalline glass eyepieces.

"What in the world?" Grigor said in disbelief.

Walking around the apparatus, Merinov pridefully took hold of the black mask. "Created this myself."

Grigor reached out, probing it, "What does it do?"

Merinov wistfully turned an eye to him, "It helps to implant thoughts, or suggestions, in the minds of the patients—to benefit them, help them to overcome things: anxiety, stress, phobias, depression." Merinov dropped the headpiece. "But you knew that already. Yes?"

Grigor nodded thoughtfully. "The theory yes, but this, no."

"Elena thought it was time."

"How does it work?"

* * * *

Sitting at the dining-room table with the *Sunday Times*, John stopped, putting his finger on a story. "Oh my God," he finished reading. "Hey, Mom?"

At the kitchen sink, her back to the room, Elena called out "Yes, dear?"

"Did you know Doctor Merinov is dead?"

Elena turned from the sink. "What?" She said in shock.

Michael, Sophia, and the rest of the family stared at John in stunned silence. John read from the paper. "Doctor Maxim Merinov, recently of New York City, was found dead yesterday, in an alley behind the Zig Zig Ale House off the Bahnhofstrasse in Zurich, Switzerland. It was believed he was shot during the course of a robbery and died of his wounds. The doctor had recently relocated to Switzerland after selling his practice in New York City." John looked up, "There's more, but mostly just background. Golly, that's terrible. Work your whole life for something and then ... to have it stripped from you like that."

Elena quietly turned back to the sink. A small crinkle creased her lips.

CHAPTER 20

1992
MOSCOW

Grupp was at a crossroads. After the failed coup of the old guard in August, things had rapidly spiraled out of control. The dinosaurs of the Soviet Union were in retreat. Even the reform-minded Mikhail Gorbachev had resigned on Christmas Day of 1991 at the same time as the dissolution of the USSR. Since assuming control of much of the remaining apparatus, Boris Yeltsin, as President of Russia, had moved to consolidate all the archives under the auspices of Russia. Included in this had been an order to move every KGB file into Russian oversight.

The fall of the Berlin Wall in 1989 had been enough of a warning for Grupp, and he'd taken precautions to move his most sensitive files out of Lubyanka's archives. They hadn't moved far, though.

Grupp then remembered a story from an old Stasi comrade who'd told him about an operative he was running in West Berlin in the sixties. Seems the woman was the assistant to the chief of the police. She had family in East Berlin and it was quite normal for her to get mail from the family. Even allowing for the inspection of anything she sent back to her family, she had been able to hide information inside baked goods or candy. For years, she'd operated in plain sight of the authorities in the West before she'd been caught.

The words *plain sight,* lurked in his thoughts one day as he stepped off the elevator for his floor. He returned to the elevator, descending into the bowels of Lubyanka. In the basement archives, blueprints of the building in hand, he moved about, inspecting the spaces. Then it came to him. There appeared to be a sizeable gap between the bathrooms and a supplies storage area just off the main passageway. In the hallway, in-between the lavatories and closet, he estimated the possible area. Slowly he nodded, a hint of a smile creasing his lips.

Quietly, he'd arranged for a new, super-secret room to be constructed at the back of the supply closet. About the size of a tennis court, it was enough space to hold all the KGB's most-damaging secrets. After completion, Grupp had arranged for the room's entryway to be hidden behind shelves holding cleaning supplies—which the East German found ironically amusing.

But there was still one file in his new treasure room that he'd retained the original record of: the one given to him personally by Orlov in the month before he died. It contained the elements of an audacious plan. Grupp had concluded long ago the likelihood it would ever come to fruition was so remote ... it was more likely Russians would stop drinking vodka first. Still, its sensitivity was beyond question—if it ever became public knowledge, it could lead to a war with the United States.

After Orlov's death, Grupp had shielded it as a mother protects her children. He denied its existence to his superiors. He even stopped drinking. What if he blurted out an indiscretion one night after too much vodka? On more than one occasion, he'd awoken in a night sweat wondering: "Is it secure in the safe behind my desk?"

Still, with the order that all KGB records be turned over to Rosarkhiv, Grupp knew he was on borrowed time. Eventually, they'd discover his hidden-records trove and then they'd seize his safe. The original file was now wrapped and sealed in plastic and safely hidden in the air-conditioning duct behind his desk. Grupp nonetheless feared it was only a matter of time until its discovery.

More than once, he'd thought of just destroying the dossier. But for reasons beyond his grasp, he found he could not. For decades, the Eastern Bloc had operated at a disadvantage against the West. True, they'd created dozens of communist states in all parts of the world to counter the capitalists. But the Americans and their allies possessed one insurmountable advantage: *freedom.* People could only be told the truth about the sacrifices needed to build a true-proletarian state for so long—before they'd throw the yoke of totalitarianism from their necks.

This plan—this grand plan he guarded—would bring glory to the Soviet Union. This would allow the motherland, and her trusted allies, to finally achieve the ultimate victory. But given its ultra-high, sensitivity and Grupp's paranoia about it, he'd decided to remove the copy of the record from the new, hidden file room while keeping the original in his possession until he could guarantee its security.

His mind whirled these facts as he stepped into the bright sun shining down on Lubyanka Square. "I have to find a new guardian." He stepped into the street.

Sudden darkness engulfed him as metal clashed on flesh and pain overcame him. Grupp never saw the bus that ran him over.

At the hospital, they transported him into the emergency room. They brought him doctors, nurses, and IVs with drugs to soften the pain. Finally, they led a priest into his room. The kindly old Orthodox cleric was in his eighties—the last relic of days before, when prelates were welcome in houses of healing. Grupp, raised a Lutheran before he became an atheist, spilled his sins onto the aged priest.

"Slow down, my child. I'm—"

"Father, I had purpose. I lived for the revolution ... but I've hurt so many people," he gasped.

The tired man of God listened passively, nodding occasionally; his eyes closed as he prayed the last rites. With a rasp, the dying man weakly reached up, clutching the confessor's robe. He pulled his head down until the priest's ear was next to his own mouth. Urgently—his will to unburden in final combat with his summoning spirit—the dying Stasi agent grunted a semi-coherent burst of chatter into the priest's ear.

With a peace often denied his victims, Grupp's body slowly fell slack. At the foot of the bed, the attending nurse shivered at the tingling hairs on her neck as the priest sat up. His face was shadowed in an expression of utter shock that brought color to his face for the first time in decades.

For a moment, he gazed at the dead man before he crossed himself and fled the room.

CHAPTER 21

1992
SAVANNAH, GEORGIA

Congressman-elect, Adam Byrnes, and his trophy wife, Penelope Jane Byrnes gave one more wave to a boisterous crowd of supporters, well-wishers, sycophants, and clingers-on.

It had taken a decade, but Byrnes finally reached the first rung on the ladder. Years of working in banking had proved to him that he had little stomach for real work. Things such as analyzing financial statements, calculating ratios, understanding business cycles and economics bored him to tears. The one thing he came to realize was that he liked the socializing at bank functions, local chamber of commerce events, church gatherings, and increasingly political soirées.

The political world especially attracted him. The power that came with elected office was mesmerizing. While he and PJ had no kids, Byrnes had still been able to get elected to the school board. Soon, it was on to the city council. Then he'd been elected mayor of Trilogy Gap Township.

As Mayor, Byrnes had been able to get a number of progressive initiatives enacted, including day care for city employees, replacing half the city's motor pool with electric cars, and expanding a public-private education program for the children of low-income families. Ambitious, he dreamt of higher office and opportunities to change the landscape.

Byrnes also proved adept at meeting and cultivating relationships with well-heeled supporters. Especially the female ones. Many a night, the Mayor stayed late at his office, serving the electorate.

PJ had drifted into her own social circles, focused mostly on the arts. At least a couple times a month, she would attend art fairs, gallery events and artist shows.

While politics and art did not cover their monthly bills, PJ's father, who owned a dozen insurance agencies across the state, supported them. Arthur Maybeck indulged his daughter while tolerating Byrnes. And the Mayor's growing political connections were proving to be useful. The run for Congress made sense for everyone.

"That went well, I imagine. Don't you, dahlin'?" he asked.

Accepting a small glass of Scotch from a staffer, PJ replied, "You are their king, sweetums." Draining the liquor, she proffered the tumbler to the aide, "And put more than a thimble of spit in this time."

Byrnes wrinkled his nose but remained silent. PJ's father had bought and paid for the election, so Byrnes needed to remain impassive in the face of his wife's indifference to the grandest night of his life. Soon enough, he would be in DC while PJ would remain in the Palmetto State.

Adam imagined that DC would offer a multitude of companionship to get through the cold winter nights.

CHAPTER 22

1992
NEW YORK

Elena blew out the candles on her cake, which in reality, was not hard. In place of eighty individual candles, there was only one candle in the shape of an eight and a zero. About the table were her sons, daughters-in-law, and grandchildren, along with Galina, her closest friend. Next to her sat Galina's daughter, Sara, with her husband Stephen and their daughter Mallory.

Her mind whispered, "What have I done?"

The news from Moscow had been like a punch to the gut. Grupp gone, and worse: apparently no one to assume control. How many times had she told that stupid Stasi moron he needed to mentor someone to take his place in case something happened?

Now, as she contemplated what she'd built since coming to New York, she wanted to go back and erase what she'd put into motion. Her mind continued its rustling, "I have to shut this down."

A tear ran down her face.

"Grandma, are you crying?" asked Chris.

Joy and regret married in sobbed laughter. Elena wiped her eyes, hugging her grandson, but, as she began to speak, a jolt shot through her neck, the left side of her body falling limp. She attempted to stand, but only succeeded in falling out of her chair. Even her cry of surprise was muted, slurred in her own ears. It was not clear to her what was happening, but Michael was already attending to her while John was dialing 911. Michael carried her to the sofa and laid her down.

"Mom? Mom!"

John came to his brother's side. "They're on their way."

Elena found she could not even smile. Her left eye kept sagging as she attempted speech that merely cascaded into thought, "So tired. I'll rest here and then get up."

CHAPTER 23

1995
NEW YORK

It had taken time, but Slaga did not mind. In many ways, the consolidation of power was like a chess match. He loved chess—the buildup of weapons on the opponent's borders, followed by the slow insertion of his forces into enemy territory. While the laws of economics were a little more refined than the laws of war, they both still required making hard decisions about the deployment and use of assets. In economics, it was called allocating scarce resources among competing demands. In Brighton Beach, it was having more bullets than the other guy.

Slaga had become an inveterate reader since his arrival in America. But one of the best quotes he'd come across was actually from his countryman, Leo Tolstoy, who wrote, "The two most powerful warriors are patience and time."

First he'd had to contend with Tino Ivchenko, his friend from St. Petersburg. The leader of a mid-level gang in Brighton Beach, Tino had carved out a sustainable niche for his gang, *Zolotoy Poyezd*—The Gold Train. They boosted cars, sold protection, and ran a string of massage parlors covering for prostitution. It had been good, but Tino was getting ambitious and the aromatic whiff of profit from narcotics and drugs had caught his attention.

Slaga and Tino had been friends from their earliest days in the army, but Tino was erratic. Famously easy to anger, he made mercurial decisions that often boomeranged with great vengeance. To protect himself, Slaga had kept himself hidden from Tino's gang. Tino appreciated Slaga's familiarity with military tactics, his insight into the way people behaved, as well as being a superior planner. Slaga would meet with Tino to discuss plans about a job, but he never directly participated.

After Slaga's arrival, they'd met a man in Tino's warehouse to discuss delivery of some stolen cassette players. A low-level criminal about to leave America to retire in Kiev, this man had stumbled into a last great boost. Tino had brought Slaga in to read the thief as they negotiated.

Holding one of the devices, Tino sought to haggle. "These are okay, not the best—what price are you thinking?"

The man looked down into his hand where he'd withdrawn a picture from his jacket. "Mr. Tino, this is my family back in Donetsk. I go soon to them. What price do you think is fair?"

"Like I said, these are not the good ones—not Sony or Panasonic."

When the elderly thief balked at the price Tino thought was fair, Tino calmly stood up, removed a gold-plated Montblanc pen and a gold-plated Glock from his briefcase; he placed them before the man on the other side of the desk.

"Which will it be?"

"*Psikh*—they said you are a lunatic!" The man began pushing his seat back.

Tino wiggled a finger at him. "*Nyet.* Now I'm going to count, and you better decide before I finish.

Suddenly realizing he was at a point of no return, his eyes turned to Slaga, seeking an appeal.

"*Odin, dva, tri*—"

Now that they had the man's attention, Slaga anticipated that Tino would un-cock the pistol. Instead, Slaga was shocked by the massive bang, acoustic pressure, and the instant tidal wave of dread accompanying the bullet as it obliterated the man's face.

Tino took the cassette players, buried the body, and dumped the truck. He then called the man's boss, a Ukrainian, to ask when the driver was coming. Initially, this tactic diverted suspicion from Tino. When word leaked that Tino was moving the tape players, the Ukrainians came at The Gold Train with everything—including assets out of Europe and the Middle East. *Assets:* a euphemism for *mercenaries.*

Mercenaries: a euphemism for *killers*. Finally, they cornered Tino down in his condo. Sending a clear message, they executed him in bed along with his wife and children.

Then they turned to Tino's goons. With brutal, quiet efficiency, they reduced Tino's outfit to rubble. But they could not find one: an unknown associate. There was some knowledge but mostly a hole. It was like he'd disappeared into the fog off Long Island.

Slaga had gone to ground, Spetsnaz discipline kicking-in after years in hibernation. Systematically, without anger or vengeance, but like a surgeon conducting a symphony, Slaga quietly picked apart the Ukrainians. He started with the lower-level soldiers. He pursued them to their watering holes, social clubs, and to the homes of their girlfriends or mistresses. He took them out when their guards were lowered. Slaga's purpose was elimination first, but also to send a message: he was coming.

The next level was more difficult.

Throughout Brooklyn and Manhattan, word spread. Death had a new messenger. They called him *the Specter*. The gang, Little Kiev, brought in specialists from Chechnya —men, and some women, who were extremely gifted at killing; they brought mercs from Odessa in the Ukraine, where it was possible they hated the Russians more than the Chechens. They formed a veritable human fortress around the leaders of Little Kiev—a fly would have needed a passport to get into the room.

Still, the killing continued. Slaga blew one boss up—along with the caravan of cars protecting him. He used an improvised explosive device made of dog-food cans and packed with C4, which he buried in the man's garbage can. Two other bosses he took out with long-range shots from his old Dragunov SVD rifle while they walked to their car. Another was found dead in his mistress's apartment, a shiv in the back of his neck and his genitals in his mouth. The back-breaking blow came when Slaga eliminated ten pins with a single ball: a strike.

On the day before a gathering of bosses to discuss how to deal with the Specter, Slaga rose early. He bathed in a silent calm, while "By the Beautiful Blue Danube" drifted from his old boom box in his comfortable, but understated, safe house. Donning a disguise, he left his home, stopping to have a sumptuous breakfast at IHOP.

The conclave of the bosses was to be held at the Club Twenty-Two, fittingly located at the intersections of Second Street and Second Avenue in Manhattan. Clad in the uniform of a ConEd utility man, he'd arrived at Club Twenty-Two at three o'clock in the morning. Feigning a terrible Puerto Rican accent, it had not taken much to bluff his way past the groggy guards with a tale of a reported gas leak in the area.

While under constant surveillance, Slaga moved back and forth between the kitchen and main dining area. He poked holes into the dining room and kitchen walls, and used a gas detector to "look" for leaks in the holes. Eventually, the thugs grew bored, their scrutiny reduced to an occasional "when are you going to be done" inquiry.

"Should be just another minute or two. I gotta run out to my truck." Returning with a commercial gas cylinder and a vacuum cleaner, he placed the cylinder next to the stove; he then commenced vacuuming up the mess he'd made in the dining room. The vacuum's loud noise drove the thugs into Club Twenty-Two's lobby. Rapidly, Slaga removed a coil of rubber hose attached to the vacuum and ran it through the two heat registers at either end of the dining room wall, up into the false ceiling, and back into the kitchen.

"Almost done!" he called.

"Yeah, yeah ... hurry!"

In the kitchen, he pulled the hoses down the wall, out of a small hole just behind the stove, and connected them to a radio-controlled T-valve he screwed into the gas cylinder, which he then wedged into a small space in the back of the stove. He finished as a guard pushed his head in.

"What you doing?" he challenged.

"Just finished. You had some leakage here and surprisingly near the fireplace—but I think I got it all. Do you guys smoke?"

Scowling, the watchman nodded.

"Well, I'd recommend not for at least an hour, should clear out the gas. Okay?" Packing his tool bag, Slaga smiled, amused at all the smoke he'd blown. He stepped to the back exit as the guard watched him go. Suspiciously, the guard knelt to look under the stove—but not understanding what he was looking at nor what to look for, he slowly came to his feet. He cast one last glance at the door Slaga had departed through, and then the thug grunted and rejoined his comrades.

In the afternoon, at the peak lunch hour, Slaga returned to Little Ukraine, parking just down Second Avenue. He got out of the car. Stopping at a deli, he bought a sandwich, chips, and a soda. He made his way down the alleyway; he'd arrived at the back entryway to Club Twenty-Two. As anticipated, he found it crawling with guards. Perfect. At a phone booth he'd discovered a few days previous, while taking a bite of his sandwich, he called the main number for Club Twenty-Two.

"Hello," came a pleasant female voice.

"*Mmmfp* ... sorry, was eating." Slaga hoped the full mouth would cover his accent enough to throw off suspicion. "Look, you don't know me, but I was paid to call in a tip. Somebody is coming for you."

After a moment, the attendant replied more timorously. "I'm sorry ... what?"

"Yes. Some crazy guy. He said 'I'm going to come through the door and kill those sons of bitches.' He paid me to call you and pass that along."

A new, gruffer man now replied. "Who is this?"

"Just some dude who wants to finish his lunch. I gotta go."

"Wait. Which door did he say?"

Slaga responded through another bite, "Didn't say. Just said to call it in."

"Where are you?"

Slaga played dumb. "I'm at ... Oh maybe I better not tell you."

"How much did he pay you?"

"Twenty ... oh and he bought me this sandwich."

"So he's coming for us?"

"That's what he said, mister. Look I gotta go." Slaga hung up the phone as he monitored the activity behind Club Twenty-Two. Suddenly, a man burst out the back onto the delivery dock. Barking orders and gesturing rapidly, he had the various thugs move previously parked cars into a defensive perimeter around the building's rear.

He then had the men take up positions behind boxes while setting a forklift in front of the back door.

Slaga nodded, certain no one could get in. Or out. Taking a final bite, and then putting down his sub, he removed a device from his pocket. Wiping his mouth on his sleeve, he pushed the red button on the center of the control panel.

CHAPTER 24

1995
NEW YORK

A fastidious man, uninterested in a family, Slaga enjoyed a life of unfettered consumption. Sex was something he took care of when the need arose—usually with high-end escorts, but the thought of exchanging his freedom for companionship had never held much appeal.

He was occasionally bothered by the idea of a legacy. What would he leave behind? He wasn't sure what he could erect that would outlast him, but it was *something*...undefined as it was.

At home, Slaga put a record of London Symphony playing Mozart's "Requiem" onto his new, hi-fi. In the kitchen, he took his time preparing dinner while thumbing through an art book he'd picked up on the way home. On his Borge Mogensen dining table, he placed his plate of pasta and mussels along with pesto sauce and a chopped salad. Opening a bottle of Mouton Cadet, he turned on the Channel Two news in time for the headline story.

"Good evening. Our lead tonight is the massacre at Club Twenty-Two earlier today. Let's go live to the scene now."

A reporter came on screen. Behind him was a beehive of activity, police, EMTs, and crime-scene personnel buzzed about. Nodding his head at his cameraman, the reporter spoke, "That's right. We're here at Club Twenty-Two, located at the intersections of Second Street and Second Avenue. Today, sometime just after one o'clock, a member of the club's wait staff entered the main meeting room and found fifteen bodies—all of them apparently dead. Initial reports indicate this was a gathering of leaders of the Ukrainian crime syndicate from the tri-state area. After lunch had been served, the room was sealed, and club staff report that no one entered the room after the meeting commenced. One curiosity has already arisen: while virtually every person in the room had a gun, either in hand or beside their body, there were no bullets fired. We've been waiting for—hold on. It looks like we're about to get an update."

The camera panned to a microphone on the steps leading up to the club where a uniformed police officer stepped forward. "I'm Captain Michael Ford of the NYPD. Earlier today, it appears fifteen men died while having lunch in the meeting room here at Club Twenty-Two. It is very preliminary in our investigation, and we have no motive and no leads, but we have recovered a commercial gas tank from the kitchen that is normally used to contain carbon monoxide. How this figures into our investigation is unknown at this time—"

A din arose from the sea of reporters. Snippets of questions flew out. "Who were they?"

"Did they shoot each other?"

"Why here?"

"Was it the Specter?" This last question brought a hush to the mayhem. Captain Ford stopped and looked directly at the questioner.

"I have no clue as to who it was. But, if the person known as the Specter is watching: if you had anything to do with this—we'll find you. That's all I have for now." Ford turned and re-entered the club.

Pandemonium erupted as reporters shouted questions while cameramen jostled to capture images of the club's interior before the front door closed behind Ford. Slaga smiled as he turned the TV off. Then a scowl intruded on his moment.

The mail had brought an unexpected arrival. He was momentarily surprised as he glanced at the return address: The Monastery of the Blessed Savior in the town of Dyutkovo, just outside of Moscow. The letter was from Misha, his cousin. Over the years, Misha—who disapproved of Slaga and his lifestyle—had still sought to keep him apprised of the family's comings and goings, usually finishing with a call for Slaga's repentance. But since Slaga's immigration to America, their contact had virtually evaporated.

Turning the envelope to open it, a sudden foreboding crept over him, but not the type of fear from danger but of the lurking unknown. He feared it more than an imminent threat. Invisible things out there that can hurt him. Always superstitious, Slaga squinted at it, was this a harbinger?

Nothing in the opening raised any alarms. Cousin *blah blah* had a baby ... Uncle *blither* is working on a collective in Siberia ... the usual prattle. Calm had returned as he finished the first page.

The next page was a little out of the ordinary. Misha described the arrival of an Orthodox priest at the monastery. He'd been in service to God since the earliest days of the Revolution, most recently serving at a hospital in Moscow. Recently diagnosed with stage-four cancer, the doctors had given him a couple of months. He'd come to Blessed Savior to finish his days at the heart of his faith. Again, Slaga's misgivings began to settle as Misha unpacked the minute detail of the priest's routine as he set about dying.

The devil returned, however, at the top of the next page. On the day the priest died, he called Misha into his cell. Misha supposed it was to hear his last confession, and indeed, the gray-bearded ancient of days unburdened himself. The last page struck Slaga like a lightning bolt.

At the end of the man's confession, Misha had begun making a sign of the cross when the dying man reached up, with surprising force to seize Misha's hand. He made Misha get a pad of paper and record the rest of his final testimony. Unconsciously, Slaga sat a bit straighter, grasping the letter tighter as if some unseen force was about to tear it from his fingers.

Years before, while working at the hospital, the priest had heard another man's deathbed confession. He had been an officer of some sort, KGB. He'd detailed a plot to groom, install, and control puppets in America. The unnamed plan was too complex for a last confession, but the dying priest had recorded where to find documents detailing the plan's particulars.

Slaga's heart pounded as he turned to the last page. Where there was ... a short sign-off. Nothing else. Frantically, he fanned the pages out—did he miss one? Nothing.

"*Der'mo*!"

Agitatedly, he checked once more before returning to the last page. A final goodbye. Then he caught it. Misha signed off:

I TRUST YOU ARE WELL. I HOPE TO SEE YOU AGAIN, PERHAPS FOR SAINT GEORGE'S DAY NEXT MONTH.

He glanced at the calendar. March? Then he remembered: Saint George, the patron saint of Moscow, is remembered by most of Christianity on his date of death, April twenty-third ... on the Gregorian calendar.

The Russian church retained, and still utilized, the old Julian calendar. In Moscow, Saint George's Day was celebrated on May sixth. Misha was probably of the mind that now that Slaga lived in America, he was on the Gregorian calendar and hence the April reference.

Forgetting the mental math of converting dates, Slaga relaxed and tried to let the reality sink in. After years of chasing a will-o'-the-wisp, at last there was confirmation of a real mind-control program. But just as quickly, the surge of discovery gave way to a new uncertainty. Confirmation of what?

His mind raced, "Where in America ... ? Who ... ?"

His ambitions began running scenarios in one part of his brain, while imagination conjured up others. Thoughts from his days in Afghanistan returned to him. "Control. Power. To know the outcome before it happens." He nodded slowly, but first, he needed to understand what Misha had found. He picked up his phone, and then put it down. It would be four in the morning in Russia. Soon enough.

He stood. At the record player, he replaced Mozart with a record of the Red Army Choir. Studying the album cover, he placed the stylus on the track of "Farewell of Slavianka" before changing his mind. Taking a bottle of Stolichnaya, he poured a hefty shot and knocked it back as the State Anthem of the Russian Federation boomed from the stereo. Grabbing the vodka, he moved to the window. Outside, the dark greeted him. Slaga liked the dark. He embraced the dark. Dark was soulless, nonjudgmental. He breathed, "Things are coming together."

CHAPTER 25

1995
NEW YORK

At his desk, Michael leaned back in his hardwood chair. Trying to find a comfortable position in a chair with no tilt in it made him grimace. He finally found some stasis by putting his feet up on his desk. He scrutinized the plastic situation board covered with pictures, names, locations, and other crime-scene evidence. In the center was a blank picture frame. Beneath it was written SPECTER. So far, there'd been no claim of ownership for the Club Twenty-Two massacre from two weeks before—not unusual, but nothing but silence from the street? What little there was seemed to point to a suspect who, in theory, did not exist.

Michael knew his sources were either scared or witless. They had mostly whispers of some Russian spec-ops guy. Spetsnaz trained. A name: *Slaga* something. But since the Berlin Wall had come down, everything in Russia was a mess. Central Red Army headquarters in Moscow was now staffed with idiots and ghosts drawing a paycheck. The only thing they had was a Slaga Dmitirev who'd died in Saint Petersburg in a house fire in 1985. Body was burnt beyond recognition. Clenching his fist, he thought, "Specter my ass. I'm going to find you."

He glanced at his watch. Eyes bulging, he lurched out of the chair, grabbing his dress-uniform jacket and raced out of the office. "Bye. I'll call in!"

His assistant barely looked up. "Tell Nic we're proud of him. Tell Sophia I said hi!"

A patrol officer walked by, "Where's the Cap going?"

The secretary looked up, beaming. “His son Nic is graduating from the academy today.”

Silently, the officer nodded. “Where they posting him?”

“Brighton Beach.”

CHAPTER 26

1995
MOSCOW

On short notice, it had taken a bit of finagling, but Slaga had been able to get out of the States with little attention. He had driven to Montreal, used his fake French passport, then flown to Paris and on to Russia. Wanting to maintain a low profile, he rented, rather than use a car service. From Sheremetyevo, he'd driven to the River Prince Hotel on Moscow's western edge. He reasoned there was less visibility staying at a hotel away from the city center. Besides, overlooking the Moskva River offered more tranquility.

And it made for a shorter trip to Dyutkovo: about an hour on the M9. At Blessed Savior, Misha had shown him around, but it soon became apparent to both men why Slaga had come. Misha took him to his compartment and closed the door.

"No locks?"

"Slaga, this is a house of God, not a barracks. No one is going to come in here without permission." Slaga disdainfully raised his eyebrows, a sneer caught in his throat as Misha challengingly tilted his head. "You doubt?"

Remembering why he was there, Slaga shook his head. Misha went to a small desk, opened the top drawer, and removed a manila envelope. He gave it to Slaga and stepped to the door.

"No one will bother you here. Use my desk." The surprise showed on Slaga's face. "Whatever this is, I'm sure I don't want any part of it." The monk opened the door to leave.

"Misha, wait."

Detecting regret in his cousin, the monk did not turn. "Slaga, I know you care for us ... in your way, but there is no need to pretend now. I'll be in the cloister when you are done.

Slaga pinched his lips; he'd wanted this to go better. He turned to his task. Opening the envelope, Slaga realized two things quickly: the first was that he did not totally understand what he was looking at; the second was the return of his fear, was he getting in over his head?

Thumbing through the documents, he was able to grasp the outlines of a grand plan, but it was like walking through a forest expecting to find something. He was not sure what it was, though he had a general concept, but pulling back that last branch and stepping into the opening—the magnitude of what he found overwhelmed his senses.

In shaky handwriting, the priest's confession—that Misha had transcribed—outlined a plan to brainwash people in the United States. It was programming specifically designed to induce them to seek out employment with the United States government. The anticipation? That a number of these *well-inserted* sleeper agents would have risen to positions of seniority within the government.

But why? The plan had never been implemented as most Soviet experiments with brainwashing had met with poor results. But there had been one case where it had worked.

That was all there was.

From Misha's notes, the man had entered the last throes of death before he could reveal anything of final substance. In his dying words, Misha gathered the man had confessed his KGB ties and the files documenting the operation lay hidden in an air duct behind his desk at Lubyanka. Slaga looked up at a crucifix on the wall.

"Moscow."

CHAPTER 27

1998
NEW YORK

Cleanly attired in a civilian suit, Nic snuck to his seat as the ceremony started. His father scowled while his mother smiled, putting a hand on his knee. Glancing down the row of seats, he saw Uncle John, Aunt Danielle, Sara and Stephen Everhill, and their daughter Mallory. Already bored, he scrutinized the program, looking for names he recognized. Disappointed, he stared at the stage where some talking head in a mortarboard and purple gown was concluding his remarks. Nic had often thought that academic gowns were too unisex, he could not tell from looking at them whether the occupant was a man or a woman. Not enough fact, too much imagination. All he needed were the facts to draw an inference.

He learned that from his grandmother, Elena. Nodding, more to himself, he reflected. *And yet feelings* rather than facts had been instrumental in cracking that case last week.

* * * *

Nic had arrived at the scene of a murder. He found a skeevy-looking thug knocked out next to a dead woman in an alley behind her apartment. Her skirt was up, her panties missing and a small dime bag of meth in her hand. The guy made his skin crawl—tats ... drill marks in his arms ... and a gun in his hand. It was a Beretta M9A3 with a round missing from the clip that matched the casing lying by the woman's body. The gun was stolen—not as clean as when gun ownership can be established, but still, it seemed an open-and-closed case.

Initial conclusions by the responders were a robbery to get drug money or a rape gone bad and the guy had shot her. Besides a welt on the back of his head, presumably from hitting his head on the pavement, there were no wounds on the perp. Still, something seemed off to Nic.

Things like the needle marks on the perp's arms looked old or completely healed as if he was off the drugs. Why were the panties missing? The way the man was laying looked off. Had the woman initially fought him off and he fell knocking himself unconscious? The suspect was left-handed but the GSR had been on his right hand. He was short—five feet, seven inches. Yet, the angle of the bullet wound suggested being shot from above. Nic looked about, there were no stairs out of the woman's building. The perp could not have been standing above the victim when firing.

Later, Nic had gone back to the crime scene. He sat for an hour at various points about the alley, rechecking his notepad.

Residents reported hearing only *one* shot. Nic checked his notepad again. The gun had a threaded muzzle on the barrel, but there was no suppressor found on the perp or nearby. A new idea occurred to Nic. What if she was dead before the perp had fired his gun? But this would require another bullet.

Nic looked about the scene; he peered into two nearby dumpsters, under them, and amongst the scattered debris in the alley. He even inspected the roof of a small shop adjacent to the backstreet. In despair, he was about to leave when the muted glint of the drainage grating caught his eye. But as he approached it, his heart skipped. Something, he couldn't tell what, was barely visible in the muck.

Suddenly panicked a flood would materialize from thin air to flush away the mire, Nic frantically grabbed a discarded two-by-four and pried off the grate cover. With his pen, he scraped away muck around the object. Hooking it, he raised it into the light. A triumphant smile cracked his face. Bullet casing. He gently wrapped it in his handkerchief.

As victorious as it felt, still, this was only half the battle. He surveyed the alleyway anew. It took a couple of scans before his eyes came to rest on something: an obscure, overlooked, dark-brown telephone pole. Like a child about a Maypole, Nic half-circled, half-danced about the stanchion. Once. Twice. It was hard because of the numerous knots, burls, and cracks. However, on his third, much slower go-round he found it. About ten feet up, there was a deep gouge and it appeared out of place.

Nic rolled a dumpster to the pole base, flipped the cover closed, and jumped onto it. Utilizing his pocketknife and cell-phone flashlight, he probed the hole. In short order, the wood about the hole flaked away. Before he could react, something popped out and fell on the dumpster top where it rolled to rest against Nic's foot. With the same pocket square, he recovered it. Holding it aloof, Nic studied the unmistakable markings of a recently fired bullet.

Driving back to the station, it had been hard to contain his sense of elation. Crime fighting wasn't so hard after all. Indeed, the tumblers to the lock dropped into place after that. The dead woman was a hooker who was trying to leave the streets. The suspect was actually a friend who'd agreed to help; he worked at a halfway house—hence the old needle marks. The victim's pimp, who also ran meth, had caught the two of them moving things out the back of her unit. The pimp, who was six feet, had knocked the suspect unconscious with a sap before shooting the hooker with silencer-suppressed gun. With a presence of mind that actually impressed Nic, the pimp had chambered another round into the Beretta, removed the silencer, put the weapon in the unconscious man's right hand, and then fired another round up into the telephone pole. What had oversold it in Nic's mind had been the dime bag the pimp put into the hooker's dead hand.

The ejected cartridge Nic found in the sewer and the bullet from the telephone pole, were exact matches for the gun used to kill the prostitute. Once confronted with the evidence, the pimp had folded like the circus leaving town.

Among other successful cases, this one would be instrumental in securing Nic's promotion.

* * * *

Applause summoned Nic from his thoughts in time to see his cousin receive his degree.

"Christopher Alexander Ford, B.A. in American History," came a voice from somewhere on the dais.

Later, waiting for Chris, Nic paused to consider that both he and his cousin were graduating at the same time. Chris arrived with his diploma in one hand and surprisingly, Mallory in his other.

"Nic!" Chris said.

"Buddy. How's it hanging?" Nic replied.

"Better, now that you're here!" Chris faced his loved ones, but before he could speak, Mallory interjected excitedly.

"We've got news—" she kissed Chris, "we're getting married!"

Nic watched in slow motion as his mom, Aunt Danielle, and Mrs. Everhill all started whooping and crying while his father, Uncle John, and Mr. Everhill offered varying degrees of smiles. A sudden image of Grandmother Elena came to Nic's mind: her dream realized—the arrival of the Fords as an American success story.

CHAPTER 28

1998
MOSCOW

It had taken Slaga three years to arrive at this moment. After painstaking, fatiguing research, bribes, and construction of a fake biography, he'd finally been hired onto the sanitation team that cleaned the KGB offices at Lubyanka. Only now, the KGB was FSB. Different initials. Same goons.

After the coup attempt in 1991, the KGB had been reorganized. The department handling Russian internal security had been assumed by the FSB. A new agency responsible for espionage and intelligence-gathering activities outside of Russia was created. The SVR, Foreign Intelligence Service, was located in the southwestern part of Moscow in the Yasenevo District.

Slaga had been able to determine that while the dead man from Misha's notes had been KGB—whose activities were now under the direction of SVR in Yasenevo—the files Slaga was after were still in the offices at Lubyanka. The vetting process to be hired had been similar to his Spetsnaz recruitment. To make it look legitimate, Slaga had taken an apartment in Kapotnya, one of Moscow's dirtiest neighborhoods. Then he'd concocted a good backstory.

Most of the narrative surrounded being a burnout veteran of the Afghan campaign. Since coming home from Afghanistan, *Bruno Shakili*, had suffered from post-traumatic stress, retreating each night into alcohol for relief. He'd even created a need to take every other month off for rehabilitation at the Red Army's Main Medical Clinical hospital. This allowed him time away to tend to his business in America. A veteran, Slaga seemed harmless enough. In exchange for less pay, the difference of which the sanitation team manager kept, he'd been hired.

The priest's notes, in Misha's possession, had referenced the dying KGB man's office had been on the fifth floor—the holy of holies. The fifth floor was the location of a host of senior offices: directors's offic-es ... Directorates for Investigations, Economic Counterintelligence, Operational Reconnaissance, and the heavyweight Military Counter-intelligence. There was also a Directorate of Records and Archives. While most records of the former USSR's foreign intelligence and recon had moved with SVR to Yasenevo, there were holdovers FSB did not want to share with SVR. These records pertained to agent networks in the Americas. None of these directly impacted FSB, but parochial interests still trumped operational necessity.

It took another year to be assigned to the fifth-floor cleaning team. The bribes to work this floor needed to be less obtrusive.

"Why the fifth floor, Bruno?" The sanitation team boss asked suspiciously.

Slaga was able to convince her the fifth floor's better ventilation helped him breathe easier, his lungs being damaged from chemicals and gases he'd ingested in Afghanistan. It was all a lie. It worked. That and the attention he'd paid to the slightly frumpy, middle-aged manager, whose husband had left her the previous year.

A month of recon on the fifth floor, and he'd still not located the office of Misha's dead KGB man. Four years before, the entire floor had undergone renovations. According to others on his shift, many of the offices looked nothing like they'd been before the upgrade. One night, as Slaga emptied the garbage, the AC came on. A *clanging* came from behind the desk of the office he was in. Tilting his head, Slaga paused his mopping to evaluate the space he'd taken for granted.

Glancing at the desk plate, Slaga's brow wrinkled in momentary confusion. Beneath the name were the words: SUB DIRECTOR, ECO-NOMIC DIRECTORATE. Slaga began to berate himself. All this time, he'd been looking for an office of someone in the intelligence area, forgetting that economics was a major area of interest to Russia. Not able to generate much of their own business research and innova-tion, Russia sought to steal it. Spying on American, European, and

Japanese businesses operating in Russia would be a large endeavor. After SVR had left the building, this particular office was turned over to the FSB deputy for economic surveillance.

Slaga came to the door, his cohort on the fifth-floor detail still at the other end of the building. Their routine was to work from opposite ends of the floor, eventually meeting in the middle. Normally, a security person would accompany them—to keep them from doing exactly what Slaga was trying to do—but the surveillance man was a boozehound and spent much of the time in the basement drinking with the other security team members.

From his cleaning cart, Slaga removed a small, high-intensity flashlight. He rapidly checked the desk. Locked. File cabinets. Same. He'd expected nothing less. Turning his attention to the area behind the desk, he ran his fingers over the wall. Nothing. A second time over the section, however, and he found a small seam joining two partitions. The seam ran to the floor, suggesting the panels had been used to cover something—like an old air duct.

To get to it would require pulling the panel away from the wall. This would leave a messy scar, alerting the occupant that someone had been poking around his office. Slaga would have to wait. He'd need tools, like a Halligan bar to pry the metal plates apart and then a soldering iron and some solder to seal them back into place. Lastly, putty and paint to restore the wall after he was done. His major concern was to dissipate the smell created by the soldering, paint, and putty work. The following Monday would be the celebration of National Victory Day. A three-day weekend—perfect. He'd start Friday night and any signs of his visit would have dissipated by Tuesday when everyone returned from the long weekend.

CHAPTER 29

1998
MOSCOW

Saturday was always a good one for General Vadik Pyotr. It was a great day to work. No distractions—just time to plan, consider, and execute. Stepping into the courtyard in front of his palatial, German-influenced, mid-century home, he savored the crisp, early morning air. Holding the door to his Volvo S90 was his butler. A frown creased Pyotr's face as he stopped to brush lint or dandruff, hard to tell, from the shoulder of the valet's suit jacket.

Stepping back, the General smiled. "Better."

"Yes sir," came a clipped, obedient reply.

Leaving the home he shared with his wife Ohxa and two children, he motored through the quiet streets of his Rublyovka subdivision. His neighbors were still asleep, probably hungover from their previous night's activities. A teetotaler, Vadik considered the massive consumption of vodka by his countrymen to be a colossal disaster that prevented Russia from taking her rightful place at the head of the table of nations.

A thirty-year plus vet of the Red Army, now the Russian Ground Forces, Pyotr had missed most of the Russian campaign in Afghanistan, but still he'd performed advisor services with Russian forces deployed in various African countries and seen action in the Georgian Civil War, Abkhazian War, Tajikistani Civil War, First Chechen War, Dagestan and the insurgencies in the North Caucasus and in Ukraine.

Fancying himself a modern-day Boyar, Pyotr had gained a reputation for being a dandy among his fellow servicemen. But no one ever said this to his face. For while Vadik Pyotr was every bit the sophisticate, he was also an early adopter of mixed martial arts. On combat tours, Pyotr had entered makeshift cages with captured enemies, offering them their freedom if they could defeat him. Few of his opponents understood prior to entering the cage, that these were battles to the death. Pyotr was rumored to have killed over twenty men.

But it wasn't just combat that spurred Pyotr, but the nominal cover these battles gave him to employ sadistic tactics designed to prolong an adversary's life while imposing the most pain he could exact.

Driving through Moscow's early morning streets, he thought again about how lucky he was to live here with buildings, cafes, trees, gardens, and sights that inspired Pushkin, Dostoevsky, Tolstoy, and Chekov—his for free. Old Novgorod-Russian architecture blended with Byzantine-revival styles of the nineteenth century melding with newer utilitarian Stalinist, Khrushchev, and Brezhnev buildings so ugly they were now *en vogue*. Vadik loved it all. He loved the lines and the collisions of design. But where the rest of Europe saw backwardness, Vadik saw a long-running historical narrative that ran back to the dawn of civilization—far earlier than any settlements in Europe.

Coming into the parking lot of the FSB building, he stopped to visit the front desk. He scanned the visitor log, always wanting to be aware of who might be in on a Saturday. Whether a senior or subordinate, Vadik wanted to let them know he was there. Still, he was just as relieved when there was no one else to concern himself with.

On the fifth floor, he made his way to his office. After his last combat tour, he'd been offered a senior position as the head of the Economic Directorate. While not as prestigious as some of the more senior military assignments, it did offer opportunities in other areas that he intended to take advantage of. First, he stopped at the maps section to pull some charts. His department oversaw the management of vast tracts of natural resources—specifically the far eastern energy resources of Chukotka and diamond mines in Sakha.

He took the graphs and maps to his office and put them on the table in the corner; he stopped when he detected the barest trace, a smell of something. Like paint. Slowly, he made his way to his desk.

Moving his chair aside, he knelt to examine the bulge in the wall where the smell was coming from. He knew that behind it was an AC vent, but nothing else. Running his finger over the edge of the panel, he perceived a slight contrast between the lip and the rest of the wall. Like a newer coat of paint versus the surrounding older latex cover.

He could not recall any maintenance being scheduled for the fifth floor. Stepping back, he scrutinized the entire wall. Other than the vent, nothing else appeared unusual. Moving to his charts table, he laid out maps that were highlighted in yellow and denoted large concentrations of natural gas and diamonds. He made notes on a pad, and moved quickly through the charts. Two hours later, he returned the charts to the maps section and departed.

That Tuesday, as he started into the FSB building, he stopped at the elevator and returned to the front desk.

"Yes, Comrade General?" asked a ramrod-straight corporal behind the counter.

"Where is the facilities department?" Vadik said.

"Second floor, General."

On the second floor, Vadik made his way through a sea of desks, each occupied by intimidated clerks unused to seeing a general officer on their floor. He found the building supervisor's office. The scruffy-looking man in the ill-fitting suit was leaning back in his chair, feet on the desk, reading *Pravda.*

"Pardon me," Vadik solicitously said.

"*Da*, leave it on my desk," the man brusquely said without looking up.

"No, I need you to look something up for me," Vadik patiently replied.

"Come back in an hour."

"I need it now."

"I said, come back in—" the paper came down huffily, but agitation on the supervisor's face morphed into shocked fear. The man bolted to his feet. "Comrade General, I'm so sorry, I did not expect—"

Vadik gently waved a hand indicating nothing was wrong. "It is of no concern; do not worry."

Greatly relieved, yet still wary, the man said, "How can I help the General?"

"Was maintenance scheduled for the fifth floor this past weekend?"

Stepping to a file drawer, the facilities man thumbed through files before closing the cabinet. "No, General."

Vadik's eyes narrowed. After a moment, a new thought came to mind. "Do you have access to the building's history records?"

"Yes, General. Is there something specific you're looking for?"

"Who were the past occupants of my office?"

* * * *

WASHINGTON

Congressman Byrnes took his place. Finally, he was making progress. Since his election in 1992, he'd been given ever more responsibility. Today he took possession of the gavel as the newly named Chairman of the House Appropriations Sub-Committee for Agriculture, Rural Development, Food and Drug Administration. Being in Washington whetted his appetite for power. But he argued to himself, that it was power for the people—to make a difference in the lives of his constituents back home.

While Congressman Byrnes would have preferred a sub-committee with more teeth—something like Defense or Homeland Security—being a sub-committee Chair was the next rung on the ladder of ascendancy. Someday, he'd reach Chair of all of Appropriations and who knew, maybe Speaker. But for today, Agriculture would play well back in South Carolina. Keep getting him elected.

The other beauty of a Chairmanship, was the need for more travel, which led to increased opportunities to satisfy his other cravings. Power was also an aphrodisiac. Women were drawn to him—his position he knew—but still it was him they would submit to.

CHAPTER 30

2003
NEW YORK

The intervening years since they'd gotten married, had flown by in a blur, yet Chris and Mallory were still in love as if on their honeymoon. To complement their domestic bliss, each embarked on careers, both financially rewarding, mentally stimulating, and that offered pathways up society's pyramid. Still, every once in a while, their self-driven whirlwind felt more like a steamroller than a finely tuned sports car.

High-intensity-packed sessions at the New York Athletic Club and good diets, kept the young power couple in shape. But the stress, good and bad, of pursuing a *Vanity Fair* worthy lifestyle nipped at them.

Posing before a ten-foot, floor-to-ceiling framed mirror, Chris double-checked the shine of his black, Hugo Boss dress shoes, ensuring his trousers with the English cuff, barely touched the top of his Oxford wing tips. Suddenly there came a throbbing in his temples. Since childhood, he'd dealt with migraines that struck from out of the blue before disappearing again for months.

Sitting on the edge of the bed, he practiced the deep breathing exercises Grigor had taught him, while gently massaging his head and neck. Quietly the pain abated. "You know, every once in a while, I wish I could see another doctor," Chris said as Mallory finished dressing. Looping his tie before the dresser mirror, he added, "Know what I mean?"

Hopping while attempting to adjust her high heel, Mallory said, "All I know is I'm late. Let's go, honey."

In the car, they made their way south on Ninth Avenue through Hell's Kitchen. Mallory's office handled cases for some of the largest real estate barons in New York. Through an associate at Glentower Realty Holdings, Mallory and Chris had found a nice "fixer upper" a couple of blocks off Columbus Circle. *Fixer* was a misnomer. About the only thing that needed fixing was updating the pulls on the kitchen cabinets. Eventually, the Fords were hoping to make their way to Central Park West with a view overlooking Tavern on the Green and Sheep Meadow.

Dropping Chris at the District Attorney's office, Mallory called out, "Don't forget the thing at the Whitney tonight!" This was met with an indifferent wave as Chris disappeared into the building.

Late that afternoon, Chris departed work, taking a car service back uptown. At Columbus Circle, he stepped from the limo, tipped the driver, and paused to savor the view. He felt like the king of the city at that moment. Checking his tie, and brushing back his already-perfect blond coiffure—every hair in place—Chris turned from Central Park and entered the Center for Right Being.

Coming out of his session, he paused at a favorite picture on the wall. It was of Elena and a young Grigor.

"Ah Christopher, she was an elegant lady. Yes?" Grigor said in his accented English.

Not taking his eyes from it, Chris replied, "Still miss her."

"She'd be well pleased with your life."

Chris turned to leave. Proffering a hand, "Have a nice weekend, Stephan. See you soon."

"Yees, and tell Mallory I said hello."

With a nod of his head, Chris departed. Coming to the plate-glass window, Grigor watched him go, lips twitching into a subtle smile.

CHAPTER 31

2003
NEW YORK

It hardly seemed like five years since that night at FSB in Moscow when Slaga had pried open the panels behind the desk in the office of Sub-Director of the Economic Directorate.

* * * *

Cautiously, Slaga put his tiny flashlight into the recess. A quick scan revealed nothing. A sense of panic and anger flooded his mind, "Another mirage?"

But then a thought occurred to him. Slowly, he lay on the ground and turned the light ... upward. There it was. A black plastic-enshrouded package taped to the duct wall. Slowly, he pulled it free, and without looking at it, stuffed it into his cleaning cart and set about rapidly repairing the damage to the panel wall.

With the file in tow, Slaga returned to his decrepit, filthy apartment. Opening a bottle of vodka, he sat staring at the package on his table. Fingers trembling for the first time since combat in Afghanistan, he unwrapped it. Heart racing, he could hardly breathe. He removed a musty, time-forgotten accordion file from the package. A name in the corner read ERICH VON GRUPP, DIRECTOR. Beneath that, there was a flap with faded wording on it. Slaga strained to make it out:

> Полярный удар. [POLAR STRIKE].
>
> Practically gulping air, he'd pried open the flap, an image of Pandora's Box flashing through his mind. In the first slot was a single piece of paper. Yellowed, but still pristine, Slaga gently laid it on the table. Beginning to

read, a chill came over him as if he were at the end of the world.

Операция полярная забастовка [OPERATION POLAR STRIKE]

With the goal of total disruption of the government of the United States of America:

Director KGB, with approval of the General Secretary and the Politburo, herewith commissions the creation of a program to place operatives into positions of authority within the US government.

The ultimate purpose will be the corrupting, reducing, degrading, and destroying the American government's capability of responding to a Soviet First Nuclear Strike.

Operatives are not to be recruited for this effort, but rather will be identified first and then will be inculcated with all the training, education, knowledge, and programming required to carry out their assigned mission, before finally being inserted.

Ideal Candidates—Infants of:

a. Russian émigrés in America still loyal to USSR
b. Americans with known sympathies for the USSR
c. Soviet diplomatic, commercial, and military personnel with open-ended assignments to the United Nations

Operatives will be unaware of their "installed" programming until activated. This program will only be implemented in the event of a Soviet Nuclear Attack.

Signed this day
4 июля 1955 [JULY 4, 1955]

Иван Александрович Серов [IVAN ALEKSANDROVICH SEROV]

Председатель Комитета по безопасности государства
[CHAIRMAN OF THE COMMITTEE FOR STATE SECURITY]

Slaga caught his breath; decades of whispers and rumors were finally confirmed and in the very hand of the Butcher himself. The rest of the file was a treasure trove of documents that a historian would have loved ... but was largely a record of ambitious failure: countless experiments to instill thought control, manipulated thoughts, or brainwashing had ended with no verifiable success. Clouds of doubt began to form again. Maybe it *was just* a myth.

The last file slot was thin, but as Slaga began to read the contents, he knew he'd hit blackjack. While most of the Soviet research into mind and thought control had been a failure, there had been one case with some upside. The documentation discussed the traction the programming was having with one patient. Slaga laughed at this reference.

* * * *

Since securing the file, Slaga had spent the last five years trying to understand what he had. While the files were thorough, Grupp, Polar Strike's last overseer, had been somewhat vague about particulars, choosing to use initials where possible. But he'd indicated that the patient and handler were in New York. So, where Grupp referred to a "Doctor G," Slaga compiled a list of psychiatrists in New York whose last name began with the letter *G*.

Six months later, he still had an encyclopedia of names to cull through. One day, as he sat in his vehicle at a stoplight, his eye was caught by a bus ad for the upcoming season at the Metropolitan Opera. "What do Americans know about opera?" As the bus pulled away, it revealed another placard on the bus-stop shelter for a free health clinic. Slaga growled as he realized he was looking for the wrong type of doctor.

In Manhattan, and the surrounding suburbs of New Jersey and Connecticut, there were thousands of doctors. Narrowing the list to names beginning with a *G*, reduced it to a more-manageable number; still, two years later, he was no nearer to identifying *Doctor G.*

He went back to Grupp's file. Doctor G. One patient. But how many others was he or she seeing? No mention of gender. Somewhere in New York City. No schools, neighborhoods. No identification of the parents. A grandparent. Grupp referred to her as *E.* The file referenced that the handler was an émigré. That stood to reason; most Americans were émigrés or descended from an émigré.

Once a month, the handler brought two patients in to see Doctor G. The file contained copies of the visit notes. It was thought the programming being instilled in the patient was taking root, largely due to the age the programming had commenced. The sessions had started early in the patient's life.

Suddenly, a monstrous thought flooded his brain. He gagged, fighting to hold down the bile in his throat. He cast the file across the room while simultaneously leaping from his dining room table as if a snake had appeared on his plate.

The handler and the grandparent were the same person.

Tears came to his eyes as he contemplated betrayal of this magnitude. It took a month to finally pick the file up, only to put it on a bookshelf, where it sat for two more months.

Eventually, military instincts reasserted themselves. This person, whoever it was, might be in a position to help him. With forced clinical detachment, he opened the file again. Émigré. Most likely a European, but from where? Who would the USSR trust with one of its most secret of secrets? It had to be a Russian.

Émigré from Russia? Grandparent. Running likely ages through his head, Slaga considered that his quarry might have arrived in America sometime in the thirties or forties.

A man, who owed Slaga a big loansharking-gambling debt, worked at Immigration and Naturalization. Through back channels, the man was able to check historic US Bureau of Immigration records. He searched generally for Russian immigrants arriving to New York, whose first name started with an *E.* A couple of weeks later, Slaga returned from lunch to find an envelope on his desk. The return address was from INS. The sense of dread—he'd first experienced with the arrival of Misha's letter years before—returned.

"Ba!" He barked dismissively. "I'm tired of old wives's fears." He closed the door to his office. Opening the envelope, he removed a single piece of paper:

ELENA AND ALEXANDER FORONOPOV

He stared at the paper. He was getting closer.

CHAPTER 32

2004
NEW YORK

The unraveling of the investigation into the Foronopovs had taken another year. Elena Foronopov—now Ford—died a decade before Slaga even knew her name. But in his research, Slaga had found the mother lode. Ford had a grandson, Christopher, who was married to his wife, Mallory.

Seeing them for the first time was like seeing for the first time. Gazing from afar, hidden behind the smoke-tint windows of his Escalade, endless possibilities passed through his head of what the young blond-haired, green-eyed prince of the city and his fair maiden could do for Slaga. Who was he? What did they do? Did they know about Polar Strike?

Slaga followed their Lexus LS 430; she was driving; he was apparently looking through files; they moved efficiently through traffic, downtown. Swooping into the District Attorney's office, the man leapt out and she was back into traffic speeding away.

Exiting his SUV, Slaga hurriedly gestured the two front-seat bodyguards, to follow the woman while he and another tough found a cafe with window seats facing the DA's building. After an hour, it became apparent that Ford worked at the office. Not wanting attention drawn to himself by over-lingering at the cafe, Slaga had his man page the others following the woman and then he left.

Back in the Escalade, Slaga queried his chauffeur.

"Drove to Deutsche Bank, where she parked below."

The other guard took it from there. "Followed her to the twenty-fifth floor. She went into a law office. Stephens Monroe. According to their receptionist, they specialize in land use and environmental law."

Slaga nodded, calculating how to learn more about the woman when suddenly, his backseat goon pointed. "Boss, he's leaving."

Chris Ford moved briskly down the steps into a waiting auto-service Lincoln Town Car. Slaga and his crew tailed the limo back uptown to Columbus Circle, where Ford exited the limo. Hesitant for a moment, he then strode purposefully across the plaza into a ground-floor office. Slaga motioned his driver to enter the parking garage. Leaving his men behind, Slaga sauntered to the lobby's building directory.

Scanning quickly, he located his information, "The Center for Right Being." Buying a cup of coffee, Slaga found a nearby bench. About an hour later, Ford left in another car-service vehicle. After checking that he was alone, Slaga pretended to be looking for an address as he stopped in front of the clinic. On the building plate:

CENTER FOR RIGHT BEING
STEPHAN GRIGOR, DIRECTOR

"Hello, Doctor G." Slaga's lip curled.

CHAPTER 33

2004
NEW YORK

Over the next few months, Slaga continued his observation of Ford. Sometimes, Mr. Ford came to the clinic alone, and other times he came with his wife. Trying to detect if there was a pattern to the programming that Grigor was supposedly giving Ford, Slaga followed him on weekdays, afternoons, weekends, and mornings. To date, Slaga saw no basis of standard or intentional design.

The Fords lived comfortably in a nice brownstone off Columbus Circle. Their nights were a mix of cocooned domesticity—home alone or with friends—and a carousel of social combat. Black-tie events all over town ... Democratic Party fundraisers ... Art exhibitions. The Yankee Stadium ... Madison Square Garden ... working out at the New York Athletic Club just off Central Park. They had a nice life.

Slaga changed his focus and commenced following Grigor. The doctor lived in a condominium overlooking the Hudson in Tribeca. He fancied himself a connoisseur of art, cuisine, high-end liquors, fashion, and ladies. But it wasn't too long before Slaga's men, Vitus and Pavel, realized the good doctor had an edge. Increasingly, they looked forward to Grigor's nocturnal activities. Fortunately, Grigor was a creature of habit and a bit sloppy, impervious to his surroundings, which made it easy to tail him. Uptown to Greenwich Village, where he'd meet women and hit a club or two. There would be music, occasionally an art gallery, then dinner, and back to his place.

"What's so unusual about this?" asked Slaga.

Pavel replied, "He has a different woman on different days of the week."

Slaga shrugged. "So?"

"So the pattern seems the same—blonde Tuesday. Brunette Thursday. Redhead on Friday—"

"Don't forget Saturday," Vitus added.

Pavel nodded. "On Saturday there's this streaked black-and-red haired one."

"So he likes variety," Slaga replied.

Pavel and Vitus exchanged looks.

"What?" Slaga asked, now intrigued.

"Nothing. They're from all over the city and seem to be living fairly routine domestic lives. But here's the rub Boss, they're all slightly overweight, a little chubby, and they're all married."

Slaga nodded, a small grin on his face. "Huh."

An idea presented itself. Most of Slaga's business revolved around import-export theft, but he also had contacts in the world of high-end escort services. He arranged for one of their best women—Kazia, a Rubenesque, Israeli natural—to *meet* Grigor at one of his clubs.

It had taken a time, but eventually, Grigor went out alone one night. He wore a fake wedding ring, and Kazia and some friends happened to sit at a table near him. Eventually the curvy, dark-haired, raven-eyed woman caught Grigor's attention. Soon, her friends faded into the night while the woman went to the ladies's room. Grigor made his move.

Positioning himself outside the restroom, he feigned an unresponsive cellphone. Realizing she'd hooked him, Kazia *helped* him get his bars back and soon they were talking over drinks. With a cover story that her husband was some low-level, overachieving, wannabe diplomat at the UN, Kazia was soon in the rotation.

Skilled at unlocking things in men they didn't even know about themselves, Kazia became Grigor's Friday-night showcase. First, it was wine at an art gallery in Chelsea before moving onto a club or two. One night, they'd landed at Olaf's, a private bar where Grigor had a vault.

"The Dalmore please," Grigor said to his waiter.

"Very good, Doctor."

"Wow, this place is amazing," Kazia cooed while rubbing his thigh.

Already self-centered, drink often unloosed a new level of pomposity. "Only the best," Grigor replied.

Kazia leaned in to whisper, "Let's go back to your place; I want to do something special tonight."

Later, as he lay in her arms, he said, "I've never had anyone do that to me before."

In the dark, Kazia just smiled.

But Grigor was fastidious about separating his personal and professional lives. The doctor even retained his own cleaning service, so a repeat of Slaga getting onto the night-janitorial team appeared out. It was impossible to get him to take Kazia to his clinic. They could make copies of keys easily, however there was an alarm system. Eventually, Kazia struck upon the idea of forcing him to unlock *her*.

"I want you in your office," Kazia whispered in his ear one night.

Grigor grunted but did not reply. This went on for a couple of weeks.

"You know I can't take you there; it would be a compromise of patient confidentiality," he said to her most-recent request.

"Why? I won't see anything."

Grigor dismissively answered. "Sorry. Can't do it."

Kazia leaned in. "I'm going to dress up in that nurse's outfit you said you want."

Suddenly aroused, Grigor huskily fought back. "So?"

"Then I'm gonna take you into your office and—"

He waited, trying to remain calmly disinterested. "Yes?" But Kazia did not reply, only nibbling his neck and ear. "What?" he asked, his tone revealing a man at war in the no man's land between duty and desire.

Kazia nibbled his neck and ear lobe, putting a hand under the covers. "I'm going to bend you over your desk—" the rest whispered into the Doctor's ear, caused his lust to boil over while simultaneously submerging his ability to reason.

It did not take long before Grigor caved in. Taking her to the clinic, he led her inside where he was about to disarm the office security system.

Dressed in a long coat, Kazia let it fall open, revealing a super-tight, white nurse's outfit that barely covered a white garter belt, hose, and white stilettos. A small doctor's bag in hand, she stepped in front of him. "Let me enter the code with my tongue," she said.

Unable to restrain himself, Grigor complied barely making it to his desk.

The code was only part of the problem, as access for Slaga and his men to Grigor's office proved to be a false start. On the first night, they entered the clinic, they'd been quick and efficient, wishing to avoid the roving building-security detail. They moved through the storage cabinets and found a file on Chris Ford. They located another on Mallory Ford, but the files were mostly medical in nature. Other than the need for her to carry an autoimmune injector to combat allergic reactions to some foods, there appeared to be nothing out of the ordinary.

Finally, as Slaga made his way around the clinic, he arrived at the locked door. He read the sign at the end of the hallway: LIGHT CHAMBER. He faced the lock; it was easily one of the hardest Slaga had ever seen. Yet after ten minutes, it *popped.* Opening the door, Slaga flipped on the wall switch; the lights came on. Nothing Slaga discovered about this Polar Strike project had prepared him for what he saw.

The walls appeared to be paneled with TV monitors, all colored in soft bluish and green. Shag carpet covered the floor. There were no pictures or decorations of any type. The device descending from the ceiling seemed intrusive, almost angry.

A long, black-metal tube—approximately four feet in length—dropped snake-like into the center of the room. From the end of the tube, a crystalline wand extended another foot. At the end of the wand was a small globe of translucent glass. A divan and a chair sat at the center of the room, facing the wand.

In the chair, he imagined was Grigor's, Slaga picked up a device that looked like a TV remote. He pushed a button. The walls came to life. Ocean scenes lit up on either side of the room accompanied by sounds of waves gently caressing the shore. Slaga quickly pushed the same button again, returning the silence. For a moment, he glanced around the room, as if trying to divine its secrets.

Concluding their inspection, but finding nothing unusual, Slaga slipped into the night.

The next morning, the receptionist at the Center for Right Being arrived at work just as the phone rang.

"Center for Right Being," she said.

A male voice replied. "I would like to schedule an appointment with Doctor Grigor."

"Have you been to see Doctor Grigor before?"

The caller, clearly not American, said, "No, but Mr. and Mrs. Ford recommended I see the Doctor."

CHAPTER 34

2004
NEW YORK

Slaga was escorted into the Director's office. Having only seen pictures of the man, he still felt the temperature in the room drop when Grigor finally entered through a door that led to his private office. Grigor's antenna immediately detected something amiss as he took Slaga in. He looked at the file on his desk.

"Meester ... James Richardson?"

"Good to meet you, Doctor."

The two men shook hands—each snatching their limbs back as if they'd touched the devil himself. Grigor gestured to the chair in front of his desk as he sat.

"How can I help you, Meester Richardson?"

Slaga removed a file from a black satchel next to his chair. Donning reading glasses, he theatrically opened the file before directing a laser-beam squint at Grigor. From a position of strength, the doctor suddenly felt a chill run through him. It was now clear the man was not here for medical attention; the visitor's next words did not surprise Grigor.

"Tell me about *Polar Strike.*"

* * * *

At home, later that night, Slaga splashed vodka into a tumbler; he sat before an open window into the dark night, and replayed the conversation in his head.

Grigor had not been completely surprised that someone had come. Yet, the timing had impressed him—eleven years since Elena's passing. Slaga had anticipated this. He'd initially put the doctor at ease, producing a fake FSB credential and telling him that after the fall of the USSR, Polar Strike had been put on ice while the leaders in the new Federation sought to read the roadmap to Russia's future and their options vis-à-vis the United States. With most of the program discredited years before, Grigor's one charge was the only active operation left.

* * * *

"But why now?" Grigor asked.

"What do you mean, 'why now?'"

"I mean, Russia and America are not really engaged in any real battles for control of the world anymore. So why look to rebuild a relic of the Cold War?" Grigor replied.

"Because you always want to have options, even old, untried ones," Slaga replied prickly, put off by the question and Grigor's sanctimonious air.

Grigor's right eyebrow twitched, but he said nothing. Slaga moved slowly in probing him for information about Ford. He paused as he recalled the point when he'd asked about projects Ford was pursuing at work. Grigor's eyes had narrowed when Slaga had inquired as to the DA's possible interest in Russian-mob activities.

"You know that's not our purpose. Why would FSB be concerned about thugs and hooligans?"

"Possible future allies or access to their networks."

This seemed to mollify Grigor and the remainder of the conversation revolved around how Grigor's network, which consisted mostly of himself after Elena Ford had died—and how there had been only radio silence from Moscow. Initially, this had worried Grigor; he thought he was under surveillance and eventually he would be found out, but nothing had happened. Elena's friend, Galina, had continued to bring Chris and her granddaughter, Mallory, in for their medical visits. And with his growing outside activities, Grigor decided it would be easier to wait to hear from Moscow rather than reaching out to reestablish contact.

* * * *

Taking a sip of vodka, Slaga realized he'd committed another cardinal sin ... he'd not asked how the whole brainwashing-thing worked. He mentally kicked himself, now worried he'd tipped his hand. Grigor would see through him and realize he was not FSB.

This game of hide-and-go-seek continued for a few more months. Slaga visited every three weeks. Grigor shared Ford's progress. He did not elaborate much and Slaga could hardly know what progress in this area even looked like, but still, it seemed there was something hidden—something Grigor knew, but was keeping behind that stony, psychiatrist wall of arrogant aloofness.

He sipped his vodka and tilted his head back, working cricks from his neck. There was always a more direct means of getting Grigor's cooperation, but he'd wait to employ those means until necessary. Ford's ultimate career ascension might prove useful, but he was young. He would wait and watch.

CHAPTER 35

2005
NEW YORK

Slate-gray sky greeted the opening of the ice rink at Rockefeller Center. Images of winter in Saint Petersburg coaxed a smile from Slaga's craggy face. He and his cousin were always sneaking out of class at the Pushkin New Technical School. Professors thought he was slow and paid little attention to him, but even at an early age, people detected a hard underbelly of cold brutality and left him alone. The two boys whiled away hours on the frozen Neva River, playing hockey, dreaming of one day starring for the fabled Red Army team.

Watching Americans attempt to skate evoked a sneer. What a soft people—they had no concept of the ransom winter demanded to let one go free every spring: the crushing cold that sapped one's life away. Most Manhattanites had probably never even been to a frozen winter lake. Instead, they came to a concrete creation surrounded by the trappings of high-end shopping and mocha coffees. They spent money, however, and that was what Slaga counted on. He would build a new Russian empire in the Americas on the backs and wallets of the clumsy oafs before him. What had Lenin said? "The Capitalists will sell us the rope with which we will hang them." He got the sentiment right, but not the outcome.

Slaga looked at his watch again. "Where is he?" he growled. "This better not be a waste of my time."

Just then, a man furtively arrived at Slaga's table. Before they could react, Slaga softly signaled Vitus and Pavel, seated at nearby tables, to remain in place. Studying the new arrival, Slaga quickly determined he possessed the right combination of weasel-like greed and desire to appease.

"Mr. Slaga?" he asked.

Slaga nodded but said nothing.

"Did you bring the money?"

"Yes."

The man squirmed uncomfortably. "Where is it?"

"Tell me about him, and stop your agitation; it will call attention to us."

Taking a deep breath, the man relaxed enough to sit back in his seat, but only barely. "He's doing very well. The DA—district—"

Slaga motioned to speed up, "Yes, yes, district attorney. Yes."

"They're moving him to the head of a task force on organized crime ... Russian organized crime."

Slaga put a hand out behind him, into which one of his assistants laid a file. Positioning it on the table between himself and the man, he opened it and scribbled something. "Most interesting. You will keep me updated. Yes?"

The weasel nodded, looking about furtively.

Slaga put his hand out to the side, this time taking an envelope from his guard. "Wait to look later. Understand?" Without glancing at it, he handed the envelope to the man, who snatched it. Slaga and his muscle quietly strode away.

In the back of his Cadillac Escalade, Slaga considered what he had heard: "Russian organized crime." Perhaps there was a way to use this to eliminate some of his competition.

"Columbus Circle," he said.

* * * *

WASHINGTON

Thirteen long years—Adam Byrnes had finally ascended to the Chairmanship of Appropriations. In an age when seniority carried less weight with the party leadership, fundraising had become the new currency of importance with regard to Congressional assignments. Good fortune, along with his father-in-law's connections in the southern states, had enabled Byrnes to become a formidable campaigner on behalf of other Congressmen and Senators in neighboring states, which ensured their support when it came time to try for the Chairmanship.

Chairmanship also carried more prestige in matters of a more personal front. Since arriving in Congress, Byrnes had set about quietly ensuring outlets for his sexual appetites, careful not to get too close to any individual partner, lest they get the idea he was looking for a new spouse. With PJ safely home in Georgia, Byrnes had found Washington to be a veritable big-game preserve—if he was careful.

With a Chairmen's term set at six years, he'd need to find another committee to start laying the groundwork for a new position or be elevated to a House leadership position such as Caucus Chair or the Whip. But for tonight, Chairman of Appropriations was just fine, especially with the comely lobbyist for some senior citizen's tax organization whose name he could not recall.

CHAPTER 36

2005
NEW YORK

"It is finally time to have a—what did the Americans call it?" Slaga rolled his tongue, "a 'come to Jesus moment.'" Grigor needed to understand some things. At the clinic, Grigor's assistant kept Slaga cooling his heels in the waiting area as the doctor finished an appointment. Opening the door to his office to escort out the patient, a scowl and eye twitch were the only signs that Grigor acknowledged his fellow Russian.

"Meesus Davis, this is my friend, Meester Richardson."

She proffered a hand to Slaga, "Pleased, I'm sure. Stephan is the best."

Slaga nodded agreeably.

Grigor continued her to the door, "Now enjoy the weekend, and I'll see you in a few weeks."

After she'd departed, Grigor said nothing as he led Slaga into his office.

"This is outside our normal meeting schedule."

Grigor's smug irritation only made things easier for Slaga. "Yes, Doctor, I'm aware of this."

Taking a seat behind his desk, Grigor removed his glasses to clean them. Affecting an academic condescension toward the Russian agent, a peon in comparison to himself, he sneeringly said, "What can I help the Russian Foreign Intelligence Service with today?"

Still standing, Slaga removed his gloves as he stepped around the desk. With a speed that shocked Grigor, he slapped the doctor across the face with the gloves. Grigor leapt to his feet. "How dare you! I'll have you shipped to Siberia, you classless pig!" He pushed the intercom button on his desk, "Greta, call Vasily at the Russian UN Office."

Slaga took a seat while eying Grigor. After a moment, the intercom squawked.

"Now why would a common doctor have a contact at the Russian UN Office?"

"Line one, Doctor."

Reaching for the phone, Grigor looked with contemptuous triumph at Slaga. Yet, the intelligence agency man just sat there as if immune to anything Grigor could summon. Grigor thought, "He must be insane." But something in the agent's demeanor had changed. There was a hardness that had not been present in their previous meetings. The threat of great physical violence lurked about him, like a cloak of fine of cloth. He could take the cloak off if need be, but Grigor sensed it worked best when its presence was merely perceived. He had broad shoulders and a hard jaw. Grigor had never noticed how big and yet gentle Slaga's hands were—the hands that had just slapped him.

Grigor pushed the intercom button. "Greta, tell him I'll call him back. Sorry for the inconvenience." Something told the doctor to sit quietly back in his chair. "Who are you, really?"

Slaga gave a slight tip of his head. "Thank you. Now we can begin anew. I should have been more forthcoming, but I needed to know who you were and what you were about."

"What do you need?"

Slaga reached into his briefcase to remove a file. "Tell me how it works."

Over the next couple of hours, Slaga explained that Grigor no longer worked for any government but the free market, namely Slaga. It was made clear that his livelihood, status in America, and network of voluptuous married women were all contingent on keeping Slaga happy. Seething inside, but unable to identify a way out at the moment, Grigor gave Slaga the barest of briefings on thought insertion, manipulation, and brainwashing. The room with the apparatus was called the Light Lab. He was going further into a person's psyche to implant thoughts that could change their life for the better. Slaga had leaned forward as Grigor explained it, like a dog waiting for his master to drop a bone. Grigor considered holding some things back, but one look at Slaga's hands gave him pause.

As the two men concluded, Slaga closed his file and put it back into his attaché case. "I'm sure I will have more questions about the techniques, but for now I would like to know what Ford is working on at the DA's office."

Shifting in his chair and about to object that this was a clear violation of doctor-patient privilege—Grigor swallowed, forcing a nod of his head.

CHAPTER 37

2005
NEW YORK

For all his intelligence, mental acumen and insight into the human mind, it had not occurred to Grigor to ask how Slaga—who he still knew only as Mister Richardson—had come into possession of the information about Polar Strike. When he finally confronted the mobster, the answer, while quite plausible, still seemed less than truthful.

"Really Doctor, I can't disclose intelligence sources and risk having them exposed."

Incredulously, Grigor challenged him. "What? You're not even KGB ... or FSB, SVR—or whatever." The Doctor studied the man seated across from him. "Why would a thu ... an underworld person have access to this information?"

Slaga squinted his eyes, wanting to be careful not to upset the tenuous balance he'd struck with Grigor. For a moment, Slaga strained to remember. "I was acquainted with ... Von Grupp."

"Who?" Grigor asked. His sole contact had been Elena, who'd died before telling him who her contact in Moscow was. It was possibly the worst thing he could have said.

In that moment, Slaga smiled quietly to himself, now aware he could manufacture a backstory to explain his knowledge of the plot. Confidently, Slaga related how he and Von Grupp had worked together during the Soviet invasion of Afghanistan. After the war, Grupp had stayed in the KGB, while Slaga went to work for the GRU, the military intelligence unit of the USSR. They'd stayed in touch, crossing paths in Moscow at times.

One night, after a round of drinking, Grupp had shared that he was worried about someone in the KGB terminating a major project Grupp was running. He'd passed on to Slaga the location of the files, just in case something happened to him.

As Grigor listened, two things occurred to him. First, Slaga was lying. Two, Grigor didn't care. However he came into possession of Polar Strike, Slaga knew of its original construction, but not its new direction. As long as Grigor feigned belief in Slaga's preposterous cover story, it bought Grigor time. But he still needed to satisfy the mobster's need for information about Chris Ford and the District Attorney's Office activities.

It had been relatively easy to get Chris to tell him what he was working on at the DA's office. As their sessions started, Grigor would play upon Chris's sense of being overworked and oppressed.

"Can't they get someone else to do that project?"

On the divan with his eyes closed, Chris began to relax. "No. Well, sorta no. It's work someone else could do, but it is work that people want to do—you know career-advancing things. So, *I* have to do it."

"Who are these people?" Grigor asked nonchalantly.

"Call themselves Bratva—The Brotherhood. Not just Russian either. Ukraine. Some Chechen. Usually connected to gangs and maybe even some government back in Russia."

"Really? Like up into de' Kremlin?"

"Possibly. Probably, but we can't prove it yet or if at all."

Grigor nodded silently.

"Anyway, I've been busy trying to get inside. Catch these guys. Very ruthless and very quiet. Stay off the grid."

"Why ees' it so hard?"

Chris related how finding CIs—confidential informants—in Brighton Beach, was almost a Sisyphean task.

Nodding knowingly, Grigor appreciated the reference to the Greek tale of Sisyphus, who'd been condemned for eternity to push a rock up a hill, forever reaching the summit, only to see it roll down again.

"Getting CIs into the gangs is ridiculously hard. Have to have the right connections—they even go as far as verifying your family background in Russia. Why do *you* want to be in the gang? What can you do for us? Hell, even getting the tattoos right is a pain in the ass."

Doctor Grigor prided himself on his street knowledge as well as high society, but while he knew body markings had significance in many cultures, he'd never really explored this. "Sorry?"

Chris continued. "Tats have meaning. For instance, drops of blood signify the number of murders you've committed. A knife through your neck might be a murder for hire. Religious icons are extremely popular. You might think a cross on the chest indicates the person is religious, right?"

"Yes, but you're going to say 'no,' right?"

"It indicates someone who is committed to the thieves's life and that they do not betray other thieves. A church on the chest or shoulder would mean the person is a thief and the number of cupolas on the church indicate the number of convictions for theft. Stars on the shoulders are for gang members in a position of authority."

Fascinated by what Chris was telling him, Grigor quietly sought to shift the discussion. "What about—what do de' call him? Specter?"

Grigor was surprised by the metamorphosis that came over Chris. Slowly, Ford sat up, swiveling to face his confessor. "How do you know about that?"

Grigor spoke in a friendly, non-invasive manner. "Well I think it's been in de' press, right? You have to admit, it ees' an unusual name to apply to a criminal."

Blinking a number of times in quick succession, "Of course." Chris nodded slowly before laying back down. "He's a gang leader in Brighton. A slippery one for sure. To the best of my knowledge, there's no good picture of him. We think he is engaged in high-end import-export theft: art, collectibles, coins, stamps, antiques. Some computers. But curiously, he dabbles in numbers. Apparently, he likes gambling."

"So this man has been giving you problems? Or ees' it de' whole Russian mob?"

"Both. Specter is for pride. The rest is for work. But you get both, probably win you the statehouse or the Senate. Don't you think?"

"Absolutely. I'm very proud of you, Chris. What remarkable progress you and Mallory are making."

Grigor stood, ending the session. But as Chris rose from the divan, he remained in place. Turning back questioningly, Grigor said, "Chris?"

"I want you to know something else. This scum. These Russian mobsters besmirch the name of generations of Russkaya who came to this country to build a new life. People, who through back-breaking work and sheer force of will, cast a future here ... and I'll be damned if I'm going to let some slobs and bullies ruin that."

Mesmerized, Grigor nodded. Breaking the momentary spell, Grigor gently took Ford's arm, escorting him to the clinic entrance. "Next week then?"

Chris nodded. "Until then. Thanks Stephan."

Grigor locked the door after him. Back in the lab, he sat down. "He's gone."

At the far end of the chamber, another door, camouflaged in the wall, popped open. Slaga stepped out and took a seat.

"Ambitious, this one."

"You got what you want. What will you do next?"

Slaga was silent, lost in thought.

"Don't you ... do anything to him. You understand?"

Slaga raised an eyebrow. "Are you threatening me, Doctor?" he said softly.

"No. Just ... don't."

Slaga sat as if in his own home, studying the doctor to the point of discomfort. Finally, Grigor huffed, "What?"

"Why the chubby women?"

"What?" Grigor replied incredulously.

"You're a reasonably handsome man. Why not a pretty woman?"

"How do you know—", Grigor's eyes narrowed, "of course." He studied the thug for a moment. "You really don't understand human nature do you? I mean, beyond de' use of fear. You can get people to do things for you through other means."

Slaga gestured for him to continue.

"A woman's greatest ally is a mirror. She looks in it and sees beauty. As she enters her prime, the mirror confirms her desirousness. She manipulates men. They serve her. But slowly, the mirror becomes an enemy. It documents her descent from the summit of desire. These ... curvaceous women are on dat' descent. As they do, many come to a realization that they're willing to do things the younger ones don't yet have to, to remain desirable."

"And you prey on these women."

Staring Slaga dead in the eye, Grigor tersely replied. "We all hunt in some fashion."

CHAPTER 38

2008
NEW YORK

Seated at his father's desk, Nic lovingly rubbed his father's police shield. "Dad, tell me again about the Specter," Nic casually asked.

Michael stopped packing up his things and sat down. His eyes roamed about his office. Plaques, certificates, and citations attested to a star-studded, success-laden career. His son's question underscored the one great failure. "Never could link him to Club Twenty-Two. No witnesses. No trail—nothing; he just up and disappeared into the mist. Best of my knowledge, we don't even have a good picture of him." Michael looked down at his hands, an old man's hands. "Really is like a—"

"We'll get him."

Both men heard the words, but neither was really listening. Looking up, Michael blinked at his son. Fordham, NYPD, marriage, Nic—forty years—where? "I know. We always do. Some just take longer to get into the boat is all."

* * * *

Chris gave Mallory a quick buss as he dashed out the door. "Going to see Stephan on the way home. See you tonight," he called.

"Don't be late; we have that black-tie at the mayor's, at seven." Uncertain if her husband heard her, she grabbed her phone to text him. Finished, she stood to refill her cup of coffee. Her gaze drifted out the window to Times Square below. College. Columbia Law. Seeing Chris move into the DA's office. Then, just last year, a new apartment on Seventh Avenue. With Chris's election to the City Council, the trajectory they'd charted for themselves ten years ago was ahead of schedule. Tonight, the mayor would appoint Chris to a special task force on water management. Not the sexiest position, but certainly a launching pad and resume builder.

Like a shark, they had to keep moving. No time to savor the moment. The primary breadwinner, Mallory continued her high profile, lucrative career track with Stephens Monroe, now handling more of the firm's major, environmental case load. Always politically correct, she knew the eco-issues also built street cred, especially in the roller-derby combat that was New York Democrat politics.

* * * *

BERLIN

Adam Byrnes stepped from the limo to enter the Ritz Carlton Hotel. Built on the vestiges of the Berlin Wall, the Ritz evoked the right sense of history. Byrnes, now the ranking Democrat on the House Foreign Affairs Committee, was enjoying the moment: an American conqueror returning to the location of triumph—first over the Nazis and then over the Soviets. General Dwight Eisenhower, an American of German descent, had led the Allies to victory over the Third Reich. A few years later as President Eisenhower, he'd been forced to watch as the Soviet Union reduced half of Germany into its own fiefdom. Ironically, it had been another Republican president, Ronald Reagan, who'd laid the groundwork for the demolition of the Wall and the Soviet Union.

On a fact-finding junket, Byrnes was in Berlin to assess German defenses and their contributions to NATO. After a moment of reflection, he remembered why he was here.

A previous European junket to Spain finished up with a conference on the island of Majorca, where a night of abandon led to a new world order ... for him. He'd been at the bar when a woman he'd seen earlier at a luncheon entered the bar. She had shocking-red hair; after a moment, her eyes registered recognition and she cautiously approached him.

"Congressman?" she asked in a crisp, almost-sophisticated British accent.

Her name was Marta. She worked for MI6, accompanying the Foreign Secretary on a visit to Spain. They hit it off. Small talk. Common interests. And the more she drank, the more her reserve evaporated. They barely made it to the elevator before her hand was in his trousers. She did things PJ would never do—or would have slapped him in the face for even suggesting. In the morning, his initial regret dissolved as she gave him an encore presentation. Later that morning, they exchanged contact info and Byrnes left for America thinking he could truly balance his yin and yang. Bill Clinton had. Jack Kennedy too.

A month later, he received a visit from a dark-haired, cool woman who projected a soft malevolence that simultaneously frightened and aroused him. She'd apparently made the appointment two months prior—something about fundraising for a charity or a college. The first thing Byrnes had noticed was a flint in her eyes and hardness about her. Tired, and hoping to make short work of this meeting, Byrnes leaned forward solicitously; he turned on his mega-watt smile and asked how he could be of assistance.

Contemptuous of Byrnes condescension, she wasted little time getting to the point. Squinting, the visitor opened her purse, removed an envelope, and tossed it onto the desk. Byrnes' sudden flare of anger was just as rapidly displaced by uncertainty and finally fear. An image of a puppet flashed across his mind: "This is how it starts." Coolly, he opened the envelope and fanned out photos from his Spanish fact-finding trip. Always possessed of a rapid, detached ability to read people and situations, Byrnes raced around to the back end of the mental debate commencing in the deep recesses of his head. He could wage a protracted campaign of denial that would slowly sink like the Titanic into the sea of political insignificance. Or—

Shaking his head as he recalled the moment from years before, Byrnes allowed a smile to crease his face as he headed to his hotel room where the hard woman was waiting. Byrnes opened his briefcase to remove an envelope of sensitive documents received from his last House Intelligence Committee hearing. She took the package and stepped to the door.

"Congressman, I hope you have a nice weekend."

As the door to the hallway closed behind her, the doorway to the bedroom opened and Marta, clad in a tight-fitting black sheath and stilettos, stepped out.

"Ready for dinner, darling?"

CHAPTER 39

2010
LONDON

The General's mouth twitched. Most taciturn in matters of personal conduct, Vadik's lips were often the only indication he was displeased. He was semi-engrossed in a panel discussion on public television. Two women were exchanging thoughts about the current state of affairs in Europe:

" ... how things play out from a security perspective will depend on Russia. Russia is weak geopolitically. Nuclear arsenal yes, but inept with regard to diplomacy, human rights, and their economy—their economy is a disaster. But their big problem is Russia seldom plays anything but the long game," summarized the first woman.

The camera cut to a man, the moderator, seated between the women on either side of a long table. "The long game?"

"Yes, Kevin," looking at the moderator, "Russia can't abide the idea of not being at the center of any discussion about Europe—even though they have been a large source of the trouble and insecurity most Europeans have experienced over the last few centuries."

Turning to the other woman, the host asked, "Does this accord with your thinking?"

Talking loudly, the second woman sniffed, "No it does not. Look, I don't think it is too hard to fathom Russia's genuine concerns. This is a rich, colorful country with a long history of being misunderstood by the rest of Europe. Since the days of Peter the Great, the West has cast a wary eye toward the country. It covers eleven time zones, vast swaths of arable land, and is a bounty of natural resources. It would be totally normal for Russia to worry about invasion. Indeed, twice in the last two centuries, their borders were violated—first by Napoleon and then by Hitler. Today, they worry an American-led Western Europe will seek to replace the duly elected government in Moscow."

The first woman cut in. "*Duly elected*? I believe this is all a chimera. They've been suspicious of the West since the days of the boyars. *All the way back* to Peter the Great, the Russian long game has been to dominate their neighbors while—additionally in the last century—seeking to influence matters in other parts of the world that prove disruptive to any Western agenda. Moscow is only interested in undermining a free Europe; as divided, Europe is much easier to manipulate."

Muting the TV, General Vadik Pyotr cast his gaze out the window of his twenty-fifth floor, Mid-town condo. "When we have control, you will be under our thumb."

CHAPTER 40

2010
NEW YORK

Exasperated, Nic threw the photo onto his desk.

"Sorry, Lieutenant," said a young detective standing before him.

Seated, Nic attempted to turn from his desk toward the window, but his government-issued chair always hitched when it caught a certain part of the swivel hub, Nic irritatedly grinded the seat, the last few degrees so he could look directly out the window. Better. At least something works—sort of.

Unwilling to sacrifice his nice view, Nic looked over his shoulder at the young cop at his desk. "Did you contact Saint Petersburg?"

A look of confusion clouded the junior officer's face.

Nic added, "Not Florida, *Russia*. You did read the file, right?"

"Oh yeah Lieutenant, sorry. Spoke to a ... " the policeman flipped pages in his spiral memo book, "Senior Lieutenant somebody or other, names are unpronounceable. They have nothing."

Nic exhaled audibly, creaking his chair.

"But ... repeated inquiries to Moscow finally generated ... this."

Hastily, Nic rotated his chair, again snagging on the offensive, unseen defect in the seat's central-swivel housing. Disgusted, he stood, kicking the chair. "What?" He grabbed a picture from his assistant's hand. It depicted a very young-looking man, clad in a nondescript military uniform. Nic could not help but wonder how such an innocent-looking man—a child almost—could be the object of his inquiry.

The junior police officer read from his notes. "Slaga Dmitriev. Age twenty. Just after reporting to Soviet Red Army Central Command Recruit center."

Slowly, as if the face staring at him would disappear, Nic picked up the grainy photo from his desk. Holding them side-by-side, Nic pursed his lips: "Can't tell."

"Saint Petersburg PD said Dmitriev died in a fire. Late nineties, I think."

Nic grunted in response, continuing to examine the picture.

"I'll keep trying, boss," the aide said. "Here and Russia."

Nic sat as the other man departed. He said to an empty office, "Yeah. *Specter.*"

CHAPTER 41

2010
BRIGHTON BEACH

After leaving the Clinic for Right Being, Slaga felt restless and had his driver stop at the Kings Arms Plaza near Mill Basin—being near water always brought a measure of peace to him. At the parking-lot rail, he paused, the soft hint of salt in the air as he stared mindlessly at boats bobbing serenely with the ebb and flow of the cove.

"What do I do with this information? I need to take precautions," he thought.

Meandering the mall, he stopped in the Constellation Book Store. Not sure what he was looking for, he roamed up and down the aisles when he came to a discount bin where one title caught his eye. He lifted the book; it was a pictorial of tattoos and their meanings from around the world.

Early in his life, Slaga had initially eschewed tattoos as a sign of a small-penis'd man seeking to make himself look bigger. In the last few years, however, he'd warmed to them ... just not on himself. A member of his *organization*—he despised the terms *gang* or *brotherhood*—bore a passing resemblance to Slaga; Nikita had arrived at Slaga's doorstep with an array of tats on his chest and arms. A loner with no family, Nikita often spent his time in bars or hooking up with various women, none of them long-term. But he liked his ink. Made him unique, he thought.

One night, after a nice boost, Slaga and the men were celebrating when one of his underbosses said, "Chief, you should get a tat to mark the occasion." This was met with great enthusiasm by the rest of his crew.

Slaga had jokingly replied, "I hate needles. Maybe we should give Nikita another tat instead."

This was equally embraced; soon, Nikita was outfitted under his left shoulder with a new tat in the shape of a treasure chest. Over the years, Nikita had become a de facto tattooed bulletin-board for Slaga. Treasure chests soon mixed with Nikita's other tats: pistols, the Madonna and child, a knife with one drop of blood, a dark-shadowed man with a machine gun, and a dove carrying a twig in its beak.

Glancing through the pictures in the book, Slaga recognized most of the tattoos, but a few were more current—ones a newer wave of toughs were inking. The anti-Soviet tats, favored by older criminals, now yielded to a changing of the guard. The new markings celebrated the glamor, klieg-light blitz and obsessive money fascination of a generation that thought nothing of spending one thousand dollars for a bottle of vodka at a high-end nightclub. There were tats of New York's skyscrapers ... one-hundred-dollar bills ... the Hollywood sign ... Rolls-Royces ... diamonds ... beautiful women.

Slaga grew bored with the publication and set it down. Next to it, there was another book. Slaga's brow wrinkled.

"Geocaching," he said to himself.

Opening it, he idly flipped pages, gleaning the subject, when suddenly he stopped. He looked up as if lightning had struck him. Taking the book to the cashier, he paid for it and left.

CHAPTER 42

2014
LONDON

Still in his bathrobe, the man opened his hotel door. Two men, lugging audio/visual equipment bags, entered.

"*Khorosho*," said the man. "Can you set it up?"

"*Da*—as quickly as we can, comrade Gen—"

The man hurriedly gestured, "Yes. Yes. Over there."

Tensely, both techs nodded and began assembling monitors and supporting apparatuses. Rapidly, they completed their work. Four video systems were set in place about the hotel desktop. The senior man adjusted knobs before turning the monitors on. Three were labeled: TOKYO, NEW YORK, and PARIS.

Their work complete, one tech headed to the door while the second showed the man how to use the system. "This one mutes your mic. Volume here. On, off." He paused before pointing to another button. "Don't touch this one or the other participants will be able to see you." As a matter of precaution, the video specialist grabbed some duct tape, ripping off a piece, placing it over the primary console camera. "There. No one can see you." He handed a remote to the man. "Your participants will be in place for the WebEx in one hour."

"Thank you. Yes, being opaque is good."

The tech team departed while the occupant commenced typing in numbers. Finished, he went into the bathroom to get cleaned up for the day. Back in the living room of his suite, he quietly savored a room service breakfast while looking down upon city. Watching Londoners scurry to their jobs, he wondered how such a small country could have dominated global events for centuries.

Finally, he grabbed his coffee and a pad of paper and then got comfortable. Checking his watch, he took a deep breath and pushed the master video-on button. Instantly, three of the screens came to life, filled with faces of men sent to carry out orders.

"Good morning, everyone."

One by one, voices chimed in their greetings.

"Please report," General Vadik Pyotr said.

On the Tokyo monitor, a bookish man consulted notes as he spoke, "General, our deal with Gazprom and Roseneft looks to be finalized. They're taking delivery of five billion cubic meters of LNG to their Sakhalin station for ultimate distribution throughout Asia. Payment through standby-letters-of-credit has been verified by Barclays in Hong Kong."

"Good. Akiva?"

In New York, a man clad in an Orthodox Jewish head covering and a thick beard said, "The next batch at Sheya mine is in dense medium separation and will commence refinement in two weeks. Nyurba run is set for delivery to De Beers next week. Moshe said the clarity, cut, and color of the last run at Suntar was brilliant and should fetch high bids at auction." The man hesitated.

"Akiva?"

"General, we have a potential labor issue at Nyurba—they want another three rubles an hour. And longer lunch."

It was silent for a moment while Pyotr scribbled on his pad. Finally, "Not unreasonable, but it would cut our margin. Offer a ruble, and ten more minutes for lunch."

"Yes, General."

"Connor?"

The Paris man leaned forward. "General, I think I found a great prospect. Michelin three-star, just off the Champs de Élysée."

"How long has the chef been there?"

"A little over three years."

"Not enough time. Let's keep looking."

"Yes, General."

"Thank you, everyone. Two weeks then." With that, Pyotr pushed a button on his remote, simultaneously killing the first three monitors and activating the fourth. After a moment, it was filled with the image of a porcelain-skinned black-haired woman with green eyes that Vadik was sure could emit lasers.

"Sigrid."

"General," she chillingly replied.

"Progress?"

"We're tracking back again through records at Red Army archives," the Moscow screen said.

"Any leads?"

"As the General knows, the man we're searching for ... well, there is no record of a *Bruno Shakli* ever being born in the Soviet Union. His documents were very good fakes."

Vadik rubbed his temples. This was old ground they were covering. In the twentieth century, the titans of Soviet state control had occupied the fifth floor at Lubyanka. His research of the previous occupants of his office had been fruitless. Famous names, yes. But, Vadik had often thought a lifetime engaged in paranoia about the West would have produced brilliant or equally crazy schemes of espionage and spy craft. So far, nothing tied to his old office.

The man from sanitation on the fifth floor—who'd possibly tampered with Vadik's office wall, with still no idea what was he looking for—had disappeared into the vapor. Pyotr was certain there had to be a reason.

"One item has come to light, General."

The General's thoughts had him lost ... "Who goes to the trouble of getting hired on a cleaning team—one with access to an area as sensitive as the fifth floor at FSB—and then vanishes? What was worth certain torture, possibly life in Siberia, or even execution if discovered? Maybe it is all a figment of my imagination. Maybe I was .... Wait, what did she say?" He spoke aloud, "Pardon me?"

"We might have something. As you know, General, Shakli's life in Kapotnya was a sham. Paid his bills. Groceries from Sadovoda Produce. Frequented the local pubs: Turliev's Bar, Cat Club and Vlaad's ... but strangely it seemed that while he was there, he wasn't really around. No football games or chess on weekends in the parks.

Whoever Bruno is, was, he blended into the background. Really well. Who has that kind of training?"

"CIA? MI6, German BND?"

"Maybe. But General, what if it *wasn't* them?"

Vadik paused, trying to think through who else it would be. "So, not a foreigner?"

"Yes ... and no."

"What does that mean?"

"General, what I'm about to suggest is ... *besynnerlig*—like, crazy stupid."

Vadik stared at the icy face on the monitor, the word running through his head. While her mother's Algerian parentage dominated her appearance, her father's Swedish idioms and taciturn perspective permeated her thoughts and she occasionally lapsed back into her native language for the right word for the moment. Sigrid was the perfect assassin.

"What if he is ... Russian—but not working for a foreign entity?" She softly said.

On occasion, Vadik liked to let things enter a sort of internal chamber in his mind where he would try to decipher a speaker's words, tone of voice, or facial expression. Divine the meaning. What was said? Implied? What was behind what was said? Where was the benefit and to whom? Like a rock tumbler, he'd roll the idea over and over, pummeling it with grit to strip away the veneer until only truth was left. Family, friends, and co-workers had come to recognize these moments and to wait while he was "away."

Sigrid took a sip of tea.

Today proved a little quicker. Ruminating but a minute, Vadik said, "A Russian living abroad."

"I think so, General."

"Why? Who?"

"Checking through immigration-control records at Sheremetyevo, we found a consistent record of entry and matching departures from 1995 to 1998 for a *Mikhail Kuznetsov*."

Vadik was guardedly optimistic but pushed back nonetheless. "So? Maybe a businessman or visiting family?"

Sigrid recognized Pyotr's rigorous back-checking protocol. "We thought of that, General. The pattern of Kuznetsov's arrivals and departures from Moscow coincided with Bruno Shakli's work schedule at Lubyanka. Kuznetsov arrives, Shakli returns to Kapotnya District and work at Lubyanka.

"Shakli leaves for his *medical treatments* at Red Army Medical, Kuznetsov departs the country. His superiors at work accepted at face value that when Bruno was gone, he was making his monthly visits to Red Army Medical. Shakli's neighbors recalled the same patterns of absences that Bruno said had to do with family duties."

Vadik rubbed his chin. "So, using family as his excuse, no one in Kapotnya—even if they were mildly suspicious—would bother to check with Army Medical; there was little likelihood that his two paths would cross."

She waited, knowing he liked to trace things on his own. "Where did this Kuznetsov come from?"

"Often arrived from different locations, but city of origin seems to be London."

Vadik nodded slowly, starting to appreciate Kuznetsov's—or Shakli's or whoever he was—cunning at covering his movements. "Sigrid, start working from London. See what contacts we have in the UK Border Control at Heathrow and Gatwick. Look for the same pattern."

"Should I bring the congressman in yet? He could get us more direct access to UK records."

When Vadik received his last promotion, he'd asked for and received a transfer to SVR. Part of his assignment was oversight of information-gathering and agent networks in the Americas. It had been during this time that Adam Byrnes had fallen into their hands. The thought had been to get him placed onto one or two of the powerful Congressional committees, Armed Services, Appropriations, Homeland Security, or Foreign Affairs and have him steal the more sensitive information he came into contact with.

After retiring from the Red Army, Vadik had maintained his contact with Byrnes, essentially privatizing this asset along with his other, growing portfolio of investments.

"No. Not yet. Let's hold him back. I want to see where his career takes us. Don't want to risk blowing him over this."

"As you wish, General."

CHAPTER 43

2016
LONDON

Vadik Pyotr stood on the soccer pitch watching his latest project with disinterest. So far, it had been a poor investment. During Boris Yeltsin's last years as President of Russia, Pyotr had quietly moved to take control of much of the diamond and natural-gas deposits in Siberia, which he'd been overseeing as the Sub-Director of the Economic Directorate at FSB. This continued after the ascension of Yeltsin's successor, Vladimir Putin.

Today, one of Russia's wealthiest oligarchs, he had homes in Moscow, Saint Petersburg, London, New York, and Beverly Hills. He owned two mega-yachts, a legitimate heavy equipment manufacturer in France, seven restaurants throughout Europe and now Sparrow Asia Football Club in East London. Sparrow FC was a member of the EFL, English Football League—one level below the Premier League, Europe's most prestigious football association. So far, the Sparrows were stuck in the middle of the table, unlikely to finish the season in position to ascend to the PL, where the big money and prestige resided.

Many Russian oligarchs, as well as other global-minded businessmen, had purchased some of the jewels of English soccer, providing them with massive infusions of cash that had bought titles, trophies, and respectability. But Pyotr's team manager had been unable to cultivate a winning spirit about the Sparrow training ground.

Disgusted, he turned away to answer his cellphone.

"*Da*".

"General."

Recognizing the voice, his pulse tightened. "*Da*," he uttered.

"We've found him."

"Where?"

"New York."

"Thank you."

Vadik turned to observe his inept soccer team going through their paces but his thoughts were elsewhere. A smile creased his face.

CHAPTER 44

2016
NEW YORK

It had been an exhilarating afternoon. Chris and Mallory had been invited to go sailing with tech billionaire Hector Orozco de Fuentes and his wife Gabriela. Sailing was actually a bit misleading. Fuentes had recently taken receipt of his latest plaything, a new superyacht that came with a one-hundred-million-dollar-plus price tag. *Southern Star*, boasted a top-end speed of thirty knots, ten master bedrooms with en-suite bathrooms, a spa with six massage rooms, disco bar, marine observation room with a glass floor for ocean viewing, indoor Zen garden, three-story library, video-game parlor, living room with floor-to-ceiling glass walls, sun deck with an infinity pool and a massive two-thousand square foot master suite with a private owner's deck.

Glass of beer in hand, Chris sat on the sun deck with Hector as the other guests mingled at the pool's edge, in the jacuzzi, or just relaxed in recliners while taking in Long Island Sound.

"You know Hector, I think we're a lot alike," Chris smilingly said.

"How is that my friend? Married above our pay grades? Successful? Devilishly handsome—at least in my case."

Both laughed good naturedly.

"No, I was thinking we both come from immigrant families that have taken full advantage of the opportunity of America. I really admire what you've accomplished. This boat—ship is amazing. And your company is making a huge difference in affordable home-solar systems."

Hector silently studied his guest. He put his flute of champagne down, removing his sunglasses. "Chris do you know where I grew up?"

"San Diego, right?"

"Yes. Actually a burb of America's Finest City, Logan Heights." Fuentes waited. When Chris, recognizing that his host had something to say, did not reply, Hector continued. "Right in the middle of the Devil's Triangle. Barrio Logan to the south, the Heights in the middle, and Mountain View to the northeast."

Fuentes took a sip of bubbly. "Idle hands are the devil's workshop—I think that's how the saying goes? Lot of down time in the Triangle. Gotta fill it some way. Drugs, murder, assault, rape—the usual pastimes. But the real killer ... what really sapped your momentum was lack of access to that opportunity you were just speaking about. That and the inherent racism that still dominates the Latino experience in America."

Chris nodded slowly. "Okay, but you got out right?"

"Totally by accident. Was trying to put myself through San Diego State. Worked nights as a janitor at a company in San Diego's tech corridor. One night the owner, Tab Kingsbury, is there working alone in the lab on some algorithms for a new solar converter when suddenly he keeled over with a heart attack. I jumped in to perform CPR and mouth-to-mouth. Brought him back."

Fuentes looked out to sea in recollection. "When Tab returned to work, he had HR call me in, wanted to thank me personally. Now someone else normally cleaned the executive spaces, so I'd never been in his office before. There I was all sweaty nervous waiting to go in, but as I was sitting there, I looked about and started seeing all the cool surfboard stuff he had on the walls. Now I love to surf, hard to do when you live in the Heights, but I still managed to learn just enough to be dangerous."

Chris nodded slowly, not sure where the story was going.

"So Tab comes out to get me and there I am slobbering over an old 1970s Dewey Weber Performer ... that's like a really rare collector board. Anyway, we got to talking and when he found out my major was Applied Physics—I've been a geek since I got my first Erector Set as a kid, he offered me a job in the lab working on solar inverters for use in mass application—converting solar energy into usable power in big systems like skyscrapers, factories, cruise ships, stuff like that."

Chris waited but when it was clear the story was over, he asked, "So the opportunity of America still could be applied to your situation? Or no."

Fuentes leaned forward. "It did, but largely by happenstance, sharing a common interest with some old tech guy? Opportunity should be merit-based, not random. So I see the opportunity you're speaking about. It's not here yet, but I believe *you* could be an architect of a new America where everyone gets a chance. I see great things for you, Chris."

Secretly flattered, Chris quietly replied, "That's quite a load to bear."

"Maybe, but I think you're the right man at the right time."

* * * *

Chris rubbed his tired eyes. Black-tie fundraisers were a political necessity that demanded a steep price. For days after the handshaking, cocktails, and canapés came the headaches. But Chris gladly accepted it all as the price of membership into an exclusive country club. At age forty, he was about to be elected to the United States Senate. The polls in New York easily pointed toward victory in the election, but raising money was an ever-constant step toward ensuring the war chest was prepared for the next fight.

Sitting in the tub soaking before dressing, he let his mind drift over the last few years: College. Dean's List at Fordham. Columbia Law. Law review. DA's office. Taking down the Specter's drug empire. City Council. Water-aqueduct renovations. Crafting the legislation to build citywide daycare. It all had changed the lives of so many working New York City residents. And now, the US Senate. Through all his achievements, the Specter case stuck in his mind. That guy had eluded detection for years, but they finally had him.

After all these years, one thing still bugged Chris—he never could figure out where the tip had come from: an anonymous message to his private email account. It had come with an identity—*Rusta Volgakoff*—and the location of his center of operations in Coney Island.

Everything in the email fit: he was a former Russian army vet; he'd been feuding with Little Kiev, the Ukrainian gang that had been decimated in 1995 in an incredible gassing incident at Club Twenty-Two.

While his life outside of his gang seemed ugly, unproven charges of rape and murder, Volgakoff was fairly low in the broader Russian mob community. Apparently, this was a cover for the massive operation he was running. The dossier of his activities, outlined in the nameless email, entailed drugs, prostitution, grand-theft auto, and protection. The strange thing had been, when arrested, Volgakoff vigorously denied knowledge of most of the charges, copping only to the grand theft. Indeed, the files recovered at Volgakoff's offices had supported this, but a raid of his CPA's office recovered numerous documents pointing to the other crimes.

Volgakoff seemed genuinely surprised when confronted with the evidence of his massive empire; he claimed he was being framed for everything. Volgakoff had been out of the country at the time of the Club Twenty-Two massacre, but a former member of his gang came forward, prepared to testify that Rusta had orchestrated the executions, using the trip abroad to provide an alibi. It was mostly circumstantial evidence, but after years of chasing a will-o'-the-wisp, Chris was confident of a conviction. But the case never came to trial. On the morning of opening arguments, Volgakoff had been found hanging in his cell—an apparent suicide.

Chris got credit for taking down the Specter and it was a huge part of his victorious campaign for the New York City Council. Still, it never quite set well with him. The only people with his private email had been Mallory, cousin Nic, his parents, and Stephan Grigor. Chris rubbed his temples again as his eyes floated to the soft, white glow emanating from the recessed lighting around the edges of the bathroom ceiling. His mind drifted back to Grigor's Light Lab at the Clinic. "Always feel good there, bad after."

"Honey, we need to get going." Mallory entered the bathroom and stopped short. "What's wrong, baby?" She asked, stepping behind the tub to massage his neck.

"Throbbing again. Always these damn headaches after seeing Stephan."

She came around to sit on the tub's edge. "Maybe we should see a specialist or something. I'll start looking tomorrow."

He reached out, taking her hand into his, relief radiating on his face. "Thanks."

Mallory stood to leave but hesitated at the door. "But you know ...."

"What?"

"Well, it's that you've been seeing Stephan—we both have—since we were children ... and I just don't want to make a big change right in the middle of such a major life moment for you. Let me get a specialist now, and then maybe we look for a new doctor after the election?"

Sagging, Chris thought for a second. "Yeah. You're right. You're always right Mal. Let's do it that way."

His wife nodded. "By the way, what do you think of the color in here? Paint too harsh?"

Barely taking his eyes from the ceiling, he said, "I'd like it a little bit more neutral I think."

"I agree." Mallory crossed her arms. "You know ... you *have* been under a lot of pressure of late. This campaign has not been easy. But look how far you've come—we've come, baby. It will be better soon."

As his wife departed, Chris slid back into the comfort of his bath, rubbing his temples.

CHAPTER 45

2016
WASHINGTON

Adam Byrnes kept hoping for two things: one, the woman seated across from him would finish up; two, he would get to have sex with her before she did. He thought he detected a Scandinavian accent as she pointed out boring statistics and details about an import bill she wanted help with.

"You will introduce this legislation—"

Byrnes pretended to look at the papers in his hand, already familiar with most of what they detailed. He laid them on his desk, studiously adjusted his tie as if late for a cover shoot for GQ Magazine, all while avoiding her gaze. "I will most certainly not. Why would I want to help a Russian company with tariff reduction, especially to the detriment of a Georgia company that makes the same thing? I'd be crucified by the Op-Ed pages of the *Savannah Morning News* and the *Journal Constitution.*"

Used to working with arrogant, condescending men who thought they knew everything, the woman softly said, "It's a bit warm in here, may I remove my coat?"

Now bored, Byrnes dismissively waved his hand.

Standing, she removed her outer jacket to reveal a black, semi-transparent shirt barely containing her ample cleavage, which threatened to burst her buttons. Reseated, she lifted her portfolio of papers while ignoring Byrnes now leaning forward in newfound interest.

Tilting her head, while slightly letting her lips part and offering a hint of her tongue, the woman subtly shifted in her seat, pulsating a tidal wave of primitive magnetism.

The lobbyist continued. "You will introduce the legislation for two reasons. First, once the tariff reduction is in place, Archangel Northstar will enter a joint-manufacturing relationship with Palmetto Fertilizer that will create four hundred jobs in your district. Simultaneously, Palmetto will be allowed to establish operations in Moscow and Vladivostok."

After a moment of silence, Byrnes said, "What's the second?"

The dispassionate ice in the woman's coal-black eyes was unnerving—and yet Byrnes could not help be inflamed with desire. Slowly, she stood. Smoothing her skirt, she glided across a massive rug. It had an outline of the Georgia crest in the center, situated before a gently flickering fireplace. She softly locked his office door before circling back around his desk. Languidly, she sat upon the desktop, forcing her skirt up just enough to move one black-stockinged, high-heeled leg across Byrnes so that she was straddling him, while simultaneously giving him just a hint of her menacing femininity.

With her right hand she pulled his head into her bosom. She put her tongue in his ear, whispering, "Tell your assistant to hold your calls. Understand?" Byrnes tried to reply, but the woman kept his head buried in her chest. "Don't speak, just nod."

Byrnes nodded. The woman yanked him by his coiffured roots.

A smothered cry died in his throat.

"Now," she hissed, pushing his head toward the speaker. Quickly, Byrnes's right hand shot out, pressing the intercom button. "Calmly," the woman added, gripping his hair even tighter.

In as even a voice as he could muster, Byrnes said, "Joy, please hold my calls for a bit. Thanks."

At her desk outside Byrnes's office, his assistant, recognizing what this meant, shook her head disgustedly. "Men are so weak," she thought.

A moment later, the box on Byrnes's desk, squawked, "Yes, sir."

* * * *

After they'd finished, the woman, composed herself and coolly gathered her things. She strode to the door where she paused, the temperature in the room dropping. Boring into his eyes with hers, she said, "Pleasure and peril reside in the same house. Introduce the legislation, or I'll be back, but for a different reason." Without a second glance, she left, disdainfully adding, "Congressman."

In her rental car, she dialed a secure phone number. After a series of pulses, buzzes, and echoes signifying the call was bouncing around the globe, it rang.

"Good evening, Sigrid. This is a secure line. How did it go?"

"He understands what we need, General."

"Good. Why don't you take some time off? You've earned it. Put it on my account and contact me when you return—I may need you to go to Amsterdam."

"Trouble?"

"One of my diamond channels is clogged. I might need you to ... clean it out."

"General," Sigrid ended the call.

CHAPTER 46

2016
NEW YORK

Slaga took out his cellphone and opened the Polaris GPS Compass app. He noted the readout and recorded the coordinates in his notebook. Since coming into possession of Polar Strike, he'd been very diligent about recording everything he'd done from the moment of finding the files in the air duct to the present second—documenting every detail in the journey to understand what the project entailed. Grigor. The Fords. How it worked. Contacts. History of the project. Maybe this was a legacy of sorts.

To date, what he'd learned had served his purposes. Through Grigor, Slaga had used Ford and the DA's office to remove most of his rivals. Claiming to have taken down the Specter, law enforcement's interest in his activities had died away. Slaga was a virtual ghost on their radar now.

Ford's continued political ascent had proved economically useful. Slaga bought land where the city water task force had proposed putting a new purification station—before it became common knowledge. After the project became public, the city, through eminent domain, had taken the land, but at triple what Slaga had paid.

Yet, with each layer of onion he peeled back, the dread magnified. Things seemed to be going too easily. Where initially Grigor's efforts had been reluctant, now it appeared as if Grigor was cooperating. Who was this woman *Elena Ford*? Who betrays blood for ideology? Was this more than some antiquated, discarded relic of the Cold War? Recalling Polar Strike's prime directive, was Ford still being groomed for something? If so ... what?

Like a pot of heated water, Slaga's guts were roiling, threatening to boil over. He'd always slept like a cat luxuriating in an afternoon ray of sunlight. Now, he was waking a couple of times a night with terrifying nightmares and headaches. These were malevolent forces from the past, threatening to consume him if he wasn't careful. All of this uncertainty had instilled a need to document what he'd found.

In the back of his head, the other thing he needed to do was dispose of any records he had. He kept some working notes; they were well-hidden in his home, but where to safeguard the main files? Today's sojourn out of Brighton had been to locate a hidden repository to safely house his dossier.

* * * *

Standing before the mirror in his bedroom, Stephan Grigor examined his appearance and found it acceptable. Fastidious, borderline fussy about his image, Grigor was equally nonchalant about things beyond his immediate concern. Since finding out that Slaga was not Russian Intelligence, Grigor began insulating himself from the thug. Given limited knowledge of the world of espionage, he was uncertain how to beef up his protection—other than changing the code to his office security system and locking all his file cabinets.

All his contact with Moscow had ceased since Elena's death in 1992. Being a good handler, Elena had never shared any information with Grigor about who she reported to. But as the time passed with only radio silence, Grigor became more confident he could continue his work as he saw fit. If communication was ever reinitiated by Moscow, he would be justified in not trying to reach out to any other Russian intelligence apparatus in America, for fear of blowing his cover.

While he'd become an American citizen years before, Grigor kept his Russian passport current; he checked in annually with the Russian Consulate—his cover that he was working with the World Health Organization. The one official he knew, his friend Vasily, was now attached to the Russian Office at the United Nations. But, comfortable with his newfound freedom, he decided against using Vasily to reinitiate contact with KGB.

* * * *

Nikita exited the ink parlor. Coming to the curb, he got into the SUV where Slaga sat in the back.

"You like the new markings?"

Turning to his boss, Nikita said, "I like the treasure chests and the rest—but lotta numbers again."

"Keeping track of our success."

The underling nodded, not totally sold; he happily accepted the envelope Slaga proffered. In the last couple of years, Slaga had begun paying him a hundred dollars for each new inking Nikita received. The tat sessions had slowed of late, partially because Nikita had been running out of space on his trunk for new markings. Ruefully, he glanced at his hands where some numbers had been recently needled.

CHAPTER 47

2016
NEW YORK

Adrift in a sea of uncertainty, he was convinced Grigor was still concealing something about Polar Strike. Slaga had been content with their "working" relationship as long as it benefited him, but after Grigor learned Slaga was *not* his new Russian Intelligence Agency handler, he'd become evasive about sharing more details. His primary dodge was claiming he didn't know much himself, as he'd been waiting all these years for Moscow to initiate contact and provide new instructions. This placated Slaga for a while, but he was certain he was only seeing the tip of the iceberg. Each of the key players knew their parts—everyone except him.

Slaga considered alternative scenarios to pry loose more information. First was to use Kazia to coax it out of him, but Grigor had grown bored with her and Slaga dismissed this option. Planting a new woman in Grigor's harem of unhappy housewives might work; still, he could not imagine the doctor sharing anything about Polar Strike with them.

Blackmailing him about his extramarital affairs seemed possible, but there might be retaliation if Grigor went directly to Ford and told him about Slaga.

He could beat it out of him, but again there was probable blowback; most likely, this would end only one way—and it would close his access to Ford.

Kazia had mentioned that Grigor had changed the code to the clinic after their last visit.

Slaga took a simple, but calculated, risk.

For a month, he had two of his men stake out the parking garage where the Center for Right Being was located. They learned the schedule, composition, habits, everything they could about the cleaning team. The group was comprised of three people: two women and a man. After a month, they had most of what they needed.

One woman had three kids at home, no apparent father and also worked a day job trying to keep food on the table. The other woman apparently liked to gamble. The man was the hardest to crack. After a month, Slaga's men had discovered he was an Army vet with severe PTSD, from two tours in Afghanistan. But the cleaning job wasn't just to earn a living. The night shift work also provided a quiet place he could withdraw to, away from noise, light, uncertainty, and encounters with people. Slaga thought he might also have a higher sense of commitment to duty.

On the next scheduled visit by the sanitation team, Slaga and his crew waited in the parking garage. When the van from the cleaning company pulled into the garage and the cleaners got out and began removing their equipment, Slaga approached them.

"I have a proposition."

Warily, they listened as Slaga outlined the offer. Open the office, but remain outside while Slaga and his men cleaned for them. Afterwards, there would be three envelopes waiting for them, each filled with ten thousand dollars.

Sure enough, the male cleaner objected. "We could lose our jobs."

"Who will know? Us being here coincides with your normal schedule inside. Nothing unusual, nothing out of the ordinary. We clean, get out, you lock up as if nothing ever happened."

Quietly to the man, both women expressed their agreement. Scowling, the male cleaner looked at Slaga, motioning him aside.

Away from the others, he looked into Slaga's eyes. He found hardness but also a spark of something more.

"Who are you guys?"

"Does it matter?"

The sanitation man nodded to his associates. "Probably not to them." He looked back at Slaga. "And probably not to me, but we work for this guy—the guy whose office you're going to toss—"

"Not toss." Slaga shook his head. "It will be as it was when he left."

"Why?"

Nodding slowly, Slaga said, "You were in the Army right?"

The man's eyes squinted, quickly realizing they'd probably been tracking him for a bit. "Tenth Mountain."

"Afghanistan?"

The man nodded.

"Me too. Eighties."

"USSR?"

"Back then, but they're gone and good riddance." Pausing, Slaga gambled, appealing to duty over money. "Look, you don't know me, but I need you to believe me. There's something bad going on here. Something evil." He paused. "You can help me to stop it."

Silently, the cleaner appeared to be considering what Slaga was saying.

"Do you remember how many times they told you—told us that what we were doing was going make the world better?"

Slowly, the maintenance man's head nodded.

"Well, tonight your actions could change things ... just a tiny bit. Take the money, it helps both of your co-workers. Probably help you a little bit—am I right?" Slaga did not wait for an answer. "And it will help to determine what this clinic is really doing."

After the man let them in, Slaga and two of his crew, made their way into the Clinic where they removed state-of-the-art bugging equipment from their cleaning cart and set about positioning bullet cameras into the AC registers and intake vents. In each room, they inserted into the wall-mounted temperature control and carbon dioxide detector boxes, omnidirectional, voice-activated microphones. The microphones and video cameras could transmit up to a hundred yards, allowing Slaga to place remote recorders above the ceiling tiles in the space over the building's public men's room down the hall from the Clinic.

Lastly, Slaga used his cellphone camera to copy Grigor's appointment book for the coming months. He knew the exact dates Ford was scheduled for appointments. The bathroom recorders had a limit of fifty hours, which necessitated replacing them once a week.

After each visit—by either Chris or Mallory—one of Slaga's men would immediately recover the recorder from the men's room, replacing it with a fresh one. Just to hedge himself against unscheduled drop-in appointments, Slaga had his men follow both Fords.

Still, after months of surveillance, nothing significant had surfaced. Chris mostly whined about the daily grind, while Mallory occasionally discussed work and how boring it was. Her co-workers came up for even more excoriation: they were vapid, vain, and too self-righteous—the environment *this* ... the environment *that*. "Jeez Stephan, save me *from* the environment," she groaned in one session. On the surface, the Fords were just another normal, aspiring power couple.

Every so often, Mallory would spend time discussing upcoming races, both national and statewide, and their impact on Chris's career. She'd talk about which person might get elected to the Senate and who would be occupying the Senate committee jobs that Chris would also want in order to continue his upward ascent. As Slaga listened and watched the tapes, he began to appreciate the woman's keen political insight. More often than not, she picked who would win various races.

But one day, as they were finishing another session, Grigor and Mallory were in the lobby saying their goodbyes.

"Tell Chris not to despair. Theengs will get better and he ees' fighting de' good fight," Grigor said.

While only a recording, the look that came over Mallory's face chilled Slaga. A laser-like glint in her eyes, head thrust pridefully upward, she replied, "Sometimes, history needs a push."

Grigor nodded slowly. "She'd be very proud."

As Mallory departed, Slaga was left confounded: "Who is this *she*?"

The words Mallory had spoken. They were familiar. Where had he heard them before? The dread returned like a fog shrouding his home.

CHAPTER 48

2016
NEW YORK

Slaga concluded he'd mined the Clinic for Right Being of all of its secrets. But something still eluded him. What was Grigor concealing? A man's last redoubt was his home, and Slaga reluctantly determined to breech Grigor's personal lair on a data mining expedition that he hoped would still his nagging anxiety. He had to chuckle though. While his conscience was usually undisturbed by his actions, with his ever-heightened scrutiny of Grigor, Slaga was beginning to feel like an policeman strip searching a suspect.

Kazia still had some hold on Grigor and was able to persuade him to take a long weekend at the Ocean Pointe Inn out in the Hamptons. Kazia had also passed to Slaga that Grigor had recently upgraded his security system at home.

Hidden, in a nondescript van outside Grigor's brownstone, Slaga and his men employed a software-defined radio to intercept the code Grigor used to arm his home security system. Ten minutes after he'd departed, they used the code to shut off the system. They knew this would send a signal to Grigor that his home security system had been deactivated; Slaga and his men waited quietly in the van. After a few minutes, Grigor's BMW returned, descending into the garage. Five minutes later, they detected Grigor rearming the system.

Ten minutes passed. Slaga's man again disabled the security mechanism. Once more, Grigor returned, this time only parking in front of the unit. Agitated, he stepped from his car and ran up the steps into his home. Using an IMSI catcher, Slaga's tech man picked up Grigor using his cellphone from inside his unit to make a call to his home security company.

After a few minutes of rechecking his system, the customer service representative assured the doctor his system was showing normal on their computers, but that if the problem continued, they would send a technician out on Monday. Grigor reset the system and departed. Slaga's tech started his cellphone timer. Ten minutes later, he disarmed the system. This time, Grigor did not return.

Posting men at each end of the block, Slaga stepped to the front door, clad as a deliveryman. Holding a box, while pretending to speak to the homeowner, he removed a lock pick set from his jacket and jimmied the door. Inside, he paused to let his eyes adjust. Slowly, he moved through the house noticing motion detectors—now disarmed—but no cameras. Good. He removed the mask he'd donned before entering and continued his progress. Big spaces. Immaculate. Large mirrors in each room. Latest design appointments. Contemporary art.

But it was so much more. The air almost smelled of his arrogance. Extraordinary decor. Modern European. Clean lines. Minimalist. Apt, considering Grigor's line of work. Where would a man like this hide something valuable? Slaga tried to apply psychology to the task. He mentally laid out what he knew of the doctor: "He thinks of himself as a sophisticate. Uses women as objects. Shows off his things and his intellect ... "

In the study, he found it. On the wall, behind a massive, executive *L*-shaped teak desk was the only thing out of sync. Inside an oversized, mid-century, stainless-steel frame was a replica of the Jean Auguste Dominique Ingres painting of *Jupiter and Thetis*.

Slaga shook his head, "Appropriate."

Testing the edges of the picture, he found that the frame swung out to reveal a simple-combination-spin wall safe: probably six-bolt, six-number combo. But as he stared at the safe, something tugged at the edge of his thoughts. It was too simple. He had heard of cases where homeowners or business people had installed easily located wall safes rigged to blow up or shoot fire or poison spray if not properly opened—or only contain small valuables designed to throw a would-be thief something but nothing of great import.

While he was uncertain if this was the case, Slaga decided to expand his search about Grigor's home.

The rest of the house offered nothing out of the ordinary, and Slaga found himself uneasily reexamining the study-wall vault. Slowly, for no reason, Slaga swung the picture back into place. His eyes squinted, "Frame is awfully heavy," he thought to himself. He reexamined both the frame and picture. Immediately, he noticed something odd.

Rather than a canvas stretched over a frame, open in the back, Grigor's version was a canvas stretched over the frame, but closed in the back, almost as if concealing something. Swinging the frame open again, he pushed on the edges where the canvas met the frame. Hollow. Slaga brought his eye to bear on the picture itself ... and there it was.

Right where Thetis's gold necklace met her crown, camouflaged in her hair, was a small brown bump. Slaga ran his fingers over it. It was almost undetectable, but unmistakably, a small button. For a moment, he weighed what to do: open the safe or push the button. Finally, he concluded that the button must be the calculated play. Rarely would someone go to the trouble of creating such a ruse, hidden in plain sight, and not use it.

Slaga slowed his breathing. Pushing the air from his lungs, he inhaled at a glacial pace, oxygen flooding his brain, sharpening his senses. He adjusted his stance to the side of the painting. He wanted to be out of harm's way in case the button triggered a booby trap. Calmly, he extended his arm until his finger barely rested on the node. He pushed the button and jumped away from the picture.

A soft rumble came from beneath a Persian carpet situated in front of the desk. Coming around the desk, he roughly yanked the carpet aside, revealing an open hole in the ground. The rumbling he'd heard was from the cover plate, now retracted out of sight along the top of the cavity. Slaga stepped back to the picture and depressed the button a second time. The cover plate slid back into place, seamlessly blending in with the floor. Only a trained eye could see the edges of the floor panel-cover plate. Slaga tapped the button one more time, reopening the chamber.

He probed the opening with his light. Perplexed, it appeared to be an empty vault. Hesitantly, he put his hand into the cavity, feeling the sides, then the bottom, and finally the top. Nothing. Slowly, he rechecked the sidewalls until he found a spot that gave with just a bit of force. Pushing, the panel receded, unleashing more mechanical noise. Slaga yanked his hand back. "*Der'mo* ... like a house of horrors."

Seconds later, a safe slowly arose from the vault. What had at first appeared to be the bottom of the chamber was actually the top of a safe. Stepping around to the front, Slaga was relieved to find a spin-combination safe instead of a biosensor device. Amidst all this complexity, finally, something he understood.

From his bag, he removed a pad of translucent drafting paper, a pen, and a doctor's stethoscope. Pulling the desk chair around, he planted himself in front of the safe. Putting the tips into his ears, he placed the diaphragm near the dial and slowly turned the dial. Left. Then right. Once acclimated to the wheel and the sounds unique to the safe, he started.

First, he rotated the spinner counterclockwise, listening for a place where there were two *clicks* in closer approximation than the others—specifically, one click softer than the other. He wrote the spinner number down on the pad.

Next, he parked the wheels by rotating the dial to the location exactly one hundred eighty degrees opposite the first spot. The *wheels* referred to the number of flywheels in the safe, which corresponded to the numbers that were the combination to open the safe—hopefully only three. Slaga set to work looking for locations on the dial where he could hear shorter intervals between clicks as he slowly rotated the dial. After three times through the process, Slaga repeated his sequence. He held his breath that he would not pick up a fourth click or a fourth number in the combination. More than three would start to introduce more permutations than he had time to try. To his relief and mild surprise, he determined there were only three numbers to the combo.

Suddenly anxious, he picked up his walkie talkie. “Anything going on out there?”

A *squawk*. “Nothing chief.”

The next part was the more time consuming. While Grigor was most likely gone for the weekend, Slaga still glanced at his watch, wishing to be done. With the back of his hand, he wiped imaginary sweat from his forehead. Something about Grigor’s home—indeed something about Grigor and Polar Strike—reeked of a different kind of evil than Slaga was used to. He shook it off and set about finding the combination numbers.

This required more time than the previous evolution. He’d need to repeat the process, each time adjusting the starting point of the dial by three numbers to the right of the last starting point. With only sixty numbers on the dial, the drill only needed to be repeated approximately twenty times.

On his pad, he marked numbers up the left side, as *X* graph and numbers on the bottom, the *Y* graph. He then repeated the layout on a second piece of paper. When he encountered a *click* followed rapidly by a second *click*, he’d mark the location on the dial for the first click on the first graph page and location on the dial for the second click on the second graph page.

Laboriously, he repeated this process until he’d made a complete rotation of the dial so that the starting point had returned to zero on the dial.

He again grabbed his communicator. “Still quiet?”

“Yeah chief. You okay?”

“Yeah, yeah. Just keep an eye out.”

Rubbing now-strained eyes, Slaga again turned to the task before him.

Taking the second graph paper, he laid it over the first. Gripping his flashlight in his mouth, he examined the graphs, circling where they intersected. Fifteen, twenty-six, sixty. Slaga returned to the safe to begin combining the numbers. He hit on the third time. Twenty-six, fifteen, sixty. The safe handle gave, but Slaga hesitated. Imagining one more layer of security, he looked about for something to rotate the handle from afar. Glancing at the closet, he had an idea. Opening the door, he found an unused clothes hanger.

He hooked the wooden device around the safe grip, moved away from the front, and gently pulled the handle down. The safe opened. Distrust, bordering on paranoia, gnawed at the gangster. Quickly, he unhitched the hanger, using it to push the door completely open. Finally confident, he stepped in front to face the open vault.

The usual suspects sat in plain sight: passport, money—Slaga reckoned two hundred thousand in dollars and euros—some jewelry, and beneath it all was a faded manila envelope. Slaga removed it, laying it on the desk.

With his cellphone, he commenced taking pictures of the sheets inside the envelope. About halfway through the papers, he stopped, eyes growing large. "*Sladkiy Gospod'*!" he huskily muttered.

The staccato bark of his walky-talky startled him. "Boss, he's coming back!"

Slaga fumbled for his radio. "What!"

"He's sitting at the stoplight. Probably two, three minutes out. Do you need me to stall him?"

Slaga weighed the advantage of having his man intercept Grigor on some premise like asking for directions, versus immediately raising the doctor's suspicions. "No—not yet!"

"*Da.* Hurry!"

Slaga rapidly completed photographing the last few pages. Putting them back into the envelope, he replaced it into the safe—exactly where he'd found it. Closing the safe door, he spun the lock, resetting it. Then he realized he didn't know how to get the safe back into the floor cavity.

"Two minutes!" his radio squawked.

"Shit!" Amidst mounting panic, Slaga smacked the safe door. Nothing! Then he jabbed at the sides. His communicator yelped, "Hurry, boss!" Finally, Slaga desperately pushed on the top. Suddenly an unseen retracting device rumbled into action, pulling the safe snugly back into the floor chamber.

"He's parking! Get out!"

At the picture, Slaga again pushed the button in Thetis's hair. The floor plate sealed the hole. Heart racing, Slaga closed the picture frame, pulled the carpet roughly back into place, and made his way to the back door. Fortunately, it was self-locking. Slaga opened the door, stepped outside, turning back to close the door as softly as possible.

In the same breath, the front door burst open.

Stephan Grigor moved into the house, quickly coming to the study. His eyes flitted about the room just as Kazia arrived. Grigor noted she looked almost relieved, as if expecting to find something that was not there.

He turned to her. "Get us some wine, okay?"

She shrugged. "Okay. Then we can leave?"

"Yes, yes. I need to check something. Now, go."

He closed the study's door. Opening the safe, he bypassed his personal effects to remove the envelope. A quick glance inside revealed nothing askew. Slowly, he replaced it. But something bugged him. He sat on the edge of his desk.

"I have the wine; are you coming out?" Kazia called.

"In a moment."

Grigor went to close the safe but stopped. Taking the envelope out, he opened it again. His brow furrowed; he closed the envelope, replaced it, and closed the safe. On his way to the door, he stopped, contemplating aloud, "I always put the papers in facing the front of the envelope, away from the flap."

Reopening the safe, he removed the envelope. Fanning the pages through his fingers, he extracted the last two pages and replaced the others. Putting the envelope back into the vault, he closed it up. Taking the sheets in his hand to his desk, he removed a cigar lighter from his desk drawer. Holding the ignitor switch, he watched as blue fire leapt out like a jet fighter.

"Stephan?" Kazia called from the other side of the door.

"In a moment," Grigor quietly replied.

The flame completed its work as the papers turned to ash in the crystal cigar holder. Closing things up, he opened the door.

"Thank you my dear, but I'm suddenly not feeling well. Let me drive you home. We'll get out to the Hamptons soon, I promise."

CHAPTER 49

2016
BROOKLYN

A few years previously, Slaga had bought the top unit at the new Galaxy Luxury Community in Brighton Beach. His twenty-first-floor unit offered a one-hundred-eighty-degree view of the coast in in both directions. It had become his personal redoubt, inaccessible to the masses and rabble below. While a sense of *having finally made it* still eluded Slaga, from his aerie, he could at least see it.

The unseen pea-soup fog of fear hovered just beyond the edges of his impregnable retreat. After he'd come home from his expedition to Grigor's home, he'd printed the cell-phone pictures of the papers from Grigor's safe.

He flipped a wall switch, bringing his gas fireplace to life; the soft flickers comforted the room. Pouring a large glass of Stolichnaya, he carried the pictures to an outsize chair near the massive bay window overlooking the Atlantic. From a side table, he removed his Polar Strike file.

Fearfully, as he commenced reading Grigor's papers, he jotted notes in the journal he'd started a few years back. Most of Grigor's notes confirmed what Slaga already knew from the file he'd purloined from Lubyanka in 1998. On the page labeled WHY CONTINUE? he'd written:

Polar Strike has no meaningful purpose. Its destination is oblivion. Why does an obscure, Manhattan doctor-psychiatrist continue implanting useless programming? Chris Ford is a sleeper agent who will never be activated.

Many pages were technical, the gist of which was a detailed description of how Grigor sought to implant the desired programming into the mind of Chris Ford. While most of it was beyond Slaga's understanding, he grasped that the primary focus was to create a layer of morals that fit over Chris Ford's primary values.

As Slaga reread this page, it seemed as best as he could understand, a new set of moral imperatives was designed to be *temporary* only to come into place if Chris was ever *activated*. Once operational, his new programming would kick into place, overriding Chris's natural sense of balance, order, and perception of right and wrong.

The trigger, was a phrase, "*The long and brutal winter gives way to spring.*" It was to be delivered to Ford via cellphone before he was to be activated. And it came with a fail-safe of sorts. If spoken to him in Russian, it was meaningless. If in English, Ford's programming was activated.

But that was it. Nothing else. The last page was what looked to be a diagram of sorts. In the background, Slaga heard the first indications his grandfather clock was commencing its hourly changing of the guard. Glancing at his watch, he closed his eyes and softly counted the chimes. Midnight. The witching hour.

Then he examined the next page. It wasn't a diagram. As best as could be determined, it looked like a table or chart. However, in his haste to complete photographing the pages as Grigor returned, this last page had come out blurry and unreadable. It was all gibberish. At the top was the beginning of something, VLA—, but that was it.

Suddenly, a flit passed like a comet through his head—an incomplete idea that whisked away into the mist. He pondered it, but as he did, cold fear jolted his gut. *Vla.*

Slaga bolted upright, the pages falling to the floor. Never taking his eyes from the papers, he backed to the massive bay window behind. Suddenly his gaze shifted down the hall. Racing to the front door, he double-checked the locks. In the living room, he took a tentative seat next to the fireplace. He stared at the papers strewn across the carpet. But the flames now cast a sinister aura about the room.

"*Zdes' obitalo zlo.*"

Evil has come to dwell here.

CHAPTER 50

2017
WASHINGTON, DC

Vadik exited immigration at Dulles International. Unobtrusively, he made his way to a dark, tinted Cadillac Escalade SUV idling at the curb. Opening the back door, he got in. As the vehicle moved off, his eyes adjusted to the darkened cabin. In the glass-partition sealed front, the driver wordlessly maneuvered onto the two-sixty-seven expressway, following the signs to Washington, DC.

Hitting a button, the glass opened. "Viktor, how are you, my friend?"

Taking his focus from the road, looking into the rear-view mirror, "Very well, General. Thank you."

"Good. Good."

Next to him, radiating polar-frigidity, Sigrid intently engaged with a laptop keyboard. "General."

After a moment, she handed the notebook computer to Vadik. "Gold is up. Diamonds down," she said.

"Thank you," he replied. Distractedly, he examined the monitor before softly closing the PC. "Is he ready to see us?"

"Yes, General." She leaned forward, tapping Viktor on the shoulder. "Now, please."

The chauffeur quickly moved the SUV into the far-right lane, exiting the expressway at Wolf Trap. Passing under the road, the SUV faded into the background of surrounding suburbs. Vadik stared out the window, fascinated at the passing landscape: trees, rolling horse properties, and small creeks interspersed with strip malls, "So much like Russia and yet not."

After a few miles of low-level evasive driving, Viktor again looked into the mirror. "I believe we are not being followed, General."

Vadik nodded silently.

"Viktor, the hotel please," Sigrid said.

Returning to Dulles, the driver made his way to the Northern Virginia Resort. In the stygian-shaded parking garage, Sigrid exited the car. After an initial check of the surroundings, she stepped to the rear of the vehicle, the back-hatch already opening. Sigrid pulled back a black tarp revealing an array of weapons. She lifted a Heckler and Koch UMP 45, but reconsidered, opting for a Glock 20. She threaded a silencer onto the tip, handing the weapon to Viktor. Taking another Glock, she repeated the process. Examining the array, she paused to rub her ear lobe. Lightly she fingered a Yamam Ari B'Lilah stiletto before selecting a jet-black Benchmade 8600 Auto Bedlam switchblade. Testing it, she popped the blade.

She turned, finding Viktor quietly studying her.

"Interesting choices."

Sigrid nodded. "When deployed, it makes more of an impression ... and I like the butterfly on the blade."

Smiling, Viktor reached past her. As he did, her eyes admiringly took note of the Spetsnaz spec-ops tat on his left wrist. Taking two loaded Glock bullet magazines, he put one his coat pocket, while locking the other into the pistol and chambering a round. Sliding the tarp back into place, she faced Viktor.

"No blades?" Sigrid asked.

Thrusting his jaw out, Viktor adjusted an already perfectly set tie while checking the lay of his coat over the Glock. "I'm trained in aikido, kung fu, and jiu-jitsu; as well as I am a small weapons expert. A blade would get in my way."

Sigrid tilted her head in quiet acknowledgement while thinking to herself, "Built like an accountant with the soul of a tortured poet. Until he's not. Intriguing mix."

With silent efficiency, Viktor moved into the parking area, making last-minute checks.

Satisfied, Sigrid opened Vadik's door. "We're clear, General."

Silently, she spun on her heel. Taking point with Viktor on rear guard, they proceeded across the garage, a caravan of stealth. On the elevator, Sigrid produced a master-override key that she inserted into the control panel. Pushing a button, the car lifted, bypassing every floor until reaching the top. Viktor stepped out. After a moment, he motioned it was safe.

At the end of the hall, Viktor used a card key to access the suite and stepped aside. Entering, Vadik was not disappointed to finally meet one of his investments: Sigrid's description had been spot-on.

"Congressman Byrnes," Vadik beamed, extending his hand, always surprised that the threshold Americans set for friendship was so low.

"General Pyotr, a pleasure," Byrnes greasily replied, his eyes flitting to Sigrid—already distracted.

"Congressman, thank you for taking this meeting."

"Of course."

Closing the door with Viktor just outside the suite, Sigrid moved to the main dining table; Vadik and Byrnes sat in two oversize chairs facing each other.

"Congressman—"

"Please, call me Adam."

Vadik nodded, "Adam. We have great things to accomplish you and I; this deal, and our future endeavors, will bring our two countries closer together."

"I'm sure you're right."

The Russian oligarch continued. "I have also arranged to wire ten million British pound sterling to the Plowshares Society. This is a PAC I control ... through surrogates. The Society will contribute to the election campaigns of House members you identify as supportive of your elevation to the Whip position. Is this acceptable?"

Byrnes smiled, "Thank you."

"Now, please to update me on the Archangel Northstar tariff relief."

"Bill is stuck in committee, I'm afraid."

Not taking her eyes from the keyboard, Sigrid icily asked, "Who?"

Uncertain as to where the power in the room was, Byrnes tentatively replied, "Sorry?"

Looking up, Sigrid locked eyes with Byrnes, tranquilizing him with imbalance. "Who is blocking it?"

Byrnes turned to Vadik, expecting he would call his guard dog off, but the general sat impassively studying him like a bug on a microscope. Uncertain, he returned his attention to Sigrid, who coldly waited. Subtly shifting in her seat caused her jacket to open, giving Byrnes a glimpse of the Glock.

"Diggins—Congressman Diggins from California. He's intractable."

Sigrid resumed typing as Vadik solicitously said, "Congressman Byrnes, soon to be the Whip I hope, thank you for your time. Like I said—a great team." Smoothly, he stood, signifying the end of the meeting. "We'll be in touch. Thank you."

Sigrid packed her things joining Vadik.

Leaping from his seat, Byrnes blurted, "Wait. I need ...." But the abyss in Sigrid's eyes silenced him. "Thank you, General," he meekly said.

* * * *

Two weeks later, while in Savannah on a recess, Byrnes was reading some documents when his assistant came in. Taking a TV remote, she turned on the news where a reporter was talking into a microphone, a car being pulled from a waterway behind her.

"Law enforcement authorities are speculating the representative lost control of his vehicle up the road here, plunging into this irrigation canal. Congressman Diggins was thrown through the windshield into the canal—where, it is surmised, he hit his head, lost consciousness, and drowned. It's believed he was driving home from a town-hall meeting in this central California town, when the accident occurred."

Byrnes felt his coat pocket vibrate. Removing his cellphone, he glanced at the number. He looked up.

"Margaret, can you give me a moment?" His assistant nodded, muting the TV as she stepped out. "Hello?"

Black cold—as from the deepest reaches of outer space—pulsed from the phone. "Reintroduce the bill." The line went dead.

Byrnes looked out the window onto the South Carolina lowlands that had often given him comfort; a fear gripped him. “Who are these people?”

CHAPTER 51

2017
SENATE OFFICES, DIRKSEN BUILDING, WASHINGTON, DC OFFICE OF THE JUNIOR SENATOR FROM NEW YORK

It had been a whirlwind, but the election last year had gone as planned—Chris Ford had carried only seventeen of New York's sixty-two counties, yet over sixty-three percent of the vote to bury his Republican opponent. It was a tour de force by any first-time candidate. Indeed, the *Times* had written:

A new Phoenix has risen in New York politics. Armed with a progressive agenda, Hollywood good looks, and a stunning, runway-model-worthy wife who is smarter and more accomplished than he is, Senator-elect Ford's arrival reminds one of a time long ago: a time called Camelot.

One of Ford's assistants had had the quote bronzed and put up next to the window looking out upon the National Mall.

With offices nationwide as well as strategically placed abroad, Stephens Monroe's environmental division operated primarily from its New York headquarters. But the firm's environmental-legislative lobbying efforts were conducted from the firm's DC base. While Chris and Mallory had discussed her moving to Washington, for the time being, she remained in New York. It was a short hop home to the city every weekend. While there, he could attend more fundraisers, shore up his political base, and see his family and Stephan Grigor.

Chris was reading a briefing paper on an upcoming agricultural bill when his intercom buzzed. "Senator Claymore is here to see you."

The Conference Chairperson, Claymore had been pursuing Chris for more party support work. "Show him in, please."

The door opened and a heavyset, balding man lumbered into the room. As if straight out of central casting from an old Hollywood studio, Claymore's paunch forced his trousers down, while his tie looked as if the wizened Illinois lawmaker used it as a handkerchief on humid, Washington days—but, appearances lie.

Claymore's mythical Rolodex supposedly had personal cell numbers of the editor-in-chief of every major paper in the country. A phone call could result in a story being printed or killed. He was instrumental in getting party leaders, committee chairs, and rising stars onto all the Sunday talk shows. Most everyone whispered in DC that he knew—not only the dirt on each member of congress, but what carpet to find it under.

"Senator Ford, always grateful when you can find time for me," said the genteel older man.

"Please, Mr. Chairperson, I'm honored to speak with a great leader of the party. Please, have a seat," Chris replied, gesturing to a couple of facing armchairs before a welcoming fireplace.

After dispensing with the expected niceties, Claymore pulled a folded piece of paper from his jacket pocket. "So Chris, tell me. Have you thought about which committees you'd like to serve on?"

Chris leaned forward in a supplicating fashion, before sitting back as if still pondering about the matter. "Well, Mr. Chairperson, I was thinking Judiciary, Foreign Relations—oh, and possibly Environment."

"Absolutely. Great choices. Here's what we can offer: Homeland Security, Judiciary, and Agriculture," Claymore put his hand up before the younger senator could object, "if *you* agree to take a leadership position on the DSCC."

"Me? But I just got here. How could—"

"Chris, you're being too modest. After what you just did in New York, well I can't think of anybody better qualified."

The Democratic Senatorial Campaign Committee was a unique organization focused solely on electing Democrats around the United

States to the Senate. It was a high-profile group with lots of reach and visibility—and required a lot of time.

Before Chris could respond, Claymore continued. "Look Senator, you stepped over about twenty—more senior, mind you—members of the New York state Democratic machine to win your seat. Now, besides looking like you stepped off the cover of GQ and oozing tons of charisma, you benefited from a fundraising effort of epic proportion. Your party is asking that you put those same efforts into electing more like-minded men and women to the Senate." Claymore paused for effect, pretending to look at his hands. "And it certainly couldn't hurt to have allies for later on down the road."

"Down the road?" Chris feigned, already knowing where this was headed.

"Son, my sources tell me that you've been running for office since you were in seventh grade." The older senator paused again for effect. "So can I tell the Leader that you'll take the DSCC offer?"

Chris thought, "What was that old saying? One hand washes the other?" He smiled broadly, standing, hand proffered. "Absolutely."

Claymore stood, "Excellent. There's someone I want you to meet. Kendall out in Idaho."

"The Governor?"

"That's right; he was in the Senate before returning home to run for governor. He's helping to coordinate the fundraising for the party's national gubernatorial efforts. He's in town for the National Governors Association annual meeting. While you're meeting with him, you might try to get some time with Johansen from Minnesota—his star is on the rise."

Chris nodded studiously. "Thank you, Senator. You stop by anytime; you're always welcome."

CHAPTER 52

2017
NEW YORK

From the earliest days in the army, the General still maintained a rigorous exercise schedule: daily six-mile runs interspersed with gym time and a personal trainer. He drew strength from his regimen. It hardened him in ways that others either could not or would not do.

In his suite at the Plaza, Vadik stood beside a grand piano at the massive floor-to-ceiling window, overlooking Central Park. He'd just finished a workout and brought a glass of organic orange juice into the living room with him, thinking, "Ah, these Americans." On the Steinway, sat a set of Russian prayer beads; he took them into his right hand, fondling them silently. While not an overtly religious man, he found the beads to be a good complement to his exercise program. Both bled away stress.

The green canopy below was one of his favorite pastimes. He let his mind wander to hunting near his Sheya diamond mine in Siberia. Prey like big Kamchatka Brown Bears were elusive, fading into the trees. On hunts, Vadik and his guide would amble through the woods—chatting, discussing sports, vodka, Tchaikovsky or Borodin—when suddenly the man would stop. Slowly, he'd descend to one knee as he listened, gleaning movement in the surrounding forest. Almost like an animal himself, he'd, sniff the air, crooking his ear in a direction, processing. Then, with a delicacy that belied his gruff exterior, the trapper would move with glacial purpose toward a copse of trees.

Again, the bear stalker would come to a stop, motioning Vadik to circle off to his right or left. From a bag, he removed an air horn and after exchanging silent nods with Vadik, he'd let off a long blast. More often than not, this elicited the desired effect. A cornered bear would flee from the cacophonous din ... right toward Vadik. For Vadik, it was his turn in the crucible—the calm that allowed him to focus, often only enough time for a single shot.

Sigrid entered the room, laptop in hand, silently taking up station on a nearby table.

"Our mystery man is out there?" He asked

"Yes, General. As you recall, we established a link between Bruno Shakli, the sanitation employee who we believe broke into your office, and a Mikhail Kuznetsov, a businessman on travel. Each time Kuznetsov entered Russia, a few days later, Shakli reported for work. Approximately thirty days later, when Shakli departed for treatments at Red Army Clinic, Kuznetsov departs Sheremetyevo. We traced Kuznetsov to London, but here things got lost in the woods."

Vadik, looked at his lieutenant, chuckling quietly at another of her odd translation of words.

"Our operative at UK Border Control was unable to find similar departure records for Kuznetsov—indicating he's a UK resident or he changes identities again for subsequent movement in or out of the UK."

Vadik interrupted, "Were there departures from Heathrow or Gatwick that coincide with Kuznetsov's arrivals and departures?"

"Yes, General. We cross-checked the dates of Kuznetsov's travel into and out of the UK and found similar arrival and departure dates for another man. His name is Ivan Petrov."

Vadik grunted. "Another common name. This ... man of mist and fog certainly looks to blend in."

Sigrid read from her laptop. "Yes. His efforts at concealment seem to confirm our increasing opinion that he is a former intelligence or Special Forces operative."

Now intrigued, Vadik turned to rest against the windowsill. "Go on."

"Petrov's movements are more asymmetrical. He comes and goes from various cities around the UK: Manchester and Birmingham in

England, Edinburgh and Glasgow in Scotland, Belfast in Northern Ireland, along with Dublin and Shannon in the Irish Republic."

"And all this activity leads to ... New York?"

"With occasional routing through Philadelphia, Newark, and Boston. We don't have an identity yet, but his background will make it easier for us to find him."

Vadik returned his gaze to the green below. "How are things in Moscow?"

"We've begun research on penetrating the records department. Your hunch that Grupp must have left something, another hint of what he was working on, is bearing fruit. Some of the people he worked with, before he died, recalled word of some secret project in *Archives*. Very hush-hush. Our ... as you call him, *mystery man*, and this project are most likely linked. Lubyanka's building engineer—the one before you arrived, who might have knowledge of Grupp's plan—is retired and no longer living in Russia. We believe he's in Europe, possibly Italy."

"Italy?"

"Yes, General. He received a large retirement payout about the time Grupp's project was completed and he quietly disappeared into the fabric."

"Italy—nice fabric."

"We have people looking now. I'll keep you posted."

Vadik nodded, "Very well."

Smiling to himself, he returned his attention to Central Park and Kamchatka Brown Bears.

CHAPTER 53

2017
NEW YORK
MARINE PARK GOLF

Nic looked up before the club made contact, leading to the inevitable topping of the ball. Disgustedly, he watched the little white object of his pain roll twenty feet.

"Hey cuz, you're not thinking of giving up your day job, now are you!" Chris laughed, calling from the other side of the fairway.

Barely finding the golf bag, Nic angrily shoved the offensive club into its slot. "Ha, ha, ha," he muttered more to himself than anyone. Nic looked over in time to see Chris gracefully launch a shot that majestically sailed across a water hazard, landing softly on the green, coming to rest about five feet from the flagstick.

"Son of—"

"Temper, temper big buddy!"

Nic salvaged some pride as his next shot easily cleared the water only to land in a green-side sand trap. Shaking his head, Nic trudged toward the bunker. Settling into his stance, he looked over at Chris quietly cleaning his ball. Nic thought, "Why does he even need to clean the ball? It never goes in a trap or hazard or mud. Geez." Nic readied his shot. "Keep your head still and stay through the shot this time." He took his sand wedge back and then forward, sliding beneath his ball. Motionless, his head intently in place, he at last looked up to see his ball land softly on the green and roll three feet into the cup.

"Nic! Great shot!"

Raking the bunker, Nic arrived on the green to retrieve his ball. For a moment, things were good. Then Chris made his putt to win the hole. In the cart, they drove to the next tee.

"Good hole, Nic."

"It was, but you still took it."

"Got lucky."

Nic nodded but said nothing. They finished their round and retired to the patio for lunch.

"You know, this is a great little course. I love coming here."

"Not as nice as Winged Foot."

"Look, you know that's Mallory's family. That's not me. I'm as comfortable here as there—you know that."

Nic nodded, a little mad at himself that his cousin's good fortune rubbed him the wrong way. "I know. So how's Mal?"

Just then, a couple of women timidly approached their table. One of them offered a scorecard. "Senator, we both voted for you and we're so excited to meet you. Could you—"

Before she could finish, Chris stood to shake their hands. "Let me sign those for you and how about a couple of selfies?"

Both golfers squealed their approval. Nic was drawn into photo duty. Then Chris signed their cards and they left in high spirits.

"Thanks, Nic. That was above and beyond the call of duty."

"No worries. I imagine that's getting to be routine?"

"A little bit. A bit unnerving." Just then, Chris rubbed his forehead.

Nic squinted but let it pass. "Mal is liking this new life?"

"I think so. Not sure when she's coming to DC. But she's good—worked to death but good. She said 'hi,' by the way."

"The same back to her. Still doesn't like golf?"

"Nah. Probably that country-club lifestyle growing up ... I don't know, but I just get the feeling she thinks golf is a little elitist or something."

Nic looked about the very egalitarian trappings of the mini course they just played. "You should bring her here. Club of the people."

Chris picked up a can of beer and a handful of French fries. "How about you? Doing okay?"

"Yeah—sorta—I don't .... " Nic's voice trailed off.

Putting a hand on his cousin's shoulder, Chris reassuringly said, "I'm sorry man. I know it's still fresh, but—it'll get better. You'll see."

Nic's divorce from his wife of six years was ten months old. It felt longer. It had not been a mutually agreed-upon separation. Maureen had wearied of Nic's constant NYPD-related absences. After receiving a partial scholarship to Brooklyn College, Maureen had taken night classes and attained an associate degree in Art Design. She and Nic were moving in opposite directions. Finances, work, and friendships came to dominate their home life, the arguments as common as meals. And secretly, Nic had occasionally imagined that Maureen compared him to his younger, more successful cousin. It was a thought Nic hated even having.

Finally, after an all-night stakeout, Nic had come home to an empty apartment and an envelope on the kitchen table. Nice, cursive spelling of his name was all the evidence he needed that he'd arrived at another death scene.

The rest was a messy soap opera. Always imagining herself to be a style-conscious fashionista, Maureen had been mesmerized by Manhattan's art-crowd community. Soon after she left, Nic was not shocked to learn she'd taken up with the owner of Canvas—an urban, self-absorbed studio that fancied itself the next great atelier. Nic soon found himself, guiltily, checking the net each weekend for listings of the gallery's showings, events, and exhibitions.

"Yeah, I know. I just never imagined something non-physical could hurt so bad." He took a pull from his beer. "So, how's the Senate treating you?"

"Good. Getting rolled up into more national party politics. But it increases my visibility they say."

"President?"

Chris choked and coughed. "I've been in the Senate less than a year and you got me moving to the big house?"

"Isn't that the long-range plan?"

"We'll see. Let me just enjoy this first."

Nic paused.

"How about the headaches?"

Chris sat back closing his eyes, rubbing his temples. "Been worse of late."

"What does Stephan say?"

"He thinks they'll pass after the stress decreases."

Nic snorted.

"Yeah, that's what I think."

The cousins finished lunch. In the parking lot, as they prepared to leave each other, Chris looked intently at Nic. "Can you do something for me?"

"Anything, man."

"If something happens to me, take care of Mal. Okay?"

"Sure," Nic replied, caught off guard.

"Thanks."

Chris turned and stepped away. In the rearview mirror of his Ford Fusion, Nic watched, perplexed, as Chris's Lincoln SUV drove off.

CHAPTER 54

2017
NEW YORK

If Stephan Grigor had a weakness, it was an unwillingness to do more than was needed. Emotional inertia is the inability to react to things, even if it might benefit someone. Like the need to change bad dietary habits just before diving into an ice cream sundae, or understanding the health risks of tobacco, as the tenth cigarette of the day flames to life—are things a person should deal with now but don't. It was something he liked to use during his sessions with patients, but he recognized that some attributes of the condition might apply to himself.

Prior to Elena Ford's death, Grigor had not known who her contact in Moscow was. After her death, and with the rapid unraveling of the USSR back into Russia and a bunch of satellite states, it was not clear to Grigor if there even was an intelligence agency in Moscow with cognizance over Polar Strike. But given that he was achieving some success with his work and now with an increasing lack of oversight, Grigor had been content to keep the status quo in place.

Grigor had greeted the arrival of "James Richardson" as his new handler with relief tinted with a mixture of skepticism—why now after all these years? Richardson's eventual revelation that he was not an intelligence officer, coupled with his threat to ruin Grigor's life, had initially cowed the doctor. But after the recent discovery of finding his Polar Strike files slightly askew in his home floor vault, and with Chris Ford's elevation to the Senate, Grigor had concluded Richardson, or whoever he was, needed to be eliminated—both as a nuisance and potential threat

He breathed and thought, "If only Elena were still alive. She was always good at these types of things."

* * * *

Life for Slaga was actually as good as it had ever been. Since Ford's departure for Washington, the mobster was enjoying a quiet success with his various pursuits. His crew typically boosted approximately fifty computers a month and resold them up and down the Eastern seaboard. When a nice piece of art—usually a copy of some great painting or new artist's work—appeared in a gallery, they'd break in to take it, often lifting other pieces or all the cash in the register as means of cover. They even occasionally spray-painted anti-bourgeois art graffiti to add fog to the crime.

The eavesdropping sessions at Grigor's office, during his sessions with Chris Ford, had proven immensely profitable. He'd kept abreast of all the NYPD's Russian mob investigations; this ensured he was always one step ahead of the police. Additionally, there'd been a few more financial windfalls from prudent investments before public disclosure of city-related building projects.

After Ford left for Washington, Slaga's interests in the rising political star diminished. With Ford gone, nothing new would be learned of NYPD activities. The real reason for his lackluster approach with the new Senator was Slaga's spiraling paranoia about Polar Strike. Often coming to mind were the images of the dread in the priest—who gave his deathbed revelation of Polar Strike's existence to his cousin Misha. "Better to let sleeping dogs lie," he thought as they said in America. "Good advice." Keeping an outline of the plan in a hidden place in his home, he'd sealed the bulk of the files up, moving them safely out of his possession.

Instinctual habits, honed by Spetsnaz training, had allowed Slaga's survival in many different environments. Saint Petersburg. The Army. Afghanistan. Being a global mercenary, and now life in New York's mob world. Over the years, he'd avoided most contact with the authorities and his rivals in large part due to two things: always being somewhere else when a crime was taking place and investing in the details.

This second one involved an almost hyper-vigilance about his surroundings as he looked for tails or cameras or things seemingly out of place. He rarely appeared in public, and only with a floppy, Patagonia sun hat, large sunglasses, and a cane used to feign a limp. With many of his rivals—Italians, Irish, South Americans, as well as Russians, in retreat or in jail—and with his decreasing interactions with Grigor, he was becoming ... if not sloppy, then more mellow.

Slaga's fears substantially dissipated. Junkets to the gaming meccas of Las Vegas, Monte Carlo, and Macau had proved profitable and relaxing. Slaga even took a girlfriend, an Argentinian woman working as a server at Tavern on the Green in Central Park. She was teaching him how to tango.

* * * *

The tip had come like a thunderbolt from the heavens. Nic Ford had been at his desk on a lazy afternoon. A caller, asking specifically for *Captain Ford.* Nic had asked his secretary who was calling. After a moment, she was back on the intercom.

" ... says he knows something about Club Twenty-Two."

The mention of a two-decade old crime, one his father had never cracked, rendered Nic mute for a second.

"Captain?" The intercom squawked.

Nic blinked, trying to clear his head.

"Cap?"

Without responding to his secretary, Nic picked up the receiver. "Captain Ford."

In the 1990s, the tipster, Roman Osinov, had been a member of Zolotoy Poyezd—the Gold Train—and knew Tino Ivchenko. He remembered the arrival of Tino's friend from Saint Petersburg. He had a strange name that started with an *S* or something, but the man had remained on the periphery of Zolotoy—almost as if he was going to night school to learn how to be a gangster. He never took part in their operations, mostly just giving advice to Tino, sort of like a consultant on crime. After the Ukrainians had derailed the Gold Train, Osinov and one other gang member had taken off for Chicago. While lying low, they'd followed the news in New York from afar.

"Why come forward now?" Nic asked the small-time hood now in his office.

Osinov regarded his hat in his hand before looking imploringly into Nic's eyes. "My wife's sister, Olga, has a son—"

Cynically, Nic beckoned the criminal with his hand. "What's he in for?"

"He got into a fight at a bar—it wasn't his fault, but the other guy is in the hospital."

"Never is. Where?"

Osinov squinted in confusion?

"Where is he now?"

"Rikers."

Nic shoved a pad of paper across the desk. "Details ... about your nephew and then everything about the Gold Train and this unknown man. Suddenly, a thought occurred to Nic. He opened his desk, rooting around unsuccessfully. Annoyed, he checked other drawers before coming to the last one. In mild desperation, he yanked out papers, piling them on his desk before finding an envelope. Opening it, he held the contents up for Osinov to see.

The man's face went ashen. "That is him."

Impatiently, Nic waved the document at Osinov. "You *know* this man?"

Osinov vigorously nodded.

The detective slowly turned the picture around to regard the old Red Army recruiting photo he'd taken from his father two decades ago. "Slaga. I never believed you were dead," he whispered.

The Specter was still alive and apparently thriving in Brighton. Nic had never truly bought the idea that Rusta Volgakoff, the goon his cousin Chris had been chasing, was the Specter. It seemed to Nic that someone, maybe the real Specter, had framed Volgakoff. The package was too neat, along with a suicide the morning he was to go trial? Nic was happy for Chris, but it still had never set well with him.

Osinov gave him what he knew, which while helpful, was also historic—and of little help with the current situation. Quietly, he'd put his ear to the ground, looking for something to trace back to the

Gold Train or Club Twenty-Two. Nic had spent his career building up trust and confidence with the merchants and thugs in Little Russia, but still, Slaga's old Army recruit photo had been greeted with shaken heads and a chorus of "*Nyet*."

But, at Red Square Ink, he hit pay dirt.

"Yeah, I think I seen him," said a diminutive, weasel-like, tattoo-coated man. He turned to rummage in a small file cabinet behind his workstation. Triumphantly, he removed a picture of a man, from the neck down, covered with treasure chests, naked women, and numbers: "Nikita D."

Nic took the picture, scrutinizing it as if it was his lost child or cousin. Given the years, the man in the picture could be Slaga. "Likes tats."

The weasel nodded.

"Nikita D?"

The inker replied, "Guys don't give their full or real name. Cops can't find 'em easier. Also don't like their face in the picture—same reason."

Nic nodded. "Can I take this?"

"Yeah. He hits the bars and cafes on Neptune. But I haven't seen him lately."

TODAY

CHAPTER 55

JANUARY
WASHINGTON, DC

Vadik Pyotr sat in his suite with CNN on the TV. A field reporter was speaking, the Capitol building in the background.

The reporter acknowledged his camera operator's cue. "Today, Adam Byrnes of Georgia was named the Speaker of the House. It was a historic election—as Mr. Byrnes becomes only the fourth representative from the Peach State and the first Democrat from Georgia since the 1800s, to be elected Speaker. On his first day as the leader—"

Muting the TV, Vadik absently said, "Very good."

At the desk on her ever-present laptop, Sigrid nodded. "What can you do with Byrnes?"

"Uncertain. We may already be getting everything we can from him."

* * * *

JULY
LOS ANGELES
CNN

The recognizable face of the network's national anchor sat at one end of a panel facing four reporters and correspondents, each with their own, unique portfolio of interests.

The anchor asked the national affairs reporter a question.

"What does the selection of Governor Johansen mean for the party?"

"Great question. In short, it means a return to its roots. The party is trying to focus on domestic issues. Foreign affairs will probably be less of a concern this election cycle. Johansen, while not a populist, is certainly attenuated to the voice of mainstream America—who are saying they want jobs and prosperity."

The anchor turned to the correspondent for national politics.

"And Johansen's selection of Senator Christopher Ford from New York—a gamble?"

The political affairs observer sought to affect a sagely look as she responded. "Possibly. He's young and hasn't been in the Senate as long as so many of his colleagues. But what I'm hearing is this is a brilliant pick. The Senator and his wife, Mallory, are super magnetic—they practically have their own solar system of political planets drawing into orbit around them. Governors, Congress, and state Democratic organizations have greatly benefitted from Ford's fundraising efforts. He's widely respected, especially in an area Governor Johansen lacks: foreign affairs."

The anchor looked to the network's blogger for Congressional matters.

"With the recent removal of New Mexico's Congressman Kenwick—because of influence peddling—and the elevation of Georgia's Adam Byrnes to the Speaker's chair, how will this affect the election? Does Byrnes have the firepower to galvanize the Dems and hold the House?"

The Op-Ed journalist nodded at the anchor. "Well, I imagine it will be an extension of the national election. Johansen and Ford offer a compelling story that resonates with voters on so many levels. Despite the Dems's massive fundraising efforts, Kenwick's corruption conviction has affected the country's perception of the party. The big question is can the Republicans take advantage of this?"

The anchor finally cast his gaze upon a studious, professorial-looking man whose specialty was foreign relations. "Doctor, how does the newly minted Democratic ticket look in the eyes of the world?"

"*Ja* ees' good for America to have domestic focus but ees' still important to remember she ees' member of de' global community and I theenk dees slate would be well received eef' elected."

The anchor added his two cents: "Thank you, professor. I'm sure many around the world would vote in this election, if they could."

* * * *

OCTOBER
NEW YORK

As Chris stepped from the stage at the University of Illinois's Foellinger Auditorium, he found Mallory beaming. Taking his face into her hands, she whispered, "I'm so proud of you and to be your wife."

Campaign aides waited an appropriate moment before intruding.

"Well done, Senator. The Governor has a few words for you," one said, proffering a cellphone.

Chris took it, keeping an arm around Mallory while rubbing his temples. "Robert?"

"Great job, Chris!" said Robert Johansen. "You ran circles around him."

The only Vice-Presidential debate had just concluded and the early flash polls had Chris defeating his Republican opponent handily, scoring particularly well on questions of the environment and foreign affairs.

Mallory felt her cellphone vibrate in her pocket. Stepping away, she answered it. "Oh, hello Stephan," she said, casting a glance at Chris. "Yes, I'm sure he looked a little stressed on TV, but I think he's doing well." She listened for a few more moments before finishing the call. "Stephan, we're within striking distance now. Good job."

CHAPTER 56

OCTOBER
MOSCOW

The video monitor in her suite came to life.

"Sigrid, how are you?"

"Very well, General."

"The Four Seasons is always perfect. They are treating you well? You have everything you need?"

"Yes, thank you."

"Good. What have you learned?"

"We found the engineer in Turin. He was most helpful. As we knew, Grupp commissioned him to create a secret file room in the Archives. This was done after the USSR collapsed and KGB was broken up. With foreign intelligence moving to SVR in Yasenevo, he thought it imperative to maintain separate copies of most of the foreign department's past and ongoing operations at Lubyanka."

"Why?"

"Unknown, General. Perhaps, the various affairs had overlapping interests or Grupp was looking for future leverage over SVR. But mostly, I think it was the efforts to stand up the national archive at Rosarkhiv that drove him. He might have worried that many KGB files were potentially incriminating or embarrassing to the agency, or both, and wanted to ensure they would never see the light of day."

"Where is this secret trove?"

Sigrid examined her notes. "These are the blueprints we secured. As you can see," she turned a chart toward the camera adjacent to her monitor, "Archives is in the basement. Down the hall from the main file room is a small closet with shelves of cleaning supplies. Behind the last shelf are stored KGB's old files."

"How do you get into this room?"

"Apparently, on the underside of the bottom cleaning-supplies storage ledge is a button, which causes the shelf to swing aside to reveal a glass door."

"When do you anticipate penetration?"

"As soon as documentation can be arranged."

"I will get it set up. Keep me posted." Vadik quickly added, "Oh, and Sigrid?"

"General?"

"The loose end in Turin is now tied off?"

"Of course."

"Accident?"

"Heart attack."

"Good. Carry on."

"General."

CHAPTER 57

OCTOBER
MOSCOW

Autumn's arrival always came with a sidecar of depression for Olegina Bortsova. The daughter of a minor party official from east of the Urals, Olegina had grown up on the Steppes of Siberia. As frigid as her youth had been, it was nothing compared to the capitol. Moscow had turned so cold and mean—citizens and party officials alike, drunk to their gills, combating winter's tentacles, and impervious to anything other than vodka and rubles. Every step of the day was calculated to be accomplished with the least amount of effort and civility.

Olegina found being an extremely competent archivist to be a defense against the crushing reality that men—drunk or not, but drunk helped—did not find her particularly attractive. In a cruel twist, the fates had ordained she'd travel through life with her father's looks and her mother's brains. It was certainly a one-way ticket to oblivion had it not been for the luck of being related to the Deputy Chief of the Ministry of Culture. He'd arranged for her to secure a position at Rosarkhiv, the Federal Archival Agency of Russia.

Of average intelligence, Olegina compensated with boa-constrictor persistence, reinforced by a willingness to go down rat holes no one else would—especially the terminally boring ones that required transposing information from old paper documents to microfiche or directly into computer files. There were days when her fingers bled from so much typing. She was ruining her eyes deciphering decades-old, faded hand scratch. At times, she imagined even the middle-age monks, who'd gone blind and permanently stooped after decades copying Bibles, would have taken one look at her assignments and fled back to their monasteries.

One task in particular though had proved more disturbing and very sensitive. It involved transcribing old KGB paper files from the forties and fifties onto the computer. Most of the records had been moved from Lubyanka to Rosarkhiv, but every so often, a new file had been found and duly sent along. Occasionally, Olegina herself would make the trip to Lubyanka, now the headquarters of the Border Guard Service of Russia. The other tenant was the Federal Security Service of the Russian Federation. While the name evoked patriotic, even noble aspirations, it could not escape the dark, evil shadow of its sinister heritage.

Down through the ages—despots, dictators, and demons tyrannized their people out of vanity, control, anger, and fear. Often, they relied upon ruthless people willing to assume the responsibility for maintaining the apparatus of government and control of the ruled. Tools like torture and murder were commonplace. But an elite few developed complex organizations that, in addition to torture and murder, placed an iron boot on the necks of their citizenry through insidious means such as mass execution, ethnic cleansing, organized famine, forced displacement, propaganda, and attempts at thought control.

The Frumentarii of Ancient Rome and China's imperial Jinyiwei wielded the truncheon of fear for centuries. Two of history's most brutal existed for relatively brief, but horrific, periods: Germany's Gestapo and Japan's Kempetai employed methods so venomous, they qualified as industrial-strength sadism. But in Olegina's mind, none enjoyed the dual distinction of being equally destructive to a country's very soul and extinguishing the destiny of so many other countries than the KGB.

Olegina always shuddered, saying a prayer when passing through Lubyanka Square. While *Iron Felix*, the statue of the Cheka's first director, Felix Dzershinsky, had been removed years ago, his presence still hung over Lubyanka. Dzershinsky had been a sadistic street thug of the first order. On Lenin's orders, he'd overseen the Red Terror that had brutalized the Russian people in the consolidation of authority after the Bolsheviks had seized power.

Not to be outdone, Joseph Stalin's carousel of security ministers—men raised up to authority before being disgraced and finally executed—recast the Cheka into the modern, more-streamlined NKVD and finally the efficiently deadly KGB. Lenin's Red Terror had been a high-school dance compared to Stalin's Great Terror of the 1930s. Purging the Communist Party, as well as the Red Army's leadership, the signature of the Terror was mass, internal deportation of whole towns to the Siberian gulags and the systemization of a police state. Stalin's cobra-like personality and paranoia about losing power had literally turned the USSR into his own personal pincushion. The agent of that destruction had been the KGB.

After the fall of the Berlin Wall, it had been en vogue to document the history of Soviet oppression against its own citizens as well as the KGB's activities abroad. For Olegina, gathering, documenting, and archiving the records had started small with files of people who'd been internally deported to Siberia in the late twenties. Then she moved on to files of people deported in the early thirties. Then to files of citizens sentenced to the Supreme Degree of Punishment or *Vysshaya Mera Nakazaniya.*

Executions became so commonplace, they moved through the system on an assembly line. Trials—whatever they were in those days—were carried out by an NKVD troika and often concluded with a brief order, something terse along the lines of "For the safety of the citizens and for crimes against the state, NAME is hereby sentenced to VMN." A trickle became a stream, which finally grew into a torrent of names.

While the scope of KGB atrocities was becoming ever more widely known, Olegina had been reminded by her superiors that nothing became personal until there were names and that she needed to maintain tight control over both the information she was archiving as well as her emotions.

"*Techeniye vremeni neset bol' proch'*," her boss, Doctor Armerian, had said to her once, as he sat at his desk gazing at the gently meandering Moskva River below: "The flow of time bears away the pain."

Stopping at Lubyanka's front desk, she noted the lobby was a bustle of activity—uniforms and suits coming and going, ignoring her. The security guard brusquely logged her in. She moved down the hall, away from the restored Neo-Baroque-influenced lobby designed to camouflage the building's sins, to an around-the-corner, out-of-sight elevator station. It was as if the country knew the ugliness of its history was so horrifying, any documentation of it were to be buried as deeply as possible with the only access hidden far from view. The old lift always creaked on its descent as if the voices of the damned were crying out to her.

Today, as Olegina stepped off the lift, the lights were flickering again. The power supply throughout the building was desperately in need of upgrading—one of the very reasons for moving the old files to the National Archives. In addition, Lubyanka could no longer maintain the required temperature and humidity for proper maintenance of paper files. At the check-in station, she found a clerk reading a fashion magazine and smoking a cigarette, another no-no at Rosarkhiv. She looked up into Olegina's eyes with a mixture of terminal boredom and catatonia. Her thoughts were visible on her façade, "My luck will never change; I'll die at this desk."

"Olegina. Good morning."

"Anna," Olegina looked around as she signed in. "Am I the onl one here?"

"*Da.*" Gesturing to the pulsing-white, harsh lights, she mutter "You know very few scholars come down anymore. And today, it's a disco in here—no one can work, so they went to Sokias."

Furrowing her brow, Olegina looked at her watch. "The ba ten in the morning."

"So? Vodka or these lights. Both give you a headache, does it cheerfully." She resumed mindlessly flipping pag think I could steal any of these files?"

Gasping, Olegina slapped Anna's hand good-natured what with them?"

Pointing to her glossy mag, Anna replied, "I could b this bag. Think how good I'd look at the Opal Palace."

"That's a mafia club—why do you go there?"

A baleful look communicated Anna's ethical indifference at her friend's question. "And I have a future here?"

Olegina gathered her things and started toward the archives storage area. "I think I only have one pickup today."

"*Da.*"

CHAPTER 58

NOVEMBER
WASHINGTON, DC

Head throbbing since leaving the office for home, Chris Ford rubbed his temples. Even sealed behind dark Ray Ban Wayfarers, the brilliant afternoon sunset forced its way into tightly closed eyes making his headache worse. Right now, he wished he could put his head in a freezer and chill the pulsing, volcanic pain. At his government-furnished, Cadillac-SUV limousine, the driver opened the back door, providing Chris respite in the car's dark, air-conditioned lair. Since the election, Chris suddenly found himself further embedded in a cocoon of security, assistants, handlers, and clingers-on—the backseat of a limo on his way home being one of the occasional exceptions.

As the vehicle pulled into traffic, the passing greenery momentarily calmed his mind. Despite the headache, he allowed himself to savor what he'd accomplished and what was within reach. Fordham. Law School. DA's office. New York City Council. Finally, the Senate. Ongoing volunteer work for the Democratic Party machine. Charity events. And now, the mountaintop—or, at least the rung below it.

Years of effort had, at long last, yielded results. Two weeks prior, the Democratic Presidential ticket of Governor Robert Johansen of Minnesota and New York Senator Christopher Ford had taken forty states while sweeping the party into control of both the Senate and the House.

The transition would be orderly but brisk. In the years after WWII, Presidents-Elect had often resided at Blair House for the week before the Inauguration. But during the period from Election Day to Inauguration Week, the President Elect and his transition team stayed at their homes, if already living in the DC area, or they rented a

Washington-area private residence, or on some occasions, a hotel in the District of Columbia, frequently the Hay Adams. Vice Presidents Elect were often an afterthought, usually making their own plans. Fortunately, Chris and Mallory could reside at their own Georgetown brownstone, Chris's residence from the time he'd been elected to the Senate. After the Inauguration, the couple would take up residence in the Vice President's official home at the United States Naval Observatory.

For Chris the excitement of the transition had been accompanied by a massive flare-up in his migraines. Since his earliest days, various specialists did not have a solution, explaining that on occasion there were *idiopathic* symptoms that were unique to an individual, *we'll just keep a watch on it*—being the best answer that medical science could provide. Since winning the election, the pain seemed worse. Doctor Grigor, his primary care physician since birth, suggested election stress as the culprit.

At the house, Mallory greeted him at the front door with a drink and another stack of files. Part of the transition process came with getting up to speed on each of the fifteen departments that comprised the President's Cabinet—as well as various intelligence groups such as CIA, FBI, NSA, DIA and programs like NASA, NOAA, NTSB, GSA, SEC—it all ran together in his head. Chris was starting to think M&Ms was a government organization. Along with his martini, Mallory handed him files from the Department of Transportation. It was promising to be an exciting evening.

From the kitchen, Mallory called out, "Don't forget to pack; we're leaving in the morning for the Hamptons."

Chris blinked his eyes shut. Half in pain, the other half contemplating the dinner tomorrow night with donors and well-wishers. Normally, this part of his job was something he looked forward to, but the strain of the last couple of weeks was grinding on him. A sudden thought gave him reprieve.

"Do I have time to see Stephan?"

"I haven't seen the schedule, but I'm sure it can be worked out."

Immediately, his headache ebbed away as he imagined the dark, sensory-calming lab and the soothing voice of Doctor Stephan Grigor guiding him up the pyramid.

CHAPTER 59

NOVEMBER
MOSCOW

The credentials Vadik had delivered to Sigrid presented her as an intelligence researcher, working for SVR. Her documents exempted her from the requirement to surrender her personal sidearm and she was issued a temporary pass. An overly patronizing guard escorted her to the elevator. As the car commenced its agonizingly slow descent to the basement, the guard allowed his eyes to roam over Sigrid.

Slowly, she put down her laptop bag and stepped to the military man, licking her lips. A sneer of joyful conquest came over his countenance as he began to unzip. She put a hand gently behind his head, pulling him closer, feigning she was about to kiss him. But the triumph on his face morphed into shock then blinding agony as the crazy bitch forcefully smashed her knee into his crotch. The sentry doubled over in fear and nauseating pain. Pulling his head close, she whispered, "*V sleduyushchiy raz ya ub'yu tebya.*" *Next time, I will kill you.*

Jerking him back by his hair, causing his garrison cap to fall off, she smiled up into his tearing eyes before pushing him roughly back. As the car hit the bottom, the door started to open; the guard scrambled to grab his hat and adjust his trousers. After stepping from the car, Sigrid turned back to the sentry, "Thank you for your help."

Behind the reception desk, a young, overly primped, red-haired woman sat staring at her cellphone. Sigrid stepped to the counter. Obliviously, the clerk continued pushing buttons until Sigrid reached in, putting her hand over the phone's screen.

"What the shit!" said the receptionist.

"Enough," replied Sigrid.

About to unleash her outrage, the file-room attendant looked angrily into the visitor's black eyes. An image of a cemetery passed through her mind. Sullenly, she terminated her cell activity before snipping, "Can I help you?"

"What is your name?"

The clerk considered lying but didn't, "Anna."

Sigrid flashed a credential that the clerk barely noted. "The America's Files Room is where please?"

The woman gestured down a hall to her right. "Down there." She pointed while crossing her arms. "There are fifty storage lockers and bins. Do you know what you are looking for?"

"Yes. Thank you."

Anna snidely said, "Would you like the code to the door?"

Coolly, Sigrid replied, "Thank you."

Jotting the access code on a piece of paper, Anna pushed it at the ice queen. "We close in an hour and a half."

Walking crisply down the hall, Sigrid's Chloe Lauren Ballerina Flats barely whispered across the ugly 1980s tile. She paused at an open room filled with study desks, each with individual lamps. Out of habit, she noted the location of the room's exits and the number of scholars—five who barely registered her existence—Sigrid continued down the hall.

At the hermetic self-sealing, revolving door to the America's File Room, she again came to a stop. Determining she was alone, Sigrid moved down the hall, away from the America's Room. Finding the door labeled MAINTENANCE, she passed it by. Turning the corner, she hung back to check the corridor she just traversed.

Empty. She quickly moved to the maintenance-room door. There was a lock, but it appeared to be broken. Sigrid turned the knob and entered the space. Inside, she closed it before turning on the lights. Two massive storage shelves ran along the wall to her left. On the other side were five storage cabinets and a mopping sink half-covered by a curtain. Bypassing the first shelf, she stooped to feel along the bottom-side of the second. She had to check her emotions when her fingers detected the presence of a button. Just like the man in Italy had said. In anticipation, she pushed the button, jumping back as the shelf rumbled, slowly pushing off the wall. It swung out, revealing a massive, thick glass door.

On the left, a red panel read PUSH. She examined it, looking for signs that it would set off an alarm. Satisfied it would not, she pushed the release. The door was more like an airlock. It hissed and then opened, releasing a rush of cool air.

Inside, she found another panel on the right side of the door, labeled PUSH. But this one not only closed the glass door, it brought the storage-shelf camouflage rumbling shut. "This better reopen," she imagined. Taking a breath, she turned to assess her surroundings. The room reminded her of a college library; the research desks were missing. There was one table in the center, as if to serve the needs of a single patron.

But as she took in the entirety of the space, she paused in mild surprise. Her eyes were not playing tricks on her. Clearly, there were four surrounding walls, the ceiling and floor, but the entire room was sealed in glass. Nodding, Sigrid realized this was for temperature, humidity, and oxygen control. Paper and other fragile documents don't like heat and do like relative humidity and temperature.

Meticulously, she set about her task, combing the black cabinets, uncertain as to what she was looking for. Each was labeled in the upper-right corner with a decade and a year. The file lockers commenced in the 1920s and stopped abruptly in 1992. Sigrid paused in thought, recalling that Von Grupp had died in 1992. Made sense.

Starting in the 1920s, she moved through the early Cheka years to GPU and finally the OGPU era—nothing unusual, just the normal espionage, recruiting agents, turning moles, and blackmail. After an hour, her eyes were crossing.

"What had that simp attendant, said? Closing time was an hour and a half?" She glanced at her SFI Rolex Submariner. Late afternoon and she was jet-lagged. She'd made it through the 1930s, but she'd need to return tomorrow. The 1940s might prove more interesting.

Gathering her things, she started for the glass door. Moving by the file lockers, she passed cabinets for 1957 before stopping in her tracks. Same as the others. Darkly obsidian. Nothing notable about it—except for the small red dot on the right rear of the cabinet. She probed it with her finger, revealing it was just a dab of paint. She checked four other bins around the 1957 repository. No red dot.

Returning to the '57 file, she pulled the drawer open only to find more documents, files, briefs, prints, and charts. Disappointment gave way to amusement. The only thing different than the 1920s and 1930s files was that the names were more colorful. *Operation Parachute. Mountain. Rainbow Death. Paris Moon. Africa Fire. Africa Fire II. Talisman. Tokyo Scimitar.*

Previously thinking the red dot had somehow been a marker of sorts, she realized it was probably just a drop of paint that randomly landed on the cabinet. Closing the file bin, something light blue, buried in the middle of the drawer, caught her eye. Pulling the surrounding paper aside, she found an accordion file labeled POLAR STRIKE.

Extracting the folder, she placed it on the center table. Uncertain as to what she would find, she casually fanned through the slots. Her brow furrowed. Something was odd about this one. Sigrid returned to start at the beginning. Slowly she strived to make some sense of the notes. Coming to an official-looking page, her eyes widened. Glancing at the signature below, Ivan Serov, Sigrid's pulse ratcheted up in shocked revelation.

* * * *

At her desk, Anna prepared to turn things over to the incoming night shift. One of her duties was to clear the Archives after official hours had concluded for the day. Part of the process was to account for all the people on the log-in sheet. As they would leave, Anna would make a check next to their name.

Today, the only late person was the nasty woman. Impatiently, she reached under her desk and flipped off the main power switch to the Archival spaces. Lights going off—leaving only the Emergency Flood lights—often had the effect of getting the last visitors out of the study and file rooms.

* * * *

Sigrid could not believe what she was reading. Removing her cellphone, she began taking pictures of the file's contents. But the pace...

flip a page, snap a picture, flip, snap, flip, snap...was laborious. She'd need to spread the file on the tabletop, allowing her to move through the data more efficiently. Putting her cellphone in her pocket, she began to clear space on the table.

Suddenly, all the lights went out, while an ominous whirring sound seemed to come from just beyond the walls. The room's air unmistakably compressed against her skin, simultaneously being sucked from her lungs.

Rapidly, she discerned the area was hermetically sealed to allow for some control over the temperature, moisture, and oxygen. But why would the air be being removed from the space? Sigrid could only divine that KGB had been utilizing old methods of preserving records that called for the vault to be kept at as low an oxygen level as possible. While maintaining a constant humidity and temperature would have been the ideal, perhaps this was not attainable at the time the space was created. Crude but semi-effective. Removing the air each day was an attempt to keep the documents as well-preserved as possible.

But why now? She glanced at the luminescent face of her watch. Just past closing time. Did the air vacuum work off a timer related to the archive's hours? Whatever it was, it was clear she needed to get out of the space or she'd suffocate.

The hair on Sigrid's neck tingled. As a child, she'd been locked in a basement by accident while her mother and father left on a three-day holiday, thinking she was at an aunt's house. When they returned and found out that Sigrid had never arrived, her panic-stricken parents dashed home to find Sigrid on a shelf in the corner of the basement. Dehydrated and hungry, she'd spent most the time battling two rats who'd chased her up onto the shelf, denying her access to the sink and a fridge with some food. After this experience, she steeled herself against all forms of fear. But she still did not like dark, enclosed spaces.

Across the room, above the entrance, a small light had come on, guiding her to the exit. But at the door, when she depressed the PUSH plate, nothing happened. Sigrid pushed it again. Nothing. She fought a small tightening in her gut. Breathing slowly, she probed the red door plate. Repeatedly pressing it, there was no response. She banged on the door, half born of frustration, half fear. Stepping back, she rubbed her ear lobe, thinking, "What am I missing?"

* * * *

At her desk, Anna again examined her watch. "Where is that bitch? I'm going out tonight." Coming around the front of her desk, she started down the barely lit hallway, toward the archives. At the main files room, nothing but empty desks greeted her. She continued on to the America's Files Room.

Punching in a numerical code, she entered but found the space devoid of life. Closing it, she was perplexed and thought to check the ladies's room. Passing the door labeled MAINTENANCE, she came to a halt thinking she'd heard something. Curiously, she pushed the door open.

* * * *

The air was clearly running out. Sigrid knew the first signs of suffocation were increased pulse and growing shortness of breath. Removing her cellphone, she activated the flashlight. Putting the device on a shelf next to the door plate, she directed the phone to bathe the door area. Stepping back, she tried to focus on the entire door. Her head was getting lighter, her thinking slowing.

"Shit!"

Sigrid's breath strained, her throat contracting. Coughing replaced breathing as she fought to retain the last vestiges of oxygen. Blinking rapidly, she forced her eyes to rotate about the door frame. Just near the left side of the door, exactly opposite the PUSH plate on the right, was a slide hatch. Pushing the piece to the left revealed a bright red lever. With her last strength, Sigrid pulled the stick as she dropped to the ground in the final stages of consciousness.

Unable to react, Sigrid could only stare, as accompanied by a *whoosh* of air flooding the vacuum of the secret files room, the door popped open. Letting the air flood her lungs, she stayed on the ground until her senses seemed restored. Slowly, she came to her feet.

Examining the red lever that seemingly saved her life, she determined it must be an emergency release in case the main door plate did not work. She also detected a cessation of the whirring from outside the room. "It must be tied to a timer somewhere," she thought.

Her breathing normalizing, accompanied a burst of anger at herself for not spending more time checking things out when she first came into the room.

She'd be more careful tomorrow.

Returning to the central file table, she began to gather up the POLAR STRIKE documents to put them back into the storage bin when another thought occurred to her. She most likely was the first person in this space in decades. It was very unlikely anyone else would come in before she returned in the morning. Sigrid opted to leave the docs splayed across the table. Gathering her things, she made her way to the door where she paused to examine the red lever again.

Cautiously, she pushed the red PUSH plate, causing the door to seal again. This was accompanied by the whirring from the vacuum pump outside the room. But this time, Sigrid quickly pulled the red lever, reversing the process. Muttering in Swedish about the room's similarity to a python, she practically leapt through the doorway into the janitor's room.

She closed the glass entry-door, observing the shelf sweep back into place, concealing the secret chamber. Just to assure herself that she could get back in, Sigrid again activated the button underneath the shelf. After the door swung open, she pushed the red plate, closing the room up again.

Lastly, she placed a small piece of black paper against the shelf floor.

Satisfied, she cracked the door open, and slipped into the hallway, pulling the door behind her. The check-in desk was empty; Sigrid had been led to believe that due to the sensitive nature of the Archives, the desk would be staffed twenty-four seven. The vapid attendant was probably in the lavatory or looking for Sigrid. Without waiting, Sigrid summoned the elevator and departed.

A few minutes later, in the maintenance room, behind a half-closed curtain covering the mopping sink, a cellphone flashlight came on. Cautiously, the owner crept into the room.

Ensuring the door was closed, Anna turned to eye the far-left storage shelf.

CHAPTER 60

NOVEMBER
MOSCOW
HIDDEN ARCHIVES ROOM

Try as she might, Anna's jaw could only hang agape in utter astonishment. After the shelf had opened to reveal the glass entry-door, she'd almost dashed from the supplies room. But at the door, she steadied herself. Mustering some spine, she made her way to the glass portal and into the secret files room.

Like a child on a scavenger hunt, she wandered amidst the metallic rows of cabinets. "What in the world is this place?" She recalled the stories, old wives's tales, of hidden secrets many thought lost in the mist of time. In the center of the room, Anna came upon the Polar Strike accordion folder. Briefly, she perused a couple documents. Some of it made sense, but most of it seemed like sci-fi gibberish.

She soon realized she did not comprehend, or even really care, what she was looking at. Then another thought came to mind. Olegina would know what this stuff was. It might be worth something to her? She thought of taking a picture, but she knew building security checked the cellphones of every employee in Archives before being allowed to depart each day. That would clearly not work. Leaving the accordion folder, Anna took the file she'd been reading and sealed the room back up.

At her desk, she realized making copies was virtually impossible. All the copiers in Lubyanka were strictly monitored. At the end of each day, the number on the counter was recorded and compared to the count at the end of the next day. Any copies made, had to be accounted for, usually via a record book with name, department, and number of copies made.

Lifting her blouse, she put the file under her skirt, down her pantyhose. Leaving the building, she went to a nearby KopiMaks copy store. But there were five people ahead of her for the two copiers. To make matters worse, both of the older machines had to be routinely stopped and restarted. Glancing at her watch, Anna shook her head.

"*Der'mo.*"

* * * *

Halfway to the Four Seasons, Sigrid realized she'd left her phone behind.

"Shit."

Returning to Lubyanka, the guard she'd battered earlier, sullenly refused to meet her eye as she re-signed the visitor's log. Good, less interaction the better. She quickly made her way to Archives. Exiting the elevator, she was surprised to find the receptionist desk was still vacant, but not tidied up, as if the attendant had departed for the day. "Where is she? In the restroom, or texting, or ... who cares." Still, if low-level employees were anything, they were predictable. Being absent for an extended period of time, even in Russia, invited scrutiny which often was not desirable. Something was off. Scowling, Sigrid set off for the maintenance room. Guardedly, she moved quietly down the low-lit hallway, relieved to encounter no one.

Once inside the supplies room, as she neared the shelf, alarm bells went off. The black piece of paper now sat in the center of the room. Inside the secret-file compartment, she found the blue Polar Strike folder just as she'd left it. Putting it down, she looked about for traces that someone was still there. Realizing anyone still in the secret files room would have suffocated by now, she still withdrew her Sig Sauer P320, threading a silencer to the barrel. Carefully, she moved through the space. After completing a sweep, she broke the weapon back down, placing it in the hollow of her back.

Her original plan had been to leave the Polar Strike folder on the center table in the secret records room, with a thought to examining it more thoroughly the next day. Return with a bigger bag, and if need be, take the file and anything else she determined was worthy, with her then. But, since the encounter with the guard in the elevator, trying to smuggle anything out today through the lobby with him on duty, might invite unwanted attention, giving the guard a reason to screw with her.

But it was clear the space had been compromised since her first departure. Gathering the Polar Strike folder, she moved down the row, to a cabinet bearing the label 1970. Opening it, she wedged it into the back, behind other folders.

* * * *

Anna again checked her watch as the KopiMaks machines continued in cranky mode. Exasperated, she huffily spun on her heel, returning to Lubyanka without making any copies. Back at her desk, Anna was about to start for the secret files room when she got a text from a friend about meeting for drinks. Putting the Polar Strike file down, she opened a drawer to remove her purse and a sweater that she put on top of the file.

* * * *

In the maintenance supplies room, Sigrid closed the shelf, again putting the black paper scrap in place. As she departed, she came to the reception desk where the attendant was back. Unsurprisingly, she was checking her phone, her desk still a mess. Anna jumped at the sight of Sigrid.

"You startled me—I thought you'd already left," she rasped.

Sigrid eyed the receptionist suspiciously. "I forgot my cellphone."

Trying to contain the thump of her pounding heart, Anna never broke eye lock with the terrifying woman. She held her own phone up. "Well, we wouldn't want that, now would we?" She said with what she hoped was just the right amount of insouciance.

"Are you the only person here?" Sigrid asked.

Snidely, Anna replied, "I'm not sure. It *is* past closing time you know."

The assassin studied her for a moment more before spinning on her heels and departing. "I'll be back in the morning."

Once the elevator door had closed, Anna collapsed in her chair thinking, "That's about as close to a snake as I ever want to be." Finally calming down, she got up and made a sweep about the Archives, ensuring that everyone had departed for the day. Satisfied, she took the Polar Strike file from her desk and walked briskly to the maintenance room. "There'll be time later in the week to get this copied," she thought. But as she reopened the secret files room, her adrenaline exploded when she found the blue Polar Strike folder had disappeared.

Looking at the file in her hand, Anna tried to think. "Whatever that bitch is doing here has to have something to do with this." Closing things up, she returned to her desk. Taking the folder, she hid it in the liner on the underside of her chair thinking, "I'll find a time to pass this to Olegina when it is safe."

As a last thought, she jotted something on a Post-It Note and put it inside the file.

CHAPTER 61

NOVEMBER
MOSCOW

"Polar Strike?" Vadik repeated.

On the monitor, Sigrid could see Vadik seated near the grand piano; she assumed he must be looking at Central Park again. "Yes, General."

"Can't say that I remember that one. Anything unusual about it?"

"Not immediately evident. But ... " she paused to look at notes, "it's an abandoned KGB program, designed in the 1950s, to undermine and control America's leadership structure in the event of an outbreak of war between USSR and America."

"How?

"As best as can be determined General, moles would be raised in America, with the intent of placing them into the American government after completing university. When activated in the event of a nuclear war, their orders would be to kill their immediate supervisor. The thought was that if enough of the leadership could be eliminated or wounded, it could significantly disrupt, or even knock out, America's nuclear response capability.

"How would ... how is this possible?"

"Mind control. Brainwashing from birth."

Sigrid could see confused amazement spread across Vadik's face. "*Vozdukh*," he half whispered.

Speaking seven languages fluently, including Russian, Sigrid understood what he'd said, but still struggled with the literal translation of the word—*vozdukh* could mean taking the spirit in and letting the spirit out. Gibberish to her mind, but brainwashing could, if effective, alter one's being.

"And it was abandoned, correct?"

"Yes, General. The USSR was never able to perfect the actual implementation of the installed programming."

"So do we know if this was Grupp's—the program he was working on when he died?"

"No, General."

"Then why the interest in this file?"

"I removed the file from Archives, made copies, and have been reviewing them in my suite. There is enough here to suggest that this was an op that Grupp had kept open."

"Why?"

"His ongoing diary entries suggest he was still running it ... but I can't be sure."

After a moment, Vadik quietly said, "Sigrid?"

"The folder is incomplete General," Sigrid said as she rubbed her left earlobe.

* * * *

Over the years, Vadik had come to recognize tells in people. Everyone had them—something indicating an internal change in their composure—elevated heart rate, eyes dilating, pursed lips, or touching a part of the body.

When he'd first met Sigrid, she was working for the SAPO: Swedish Security Service. It was Sweden's CIA or KGB. Sigrid had been assigned to Moscow and was running an asset at the Russian Ministry of Industry and Trade. It was early in her career, but already she displayed an aptitude for drawing people into her spider's web of deceit. Human frailty wed to blackmail.

The ministry official she was working had been on FSB's radar for a couple of months. What had perplexed the Russians was how this ice maiden instilled in her source both deadly fear and yet a primal sexual attraction. She was the essence of a black widow.

Finally, FSB rolled her up along with the ministry stooge, hauling them into Lubyanka for interrogation. As Vadik and his team questioned the pair, the crying Russian was regretful, but Sigrid

Magnussen seemed detached, almost aloof. Things turned physical. With Vadik watching from the other side of a two-way mirror, his chief goon stood at one point and grabbed Sigrid by the hair, shaking her before letting go. Then, she rubbed her left earlobe. What came next shocked Vadik.

Sigrid didn't jump up; she *glided* to her feet. With blinding speed, she shocked the interrogator, jabbing a finger into his throat, while simultaneously kicking his legs from under him, before finally smashing his head on the table to knock him unconscious. Even though securely removed on the other side of the mirror, Vadik'd still involuntarily reached for the sidearm in his shoulder holster.

The Trade Ministry official was sent to a Siberian labor camp, his wife and daughter evicted from their state-subsidized apartment. They moved in with a neighbor, a low-level police officer, for whom the woman eventually divorced her husband—then she discovered her daughter was also sleeping with the policeman. Out on the street, the woman eventually became an escort.

The Swedish agent got off relatively unscathed. FSB released Sigrid to the Deputy Chief of the Swedish Mission who'd escorted her to Sheremetyevo Airport, where she was declared persona non grata and deported back to Stockholm. Returning to SAPO HQ, she'd wallowed in a desk job for a year. At the same time, Sweden was waking up to the growing threat from the pool of recent Middle Eastern immigrants. Sigrid's next assignment was Madrid where she utilized her language skills, appearance, and social camouflage to recruit assets from fringe terrorist groups in North Africa.

But Vadik had never forgotten that day in interrogation. He monitored her career from a distance. After he left FSB, he tracked her to the Spanish port town of Malaga where Sigrid had befriended a French woman married to a Tunisian cleric running a cell of the Desert New Day group. DND had its tentacles into a number of immigrant groups in Northern Europe and had already committed some low-level terrorist acts around Stockholm, Malmo, and Orebro.

SAPO was interested in dismantling DND and had given Sigrid wide latitude in discharging this assignment. The French woman was also bisexual, which Sigrid exploited to get close to her, the cleric, and his cell; she convinced them she could open some doors in Sweden.

One day, Vadik followed her and the woman to a cruddy port hotel. In the room, Sigrid had surreptitiously taken a number of selfies with the woman en flagrante, careful to omit her own face. Prior to the assignation, Sigrid had tipped the cleric to look for his wife at the hotel. He'd burst in to find her in bed with Sigrid. Momentarily shocked, he started punching his wife, never seeing the silencer-equipped pistol that Sigrid removed from under the pillow.

Calmly, she put it to his head and pulled the trigger. Before he'd even hit the ground, she fired twice into the woman's head and then put the gun in the dead cleric's hand and fired once more into his dead wife's body. Unthreading the silencer, she'd placed the pistol back into the man's hand. From a drawer, she removed a small portable cellphone attachment that she used to print copies of the selfies, which she placed near the dead man's body.

Set to remove her prints and presence from the room, the door had unexpectedly opened. Before she could react—Vadik, accompanied by two gun-wielding thugs, entered.

"Tsk tsk," he said, looking about. "I see you've found new pursuits since last we met Ms. Magnussen."

It took a moment for her to remember. "General Pyotr," she'd tersely replied.

Vadik looked about the hotel suite, "Busy day?"

She tipped her head. "A bit. Still have a ... cell to clean out."

"Need help?"

She squinted, shaking her head. "Only seven. I should be okay."

"Very well. When you've finished, may I invite you to join me for a drink? I have an offer you might find interesting. The Miramar Rooftop Bar ... at, shall we say, six?"

Sigrid nodded, "General."

Over drinks, Scotch for her, martini for him, Vadik had offered her a million dollars a year to leave SAPO and work exclusively for him. Expecting as much, she'd come prepared. She wanted a five-million dollar signing bonus. Full health care, new apartment in Manhattan overlooking Central Park, a condo in Stockholm, and a defined benefit plan that would pay her half a million a year in retirement. Vadik had accepted without blinking.

Twelve years later, Vadik had not regretted a penny spent on her. Curiously, when he'd asked her why she'd consider leaving SAPO, she'd replied, "I've discovered certain things about myself that my current employer might object to."

"Such as?"

"I don't feel any sense of loyalty to them."

"Why?"

She'd answered straightforwardly, but before doing so, she pulled on her left earlobe. "Most of them are *tölps* ... dolts. Same prep schools. Same families. Same deceptions. They control the sheep. The way I see it, borders don't matter anymore; I will control me."

The earlobe gesture was her way of communicating an internal discomfort with what she was saying or about to say.

She was the best fixer he had.

* * * *

Vadik found that with most subordinates, he would occasionally need to get their attention when they made a mistake. Not with Sigrid, who was harder on herself than he could ever be. And, truthfully, he was a tiny bit unsure of her.

"Where is the original Polar Strike file?"

"Safely in the 1957 cabinet, in the secret files room."

"And you suspect something is missing because the black paper signal you left on the bookshelf was out of place on your return?"

"Yes, General."

"No chance it fell off the shelf?"

"No, General. It was set such that only the opening of the bookshelf would have dislodged it. But I believe someone may have ... learned of the room, possibly while I was in it, then entered after me and removed something."

"If something was taken, can it be recovered?"

"We are seeking to penetrate the working circle of Archives personnel. We should know more soon."

Sigrid could see on her monitor that Vadik looked pensive, obviously distracted. She waited.

"What *do* we know?"

Sigrid re-summarized Grupp's notes, the technical jargon about brainwashing, as well as the clinical test results.

"But it was abandoned, right?" Vadik said.

"Yes, General. The USSR was never able to perfect the actual implementation of installed programming."

More to himself than anything, Vadik mused, "Is it possible there was a tiny success? Something that KGB missed? Why would this mystery man, this ... *Ivan Petrov*, correct? Why would he risk breaking into my office in Lubyanka for an extinct program? Something important is missing from that folder. We have to have it."

"Our efforts will pay off soon. I have Yuri and his crew working on that now, General."

"Yes, I'm sure." Again, Vadik drifted off and Sigrid realized he was *away*.

Finally, after a few minutes, Vadik said, "What if we could control America's leadership? How many business leaders or heads of state would seek influence over America? We could sell access to the Oval Office the world over." Vadik looked at some notes he'd been jotting. "Please continue your efforts to find it," he added, "but carefully. We don't want my old fellows at FSB *or* SVR to know what is under their noses."

"General."

The monitor went black.

CHAPTER 62

NOVEMBER
NEW YORK

The Secret Service would have preferred underground parking, but denied this, prepared for a rapid insertion across a crowded plaza. As one agent opened the back door to a jet-black Cadillac SUV, Seth, the Secret Service agent in charge of Chris Ford's detail, quietly mouthed into his cuff microphone. "Crystal Star is moving."

A little ambivalent about his new code name, Chris was nonetheless enjoying his new celebrity. He stepped from the limo as a Roman emperor might have descended from a chariot. Quickly surrounded, his phalanx rapidly crossed the sidewalk into the Clinic for Right Being as bystanders, restrained by more agents, tittered, nervously snapping out-of-focus cellphone pics. In the lobby was more of the same as the staff, Doctor Stephan Grigor front and center, gathered to greet the Vice-President Elect.

"Mr. Vice-President Elect, ees' always a pleasure to see you."

"Stephan, thank you for seeing me on such short notice."

"I am at your disposal—whenever necessary."

Once behind the doors separating the lobby from the interior offices, Chris sagged, putting a hand to his head. Doctor Grigor steadied his patient and friend.

"Stephan, the headaches have been awful the last two weeks."

"Stress, most likely."

The physician led Chris into the Light Lab. Besides the expected long, black metal tube with the crystalline wand extension, there were some new furnishings: a new divan, two leather chairs, and an ottoman. Next to the chair was an antique coffee-table lamp with a

Lalique frosted-glass image of a diaphanous, barely covered woman reaching for a half-seen orb. From unseen speakers, classical music softly bathed the room.

Grigor guided Chris to the chair with the ottoman. Sitting, the two men faced each other. On a remote, Grigor hit a button. Instantly, the sound of gently falling rain replaced the music.

"New?" Chris asked.

"Yes. Kind of you to notice. So Chris—sorry, Mister Vice President—"

"Stephan, please call me Chris. Nothing's changed."

"Of course. Thank you."

"So, please to sit back," the doctor reached into a drawer in the coffee table, extracting a set of jet-black goggles affixed to a head strap. From the back of the headset, a semi-circular cable extended forward, from which dangled a small, mirrored disco-ball with a tiny opening on its top surface. Chris dutifully donned the mask and laid back into the comfortable chair. Doctor Grigor dimmed the lights while flipping a switch on a console beside his chair. From the ceiling, a stream of blue light pulsed. Adjusting buttons on the console, he guided the beam into the slit atop the goggle disco-ball. The light was redirected into receptors on either side of the black-glassed mask.

"Now Chris, tell me these last few weeks."

As the light disappeared into the goggles, unseen receptors directed it into a central processor in the middle of the front plane where, at last, it was micro-adjusted for Chris and beamed into his eyes. Soft translucent light found its way into the hypothalamus at the base of Chris's neck. This, in turn, dialed down the signals to the pituitary gland and adrenals.

Quickly, the anxiety and throbbing lifted. Like a vault door swinging open, Chris unburdened himself of the rigors of moving to Washington, finding a place to live, the constant briefings, working with Mallory to select china, carpet, and linen patterns for the Vice President's residence, attending more fundraising events, meeting with the House and Senate leadership.

Seated nearby, Grigor jotted notes into his journal. Chris prattled on for a couple of minutes, when Grigor gently took the note pad in his lap and placed it on the side table. He leaned over and whispered into Chris's ear, "Come to me." Grigor snapped his fingers and sat back.

With a gasp, Chris sat upright, his breathing heavy. Before he could remove the mask, Grigor put a hand on his shoulder, calming him.

"Stephan, the dream changed again!"

"Tell me."

"It's the one with those words: *The long and brutal winter gives way to spring.* But now after the words, instead of immediately killing the ... "

"What do you see Christopher?"

Chris relaxed; a smile creased his face. "Actually, nothing. I'm just to feign a heart attack and fall to the ground."

"Very good, and the injector pen?"

"Will be in my jacket pocket. I'll be ready."

"Excellent. Excellent, you're doing very well, Chris." Grigor snapped his fingers again. "Return."

Chris sagged into the sofa. A moment later his eyes fluttered open, breathing returning to normal.

"Go on, Chris."

Lying immobile, he searched his memory. "Sorry Stephan, what were we talking about?"

"You were telling me about being Vice President."

Chris nodded. It was an old refrain he'd heard before but now was getting to experience firsthand. Recent Presidents had sought to include their Vice's in the day-to-day operations of government, but the role of Vice President largely remained that of a glorified lady-in-waiting. How to change that.

Nodding, at times, Grigor resumed jotting notes, and listening to the rain.

CHAPTER 63

DECEMBER
MOSCOW
ONE MONTH TO INAUGURATION

The previous evening's cooling touch had departed with the setting sun. This morning, the Siberian Express had pulled into town. Olegina leaned hard into a bitter cold, hammering wind as she fought her way to the Metro. Images of her last vacation on Spain's Costa del Sol flitted through her mind, but just as quickly faded once she'd reached the safety of Universitet Metro Station. Unlike many Russians, Olegina liked travel, considering herself worldly. She was proud of the passport stamps she'd acquired in ten different countries. Even Egypt. But never America.

Last night had been another disappointment. Anna had goaded her into hitting the clubs, whisking her to the Opal Palace—Moscow's newest techno mafia-club. Before leaving her apartment, Anna had given Olegina a mini-makeover. But when she stepped out to answer her phone, Olegina had stolen a look in the mirror. She was stunned at the metamorphosis.

Later, at the club, Anna wore new Louboutin heels; she wouldn't say where they came from—strutting like it was Fashion Week in Milan. Heads turned and Olegina found herself enjoying the reflected attention. "Maybe I'll get a pair," she imagined. This thought crashed to earth, felled by two conjoined sobering and depressing thoughts: she couldn't afford them, and they wouldn't make a difference anyway.

The Palace had been off-the-hook crazy. Strobe lights, that instantly punished her eyes and brain, striped the tables and floor as if searching for escaped felons. Ranging along the walls like skyboxes were booths set up for bottle service. Oligarchs and moneymen held court while anxious women orbited them, seeking a ticket out of the drabness of their lives. On the dance floor, cologne-drenched men in blazers, designer shirts without ties, and sharkskin slacks gyrated with women in skin-tight dresses, skyscraper-high stilettos, and neon-bright lipstick; they whirled like dervishes into their own ecstasy. To Olegina's eyes, the whole scene was a pulsing noir of nihilism.

Mildly surprised as Anna started up to the boxes, Olegina hesitated before dutifully following. Watching Anna's new heels ascend each step, Olegina suddenly realized where and whom they were from; it became clear a moment later when a slick-haired tough stood up to give her a kiss. Anna smiled, then stepped back to introduce Olegina. A cool dread passed through Olegina as she looked into eyes that betrayed vulgarity wedded to death. Olegina thought: "Dance with me, and you'll die," as she unconsciously snatched her hand out of his.

"Yuri, this is Olegina," Anna yelled into the gangster's ear.

Nodding, he gestured to a sofa, while escorting Anna to a divan next to his. Olegina was seated beside a bullish man bedecked in a garish suit resembling a Bedouin's tent and drowning in Polo, clearly attempting to cover up nervous sweat and other inadequacies. Reaching toward the table, the coat opened, revealing a large holstered pistol. Filling a glass with ice and then Johnny Walker—Blue Label, he handed it to Olegina. "Drink. It's American Scotch."

"Isn't it from Scotland?" Olegina replied.

The goon just grunted. She took a sip, but unaccustomed to the pungency of the amber liquid, she sputtered, eyes watering. "Thank you," she said to the man she now surmised worked for Yuri. Another grunt as he lit a cigarette. On Olegina's other side was an emaciated woman on a cocaine diet. Her tight-fitting black dress could barely contain oversized breast-implants that projected her desperation. Next to her were two more similarly attired women deep in heavy kissing.

The music faded away, leaving headaches and time to adjust. Girls mostly looked to secure their partners for the evening while men strutted like peacocks. Olegina was already bored when Yuri asked her, "So Gina, where do you work?"

"It's *Ole*gina," she said, never liking the shortened version of her name. Yuri squinted but said nothing; the menace in the way he stroked Anna's hair made it clear he'd call her whatever he wanted. Glancing down, Olegina noticed Yuri's expensive Hugo Boss shoes. She awkwardly added, "Rosarkhiv." But, by now, Yuri was kissing and pawing Anna. Suddenly they were up, but while Olegina thought they were going to dance, instead the couple disappeared through a curtain behind the box.

Seeing her perplexity, the thin woman leaned in toward Olegina. "Going to his office."

"Office?"

Mildly amused by Olegina's naiveté, the skeleton condescendingly replied, "It's not that kind of office, but there's business being transacted."

Olegina slowly nodded. She took another sip of her drink, eyes wandering to the curtain.

* * * *

Having left the Opal Palace before Anna returned, Olegina was curious to see how the rest of the evening had unfolded. Entering Lubyanka, she removed her gloves to sign in and made her way to the elevator. As the car ponderously descended, the creaking dulled her thoughts when suddenly she heard what sounded like a scream—not imagined, but a real one, then came another. "What in the world?" she thought. "There must be a logical explanation," but unconsciously, Olegina drew to the control-panel side of the elevator, out of sight, just as the door opened.

An unseen male voice—from where, she could not tell—barked, "Check the America's files!"

"I already looked. It's not there!" came a nervous response.

"Are you sure?" said the first man, the voice now a little familiar.

"It's not there, and the clerk is dead—ask your bitch where it is!"

A cold terror gripped Olegina. Lifting the hand with her gloves to her mouth muffled her gasps. Something caught the edge of her vision. Bloody fingers appeared at the base of the check-in desk. Just then, the elevator bell signaled the door had been held open beyond the allotted time. Terrified beyond a rational ability to comprehend, Olegina leapt away from the clanging bell to the reception counter. Eyes bulging, she looked over to find Anna lying in a swimming pool of blood. Olegina rapidly came around, kneeling over the mortally wounded woman. In the distance, she heard one of the voices.

"What was that?" said the first man.

"The main elevator. We came in through the service elevator in the back, but security people will be coming down from the lobby. We have to go!"

"Damn it. We can't leave without it!"

"Come!"

Olegina started to cry as she looked for cover. She jumped when Anna put a hand on her arm. "Under there," Anna gasped, pointing beneath her desk. "It's ... " red phlegm spewed from her lips. Burrowing as far under the desk as possible, Olegina turned toward her dying friend. Meeting her eyes, Anna nodded at a bloody file near her hand. Not understanding, Olegina violently shook her head. But with her last strength Anna shoved it to Olegina. The men arrived as Anna coughed one more time, her eyes going dull.

"Dead already. Damn it!" said the voice that sounded familiar.

Shoes appeared adjacent to Anna's body. Hugo Boss. Olegina bit her lip in a desperate attempt to keep quiet. The thug tossed papers off Anna's desk and rifled drawers before finally kicking the dead woman's head.

"*Stupid zoloto kopatel*!"

"Yuri! Now!" hissed the other man.

"Da!"

A last pawing on the desk resembled the sound of a slithering snake. Olegina hugged herself, eyes closed, cold dread locking her jaw tight. She silently pleaded, "Go now."

"Yuri!"

Scraping and tossing of paper ceased. "Okay!"

Silence. Closing her eyes to avoid looking into Anna's, Olegina cried noiselessly. It seemed an eternity before she realized they'd departed. She stayed motionless for the longest time before summoning the will to come out. Legs cramped from being on her knees, she wobbled and leaned on the desk for support. As her hand landed in a pool of sticky, drying blood, she recoiled in revulsion. Retreating to a corner, she could no longer deny her senses and she screamed into her gloves from the depth of her being.

Finally, her heart slowed enough to process beyond survival. "Call someone." Standing, she approached Anna's station, but the destruction was enough to divert her to another desk. Despite an established history of routinely visiting the archives, Olegina was nonetheless fearful about her presence among such carnage.

Lifting the phone receiver, she hesitated, then slowly replaced it. "America's files?" Glacially, the words of Yuri and his goon dropped into her mind like parachutes.

Turning slowly, she cautiously inched past Anna's desk, down the hall. She came to a locked door reading SPETSIAL'NAYA KOMNATA AMERIKA: SPECIAL AMERICA'S FILES ROOM. She'd heard of this place. It was the repository for documentation about covert actions—uncovered by FSB—that America had committed against Russia. Supposedly, it was a treasure chest of espionage, spy networks, lists of agent runners and double agents that FSB maintained to combat ongoing US actions.

Olegina remembered that SVR—the Foreign Intelligence Service—had moved its files detailing Russian covert activities abroad to its new headquarters in Yasenevo District. The old KGB files Olegina was occasionally sent to Lubyanka to retrieve for Rosarkhiv should have gone with SVR to Yasenevo.

The keypad-accessible door was cracked open. Gently pushing it, she warily entered. While she'd thought it possible there could be more casualties, she was still shocked to find three more bodies: two women and a man. Quickly determining they were dead, she put a hand to her mouth, eyes brimming with tears.

She needed to get out; she needed to alert someone, but as she let her eyes wander the room, curiosity slowly pushed aside fear. Never had she expected to be allowed into to this directory—need-to-know access only. The cooler atmosphere was the first indicator things in the space were treated with higher attention

More humid air. Then there were the bins. Museum-quality Viking storage cabinets. Oddly, they were all locked. What in the world had the thugs been looking for? What could have cost four people their lives?

Sudden pulsing from her bag jolted already-frayed nerves. Frightened, then annoyed, she opened her purse to find her vibrating cellphone. She sent it to voicemail and made a rapid sweep of the room. Nothing. Disappointed, she came back to reality. Need to go *now*.

Outside the room, she retrieved her cellphone from her purse to find a text ad for a nearby restaurant. "Bah!" Angrily shoving the phone into her pocket, a new thought popped into her head. Whatever had happened here, was probably related to the file Anna had tried to give her.

She moved quickly back to reception, but when the blood pool came into sight, her gut tightened in fear. Back at Anna's desk, her revulsion and shock returned. Fighting back tears, she carefully avoided the drying pools of blood. Behind Anna's desk, she scanned the cubby below, where she'd been hiding. There it was. Using a pen from Anna's desk, Olegina gingerly pulled the file toward her.

Opening it, she scanned the pages. But before she could dive into the file's contents, she returned to the Post-It note stuck to the inside cover. As she read it, her brow furrowed before a look of astonishment broke across her face.

"*Der'mo,*" she whispered.

Taking the note, she went back down the hall, but passed the America's Files Room and found a door marked MAINTENANCE. Pushing it open, she turned on the light switch.

It was a supplies room. Following the instructions on the note, she came to the shelf closest the wall. Shaking her head in doubt, she knelt and began fumbling her fingers along the underside of the bottom shelf.

"I can't believe I'm doing—this is stupid."

But a second later, she was shocked to hit a bump. "What the—"

She lowered her face into a position to see a small black protrusion from the metal rack casing. Hesitantly, she moved into a kneeling position and then pushed the button.

Disbelief gave way to astonishment when suddenly the supplies ledge began sliding from the wall toward Olegina. Barely jumping clear, the shelf moved back to reveal a glass door

Her blood ran cold. "*Trakhat' menya*," she breathed in amazement.

On the wall was a red plate. PUSH.

Pressing it, Olegina was less shocked when the glass door hissed open. Her eyes moved about the door, especially the edges, ringed with a sort of rubber gasket that probably worked to keep unwanted humidity and other corrosive substances from entering the room. She'd read of this before, supposedly at the Vatican Archives. A hermetically sealed space dedicated to maintaining proper humidity and temperature. But nothing prepared her for what came next.

Cautiously, she stepped through the entryway; it was if she'd been transported to a movie set frozen in time. There were rows and rows of storage bins, cabinets, and lockers ... relics from the past waiting to be summoned.

Unlike the Americas' Room, none were locked. Like she was a girl again, outside the Central Children's Toy Store on Christmas Eve, she wandered agog past lockers labeled by decades and years. Another phone vibration reminded her time was evaporating. "I need to come back later. What were they looking for?"

Still, she lingered. Her hand reached out to touch one of the cabinets. Everything in the room was in pristine order, nothing out of the ordinary. But on the only researcher's table in the room's center was a half-opened, light-blue accordion folder. Olegina squinted. Did this mean something? Had Yuri and the other psychopath known about this room and probably this file? Had they been through the folder looking for something?

Olegina glanced at the Post-It note and then her mind drifted to the file on Anna's desk and finally back to the blue folder. Quickly, she packaged up the dossier and moved to the door.

Uncertain how the apparatus worked in reverse, Olegina stepped into the supplies room and then pushed the red plate lever. As the glass door slammed into place, Olegina once again was forced to dodge the storage shelf of supplies now reversing, concealing the glass door.

"Whoever created this room, surely did not want it found." She thought.

Back at Anna's desk she evaluated her options. Wanting to begin perusing both the blue folder and the file Anna had given her, Olegina realized she was out of time. She opened the blue folder, roughly shoving Anna's file into it, before placing both into her rolling bag. At an adjacent desk, she picked up the phone receiver. Taking a deep breath, and then dialed the lobby.

"Security," answered a bored voice.

"Oh my God! There's blood everywhere! You have to come now!"

"What? Who is this?" asked the now duly alarmed guard.

"Are you an idiot? The Archives! Come now!"

With a work history of entering and departing Lubyanka to pick up files, it had been easy to justify her presence in Archives. When asked about the long gap between her entry and finally summoning help, Olegina had detailed her initial shock and fear the killers were still nearby. She said she chose to hide in a closet until she felt safe. After determining they'd left, she commenced checking for other people, finding them all dead.

Combing the Archives, the only anomaly had been the open door to the Special America's Files room. Whatever the killers had been looking for, they had it and were gone. Olegina knew they would secure the entire space and pore through every file locker in a vain attempt to understand what they'd been in search of.

They put her in a special room and interrogated her. Checking her rolling bag, they found the blue folder, thankfully overlooking the one red-stained file Anna had given her. Olegina had fabricated a story about being sent to retrieve the file which explained her presence at Lubyanka in the first place. The lead investigator poked the blue folder, before squinting suspiciously at Olegina. Finally, he shrugged, grunted, and left the room. After a couple of hours, FSB officials, uncertain as to how Olegina fit into the grisly murder scene, let her leave. It had taken every shred of calm to depart the building, walk to the Metro, and ride home—without looking into her rolling bag.

In her apartment, Olegina slammed the door and wobbled into the kitchen. From a cabinet, she grabbed a rarely opened bottle of vodka and took a big slug. Pouring a glass, she took it to her dining-room table, placing it next to the folder. Tentatively, she opened it, noticing for the first time the name on the side.

"Polar Strike?"

CHAPTER 64

DECEMBER
NEW YORK
ONE MONTH TO INAUGURATION

Vadik put his coffee cup down on the piano. "You've made quite a mess."

On the monitor, Sigrid coldly answered. "Could not be helped, General—Yuri and his men are very good at extracting ... things we want to know, but given the limited space and time constraints, they were unable to get the receptionist or clerks to divulge anything useful."

"Did this Anna, who you most suspected, ever indicate she had the file or missing information from the blue folder?"

"Unknown, General."

"Did she know about Grupp's secret room?"

"Also undetermined." Sigrid unconsciously pulled her earlobe, pained to speak the next words out of her mouth. "I'm sorry, General, but this woman was either truly ignorant, or had a high pain threshold, but we could get nothing from her or her colleagues."

Vadik turned from the monitor, concealing his irritation. The killings at Lubyanka would point to an insider, someone who'd worked there or had extensive knowledge of the Archives. Either way, it could bring unwanted attention to him.

Calmly, Vadik inquired, "Very well. What about our mystery man?"

Without betraying her relief, Sigrid replied, "Our contacts at INS finally got something on Ivan Petrov. They ran to ground a picture from the overhead camera at Immigration from the last time he passed through Kennedy. From there, they were able to track his progress to a car-ride service from the airport to Brighton Beach. We got a copy of the credit card he used and found the driver who gave us the address where he dropped Petrov."

* * * *

It had been so long that he missed the telltale signs. Just after one in the morning, Slaga had dropped his girlfriend off and was heading home. While he still employed his bodyguards, it was with nowhere near the frequency before, and on nights when he went dancing, the men had the night off.

In his Toyota Avalon, Slaga pulled from the curb. He replayed in his mind the evening at the Patagonia Club. It had been a night of triumph; he'd finally been able to execute the Colgada—one of tango's more challenging moves—without a break in stride. He and Olivia were now among the more-accomplished members at Patagonia. They were even talking about a trip to Olivia's home in Buenos Aires.

Leaving SoHo, Slaga normally would have taken Broadway south to the Carey Tunnel to Brooklyn, but tonight, he wanted to see city lights. He moved down Delancey Street onto the Williamsburg Bridge across the East River, savoring the bright Brooklyn night.

He continued onto I-278 to the Prospect Expressway, which, near Kensington, became Ocean Parkway. He originally intended to drive straight home but thought to stop and get some *ptichye moloko* cake at the Violin Cafe. Just after crossing Kings Highway, something in the trailing traffic pattern blipped on Slaga's radar. As one car turned off Ocean onto Kings, another car, a beat-up Chevrolet, turned too quickly it seemed, onto Ocean from Kings. By itself, this would be nothing, but something about the vehicle that turned onto Ocean seemed familiar. His mind raced. "Did I see that beat-up Chevy, back in Manhattan?"

Slaga's senses shifted into a higher gear. He turned at a Starbucks. The Chevy continued past the parking lot. Slaga feigned stepping from his car, but then restarted the engine. Backing out, he turned right, back onto Ocean and then immediately right onto the next street. He took the next right and once more back onto Kings, before quickly parking and turning off the engine and lights.

Two minutes later, the Chevy slowly motored down Kings Avenue. Distracted, the driver appeared to be looking for something and failed to see Slaga's darkened vehicle tucked quietly against the curb behind a pickup truck. The Chevy came to a stop in the middle of the deserted street as a minivan approached from the opposite direction. Both vehicles stopped, the drivers gesturing excitedly. Finally, the van circled behind the Chevy and both turned onto Ocean Parkway, heading toward Brighton.

Slaga took up his cellphone and dialed.

"Everything okay, boss?" said Nikita.

"Not sure, Niki. Call some of the boys and meet me at the Galaxy."

"*Da.*"

Slaga waited a few minutes before continuing toward Brighton. Before reaching the Galaxy, Slaga pulled off into a darkened alley, killed the engine, and got out. Hugging the shadows, he stealthily inched his way toward his building. Finding a good observation spot, he watched as his men arrived and entered the building. After a few moments, the lights on the top floor came on.

His cellphone rang.

Slaga answered. "*Da*?"

"Boss, you coming?" asked Nikita.

Years of interrogation had honed a sixth sense in Slaga: an ability to recognize changes in vocal patterns. The rising tension in Nikita's voice was unmistakable. Whoever had been tailing him was already in his home. Checking his hunch, Slaga said, "Tell them I will be there in a moment."

Slaga could hear Nikita's mouth move slightly away from the phone. "He'll be .... Wait, what boss?" Suddenly there was screaming and agitation.

The telltale sound of silencer-suppressed gunshots was followed by cries and then quiet. The voice on the phone was the essence of death itself. He'd been right about distancing himself from Polar Strike—just not far enough.

"Bruno? Bruno Shakli? Or is it Mikhail Kuznetsov? Perhaps it's Ivan Petrov—*Da*?" A frost-laden voice asked.

"What do you want?" Slaga always found that when on the defensive and short of information, the best choice was to stall until the enemy tipped their hand.

"We should talk."

"Is Nikita able to speak?"

"I'm afraid he—and the rest of your men—won't be taking any phone calls for a while."

Slaga hung up, opened the phone, removed the SIM card, dropped it to the ground, crushing it beneath his shoe. Rapidly, he retreated to his car. Inside, he opened the glove box to remove another, never-used burner phone that he activated. Dialing a number, he followed a series of prompts. After a minute, he terminated the call and destroyed this phone.

Exiting the vehicle, he softly opened his trunk, removing a Beretta 92 from the tire well. Quietly, but rapidly, he closed the distance to the back of the Galaxy. Taking inventory of his surroundings, he opened the service entrance with a spare key the super had given him. Softly closing the door, he waited for his eyes to adjust.

He made his way to the service elevator, taking it to the twentieth floor. As the door opened, he braced himself for a firefight but only the quiet of plush carpet and aquamarine-colored walls greeted him. His penthouse unit was one floor above. Years before—Slaga had determined a panic room in his unit could still be breached. Instead, he'd bought the unit right beneath his, constructing a secret staircase to the unit.

Senses on high alert, Slaga crept down the hall to his condo retreat. Inside, he closed the door, hovering near it, listening intently for activity in the townhouse as well as from the hallway outside. Finally, he gave himself permission to sag just a bit.

Quickly, he moved to the den where he turned on his desktop. A security app displayed images from various vantage points in his unit above. A combat-hardened vet, Slaga was shocked at the amount of blood. Whoever this was, they'd been savagely efficient.

Nikita and all his men were dead, shot and throats cut, their bodies strewn about the massive living room. The killers were professionals. All wore hats and gloves. No facial images. Nothing. But one image of the sole female chilled Slaga. Something about the way she moved conveyed an ease with death...almost as if tending a flower garden.

Foreboding permeated his being as he summoned a view of his fireplace. Bricks strewn about instantly confirmed his worst fears. While moving copies of the file—with his notes and the most sensitive parts of Polar Strike—to a secure location, he'd kept a small working file of the operation in a super-secret safe hidden in a false-bottom part of the hearth. How in the world did they find it?

"*Der'mo*!" He angrily spat. "What a fool I am." The working file had information about Polar Strike, the Fords, and Grigor—the whole thing was blown now.

He needed to disappear.

CHAPTER 65

DECEMBER
NEW YORK
ONE MONTH TO INAUGURATION

Vadik sat on his sofa glancing at Sigrid, Viktor, Yuri, and a couple of his men. "He got ... *away*?"

"Yes, General."

"Did you ever find anything that indicated who he really was?"

"Nothing, General. He was very thorough. Even his men did not know his name—they just called him: Boss." Sigrid paused to lift a folder in her hand. "Had this file hidden in a false-bottomed log holder by the hearth. Yuri found it when he was searching the fireplace."

Distracted by the idea that the object of years of pursuit had slipped his net—again, Vadik harrumphed, "Anything else?"

"Passports for Bruno Shakli, Mikhail Kuznetsov, and Ivan Petrov."

Vadik looked up. "He may still be alive, but his ability to travel has been impaired."

Silence prompted Vadik to look her way.

"You think he has more passports?" Vadik asked, then answered his own question. "Of course he would. Or at least the resources to get another." He paused a moment to play out scenarios in his rock tumbler. "Well, of no matter. He's probably in the wind as we speak." Vadik strolled to the window. Snow laid a quilt of depression across Central Park below.

"General?"

Vadik recognized the tone in Sigrid's voice—it was one he rarely heard, except in times of great importance or danger. Slowly, he turned. "Yes?" He asked, mildly curious by the barest glint in Sigrid's eyes.

"This file confirms that KGB was working on something in the 1950s to undermine America's leadership. It relied heavily on brainwashing, but as we know, it was never implemented because of the consistent failure of the installed reprogramming to take in the potential sleeper agents."

Vadik threw his hands up futilely. "Yes, well how does that help us now? It seems that this Bruno Shakli went to a lot of trouble to secure files for a program that history forgot."

Sigrid lifted the file up. "General, there was one success."

Vadik's eyes narrowed. He crossed his legs, settling back in his seat. "Go on."

Sigrid briefed Vadik on what they'd recovered from the fireplace file: the situation with Chris Ford, his history with the Center for Right Being, and his programming—and how he was now about to become the Vice President of the United States.

As if rescued from the gallows, and made Tsar of all the Russias—Vadik's face reflected shocked jubilation. Standing, he went to his Central Park overlook. For a few minutes, his eyes hazed over, lost in thought.

Finally, he turned. Nodding, he said, "This ... is extraordinary. Ford kills Johansen, then gets removed from office and the Speaker assumes the Presidency." Vadik allowed a slight sneer to crease his face. "Finally, we can tip the balance of power away from these arrogant bastards. We'd be the masters of the world." The oligarch allowed himself a smile as he considered the wealth and power.

Vadik sat, eyes closed, rubbing his left index finger with his right, a sign he was again in deep thought. Finally, he said, "And according to this ... Doctor Grigor's files... Ford is not aware he has been programmed, correct?"

"Yes, General."

"So, if we could activate him, he'd kill the President."

"Correct."

"Do we know how he could be activated? What causes Ford to go from a sleeper agent to active status?"

"Unknown. I think a visit with Doctor Grigor might be appropriate."

"Alive."

"Of course, General."

Again, he let his mind drift to sitting behind the desk in the Oval Office. After a moment, he noted Sigrid in a holding pattern, waiting to land a final plane. "You have more."

"One last wrinkle, General. Probably nothing, but the archivist from Rosarkhiv—you know the first on the scene after Yuri and his men departed—an Olegina Bortsova, has been out sick from work the last couple of days."

"Sounds plausible—after what she saw. What is your concern?"

"Uncertain General, but what if she found something we overlooked and took it with her?"

"We have what she may or may not have, right? What could she do?"

"Alert the authorities who, to avoid a backlash against Russia, might alert the Americans. I would like to keep tabs on her."

Vadik nodded. "Yes. Yes, of course."

CHAPTER 66

DECEMBER
NEW YORK
ONE MONTH TO INAUGURATION

"I thought it was *warming*, not global freezing." Nic Ford muttered as he stepped from his NYPD-issue Chevrolet, grossly out of place next to the countless Mercedes Benz, Lexus, and Range Rovers oozing wealth in the parking spots of the Galaxy Luxury Community in Brighton Beach. His breath vaporized into a heavy fog that whisked away in the still, frozen early-morning air.

In his youth, his grandmother, Elena, often regaled Nic with stories from her childhood in Russia. Many was the time she spat: "America cold is *slabby chay* ... weak tea." Nic struggled to recall her name for winter in Russkaya.

A young patrol officer seemingly appeared from out of the mist like a ghost. Pointing to an upscale building, he quietly said, "This way, Inspector."

Nic's gaze drifted upward when the stabbing pain in his neck reminded him of a visit many years ago to Brighton.

At another crime scene, he'd noticed a man who looked out of place. On a hunch, he'd started over to speak with him when the man suddenly turned, first walking rapidly away, and then ducking into a dark alley. Nic followed him. Somehow, the tough had gotten into a position behind him, first kneeing him in the back before going for a chokehold with his arm around the policeman's neck.

Attempting to break free, Nic felt his airway being slowly crushed when he'd remembered the Bic pen in his pocket. With his last gasp,

Nic had thrust the pen into the thug's neck. Yelping in great pain, the killer momentarily relaxed his death grip enough for Nic to break free. Lurching away, Nic had yanked his service revolver from its holster. "Please give me a reason."

Blood pouring from his neck, the mobster grudgingly surrendered, finally cuffed with the pen still protruding from below his ear. Ever since, Nic had been over-sensitive to people being behind him and had occasional stabs of neck pain when he moved his head suddenly.

Ruefully, Nic rubbed his neck. "Top floor?"

Silently, the patrol officer nodded.

"How many?"

"Five."

Lost in thought, Nic looked up again before slowly lowering his gaze to the patrol officer silently observing him. Nic smiled as he extended his hand. "Sorry, Nic Ford. What's your name, son?"

"Paddock, sir."

"All right, so who's the owner?"

Earnest to please, the patrol officer ducked into his notebook. "Title came back to a shell corp. Hermitage Holdings—"

"Slaga Dmitriev ... well we never made the complete connection."

The officer looked blank? "Who sir?"

Nic realized the patrol officer knew nothing of Club Twenty-Two, the Gold Train, or the Specter. "Nothing. Where is the lead officer?"

"He and evidence collection have already started to gather up things. I think they're down in the garage now looking for clues. Should I call him?"

"No, I'll catch him later."

The patrol officer nodded silently.

"Who called it in?" Nic asked.

"Cleaning lady. Arrived and found ... "

Something in his demeanor made Nic pause. "Your first homicide?"

"No sir ... just never one like this."

Nic squinted but said nothing. Ignoring his neck, he looked up at Penthouse *A* in the Tolstoy building with its expansive view of the Atlantic Ocean. Long the destination of choice for Russian and Ukrainian mobsters, Russian oligarchs, Old Politburo bosses, retired or in-hiding ex-KGB spooks, and Russian wannabes, the Galaxy, was an upscale respite in Brighton's gentrifying, crud-filled landscape. And yet, something was off. Normally, a Russian gang would not have been so defenseless. There was always gang security to prevent outsiders from getting in.

Stepping from the elevator into the foyer of Pent *A*, Nic admired the black-and-white, fully matted photographs on the walls. At the open front door to the penthouse, he stopped to admire the print: a naked, reclining woman turned away from the camera, covered with curvy stripes.

"Brodovitch."

"Pardon, Inspector?"

Nic looked over his shoulder at the forgotten officer. "Sorry. These are works by a famous Russian photographer from the mid-twentieth century, Alexey Brodovitch." Nic rubbed his head. "If this is real, probably worth ... well more than you and I make."

Moving across the threshold was like stepping into a photo layout from *Architectural Digest*. The travertine floors were draped with brilliantly colored Persian rugs. Black lacquer Danish Modern furniture posed invitingly. Walls painted in varying colors—red so bright it gave him a headache; a forebodingly dark black and one wall of virginal white, were covered with more Brodovitch prints. The kitchen was a blend of ecru-colored concrete counter tops accented with small dashes of red and black that complemented the walls. Nic noted the Wolf professional gas range, Miele dishwasher, and Jura Giga coffee machine. The fridge, a Meneghini Aradementi, took up a whole wall. They were all names that dripped dollar signs.

An image of his wife—ex-wife—leaving for the arms of a wealthy arts dealer passed through his mind. Nic shook his head, thinking of his old Mr. Coffee at home. "Okay, where next?"

"This way, sir," the young officer's tone reminded Nic of his first days out of the academy.

They made their way through the dining room, down a hall to a great room flooded with light. Beyond the floor-to-ceiling plate-glass windows, white caps restlessly agitated in the cloud-covered Atlantic. To his left, a colossal, wall-mounted flat-panel TV reigned above a fireplace worthy of the great homes in Newport that stood guard over the rest of the room. Situated on either side of the fireplace were two obscenely expensive leather sofas flanked by side tables with hi-tech jet-black lamps all seemingly sinking into a mammoth, black bear-skin rug. Recessed ceiling lighting bathed the fireplace with angelic admiration.

However, it was on the wall opposite that drew Nic's eyes. A *National Geographic* worthy black-and-white photo of a monstrous polar bear squinting at the camera dominated the room. Beneath the wall-mounted print were five bodies. Each shot once in the head, execution style, with their throats cut. Normally, a crime scene this graphic would be the focal point for any preliminary examination, but it was the bizarre scrawl next to the picture that had Nic's attention. In blood, was a line from the frame that descended at an angle, and then zagged back in the opposite direction before appearing to stop suddenly and descend in an incoherent mess to the floor. "IDs?"

"No, sir."

The picture Nic had of Slaga Dmitriev was back in his office. But he wasn't sure it would be of much use; each of the dead men's faces were virtually unrecognizable—gouged eyes and teeth shattered beyond imagination.

"Ollie ollie auction—holy mother of ... "

Both turned to find a female uniform stopped in the doorway. Behind her were two techs with a gurney. Nic's eyes were drawn to the woman's stunning red hair. The policewoman joined the police officers.

She offered her hand, "Tasha O'Riley. ME's office."

"Nic Ford," he gestured to the police officer, "Officer Paddock."

Tasha nodded to both before donning a set of latex gloves. "Never seen a dead man using a wall like a coloring book. Whataya suppose he was writing—last will? Who's the vic?"

"Uncertain. Possibly Slaga Dmitriev."

A long whistle poured from the examiner. "Don't know who that is, but this is messed up. Somebody must have had a real hard-on—"

"Okay, okay. Let's hold the commentary." Nic crooked his head quizzically. "What can you tell from this?"

"Well Inspector, other than this looks like a three-ring circus ... someone clearly did not want these guys easily identified. But," the ME knelt as she paused to muscle a second pair of gloves over her first set. She noted Nic's raised eyebrows, "What? Bit messy you know?" She raised one of the victim's shirts exposing a heavily tattooed body, "Ink might help."

Nic nodded, "We'll let you get to it while we check the rest of the place." Other than more reminders of his paltry paycheck, Nic did not find anything else of interest in the living room. In the master bedroom, an exquisite teak bookshelf stood empty, its former residents strewn about the room. There was an outsize collection of furniture that Nic remembered from a catalog. *Drexel? Thomasville?* The bedding and throw pillows had been gutted and thrown aside. The ocean-liner sized corner desk was rifled like the bed, bookshelf, and carpet. Nic donned gloves to check the desk, but after a moment, turned to the debris field on the floor. Books, mostly in Russian but some English, had been shaken, then dropped.

"I wonder what they were looking for?" Officer Paddock's voice broke the stillness.

On one knee, Nic shook his head slowly. "Not sure, but doesn't look like they found it."

"How can you tell?"

"Well ... whoever it was, it doesn't appear they stopped suddenly, you know as if they found what they were looking for and didn't need to keep searching. The rifling appears total."

Nic stood and was about to leave the room when his eyes came to rest on one book on the floor. He turned the book with his shoe such that he could read the title. THE BASICS OF GEOCACHING. "What would a Russian thug be doing with this?" Ford opened the tome, but finding nothing unusual, he closed it. About to drop it back among the other scattered texts, he felt a tiny bulge. He opened the back cover and found an object taped into a small cut-out depression. A solid gold key with a diamond-encrusted Russian Orthodox Cross on the top, it looked nothing like anything he'd ever seen. Instead of leaving it, he took the book with him.

"Officer Paddock, please make a note that Inspector Ford is removing this book and key for examination. I'll place it into evidence at the station."

"Yes, Inspector."

"Please go see if there's anything out of the ordinary in the bathroom. I'm going to check in with the ME."

In the great room, Nic found Tasha with her arms crossed in her OCME jacket that was two sizes too big. Perplexed, she was examining the splattered wall from an angle. "So what does the Office of the Chief Medical Examiner think?"

Without moving her head, Tasha's eyes shifted to Nic's. "Not sure but look at this." She pointed to the start of the bloody scrawl. "Can't tell if he was writing something in English or Cyrillic."

"Why?"

"Well, you can see the first downward stroke before doubling back—could be start of an X, Y or Z ... in either language but doesn't seem to make sense."

"Why?"

Tasha turned to face Nic. "Because people don't normally start letters this way."

"Like what?"

"Like the letters were started back to front rather than the normal front to back."

"Maybe he died before he could finish."

Nic and Tasha turned to Officer Paddock who immediately shrank back, "Sorry sir, didn't mean to intrude. Nothing in the bathroom looked out of order."

"No worries. What letters do they look like to you?" Nic asked.

"Well sir, I was thinking more like the start of a number or some code."

Silence descended over the room as Paddock's thoughts drifted down the hallway. One of the med-assistants cleared his voice.

"Sorry Tash, you ready to move 'em?"

Momentarily lost in thought, Tasha did not hear the technician.

"Tash?"

Staring vacantly at the blood scrawl, Tasha suddenly shook her head. "Sorry—what?"

"You okay? We were thinking we should start to bag these guys."

"Yeah, yeah." She stepped aside as the techs moved the gurney into place. "Just mesmerized by this picture—" Everyone waited for her to finish her thought. Tasha blinked a couple of times before continuing. "Nothing. Okay, let's go."

Opening a duffel case, a tech removed five large, black, body bags casting a pall across the room. The forensic assistants began their grim routine. Turning, she faced Nic and Officer Paddock. "Inspector, I'll get you the photos and preliminary summary from the autopsy ASAP." Packing her med-bag, she hesitated, "By the way, I looked to see who the lead investigator on this case was before I arrived." Tasha paused. "Why is a twenty-year vet, an Inspector of all things, working what appears to be a—sensational, no doubt, but—routine murder?"

Nic smiled before nodding. "I'm on a special task force assigned to ... well let's just call it: Organized Russian Business Activities of a Questionable Nature. Mayor wants to dial down their image."

Tasha raised her eyebrows, "*Rossiyane v N'yu-Yorke ne khorosho dlya biznesa*?"

It was Nic's turn to tilt his head admiringly. "Well, probably not good for this guy anyway," he said gesturing to the body-bagged, gurney-strapped dead man being rolled past them. "*Vy govorite bezuprechno.*"

"Thank you. Learned from my mother. Where'd you learn Russkiy?"

"Father, Grandmother—mostly Grandmother."

Officer Paddock broke up the mutual-admiration session. "Sir, I'll meet you at the elevator."

Tasha said, "Yeah, I gotta go. I'll get that work to you Inspector ... and I'll get you some extra detail on the tattoos; probably mean something."

Wanting the conversation not to be over, Nic reluctantly said, "Thanks."

Nic turned back to examine the wall again. Russians don't make a mess like this at home. Something was off. Starting for the front door, he stopped suddenly. His grandmother's name for the Russian winter came to him ... *Resplata*—The Reckoning.

CHAPTER 67

DECEMBER
BRIGHTON BEACH MURDERS
BROOKLYN
KINGS COUNTY HOSPITAL
ONE WEEK AFTER

Cupping his cellphone to his ear with his shoulder, Nic rubbed his eyes, then his temples as he listened to on-hold music from the sixties. His gaze drifted to some papers he'd brought from his office. "Have to get those filed. I hate forms."

While normally rotating between offices in Manhattan and the Sixtieth Precinct in Brighton Beach, Nic had come to the police morgue facility at the Kings County Hospital after his conversation with the ME on the case. Sitting in an empty office, staring out a grimed-up window at a salvage yard where three workers were trying to open a mangled car door, he fought his depression and nagging fear that nothing the police ever did, stopped the seeming tidal wave of crime.

"Inspector?"

Turning from the salvage-yard opera outside, Nic pulled the phone from his ear to find Tasha O'Riley just inside the door. Suddenly, his mood changed. Nic held the phone from his ear for a moment before pressing the END button.

"I hope I didn't interrupt anything," the ME said.

"Nah, I was tired of the trip to way-back anyway." Her perplexed look caused Nic to hurriedly follow up. "On-hold music from ... never mind."

Nic found himself distracted by O'Riley. Her manner of speech, appearance, and red hair reminded him that he'd not been on a date in over a year. "So, what's up?" he asked.

"Just wanted to update you on the vics from Brighton Beach. You gotta sec?"

"Sure."

Without waiting, O'Riley wheeled and started down the hall. Momentarily surprised at her casual attitude toward rank, he gathered his things and trailed after her.

"In a hurry, Officer O'Riley?"

"Not at all, Inspector. I want to give you as much time as possible but also have a class to get to."

In the morgue, there were ten slab tables, all occupied. O'Riley led Nic past them into a large meeting room. The table was covered with manila folders. Tasha sat, gesturing for Nic to the open seat across the table. "We've completed our examination of the five bodies from the Galaxy and released them to their families. All but one."

Nic's brow furrowed but before he could speak, she opened one envelope and emptied the contents onto the table. Out poured photos of the bodies and from the Galaxy murder scene.

Flipping one around toward Nic, she asked, "You recognize this man?"

Nic lifted the photo. On the body, a kaleidoscope of colorful tattoos did battle for space on the dead canvas. Impassively, the grizzled cop studied it. Broken teeth, missing fingers, gouged eyes. It was savagery Nic no longer invested in. Slowly from his pocket, he removed the photo from Red Square Ink of the tattooed body of Nikita D, comparing the two. "Probably Slaga Dmitriev. So whataya got?"

"Come with me, Inspector." Tasha stood, leading Nic back into the examination room to one of the tables. Pulling back the sheet, she said, "No one claimed this guy."

Nic lifted both photos in his hand. "Same guy, right?"

"Correct, Inspector. Even the families of the other dead men that we released vaguely recognized him—they called him ..." Tasha paused to look in her exam notebook. "Called him *Nikita*—"

Nic looked up sharply but said nothing.

The ME continued. "But no one knew him well or if he had family. Probably confirms your theory he's this Slaga guy you're looking for."

Slowly, Nic circled the body, uncertain whether to believe it was the Specter. Still something gnawed at him. He studied the Red Square Ink photo in detail before handing it to Tasha. "If this *is* Nikita or Slaga, could he have had some more tats done since this picture was taken?"

Examining the picture, the ME nodded. "Possibly. There are some markings on the body that aren't in the picture. Might even explain a couple of things I've been wondering about." Tasha handed the picture back to Nic.

"How so?" Nic asked.

Tasha pointed to the photo and then to the body on the table. "As you know Inspector, all this ink means something."

Certain that after twenty-plus years on the force, Nic was familiar with the meaning of most Russian and Ukrainian tattoos, but wanting to listen to her voice, he nodded for her to continue.

"On the chest, suns might indicate a number of times the person has been sent to prison. A cross suggests he was a thief; a skull, a murderer. A snake intertwined with a woman, a passive homosexual, usually forced onto the recipient. Crowns on the hand, a criminal boss or mobster. Shoulder epaulettes, a senior boss. Machine gun wrapped in dollars beneath a skyscraper usually suggests a love of things American. Russian church dome, devotion to crime, etcetera, etcetera." She paused to see if she still had his attention. "Sometimes, we see new markings that we don't quite understand yet. See anything unusual on this vic, Inspector?"

Nic slowly moved about the table, inspecting the corpse. The casual tour across the body came to a sudden stop, his eyes locking onto the base of a skyscraper in the middle of the dead man's lower left side. "What is that?"

"Good eye, Inspector." Tasha came around to join him, her closeness unsettling him. She picked up a magnifying glass and handed it to him.

Enlarging the image, he hesitantly mumbled, "Looks like an old pirate's treasure chest?"

"Exactly."

Genuinely confused, he looked up into Tasha's ocean-blue eyes. Just as quickly, he returned his gaze to the body. "What does it mean?"

"You tell me. Never seen this on a Russkaya before."

"And what ... what are those markings?"

"On the corners?"

"Yeah."

"Here, you'll need this." Before Nic could speak, Tasha offered him a new magnifying glass.

Extra-strength magnification enhanced the marks at the edges of the chest. "Are these—"

"Numbers? Yeah."

"Four?" he asked.

"Good eye."

"Umm." Satisfied there was nothing else to see, Nic stood back. "What are they?

Tasha picked up a pad from her examiner's table. "On the top left, four-one. Top right one-one. Bottom left one-zero. Bottom right seven-eight."

Running scenarios through his head, Nic shook his head slowly. "Odd sequence. Combination to a lock?"

"Maybe. Were also thinking bank account, chemical polymers, Fibonacci sequence, or—"

"GPS coordinates?"

"Yes, but that doesn't seem to play out."

"Why?"

Tasha crossed her arms, relishing the dispensing of information. "Would only be enough numbers for part of a set. You know you need both latitude and longitude for GPS."

Nic flashed back on finding the geocaching book at the Galaxy. "No other random numbers? Maybe the other half?"

The ME shook her head, watching in silent amusement as Nic reexamined the body. "Men always think you've missed something."

"Any other weird tats?"

"One. On his back is a line from one spot on the left shoulder around to a spot on the right shoulder. Almost like a string. Can't fathom the meaning."

Nic stared, out of words. "That's it. Nothing else?"

The medical examiner shook her head. Nic disgustedly handed the magnifier back, mildly snarling at the body. "C'mon Slaga, what the hell are you hiding?"

"Sorry, Inspector. I'll keep looking for something. Not sure if I'll find anything else, but I just wanted to brief you."

Nic realized that their time together was drawing to a close. Nodding absent-mindedly, Nic mumbled, "Okay, thanks." He blurted, "What class are you off to?"

"Kempo—no wait." She glanced at her smartwatch. "Sorry, today is Tuesday, Taekwondo."

"Martial-arts junkie?"

"A little. Mostly helps to blow the stress out of," she gestured about the room, "all this love."

Nic snorted before reluctantly turning away. At the door, he couldn't help himself and stopped to look back at Tasha. She was bent over the body when she caught his eye.

"Anything else, Inspector?"

"No. Thanks again," he mumbled before leaving.

CHAPTER 68

JANUARY
MOSCOW
THREE DAYS TO INAUGURATION

In her apartment, Olegina wiped tears as she tossed from side to side in her bed. Finally, she got up and made a cup of tea. Unable to sleep since the bloodbath at Lubyanka, her superiors had given her time off to recuperate, but she'd finally returned to work just to take her mind off the nightmares.

While she couldn't prove it, she was certain she was being followed and that someone had been in her apartment. Her eyes lifted to the ceiling tile, above which she'd hidden the file. It had remained there, untouched since the massacre. But she'd finally had enough.

Pulling a chair over, she rose, lifted the tile ... and stopped at the sight of the red-stained folder she'd removed from Lubyanka. Stepping off the chair, she returned to the kitchen to get rubber gloves from beneath her sink. Back on top of the chair, Olegina donned the gloves and hesitantly removed the folder. Casting about, her eyes landed on yesterday's *Izvestiya*. On her table, she opened the paper and then lay the folder on it.

She sat staring at it for a moment, her memories flooded with pain and death. Finally summoning the courage, she gently opened the folder, as if this would lessen the terror within. But the fear was up against a stronger force. Her anger. Something in these files had taken the life of her friend and three co-workers.

Slowly, she moved through the record—pausing at times to marvel at the plot's detail and at times savoring what few historians would ever have a chance to see. KGB had concocted an intricate scheme to plant moles in America. But the complexity of the plan, named Polar Strike, had seemed beyond reach. Indeed, from what she could understand in the file's techno-jargon, most of the old KGB's efforts and thought manipulation—brainwashing, had been a failure.

She flipped pages, mindlessly lost in the minutia of detail and certain the operation was destined for historical oblivion, when she arrived at the bloodstained manila file that Anna had given with her last breath. She briefly considered using tissues to open the folder, but quickly realized the blood was dry and could not hurt her. Slowly, she waded into the contents. Her eyes widened. Her hand shot to her mouth as she bolted upright, unable to breath.

One test case had proven successful—*and was still active.*

Rapidly, she moved through the rest of the file. She reread that last couple of pages a second time, unwilling to believe what her eyes conveyed. In a flash, what had been a remote plan, frozen in a glacier, suddenly lurked outside her window in the darkness. The names were vaguely familiar. Cold terror pulsed through her veins like a neon light. Falteringly, she stood. In the kitchen, she found today's newspaper face down on the counter. Taking it back to the table, she looked at the Polar Strike file detailing the American test case: CHRISTOPHER FORD.

Olegina gasped as she looked at the *Isvestiya's* headline:

> JOHANSEN-FORD PREPARE TO TAKE POWER IN UNITED STATES

The installation of the new American leadership was set to commence in days. Olegina pulled her hands inside the sleeves of her sweater before putting them over her face. She wept; now she understood ... why someone wanted this information ... would kill for it. Looking across the room at a map of America, she could only shake her head. "What to do?"

Then a new thought came to her. She glanced down at her phone. Slowly, as atop a tightrope, she took it up, opening her contacts and scrolling to an entry. About to dial, she stopped. The call would be monitored. Not sure who could be trusted with this, Olegina gathered the folder along with her things and left her apartment. In the lobby, she encountered two men in blue overalls with toolboxes. They appeared lost.

"Can I help you?" she asked.

"We've had a call about tenants power going in and out. Do you live here?" Their attitudes were a bit too friendly for members of the tradecraft who often were boorish, drunk, or on their way to being drunk.

Unconsciously, Olegina turned away in doubt. "Uh no, I was just visiting my aunt. Good luck."

One tried to grab her sleeve, "Miss, wait—"

But radar on high alert now, Olegina ducked out the front entrance and walked as unhurried as she could feign to the corner phone booth.

Inside, she cast furtive glances outside. At the entrance to her building, she could swear one of the men was looking out the glass door at her, talking into his cellphone. Unlocking her phone, she relocated the name in her contacts. Using her Moscow Calling phone card, she placed the call.

The previous year, she'd attended a seminar at Moscow University on money laundering, integration, and placement. There, she'd met an African-American, female FBI agent who worked in the Bureau's National Security Branch. More direct, and sometimes rough around the edges, Shelby and Olegina had bonded immediately. She answered on the first ring.

"Littlejohn," said a voice, efficiently.

Olegina opened her mouth, but the image of Anna's bloody face, flashed across her mind. Raspy, she choked before hanging up. But a moment later, she stood erect, wiped her tears, and inhaled new courage. "*Nyet*," she angrily redialed the number. It rang once.

"Who the fuck is this?" came a terse answer.

"Shelby?"

"That's right." A long pause before the woman said, "Wellll? You gonna start gasping again, tell me dirty things or—"

"Shelby it is Olegina ... Olegina Bortsova from—"

"Russia ... Olie—I got you. How you doin' girl? Man, I thought you were—hell never mind. Where you calling me from? Like the moon? And what's with all the heavy breathing and all?"

Olegina fought to hold her composure. "I'm in ... I need your help."

Instantly, the FBI woman's tone changed. "Where are ... You in Moscow? Are you at a place where you can talk?"

Olegina looked outside the booth. "I'm not sure. Probably not."

A moment to assess before Shelby said, "Okay, look. I want you to go the American Embassy. Right now! I have a contact there I'm gonna call as soon as I hang up with you. He'll meet you there and—"

"I don't need asylum, Shelby."

"No, of course not, but there are secure phones in our department there. Then you call me back."

"Oh yes, of course."

"Now, go girl." The line went dead.

Grabbing her backpack, Olegina again checked her surroundings as the two maintenance men left her building. Without a glance at her, they got in their vehicle and slowly motored down the avenue toward her. Olegina pretended to be reading a magazine at a small news stand next to the phone booth. As the repair van moved past, the men again ignored her but the passenger on his cellphone, cast a surreptitious glance her way.

Once the truck turned the corner, Olegina paid for the magazine and whispered something to the old man behind the kiosk counter. He motioned to her.

A moment later the van came back around the corner. Quickly, it pulled up to the kiosk, rolling down the window, the passenger called out.

"Hey Tolstoy! Did you see where that girl went? I forgot to give her an invoice."

The old man nodded, gesturing down the street. The man waved and they drove off. After a moment, the vendor tapped Olegina down behind his counter. "They're gone."

Olegina stood up and grabbed her pack.

The man smiled. "Old boyfriends are a pain."

"Thank you," she said as she gave him a small kiss on the cheek.

"Go down the alley here. It'll get you to the Metro quicker."

Offering her thanks once more, Olegina, disappeared down the backstreet and made her way to the Metro. The whole way across town, it seemed as if every person was looking right at her. Nervously, she came up the stairs at Krasnopresnenskaya Station. Pausing to assess the lay of the land, she pulled the hood of her jacket up over her head and set out for the American Embassy down the street.

It had to be her imagination, but a black SUV, keeping a distance of a hundred feet, appeared to inch along behind her. Thank goodness for people still out and about their errands and such. Finally, she stood across the avenue from her destination. The SUV seemed to accelerate toward her and with the last shred of courage she had, she dashed across the boulevard to the Embassy. Reaching the driveway, she was shocked when the SUV cut her off and three men leapt out.

"Help!" Olegina screamed.

Two accosted her, each taking an arm. They muscled her toward the SUV, the third opening the door.

Four US Marines burst from a security office.

"Halt! Let her go!"

The driver exited the vehicle. Hands up, he approached the guards, waving a badge in his hand. "I'm Moscow police, this woman is—"

"He's lying!" Olegina yelled.

One of the men holding her, viciously slapped Olegina. "Shut up!"

The lead Marine's eyes tightened. Unstrapping his side arm, he said, "Stand down and release her."

The badge man said, "You have no jurisdiction here. This is an internal Russian matter. Now step back—"

But the Marines took up a perimeter around the SUV. The Marine said, "Sir, this driveway is an extension of the Embassy and constitutes American territory. You and your men are standing on soil of the United States. This is your last warning. Stand down and let her go!"

Grudgingly, the four Russians released Olegina, retreating to the SUV. The Marines hustled Olegina inside as the SUV screeched angrily away.

Escorting her to a reception desk, the lead Marine sat opposite her. "Ma'am are you all right?"

Nodding, Olegina, wiped her eyes with her shirt sleeve before the American offered her a box of tissues from a desk drawer.

Taking a couple, she noddingly smiled. "Thank you."

Putting the box next to her, the Marine comfortingly asked, "Now, how can we help you?"

"Yes, I'm here to see ..." Olegina replayed the call with Shelby Littlejohn in her head. "I'm—I'm not sure who I'm supposed to see."

"No worries ma'am; give me just a moment, please." Standing, the officer added, "Those friends of yours aren't coming back are they?"

Olegina fearfully shook her head.

The Marine went into a glass-enclosed office overlooking the reception area and picked up a phone. In what seemed no time, a man in a suit much nicer than any Russian suit she'd ever seen, arrived into the office.

"Ms. Bortsova?"

Olegina nodded vigorously, "Yes."

"I'm with the US Diplomatic Security Service. Ms. Littlejohn alerted me to your arrival." He nodded to the guard. "This one's off the books, Sergeant."

The Marine crisply replied, "Aye aye," closing the visitor log with no record of entry.

Nodding, the man said, "Ms. Bortsova, this way please." The man escorted her into the embassy proper, as a great weight seemed to lift from her shoulders. Inside, he directed her down a hall, through two massive, airtight doors and into a room. "This is the SCIF, you can—"

"Skiff?"

"Sorry. Sensitive Compartmented Information Facility. We call it the skiff for short."

Olegina nodded hesitantly.

"This phone is connected directly to the FBI in Washington. Ms. Littlejohn is waiting. When you are ready, just lift the receiver and the call will be placed for you. I will be in that glass compartment there. I will be unable to hear your conversation, but as you can understand, we can't have a Russian national in here alone."

Before she could say anything, the man stepped into the glass room, sealing the door behind him.

Olegina looked about the sterile room; it was softly carpeted, with sound baffling on the walls and painted in muted blues and greens; it was nicer than any room she'd ever seen and yet the most sterile she'd ever been in. The man gestured to her to pick up the phone.

Putting the receiver to her ear, she heard a series of switches and changing dial tones indicating the call was being rerouted and scrubbed of bugs or tails. It rang once.

"Littlejohn."

"Shelby. It is Olegina."

"No kidding. I thought it was Joe Stalin himself."

Olegina immediately remembered what she liked about the FBI agent. "Thank you for arranging this."

"No worries. So, what's going on?"

"I'm not sure."

Olegina could feel the irritation at the other end. "I don't know? You kidding me? I just arranged for you to call me from a SCIF in the American Embassy for 'I don't know.'"

"Okay. Please make your ... pie hole to be filled."

After a moment, laughter poured from the phone receiver. Finally, "I love it when you try to speak American slang. Okay Olegina, let's start at the beginning."

For the next ten minutes, Olegina detailed her job at Archives; she was careful to leave out anything that could be portrayed as damaging to Russia. This was not about betraying her country. She relayed her interactions with Anna, the Opal Palace, and Anna's clubbing thug-buddies, before concluding with the last few hours.

"Shit girl, that's like out of Hollywood or something. You okay now?"

"Yes. But very frightened."

She could hear Shelby thinking. "You have this file with you now?"

"Yes."

More silence before Shelby softly said, "Olie I need you to listen to what I'm about to say to you. And you need to do it without thinking about it, okay?"

"Yes. What?"

"Do you have a passport?"

"Yes. But ... "

"You don't have it with you, correct?"

"*Da*—yes."

"Where is it?

"At my office."

"How far is that?"

"Not far." Recalling the black SUV outside, she quickly added, "Too far. I keep it at the office. Security reasons and they want to keep ... how you say—"

"Keep tabs on you?" Shelby prompted.

"Yes."

"Okay, never mind. We're gonna have to do without it for now."

"For now ... what?" Olegina skeptically asked.

"The Diplomatic Security agent—his name is Joe—is going to take things from here. Please follow his instructions."

"Why? Where am I going?"

The line had gone dead. In the control booth, Joe picked up a flashing line, nodded a couple of times, hung up, and came out.

"You ready?"

"For?" Olegina replied fearfully.

"I'll brief you in the car."

In the basement, they met three other agents. They piled into two Lada Largus SUVs with tinted windows. In the second vehicle, Olegina was pushed down on the floor. Both Ladas came up out of the basement, rapidly merging with traffic.

In the passenger seat, Joe turned to face Olegina. "We are driving you to Sheremetyevo. We have a pre-assigned hangar there where a private jet, cleared for immediate takeoff, is waiting."

"What about a passport?"

"Won't need it. On a diplomatic departure, we don't have to declare a manifest, so your presence will be unlogged. Your superiors will find your passport right where it should be and they'll think you're somewhere—on a bender, at Grandma's, or dead, but still in Russia."

Olegina panicked. "Where am I going?"

"Washington."

CHAPTER 69

JANUARY
WASHINGTON, DC
JOINT BASE ANDREWS
TWO DAYS TO INAUGURATION

Knowing her destination, Olegina had still been both surprised and impressed, when the DSEC Service agents had delivered her to the diplomatic terminal at Sheremetyevo, where they placed her aboard a waiting jet and then departed. Quietly, a sparse flight crew welcomed her: two cabin attendants and two pilots, all armed. After takeoff, the attendants removed to their crew stations, one in front, the other aft, leaving her alone in the spacious cabin of the Gulfstream *V* jet.

* * * *

From the diplomatic terminal, Joe watched as the plane climbed into the night sky. He dialed a number.

In Washington, a burner phone rang. Answering it, a voice said, "X-ray, bingo, star."

"Bingo, star. The package is in the air," Joe said and then hung up.

Terminating the call, the recipient dialed a new number.

The call was answered, "X-ray, star."

In Washington, the caller replied, "She's flown," and hung up.

* * * *

Over the Baltic Sea, Olegina's fear slowly evaporated, and she finally surrendered to a crushing exhaustion. She slept across the Atlantic, awakening about an hour from America's Eastern Seaboard. One of the attendants arrived, guiding her to the jet's aft bathroom. Another surprise awaited: a small shower. Gratefully, she cleaned up, standing for five minutes beneath the cascade of hot water, washing away the last few days.

Stepping out, she was greeted with shopping bags on the vanity. In the first bag were some toiletries along with three unopened packages of underwear—large, medium, and small. A smile creased her face. The second contained jeans, a number of long-sleeve tops and a pair of athletic shoes.

Cleaned up and newly dressed, she retook her seat in time for the plane's final banking maneuvers toward Andrews. Olegina stared awestruck as the early morning sun bathed the capitol, light creeping up the unbelievable Washington Monument.

After touchdown, the Gulfstream taxied to an out-of-the-way building resembling more of a Quonset hut than a terminal. A black GMC Tahoe, with dark, black-tinted windows, sat in front. The plane stopped and one of the attendants escorted Olegina to the forward door as the jet's air stairs descended to the tarmac.

"Thank you," Olegina nervously smiled as she left.

The Tahoe's driver-side door opened. Out stepped a dynamo: Littlejohn.

Relatively short at five four—Shelby Littlejohn had graduated second in her class at the FBI Training Academy at Quantico. Being second had been a burr under the saddle for Shelby; it drove her to excel at everything she attempted from top-notch performance appraisals to three-time finisher of the Ironman in Hawaii to a master's in psychology and European studies from Georgetown to being fluent in Russian and German.

Just two years in the field, she'd been instrumental in the takedown of a Boston area mobster, Micky "Double Tap" Gasparé. DT as he was known for short, got his nickname from a propensity to shoot victims twice in the head to ensure they actually died. A particularly vicious thug, he'd dump bodies in the various landfills he owned, leaving families to wonder what happened to their loved ones.

Assigned to surveillance, Shelby was working a stakeout at the Red Pine Landfill outside of Pittsfield in western Massachusetts. The

FBI had been tracking the movement of a shipment of cocaine that Washington believed Gasparé's gang was going to stash at Red Pine before commencing distribution.

The FBI also had a mole inside Gasparé's, operation. The agent, Robert Carrier, had tipped the Feds to a couple of the syndicate's earlier drug drops, which the FBI had been happy to share with the Massachusetts State Police. But unbeknownst to either FBI or MSP, Gasparé had his own double agent inside the State Police. This person tipped them off about Carrier.

One day, Shelby's team was observing a drone camera feed of Gasparé and his men driving into Red Pine. Exiting their vehicles, they stepped to the back of one. Shelby and her fellow agents, were shocked as the thugs yanked Carrier, bound and gagged from the trunk. Shelby's team watched horrified as the mobsters dragged the FBI agent toward a giant wood waste chopper at the base of a small crane. Before her lead agent could react, Shelby was out of their surveillance vehicle and racing the five hundred yards of space between the FBI van and Red Pine.

As she ran, she drew her sidearm. Stopping to take aim, she fired three quick shots in the direction of a crane in the center of the dump. The rounds ricocheted off in various directions, touching off pandemonium among Gasparé's men who began firing in general chaos at imagined intruders.

Shelby quickly scaled the perimeter fence, and under a hail of fire, made her way to an office building near the entrance to the fill. By then, Gasparé had been able to restore some order among his goons.

"Stop firing! That's what they want you to do!" He motioned to a couple of his men, "You three cover the entrance and kill that bitch!" Gasparé turned to another, "Let's get rid of this piece of shit before the Feds get here. Turn on the chopper." Snarling at Agent Carrier, Gasparé said, "We're gonna shred the evidence."

The industrial strength wood and waste crusher was designed to reduce anything to small pieces, which could then be easily moved into the dump. As it roared to life, Gasparé's men grabbed Carrier, muscling him toward the murderous grinders.

Sirens could be heard as Shelby's team bore down on the landfill, but it was clear they would not get there in time. Near the office where she'd found cover, there was a huge electric box with a unmistakable red handle in the up position. But pinned under intense strafing fire, Shelby improvised. Picking up a nearby block of discarded wood, she jumped out for a second, momentarily startling the closing gunmen, but it was just enough time to simulate using her mouth to pull a pin from an imaginary hand grenade and toss it toward the three approaching mobsters.

It had the desired effect as all three dove for cover. This allowed Shelby enough time to yank the red handle down, bringing the wood chopper to a halt as Gasparé's men were pushing the screaming Agent Carrier into the chopper's gapping maw. Dashing back for cover, one gunman successfully caught Shelby with a hit to her thigh. Nonetheless, she kept the killers at bay just long enough for a squadron of FBI vehicles to burst into Red Pine.

Shelby was awarded the FBI Shield of Bravery for conspicuous courage in the face of grave danger and for saving Agent Carrier. Simultaneously, a Letter of Caution, was placed in her service jacket, discouraging bold, but rash actions that could potentially imperil herself and possibly her fellow FBI agents.

Shelby had ascended rapidly through the ranks: probationary agent, Special Agent, Senior Special Agent, and finally Supervising Special Agent—and back to Senior Special Agent after a botched surveillance-op had blown back on her. The suspected spy was an American working as an analyst and translator at the United Nations. Secretly, she'd been passing sensitive information about terrorist activities, received from UN peacekeeping forces in the Middle East, to her lover, an economic attaché in the Cuban Mission to the UN.

About to move on the two, one of Shelby's new agents had inadvertently tipped his confidential informant in the Cuban Mission they were about to strike. The CI had then bartered the information with his superiors for a promotion. The woman and her handler had gotten to JFK and onto Iberia Airline's last flight to Havana, one step ahead of the FBI. Shelby had been demoted and transferred to the

National Security Desk in Washington, where she was assigned routine support and liaison with local law-enforcement duties.

But her instincts and analytical ability to predict where foreign governments and anarchist black-hat organizations would attempt hacks into the American intelligence apparatus had proved invaluable and eventually she was put onto tracking money laundering and narcotics trafficking emanating from Eastern Europe, the Baltic States, and Russia.

She and Olegina hugged. Shelby looked up into Olegina's eyes, seeing the fear in them. Before Olegina could speak, Shelby grabbed her bag, along with Olegina's arm, and escorted her to the truck. Inside, she turned to the Russian.

"All right, from the beginning, tell me what's going on."

The FBI woman listened intently as Olegina unburdened herself. Shelby squinted or grunted at times but said nothing, pausing only to remove tissues from her purse that she gave to the sobbing Russian.

"You have the Polar Strike files with you?" Shelby asked.

Olegina nodded, pulling them from her backpack.

"Good. I've been cross-checking some of what you told me on the phone with what we know here. Vice President-elect Ford has been staying out in Georgetown as he and President-elect Johansen prepare for the Inauguration. So far, he's made five trips back to New York where he visits his wife, family, friends, fundraisers, and a Doctor Stephan Grigor, the family physician he's been seeing since birth. I'm betting that's where the brainwashing is taking place."

"Brainwashing is one thing ... but what would cause Ford to go active?"

"What does the file say?" Shelby asked.

"The file is silent on this."

Shelby nodded as she considered this.

"And for what purpose?" Olegina asked.

Shelby replied, "Not sure. Let's start with what we have. A dusty, time-forgotten plot to disrupt the government of the United States. We sort of know the mechanics of how the plot works. Brainwashing of ... potential moles from birth with the intent of securing jobs for them in the American government. Correct?"

"Yes."

"If activated, the moles are to kill their immediate supervisor." Shelby stopped in thought. "Which I imagine if there were enough moles in place, could seriously impede an American response to a Soviet, now Russian, attack."

"Yes."

Shelby continued. "So, we know possibly who—probably Ford—what, and why, but not when, where, or how."

Olegina nodded but said nothing.

"I'm going out on a limb ... that's an American expression—"

Exasperated, Olegina gestured. "Yes, yes—I know. Please continue."

Eyes closed, Shelby tapped her forehead with her fingers as if divining the answers. "I think we can guess when and where. In two days at the Capitol, Johansen is about to be sworn in as President, if activated, Ford assassinates Johansen, his immediate supervisor."

"If we tell the authorities, couldn't they stop it, or just remove Mr. Ford?" Olegina offered.

Shelby absently shook her head. "No evidence. Just an old file that references *Christopher Ford*. What if it is another Christopher Ford?"

Olegina waved the file. "Another Ford? In New York? With a Russian patriliny?"

Shelby stared out the window, extrapolating possibilities.

Olegina angrily added, "And why would someone be killing people at Lubyanka for this information?"

"Just hold on for one damn second, okay?" Shelby snapped back.

Olegina glanced out the window. Had it been a mistake to trust the FBI woman? Finally, Shelby said, "Maybe it's for another reason."

"Like what?"

"Like maybe I don't know."

The Russian studied Shelby for a moment before nodding in agreement. "Okay."

Shelby's phone vibrated. Removing it, she read a text. Grimacing, she turned to Olegina. "Now, I'm already in a little hot water. My boss was not happy about the cost of a diplomatic shuttle between Moscow and Washington—so before we go to the Desk Chief, we gotta know what Ford's trigger or triggers are." She turned, starting the Tahoe.

"Where are we going?"

"FBI headquarters. Want to introduce you to my boss."

Leaving the base, Shelby guided the Tahoe out the Pearl Harbor Gate, turning onto Dower House Road.

"This back road should be quiet and quick. We'll take this to the Interstate and into DC; should be a little slower at this time of day."

Olegina absently nodded but said nothing. As the SUV passed the first cross street, a blur at the edge of her right eye caught her attention. A millisecond later, there came a horrible crushing of metal and the Tahoe spun like a top, tossed across the empty street into a ditch. Both women screamed, but just as the truck came to a stop, Shelby, with Sig Sauer P226 in hand, launched out her door as the first round of gunfire hit the Tahoe.

Rolling to her left, she came to a crouch, and popped off three rounds before continuing around to Olegina's, now-smashed side of the SUV. Prying the door away, she pulled the stunned, wounded Russian to safety behind a brick wall.

"Were you hit?" Shelby asked.

"I think the arm."

The FBI agent rapidly located the bleeding. "A scrape, you'll be okay. Removing a handkerchief from her coat, she pushed into Olegina's hand. "Put pressure on it with this. I'll be right back!"

She crawled to the end of the wall. Removing a small, telescoping mirror stick from her jacket, she slowly extended it around the barrier. Two men, with Uzi Pro pistols, approached the Tahoe. To the right of the assassins was a large propane tank. As they caught sight of her arm and mirror, they opened fire.

Under murderous hail, Shelby was forced to remain behind the wall. Using the mirror, she took aim as best she could before popping off four rounds toward the gas container. The last one striking true.

A deafening blast launched plumes of fire into the surrounding atmosphere. Like a crocodile snatching a victim from the safety of shore to a watery death, the murderous fire swept out, engulfing the closest killer. Now a human candle, he dropped his weapon to fight the flames, his dying shrieks piercing the air. Momentarily distracted, the other assailant turned toward his mate.

Shelby calmly stood up, firing one shot into the man's head and then another at the assassin on the ground. After checking that both were dead, she came to Olegina's side.

"How's it going?"

"Bleeding has stopped. Who were they?"

"Was gonna ask you. The Diplomatic Service agent in Moscow told me he thought you'd been followed. While Russian security can't get into our hangar space at Sheremetyevo, they can certainly note a plane's tail number. Every plane has to file a flight plan, even black flights. Whoever they are, they have access to air-traffic-control resources, both here and in Russia. They must have tracked the tail number of your plane here."

"But if there was no manifest of me being aboard, how did they know I was here?"

Shelby noddingly replied, "I don't know. But they probably saw you get off the plane a few minutes ago. This is a secure air base, but with remote-controlled drones, how hard would it be to observe who is stepping off an airplane?"

Olegina looked anguished. "So now my bosses know I've left Russia?"

"Not necessarily. I'm pretty sure no one at Rosarkhiv or Lubyanka, sent assassins to kill you just because you're not at work."

Nodding uncertainly, Olegina checked her wounded arm. "So, now what?"

Shelby looked at her now-totaled Tahoe and then at the assassin's, barely damaged Hummer. "Grab your things." At the Tahoe, both women removed bags and personal items. "Come on."

They hustled to the SUV, where the keys were still in the ignition. From her field bag, Shelby removed two sets of latex gloves, handing one to Olegina. "Keep your hands off everything; we'll have to dump this later." Shelby started it and put them on the road. She looked at the still-shocked Russian.

"Two days to the inauguration, someone's put this Polar Strike into play and they don't want you—now us—to mucky it up."

"Mucky?"

"Yeah, mucky. Don't they have words in Russian that describe a fucked-up situation that's only getting cloudier or more opaque?"

Olegina stared angrily at Shelby. "I have been just been shot and you're lecturing me on words?"

"It's *just been shot*, not *been just been* ... " Shelby's voice trailed off as Olegina's light-green eyes lit her up like a pinball machine.

Olegina turned to slap the door window. "*Nechuvstvitel'naya trakhayushchaya suka*!"

"Hey, I got some of that."

Olegina turned back. "Really? How much? Maybe is too much mucky—huh?"

Shelby pulled the vehicle over. She put her hands up defensively. "Okay, I get it. Sorry. I've got a wounded woman who I've secreted out of Russia, a plot to kill the president, bullets flying everywhere, two dead assassins, and now a stolen vehicle. I'm just as frightened as you."

Both exhaled.

"What do we do next?"

Shelby thought for a moment. "I think we have to know what the trigger is that activates the Vice President. Whoever sent those guys either have that information already—and were just trying to eliminate a possible threat to their plan—or haven't found it yet and don't want us muck– *messing*, things up for them."

"New York," Olegina replied without thinking.

"Pardon me?"

Olegina opened the file. "This stuff all seems to start with this Doctor Grigor. We have to find him."

Newly impressed with Olegina's sudden determination, Shelby put the Hummer in drive. "Let's go."

CHAPTER 70

JANUARY
NEW YORK
TWO DAYS TO INAUGURATION

As they drove, Shelby, opened the contacts on her phone. Scrolling to a listing for Sarah Boxer, she pinched her lips before dialing.

After one ring, a gruff-sounding voice answered, "Damn it Little-john, where the hell are you?"

"Hey boss, good talking to you also."

"Don't give me that shit—I'll demote you to bingo fraud enforcement in Eastwhatthefuck! You got me? I'm already up to it! A firefight? Dead guys? Secret flights—what is this, a James Bond movie? Do you know how much it costs to run a black-box flight out of Moscow?" Without waiting, Boxer continued. "I didn't think so. And who *is* this Russian national you brought out?"

"Boss, hold on. Look, she has very reliable information about a potential plot to assassinate the President."

After a long silence, Boxer said, "I'm listening."

Shelby told her boss about Olegina, Polar Strike, and the attack outside of Andrews Air Base.

"That's ... like a sci-fi story or something."

"I know—I know, but it can't be a coincidence someone tried to kill us right after we left the base."

"Okay. Bring her—this Bortsova woman—bring her in and let's take it from there."

Olegina could not hear the total conversation but Shelby's body language suggested she was moving into uncharted territory.

"Actually boss, there is one part of the plot we don't understand."

"What's that?"

"The Senator's trigger. Like what causes him to become activated."

"Sooo ... what?"

"So I'd like to run that down."

"How?"

Shelby glanced at Olegina, giving her an unconvincing nod. "Find and debrief Senator Ford's doctor."

"What? Where—New York?"

As meekly as Shelby could muster, she replied, "Yes, boss."

"Out of the question. This is insane. I can't have a Federal agent snooping around the background of the incoming Vice President of the United States. It's—"

"Look boss, what if this is real? Weird stuff happens more than we think. We still haven't found the air hijacker, D.B. Cooper. The Black Dahlia murder in Los Angeles, never solved. The Atlanta Olympic Bomber in 1996, we had the wrong guy for the longest time. Robert Hanssen, one of our own, selling intel to the Soviets for twenty years. The Bureau missed the nine-eleven bombers—wasn't there a memo out of Phoenix in 2001, something about Middle Eastern guys taking flight training, learning to take off but not land airplanes and seeking information on how to penetrate airport security? It got stuck in the chain of command because no one could make heads or tails out it. I don't want us to make the same mistake. It sounds crazy I know, but we should run it down."

After a moment, Boxer tersely said, "Okay. A day. Up and back and stay connected. You got me agent?"

"Yes ma'am."

After a four-hour drive, the Tahoe emerged from the Holland Tunnel into lower Manhattan. Making their way uptown, Olegina momentarily forgot the last two days as her neck swiveled like that of a child's doll. New York was everything imaginable. The sidewalks were filled with people moving with purpose. While she knew Americans suffered the same daily indignities that Russians did—bills to pay, weather, health issues, failed relationships—these people seemed to be shrugging it off in a hurry to get to the next adventure, or maybe she was wrong altogether. Either way, it was all very exhilarating.

Hypervigilant, Shelby drove slowly, checking her mirrors every ten seconds.

"You hungry?"

Olegina had not even thought about this until she was asked. "Yes."

"Okay. Let's ditch the Hummer. I'm sure the mess at Andrews is on the wire already."

"The wire?"

Shelby said nothing while trying to find CBS 1010, New York's all-news station on the radio.

"What are we going to do?" Olegina softly asked.

Shelby looked away from the road. "Somebody just tried to kill us for one of two things: for the file itself or to keep us from letting someone know what's in it. Either way, I'm not sure whom to trust with this. This is a mess."

Olegina's head bobbed in agreement.

"But the one thing we don't know is what triggers Ford to activate his programming."

Shelby pulled into a parking garage, found a buried space in back, parked the Hummer, and began wiping down the steering wheel. Olegina did the same. Exiting, they joined the sidewalk stream. At a nondescript cafe, Shelby guided them inside. Taking a booth away from the windows, but with good sightlines, Shelby handed Olegina a menu while watching the door.

"I think we're okay for the moment. Try the Denver omelet."

"What is a Denver *umlet*?"

"Trust me, you'll like it. Hey, let me see the file again."

Beneath the table, the Russian gave the dossier to her, but after a minute of looking through it, Shelby quietly put it down. "This thing is like a jargon swamp." She turned to look out the window.

In no time, their food arrived, just as two men drifted down the other side of the street. The FBI agent's senses went on high alert when a third man, opposite the two across the street, meandered down their side of the avenue.

"Go to the bathroom," Shelby said under her breath.

"What, the food just—" but Shelby's alarmed demeanor killed off her protest. "I'll meet you there."

Olegina left while Shelby waited. As the man passed the cafe, Shelby lifted her cellphone, turned toward the wall, and feigned having a conversation. Once the man had moved by without stopping, she pocketed her phone, dropped a twenty on the table, grabbed the file, and walked to the bathroom.

But the ladies's room was empty.

"Olie?" Shelby checked the stalls. "Olie!"

Outside the window, came a muffled cry. Shelby raced to the back door in time to see three men shoving the struggling Russian woman into a Suburban. As they piled in, a dark-haired female, holding the door, shot Shelby a lethal glance before sneeringly jumping into the passenger seat.

"Ah, shit!"

Shelby drew her side arm, but unwilling to risk hitting Olegina, watched angrily as the vehicle tore down the alley, fishtailing away into traffic.

Options raced through her mind when finally a thought surfaced, "Ford's trigger. That's what they're looking for."

Shelby returned to the stolen Hummer they'd dumped earlier. Inside, she weighed her options. Suddenly her cellphone rang: an unrecognized number.

"Hello?"

"Agent Littlejohn, bring the folder to Times Square. One hour. You'll be contacted there." The line went dead.

Shelby fought back an urge to cry in rage. She slowed her thoughts. "They have her and they're controlling the situation. But ... how did they get my number?"

Her eyes returned to her phone, then to the Hummer's dashboard. Cellphone or vehicle, her movements were being tracked. She needed to change up the dialogue.

Dropping her phone on the vehicle's floor, she took the blue folder and exited. At the first convenience store, she used cash to buy a cheap throwaway phone and a protein shake. Taking a sip, Shelby grimaced remembering that she and Olegina had not eaten breakfast. The archivist had to be famished, in addition to being terrified.

Shelby ran a diagnostic on her situation. She was off the reservation now. Her little field trip to New York had blown up and there was no good outcome for Olegina—or the last shred of Shelby's career if she didn't get the Russian and the folder *and* Ford's trigger back to DC.

Shelby slowed her breathing. "Time to make some changes here. I'm tired of being on the receiving end." In a small park, she found a bench and sat down. They'd be looking for her before she ever stepped into Times Square. Whoever these people were, they would have seen by now that her cellphone had not moved in ten minutes, alerting them that she was onto them.

Looking at a nearby garbage can, she got an idea.

CHAPTER 71

JANUARY
NEW YORK
TWO DAYS TO INAUGURATION

Olegina blinked as a black hood over her head was brusquely yanked off. A second later came a vicious slap across the face. Tears pooled as her eyes came to focus on a strikingly beautiful, dark-haired woman, hood in hand before her. Olegina was tied to an extremely uncomfortable, wooden, foldout chair. On a table next to her was her cellphone—now plugged into a scanner—and some surgical knives. Glancing about revealed only that she was in a dark, windowless room. She could hear traffic in the background.

"Good. I have your attention," Sigrid said.

From behind the woman came a man she immediately recognized.

"Yuri," Olegina whispered, voice tinged with both fear and hate.

The thug smirked but said nothing.

"We know you brought the file from Lubyanka to Washington. What's in it?"

Olegina stared dumbstruck before quickly filling in the blanks between Anna, Yuri, this woman, and the secret files room. "I've scanned it once, but I'm unfamiliar with the folder's contents."

Another hard slap. "Why bring it here?"

Whimpering, Olegina yelped, "When I saw Ford's name, I knew I was in beyond my ability. I met an FBI agent last year who I thought could help."

"Why'd you leave Washington?" The woman asked like a biologist examining a fly beneath a microscope.

Olegina hesitated, never seeing the woman's fist as it smashed her left ear.

"*Der'mo*! Stop hitting me, you psycho bitch!"

"Do you see Yuri?"

Olegina's eyes flickered from her interrogator to Anna's killer. "He's a pig and vulgar, but he's expressed interest in spending some quality time with you." Sigrid grabbed the terrified archivist's blonde hair. "Now, why are you and Agent Littlejohn here?"

At the mention of Shelby's name, Olegina shot a glance at Sigrid, who hissed, "We know who she is, and we're going to kill her and you. Now again, why are you here?"

Rapidly deducing she had little negotiating leverage, a sudden calm came over Olegina. "You're going to activate Ford," she gasped, "but you're missing something. That's why you need the folder."

The temperature in the room suddenly dropped as Sigrid's eyes became slits. Wordlessly, she nodded at Yuri, "We need her for the swap. But after we have the file and have killed the FBI woman," Sigrid smiled evilly at Olegina, "she's yours."

Turning to examine her cellphone, Sigrid said, "I'll be back in half an hour, have her ready."

CHAPTER 72

JANUARY
NEW YORK
TIMES SQUARE
TWO DAYS TO INAUGURATION

Beneath a large billboard for the *Phantom of the Opera* across from a busy pretzel kiosk were a banquette of concrete barriers that tourists sat upon. Unlike Moscow, Olegina had never seen so many people happy to stand in line to pay exorbitant sums for a snack that cost pennies to produce. She envied them.

Next to her sat Yuri, who was strangely more nervous than Olegina. They were at the end of a bench, Yuri seated against a plastic display case with bus schedules. The thug had his arm around her, his hand over her breast. Just inside his expensive, Italian leather jacket, he fingered a built-in silencer Maxim Nine pistol, hard up against Olegina's ribs. Sitting in thirty-two-degree weather, Yuri's body heat actually felt good.

"Where is she?" Yuri said, frost and agitation wrapping his words like a snow parka. Glancing at his watch provided no insight. "I need a fuckin' cigarette."

Olegina turned, condescendingly inspecting her captor. Yuri did not take kindly to her examination, shoving his pistol harder into her side. "What?"

She grunted. "Any harder, we'll have to get a room."

"Shut up, bitch."

Just then, a NYC sanitation cart pulled up, partially blocking their view of the kiosk. A worker began sweeping around them.

Yuri pushed the worker. "Hey, get this thing away from—"

The worker, an African-American woman turned, leaning in toward them. "Sorry sir, I didn't mean anything." Recognition came too late. Yuri never felt the Taser sting that immobilized him. Shelby pushed Yuri's weapon down, but with his last convulsion, his finger pressed the trigger, discharging a silenced round quietly and safely into the street; it hit a bus tire—the blowout being masked by traffic.

Shelby rapidly removed the pistol from his grip, simultaneously zip-tying his hands to a belt loop on his trousers and then to the bench. Removing a small rubber ball, she wedged it into his mouth before turning to Olegina.

The Russian woman's face was frozen in shock as Yuri, while conscious, could only moan. Shelby leaned the thug against a light pole, pulling his jacket over his hands.

Loudly, she said, "Yes sir, I'm sorry. I'll move the cart now."

Firmly grasping Olegina's arm, Shelby muscled her up. "They're watching us. Let's go!" Shelby whispered into her ear.

Like a cornered animal, Olegina glanced about the square wildly. "Who?"

Roughly shoving Olegina down, she pulled a flap aside on the cart. "Get in!"

A bullet hit the concrete next to them. Olegina's reflexes took over as she lurched into the cart. "Go!"

Now reacting to an unknown, but immediately evident danger, the crowd awkwardly cast about for perspective on where the threat lay while simultaneously looking for a way out. Confusion morphed into panic as more bullets ricocheted about them, but the dispersing mob rapidly created cover, as Shelby pushed the cart through traffic to a fast-food store. Once inside, she yanked Olegina from below and raced for the alleyway exit behind the store's cooking area.

Outside, she stripped off the coveralls, revealing the dirty clothes she'd been wearing since early in the morning. Noticing the perplexed look on Olegina's face, she said, "I sort of borrowed them ... the cart and a truck from a sanitation worker at Washington Park. I'll get em' back—look, are you okay?"

Heavily breathing, Olegina fought back tears. "What is going on? He was going to kill me!"

Shelby attempted to calm her hysteria. "Look, you're out of danger. I've got the folder. We'll just go back to Washington, brief the desk chief, and let them deal with it. You've done enough. Either way, I'm not putting you at any more risk."

Smothering her lips with her hand, Olegina turned away, seeking comfort from the alley's grimy brick wall. Her internal voice shouted, "Should never have opened my mouth. This whole mess is fucking me. Let the bosses figure it out." But then an image passed through her mind.

A scrolling loop of the documentation she'd been forced to digest in her work at Rosarkhiv. Orders of routine executions of countless innocents, to preserve a soulless machine of feckless and bureaucratic merchants of evil. How many families had been wiped clean, loved ones lost—or been banished to Stalin's Death Ring—because people in a position to know otherwise or to stop it, had not stood up to history's thugs?

Wiping frozen tears from her eyes, she swiveled to Shelby. "We are not done yet. We need Ford's trigger, yes?"

While not friends, Shelby wanted to make things right. "You sure?"

The Russian woman nodded emphatically.

Shelby inclined her head, smiling. "Let's see what we can find at this Doctor Grigor's clinic."

CHAPTER 73

JANUARY
BROOKLYN
TWO DAYS TO INAUGURATION

Outside the hospital, Nic made his way toward his car, his mind wandering, "What could those numbers mean." Again, an image of the geocaching book came to mind. His phone rang. It was Chris.

"Yo, cuz how's it hanging? Ready for the big day?"

"Yeah."

Fear and apprehension radiated through his phone.

"What's going on? You sound stressed."

A moment of silence before Chris spoke. "Look, it may be nothing, but I called Stephan a couple of times yesterday and again this morning, but he's not responded. Could you swing by and see if he's okay?"

"Yeah sure. Clinic or house?"

"I don't know. Both. He may just be sick, but I know we were supposed to talk this week."

"On it. I'll call you back." Before hanging up, Nic added, "You sure you're okay?"

"Thanks man. See you in a couple of days." Chris hung up.

Examining the dead phone, Nic shrugged and started for his patrol car. As he walked, he thought, "Not like Chris to sound spooked. Maybe just the inauguration stress." Still, it gave Nic a slight chill.

In the car, he checked the geographic-information system for Grigor's addresses and then set a course for Manhattan. As he drove, he called both known numbers for the Doctor. House, then clinic, but to no avail.

It had been a few years since he was on patrol and he paused to recall the procedures for a police welfare check. At its very essence, this type of check required no court order or approval. At the request of a community member who has reason to believe someone might be in trouble, police may enter a premises or place of business. Still, this being Doctor Grigor, Nic was a little hesitant to barge in without a clear-and-present danger.

The other thing inducing his reluctance was a basic uncertainty about Stephan Grigor. Being seven years older than Chris, and living three subway trains away, his Grandmother Elena had not taken him to see Grigor. He'd appeared on the scene about the time that Doctor Merinov had retired. Nothing extraordinary about that, still Nic had never really felt comfortable around the hard-to-understand Russian. But he appeared to have the confidence of both Chris and Mallory, so what did Nic know?

At Grigor's brownstone, Nic drove by the front and then around the back. He parked. Back door. Locked. No apparent activity inside. He redialed the home number. While the phone rang from within the unit, Nic detected nothing unusual and returned to his unmarked police interceptor.

At Columbus Circle, he parked in the garage and made his way upstairs. The clinic had both a public entrance and a back entrance, for use by the building's maintenance department, the cleaning company, and other service providers. On the main floor, he opted to take the building's internal common corridor, which took him by the Clinic for Right Being's rear-access way. While the door would be locked, he'd be able to partially ascertain if something was amiss before moving into the public area and around to the CRB's main entrance.

Reaching the landing to the back corridor, he paused to catch his breath, thinking, "This beat duty is definitely for the kids."

But as he opened the door, he could hear what sounded like hushed voices from around the corridor's corner. Brow furrowed, he leaned back against the wall. Heart beating faster than it had in years, his hand fumbled into his jacket, closing assuredly around the grip of his service revolver. Slowly, Nic inched his way along the wall toward the whispering.

"I think it's locked."

"I have a lock-picking device—hold on."

Uncertain as to what was going on, he considered going back and radioing in for back up.

"Even if we get in, how do we know what to look for?"

"Something related to Christopher Ford, I imagine."

Nic's gut tightened. Removing his flashlight, he laid it along the top of his gun, turned it on, and stepped around the corner.

Two intruders were testing the door to the Clinic for Right Being.

Nic's voice wavered, "Freeze, do not move! Put your hands above your head and turn toward me! Slowly!"

Hands raised, the burglars glacially rotated toward the intensely alert but uncertain Inspector.

CHAPTER 74

JANUARY
THE PLAZA HOTEL
VADIK'S SUITE
TWO DAYS TO INAUGURATION

Sigrid sat at a writing desk while Vadik relaxed on the sofa, a cold washcloth over his eyes. Without looking up from her laptop, she said, "We're very close to being active."

Removing the cloth, he rubbed his eyes. Gently dismissing her, Vadik said, "First things first, where is she?" He tersely asked as if wiping lint from his suit.

"She is gone," Sigrid replied. Vadik's scowl induced her to continue. "Yuri was set to make the exchange in Times Square when the FBI agent, Littlejohn, camouflaged herself as a city worker and freed the archivist while immobilizing Yuri."

Bringing his hands together, Vadik rubbed his fingertips. "I've never been displeased with your services, but I must say this particular operation has produced an unusual number of ... *setbacks*. Can Yuri be traced to us?"

"No, General. He is in police custody, but he has no ID on him and we have his passport. The authorities will make inquiries in the Russian community, but he is untraceable."

"Can he be ... eliminated?"

"Our contact at NYPD thinks it can be handled tonight."

Satisfied, Vadik nodded before continuing. "And the archivist? Any idea of her location?"

"Uncertain, General. She escaped with the FBI woman and we are looking for them."

“But we don’t need Bortsova if we have Grigor’s information and files, correct?”

“Yes, General,” she rubbed her earlobe, “but I’m not sure we have his complete cooperation.”

Imperiously, Vadik lifted his chin, growing displeased with the tepidly, incomplete responses. “How so?”

“Uncertain. Please don’t misunderstand—he was most forthcoming,” Sigrid replied with a hint of thaw.

Vadik could tell she likely employed some of her favored tools of persuasion. As long as he got what he wanted, he was fine with her satisfying her needs. “Why? Will activating Ford prove difficult?”

“Not as hard as I would have thought.”

Vadik nodded slowly. “What is his trigger?”

Sigrid paused. “A phrase.”

“Just a phrase?” Vadik asked, mildly curious. “A simple phrase will set in motion one of the most dramatic changes in world history?” His mind drifted to flushing bears from cover. “What is it?”

Sigrid crossed her hands in her lap, clearly relishing the moment. “The long and brutal winter gives way to spring.”

Blinking rapidly, Vadik’s mouth opened but he could only stare. Finally, “That’s it?”

“Yes, General. Seems the programming worked best for Mr. Ford when the commands were simple and easy to follow.”

“Is he programmed now?”

“Programmed, yes. Activated, no. If ever the plan was to be implemented, Grigor was to deliver the phrase via a phone call.”

“So how will we—”

“Doctor Grigor will deliver the phrase in a phone call the morning of the inauguration.”

Vadik beamed, “Excellent.” Then another thought clouded his face. “What keeps Ford from attacking the president the first time he sees him?”

“I had the same thought, General. As you recall the programming only calls for a sleeper agent—once activated—to kill his or her immediate supervisor. As we understand the Polar Strike file, Ford will kill his immediate supervisor, the President, only after Johansen has completed the Oath of Office, becoming Christopher Ford's boss."

Vadik stood and moved to the window overlooking Central Park. "Simple and yet effective."

"This year, there is a deviation in the Inaugural schedule. After Johansen is sworn in, he will retake his seat while opera star Miko Devanney sings 'America the Beautiful.' Afterward, Johansen delivers his inaugural remarks. While Ms. Devanney is performing, Ford will kill the president."

"How?"

"Mrs. Ford suffers from allergies and she carries an autoimmune injector to counter the sudden onset of symptoms that can kill her. Unknown to her, the injector's medicine will be replaced with phenol. Now, for the ceremony, guests are required to leave purses, bags, and cases with security in the Capitol prior to moving onto the Inaugural platform. Vice President Ford will be carrying his wife's injector in his coat pocket for the duration of the ceremony. Once Johansen retakes his seat next to Ford, the Vice President will use his wife's medical device to inject the President."

Confusion came over the General's face. "So, why the concern?"

The Swedish assassin paused, unable to articulate a clear response. "Something seems off about the Doctor. Grigor gave us everything we wanted, but as if he was keeping—how do the Americans call it—an ace in the hole?"

Rather than following along, Vadik appeared distant.

Finally Sigrid asked, "Is there another thought on the General's mind?"

"Just wondering," Vadik rubbed imaginary stubble on his face, "why is the plot still in place?"

"General?"

"I mean, if Polar Strike was largely a failure, why did the KGB keep it in motion?"

Sigrid put down her laptop, "While the program was discredited, because of the lack of brainwashing successes, Grupp continued it. Perhaps out of pride. Maybe a hope it might eventually work, a sense of destiny—there could be a multitude of reasons we're not privy to.

And while not a rogue operation, it was off the books. As the General is aware, Grupp never reported up the chain of command that Polar Strike was still in play."

"Could this be what you're alluding to with Grigor—his sense of duty?"

"Possibly. But I share the General's curiosity. Would Doctor Grigor have activated Ford even if we had not contacted him?"

Vadik firmly responded. "No, I don't believe so. If he's worked with Ford since childhood, it is probable he has formed an emotional bond with the man. I imagine the plot was never going to be activated. And yet Doctor Grigor's pride in his work prevented him from the cessation of programming Senator Ford, his one success." Vadik paused, then added, "Tell me, did the Doctor seem surprised we'd contacted him?"

Sigrid crossed her arms in thought, "Actually, no. Bruno Shakli, our mystery man who broke into your office, had been leaning on Doctor Grigor for years in an attempt to stay abreast of what Ford and the District Attorney's office were investigating. Areas of inquiry, persons of interest—mostly a form of surveillance and to keep the DA from Shakli's front door, I presume. Shakli originally posed as KGB before revealing himself to Grigor. So, when we met him, Grigor initially thought we were connected to Shakli. But after dispelling that—I made clear who we were and that we wanted Polar Strike activated—he seemed ... almost relieved."

Wrinkling his brow, Vadik stood and went to the dining-room table. Absently, he poured a cup of coffee. "We still need the archivist tracked down. She and the FBI woman are loose ends."

"Already in motion. We have some contacts in the Department of Justice. When the FBI woman resurfaces, we'll know, and those threads will be tied off. Then, we'll have the file Ms. Bortsova brought to America; thus eliminating everyone who has knowledge of Polar Strike."

"With the exception of Bruno Shakli. But I'm willing to bet he's running now. We won't hear from him again."

"Yes, General."

"So, what could Grigor be holding back?" Coffee in hand, he drifted to the window, looking down upon the Park, he mused. "I think you should spend some more time with the good Doctor."

A tiny smile creased Sigrid's face. "Yes, General."

CHAPTER 75

JANUARY
COLUMBUS CIRCLE
NYPD TRANSIT BUREAU DISTRICT
TWO DAYS TO INAUGURATION

Seated in an uncomfortable, gunmetal-gray chair, legs crossed to affect a relaxed manner, Nic studied the two women before him. After the African-American woman had identified herself as FBI, he'd brought both of them across the street to the Transit Bureau offices. In handcuffs. The other woman was clearly Russian and had said little since their arrival.

With Littlejohn's ID in hand, Nic grilled the women. "Why don't you want me to contact your office again?"

"Officer ... what is your name, again?" Shelby snidely asked, clearly bothered that she was still handcuffed to the interrogation-room table—a role reversal from her years of grilling suspects under similar circumstances.

"Why does that matter?" Nic testily replied as he thought, "Something about these two isn't right." He glanced at the other woman who refused to meet his eyes.

"Look, I've identified myself to a fellow law enforcement professional. I would think you could extend me some professional courtesy and uncuff us."

"Why were you trying to break into the Clinic for Right Being? Why don't you want me to call FBI headquarters in DC?"

"I told you—" Shelby barked, before catching herself. It was time to lay some of her cards out. "Officer, we're trying to run to ground a potential lead on a national security investigation."

Nic's brow furrowed, his eyes drifting to the folder sitting to his right on the desk. "Does it have something to do with ... " he rotated the fading red file so he could read it. "My Cyrillic alphabet is rusty, but not my limited understanding of forensics. What does this say? And of equal consideration ... why is part of it covered in dried blood?"

Secured to separate handcuff rings in the center of the table, the two women unconsciously exchanged nervous glances. This only agitated their interrogator.

"Okay, ladies. I've been patient, but my next—" A knock outside the interrogation room derailed Nic's thought. "Come!" He bellowed.

A uniformed police officer stepped in, handing a note to Nic. "Inspector Ford, the number for the FBI's National Security duty office."

Shelby and Olegina looked from the police woman to Nic who was momentarily distracted scanning the paper. As the officer left, Nic looked up into two sets of astonished eyes. "What?" He stuttered, a chill passing through him.

"Nicholas Ford? Cousin of the incoming Vice President?" Shelby whispered.

"Yeah?" Nic's gaze bounced between the FBI agent to the Russian woman, finally coming to the folder on the table and back again. Coming erect, he slammed the desk top. "What the hell is this? You better start talking right now," he said with false bravado.

Shelby nodded before drilling Nic with hard eyes. "You're not going to believe me," she hesitated for effect. "But you better. Un-cuff us and give me the folder."

An image of winter and his grandmother's adage passed through his mind: "The reckoning." Reluctantly, Nic freed them. He pushed the folder to Shelby, who in-turn, gave it to Olegina.

Tapping the folder, Shelby looked into the historian's eyes before gesturing with her head toward Nic. "Talk."

CHAPTER 76

JANUARY
STEPHAN GRIGOR'S BROWNSTONE
TWO DAYS TO INAUGURATION

Seated at Grigor's modern, teak desk, Vadik admired the *Jupiter and Thetis* portrait. "Doctor, I really commend your aesthetic. Your home is most tasteful." Slowly, he swiveled the chair to face front where Grigor sat naked, gagged, and secured to one of his dining-table chairs.

Next to him stood Sigrid, clad in a black, skin-tight dress and stiletto heels. In one hand, she clutched a handheld stun gun, in the other, Grigor's hair.

Vadik softly asked, "Now Doctor, I want to know everything. Surely you don't need another dose of persuasion from my assistant." This produced muffled screaming from Grigor. Vadik nodded and Sigrid pulled the ball gag from Grigor's mouth.

"You know everything! There's nothing else to tell! Please!" Sigrid took up the stun gun as Grigor bent over to protect himself. "No!" He whimpered.

"Doctor?" Vadik inquired.

Sigrid's lips creased with a hint of mirth as she leaned in. "I understand your balls will never work the same after I'm through." She placed the gun next to Grigor's ear, but before she turned it on, Grigor jerked away.

"Okay! Enough," he dejectedly said, his last shred of dignity evaporating. "There's one wrinkle. When the call is placed to Ford, if the triggering phrase is in Russian, it's meaningless. In English, it will activate Ford's programming."

Vadik leaned forward. "Most revealing. Why hold this back? Were you planning to try to deceive us?"

Before Grigor could reply, Sigrid wedged the gag back into place.

"Perhaps you have more to share? I'm going to step out for a moment while my assistant continues to debrief you."

This was met with violent, smothered screams from Grigor, but Sigrid was already closing the door after Vadik. Donning latex gloves, she turned the stun gun on; Grigor wet himself.

* * * *

Byrnes sat at his desk in the Capitol reviewing, for the umpteenth time, the briefing book for the Inaugural Ceremony. As Speaker of the House—and number three in line for the Presidency—he would be seated adjacent the incoming President and Vice President. Just then, his assistant buzzed him.

"Mr. Speaker, the Secret Service is here to review tomorrow's security protocol." Every four years, Congress would organize a Joint Committee of Inaugural Ceremonies. While the Chairperson of the group was historically a senator from the party in charge of the Senate, the Speaker, regardless of party, always provided significant input to the order of ceremonies. A major part of this was protecting the President, President-elect, and the vast array of assembled dignitaries on the dais for the Inauguration.

Tapping the intercom button, he said, "Thank you, I'll be right out."

His private cell vibrated from inside his coat watch-pocket. The special phone—the one he was increasingly fearful of, but lusted for nonetheless, as it promised a visit from the caller's assistant.

Since being named Speaker, Sigrid had made three visits, each time presenting him with something General Pyotr would like introduced ... or added to, pending legislation. Each had been spending or appropriations related—all things that would benefit the Russian's vast network of businesses, investments, or interests. And, not inconsequentially, each also benefited a business in Byrnes's district or somewhere in the Palmetto State. Not once had there been anything that could be interpreted as threatening to American national security.

So, why the increasing nervousness about taking his calls? When being handled by the KGB and passing information to Marta—who'd since disappeared after General Pyotr arrived on the scene—he'd been actually doing more damage to America than now. Perhaps it was the perception of having fallen into a spider's web. The things Sigrid did to him were depraved and yet he could not break her spell.

"Hello Vad—General," Byrnes said with guarded neutrality.

"Mr. Speaker. Good morning, I hope I am calling at a good time."

"Just about to take a meeting with the Secret Service."

"Ah yes, of course. The ceremony, no doubt. I really didn't want to intrude, just to say hello and that I'm looking forward to another year of great accomplishments. Is there anything we can do for you right now?"

"Not now, but perhaps ... in the next week, Sigrid could brief me on your thoughts for the coming year?"

"Most excellent. She'll be in contact. I hope the Inauguration is the best ever. You've worked very hard, I'm sure, putting it together."

"Thank you, General. Please have her call me when it is convenient."

"Mr. Speaker."

Byrnes stared at the silent phone: a promise and a threat.

CHAPTER 77

JANUARY
COLUMBUS CIRCLE
NYPD TRANSIT BUREAU DISTRICT
TWO DAYS TO INAUGURATION

Nic stared at the two women as if they'd arrived from another planet.

"Inspector, you can't kick us. I know it's bizarre, but you gotta believe it."

Shaking his head, Nic gestured at the open file in the table center. "This is just too outlandish."

"Is it really? Look closer at the wording—"

"At what?" Nic snapped.

Shelby reached in, randomly flipping pages. "Even if you can't read Russian, look how many times the name *Ford* is mentioned. *Even you* can read Cyrillic for the name of *Christopher* and," Shelby hesitated, "this one." She pointed to a name, leaving her finger next to it for emphasis.

Nic nodded slowly. "Elena."

"Your grandmother, if I'm correct?"

He looked up—first at Shelby, then Olegina, looking for signs of duplicity. "I need to call Chris."

"No!"

The two law-enforcement agents turned to regard the until-now silent Russian.

Practically pleading, Olegina said, "Inspector, I left Moscow one step ahead of the people who killed my friend at Lubyanka. If you need, you can call the police in Moscow. I'm sure they can confirm the archive killings. But we don't know Mr. Ford's—your cousin's—triggers. I'm sure if we found them, we could prevent them from being activated."

"That's why we were at the Clinic."

Nic put his hand up. "Okay. Let me try Stephan—Doctor Grigor—again." He dialed the clinic.

The receptionist answered, "Clinic for Right Being, the offices of Stephan Grigor."

"Hi Erika, this is Christopher Ford's cousin, Nic Ford. Is Doctor Grigor in?" From the other side of the table, Shelby and Olegina could detect the tension in the woman's voice. "I see. Okay, if you hear from him, please ask him to call me ASAP. It's very important." Putting his cellphone on the table, Nic said, "He didn't come in today and his assistant said it is very unusual for him not to call in when sick or planning on being out."

Suddenly, their vacuum of uncertainty was flooded with a tidal wave of dread; all three knew something awful had taken place that would lead to something even worse. Nic thought for a moment before bolting up. Taking the file, he handed it to Olegina.

"All right you two, let's go."

CHAPTER 78

JANUARY
STEPHAN GRIGOR'S BROWNSTONE
TWO DAYS TO INAUGURATION

A dim bulb—seemingly unsuited for its purpose—cast dark light over the back patio, portending a grim outcome. He knocked once out of habit; then Nic removed a sleeve of lock-pick tools and set to jimmying the door.

"I'll pretend I did not witness this," Shelby jokingly offered.

Nic grunted. "Wouldn't want the FBI to compromise those Olympian standards of theirs."

"Touché."

Unfamiliar with American legal concepts, Olegina was still certain that forcing a man's door open was out-of-bounds. Listening to the two law-enforcement agents exchange barbs, Olegina grasped the nuances of the tension-breaking humor and joined them in a halfhearted chuckle.

The door *popped*. Inside, both Nic and Shelby drew their sidearms.

Shelby whispered to Olegina, "Stay here. I'll come back after we determine it's safe. You got me?" Before she could say anything, the FBI woman faded into the darkness.

Vaguely familiar with the layout from previous visits, Nic instinctively made his way across the kitchen. He paused at a pocket bathroom before moving quietly through the living room into the foyer. On previous visits, he'd never been invited to this side of the house. Creeping down a hall, he abruptly came to a stop. His gut tightened as he took note of the low light emanating under the closed door to the study. Shelby came alongside.

Exchanging silent hand signals, they took up station on either side of the door.

"Stephan?"

No answer.

"Stephan? It's Nic Ford. Are you in there?"

Moaning came from beyond the door. Nic did not hesitate, pushing the door aside. The two law enforcement agents moved inside, first determining the room was secure before approaching a still-naked Grigor, sprawled on the floor. He'd been tortured and left to die.

"Stephan!" Finding a throw on the sofa, Nic covered the beaten psychiatrist. Glancing at Shelby, he said, "Get some water please, then bring Ms. Bortsova inside, lock the door, and call an ambulance!"

Grigor was a man Nic had known from afar most of his life; still, the Inspector was filled with rage at the shattered husk before him. He set about making him as comfortable as possible. Shelby and Olegina quietly arrived. Taking a bottle of water from Shelby, Nic held it to Grigor's bleeding lips.

"Stephan, who did this?"

Gasping, Grigor cried as he sucked water. "After Chris and ... " more water and shaking, "Polar Strike."

At this, Olegina gripped Shelby's arm, her eyes as large as moons. Shelby knelt next to Nic.

"Doctor, who? What did they want?"

"The trigger."

Shelby and Nic exchanged glances. "What is it, Doctor?" she asked.

Gasping, Grigor said, "I told—"

Nic jumped in. "Told them what? Stephan, told them *what*?"

Grigor grunted, "The long and brutal winter gives way to spring."

"What is—is that the trigger?" Shelby agitatedly asked.

"Yes. But ... English no—" Grigor spit up blood. "No good. Russian ... " the rest of his words softened to gibberish.

Shelby shook Grigor. "In Russian what? What!"

Grigor's eyes glassed over. And then, as if someone unseen had called his name, Grigor opened his eyes, but all he could see was the Red Square May Day parades of his youth and the Russian national anthem pouring across a proud people gathered to honor its heroes. He started crying as the Premier pointed to him and everyone turned to clap as he received the Order of Lenin.

Shelby slapped the doctor, bringing a momentary return of his senses. "What about Russian!"

"Russian, activates Chris programming." Grigor's breath rasped.

"How?" Nic yelled at Grigor.

Grigor pulled Nic's head down to his mouth. Nic nodded desperately, before sitting up, staring at Grigor incomprehensibly.

"Cellphone? What does it do?" Nic asked.

Convulsing, Grigor muttered, "Activates—"

Nic appeared to be in shock as he processed what this meant.

"How, Doctor?" Ignoring Nic's stern glare, Shelby gently shook Grigor. "How does the trigger work?"

"*No ya obmanul vsekh.*"

"What?" Shelby barked, shaking Grigor. "Son of a bitch!" She turned to Olegina who appeared to be thinking, her brow wrinkled. "What was that?"

"He said—"

Grigor shot a hand out to Nic. "Thetis ... " But this was all he could muster, his breath dying on his last word—lungs decompressing, Grigor's body fell slack, his spirit summoning him. Nic stared catatonically at the body as Shelby gently draped the blanket over Grigor's face.

After a moment, his face scowled. "What?" First at Shelby, then to Olegina. "What did he say?"

"Thetis?" Shelby replied, equally perplexed.

From the door, came a whisper: "The picture." Nic and Shelby looked up at Olegina, who slowly pointed.

Nic and Shelby were both shocked by the massive painting they'd initially missed; it dominated the room. Nic arose and went around behind Grigor's desk. "Olegina, please turn the overhead light on." Simultaneously, Nic rotated the desk lamp, directing its beam at the canvas. He studied it futilely. "Sooo, what am I looking at?"

The women joined him. Nic removed his pocket flashlight. "Light is bad in here." Probing the surface yielded nothing.

"Wait. Go back," Olegina said. "There, in Thetis's hair." She took the torch from Nic, using it to highlight a section of the painting. Without hesitation, she pushed the hidden release buried in the brown locks. All three jumped. From beneath the carpet, the plate concealing the floor recess ratcheted open.

Stripping the rug away, they were dumbfounded by Grigor's last redoubt. "I've seen these before. Here, give me some light." Olegina illuminated the recess as Nic pushed the sides. Hitting on the second push, Nic was still surprised as rumbling came from the hole. As if the day could get any stranger, a safe emerged from the floor into view.

All three exchanged looks, afraid to take their eyes off the vault. Hesitantly, Nic skirted the vault, gently probing it with the flashlight, before coming back in front. He poked the combination spinner, glancing at Grigor's body, "Now what?"

"Ahh, shit." The other two glanced at Shelby just in time to see her withdraw her sidearm. "Sorry, Inspector, we don't have time for this. Stand back."

At the sight of the weapon, images of Lubyanka flashed through Olegina's mind. A terrified sob escaped her mouth as without a second thought, Shelby aimed dead center at the dial and fired. The cacophonous *bang* died away, leaving a dial-less safe. Nic hesitantly rotated the handle and the door swung open. Quickly setting aside his misgivings about lawful search and seizure, he pulled money, documents, and jewelry aside, before finding a file labeled: FORD.

Tears welled in his eyes, momentarily thinking of reading it, before he handed the file to Shelby. Taking it to the desk, she motioned for the still-shaking Olegina to join her. Opening it, they quickly dissected it. After a moment, they paused. Shelby looked up into Nic's distraught eyes.

"What?"

She shook her head, "Inspector—Nic, you sure you want—"

"Tell me, damn it."

Shelby looked up as Olegina gently nodded, putting a hand on the agent's shoulder.

"Okay." Shelby gathered herself. "It's all here. Everything we told you back at the station. Polar Strike was born in the fifties, nursed to life by some guy named Ivan Serov."

"The Butcher," Olegina whispered. Aware of the silence in the room, she added, "Worked for Beria and then was the KGB Chairman after Stalin died. Removed by Khrushchev. Vicious man."

"So, why would this be in Grigor's safe?" As if answering his own question, Nic sat down. "Stephan was brainwashing Chris."

"Broader plan was intended to gut American leadership in the event of a nuclear war; they were using brainwashed moles, inserted into various positions within the American government, who—when activated—would kill their immediate supervisors."

"Why?" Nic asked.

Shelby looked up from the file. "Probably to disrupt the chain of command, create chaos, fear, or paralyze the American response to a Soviet first strike. But eventually, the Kremlin deactivated the program. Apparently, over the decades, the Russians found that the brainwashing was really ineffective ... except—" Shelby's voice trailed off, pursing her lips, eyes not meeting Nic's.

"What?" he asked.

Looking up into the distraught detective's eyes, she could hardly speak. "There was one successful case. Christopher Ford. Grigor ... and your grandmother, were running this op." She let this sink in for a moment before adding, "But it doesn't say for what purpose."

Angry, Nic forced himself to concentrate. "Is the plot still active?"

The FBI woman gestured to Grigor's covered body. "Someone still thinks it is. Everything in this file confirms what we already knew. Except for Senator Ford's trigger, which we just learned from Grigor. But the reality is, Grigor's killers got the wrong trigger—or at least the language to deliver it in. Grigor crossed them up. He just told us if Senator Ford hears, *'The long and brutal winter gives way to spring,'* in English it is meaningless, but in Russian, it activates his programming. The doctor's murderers will call your cousin and deliver the message in English—leaving Senator Ford inactive."

As a collective sigh helped to ease the tension in the room, Shelby's brow furrowed. Turning to Olegina, she asked, "What did Grigor say?"

"Sorry?"

"Just before he pointed to the painting, Grigor said something in Russian. What was it?"

Looking down in recollection, Olegina slowly looked up, an ominous countenance clouding her face. "He said, 'But I deceived everyone.'"

CHAPTER 79

JANUARY
NIC FORD'S HOME
ONE DAY TO INAUGURATION

Shelby rubbed her eyes awake. It took a moment to recognize the guest room at Nic's condo. The other bed in the room was empty. Donning a now two-day-old shirt and jacket, her nose wrinkled, "I need some fresh clothes."

She suddenly remembered she'd not checked in with her boss in the last twelve hours. Using the burner phone she'd purchased, she called FBI headquarters, identifying herself. She was put through to Boxer's office where her assistant answered.

"Desk Chief's office."

"This is Special Agent Littlejohn, is the Chief available?"

Placed on a brief hold, Shelby had to hold the phone away from her ear when Boxer picked up.

"Littlejohn, where the hell are you?"

"Sorry boss. Still in New York—"

"What! When are you coming back and what number are you calling from?"

"Sorry. I Had to ditch my cell as a security maneuver. I wasn't sure if someone had compromised my phone. Coming back today."

"Fine. Look I'm going into a briefing on security protocols for the inauguration, what do you have for me?"

Shelby brought the Desk Chief up to speed on what she'd discovered about the trigger and sequence to activate Senator Ford's programming as well as the murder of Ford's doctor.

"Damn, Shelby, that's fine work. Very fine work. Look, please get back here as soon as you can and stay in contact this time. We need to brief the Director and probably Secret Service, NSA, and—with the Russian involvement—maybe even CIA."

Beaming at the grudging compliment, Shelby replied, "Thank you, boss."

In the kitchen, Nic poked at bacon sizzling in a pan, while over-cooking pancakes on a skillet. In the corner, Olegina drank coffee, mesmerized by the fashion and high style of the *Today Show*. Nic looked up with just barely enough humanity to nod. She couldn't blame him. In only one day, she and Olegina had managed to shatter his entire worldview of his family. The last twenty-four hours seemed a blur.

The Ford's trusted family doctor had been experimenting in thought control for years. His grandmother had been a KGB operative since the Bolshevik Revolution, and his cousin was now a programmed sleeper agent—one step from assassinating the soon-to-be President of the United States. After leaving Stephan Grigor's brownstone, the three of them had had a moment to decompress and consider what they'd learned.

Even hearing the thoughts in her mind summarizing what they'd learned for the umpteenth time, Shelby could only shake her head. Chris Ford's decades-long brainwashing would cause him, if ever activated, to murder his immediate supervisor. The trigger was a phrase. Delivered in Russian, activated his programming, in English, would leave him in a dormant state. Before dying, Doctor Grigor had whispered into Nic's ear, that he'd duped his captors, telling them exactly the opposite information.

Thus, when Grigor's murderers sought to activate Ford at the Inauguration, telling him in English, they'd actually be leaving Ford inactive. The killers had taken Grigor's cell, presumably to call Chris sometime the next morning. Ford would see the incoming call, think it was his doctor, and answer it—never knowing the next words he'd hear could have changed history. But Grigor had died before saying why they wanted Johansen and Ford removed before they even took office.

And yet, why kill Grigor for a plan to assassinate the President? While she, Nic, and Olegina left Doctor Grigor's home under the impression that Chris Ford would remain a dormant sleeper agent, they'd determined to alert Chris after the Inauguration. Perhaps there was a way to deprogram him. Vice President Ford couldn't spend the next four years a heartbeat from the Presidency, brainwashed to terminate that very heartbeat if activated, even accidently.

Then a new train of thought pulled into the station. The randomness of history would argue that sometimes weird things happen. The plot to assassinate Abraham Lincoln had also been a part of a larger plan to decapitate the American government. John Wilkes Booth and his fellow conspirators had also intended to kill Vice President Andrew Johnson, General Ulysses Grant, and Secretary of State William Seward. But fate dictated otherwise as Grant left town the night of the assassination to see his family. Seward survived the attack on him, and the assassin sent to kill Johnson, lost his nerve at the last moment.

In World War II, Operation Valkyrie had been a plot to decapitate the Nazi High Command by assassinating Adolf Hitler and establish a new government that would seek to end the war on terms more favorable to Germany. But again, fate had dealt a blow to the plot as Hitler survived the assassination attempt, leading to Germany's complete and total defeat.

But while Polar Strike nominally fell into this category, most of the plot had fallen into history's dustbin when the Soviets had been unable to develop reliable sleeper agents. So who would go to so much effort to keep it active? Was it Grigor's apparent pride in his work or blind loyalty to a dead government? Somebody would benefit from this, but who?

While they probably had neutralized the threat from Grigor's killers, Shelby still thought increased scrutiny on the incoming President and Vice President would be needed after the Inauguration. Once installed, Ford could be safely debriefed and they could begin the process of deprogramming—if, indeed, it could be done.

Still, the whole thing seemed blurry? Had they missed something? Before she could vocalize her thoughts, Nic's cell rang.

Nic handed the spatula to Shelby while taking up his phone from the kitchen counter. “Ford.”

It was Tasha O’Riley. “Inspector, I may have found something. How soon can you come in?”

CHAPTER 80

JANUARY
BROOKLYN
KINGS COUNTY HOSPITAL
ONE DAY TO INAUGURATION

Tasha entered the multimedia pod where Nic, Shelby, and Olegina stood at an expansive conference table. At the end of the room was an immense white board descended from the ceiling, partially covered by a screen. Next to the board was a large, flat-panel monitor. On an adjacent table sat a globe and lamp. Nic made introductions before escorting the women to a smaller nearby room.

"Protocol. Need to know," Nic said defensively. "We'll be out of here in no time."

Shelby—newly attired in a velour sweat-suit—and Olegina, reluctantly nodded.

In the multimedia pod, Nic sat. Tasha brushed by to get down the table toward the screen, trailing a suggestion of something fresh that also hinted at a night of quiet jazz and single-malt Scotch. Why did she always distract him?

"Thanks for coming, Inspector," Tasha said. "I thought you'd be in Washington by today."

"Me too, but something ... came up. What d'ya got?"

The ME glanced at the two outsiders in the other room.

Casually gesturing, Nic nodded. "They're okay."

"Very good." Tasha picked up a remote, pointing it at a projector hung from the ceiling, a wall mounted monitor came to life with images of the dead men from the murders the previous month at the Galaxy Condominium.

"Recognize these, Inspector?"

Quickly, Nic recalled being in the morgue with Tasha. His memory wasn't necessarily of the tatted bodies, but of being in Tasha's presence. "I got it. Last month. Brighton Beach." Nic pointed to one of the pictures on-screen. "That one, he had some sort of odd tats—treasure chest with numbers around it?"

"That's correct."

Nic stared, enthralled to be in Tasha's presence, but fidgeting to get on with his travel plans. "Okay." He raised his eyebrows waiting. "Something new?"

"Maybe. As you recall, the numbers we got from the treasure-chest tat were these." The ME pointed and clicked the remote. On the screen came four-one, one-one, one-zero and seven-eight. "These are clearly not Fibonacci sequencing. We ruled out zip codes, chemical polymers, variants of pi, genome sequencing, ciphers ... we checked with various banks in the area, and none have this combination of numbers. On a hunch, I tried GPS coordinates and I thought we had a match. Part of a match, anyway."

Lost, Nic reflected for a moment. "Part?"

"Before I address that, let me return to the tattoos again. Do you remember this?" Tasha pushed the remote again. A new image appeared, that of a red line running from the left shoulder to the right shoulder.

"I remember this—same guy. I remember you talking about it. A string or something right?"

"Correct. A line seemingly connecting two spots on the body."

"Shoulder to shoulder right?"

"Yes."

Thinking they'd just derailed a potential assassination plot, a new sense of fear crept into his gut as tingling buzzed up his neck. "What do they mean?"

"I don't want to upset you Inspector, but—"

Nic grimly gestured for her to continue.

"I'm not sure yet. But I've been reading up on new technology in tattoos. One of the latest processes in body art is using inks that can only be seen under ultraviolet light. This type of tattoo is very popular right now in the rave scene. Your tat is invisible during the day when you're at work, all respectable and such. But at night clubs with special illumination, you become a billboard for whoever you're trying to attract. On a hunch, I exposed the line and the two circles to a UV light and this is what I found."

Upon the white screen, appeared two forms side by side. "The left image is of the point on the left shoulder, the right image is the right shoulder point."

Leaning forward in his chair, Nic squinted. "It's the two points, so?"

Nodding silently, Tasha pushed her clicker summoning a new image. Two new images appeared. On the left was a point with two letters in the center: PS. On the right, a point with two letters: CF.

She continued, "This next image is the red line under UV."

Replacing the two circles was the red line. In the center were the words CONNECT THE DOTS. On either side of the words were a series of marks.

"What are those ... "

"Dashes and dots." She waited for recognition.

"Morse code?"

"Correct."

His throat suddenly dry, Nic tried to swallow. "Officer O'Riley—"

"Tasha."

Despite his anxiety, Nic smiled. "Tasha. What does all this mean?"

"Uncertain, but I think it's the missing half of the GPS numbers that complete the coordinates from the front of the vic's body." On screen came a new image: 74.026887."

Nic blinked, heart pumping pure adrenaline. He barely heard her next words. "The numbers could be the missing longitude, and *connect the dots*, seems straight forward, but do the letters or ... any of this mean something, Inspector?"

When nothing came from the detective, Tasha slowly turned to an ashen-faced Nic.

"Inspector?"

Nic lowered his head into his hands. After a moment, he wiped tears from his eyes as he nodded. "Sit down, I have to tell you something. But I need the others." Opening the door, Nic gathered Shelby and Olegina, bringing them into the conference room.

Uncertainly, they took seats at the table. Tasha looked first at the FBI woman then the Russian and finally back at Nic who appeared as if he was standing at the edge of the Rubicon. Finally, he exhaled. Lowering his head, he looked at Tasha. "What we're about to reveal to you is highly classified and can't leave this room. Understood?"

"Inspector, I'm a professional—"

Nic snapped, "Do ... you ... understand?"

Silently, Tasha nodded. Nic tipped his head at Shelby and Olegina. Opening Olegina's blue folder, they spread the documents out on the table. Slowly, but with gathering steam, they briefed the ME on what they'd uncovered of the assassination plot.

In disbelief, Tasha's eyes probed Nic, Shelby, and Olegina, searching for a sign that they were joking. "Holy fu—"

"Exactly," Nic finished. "Now, can you bring us current on what've you found?"

"Absolutely." Tasha reset the latitude coordinates on the treasure box. Rapidly, she recounted her findings. With the picture of the string-embedded message on screen, Tasha paused. "You all with me?"

"So, why does some victim from a random Russian mob hit have details of our plot inked on his body?" Shelby skeptically asked.

"Not sure, but starting to think these numbers are a clue."

"A clue to what?" asked Shelby.

"GPS coordinates."

"But don't GPS coordinates usually include letters, like *N* for north or *E* for east?"

Tasha nodded as she moved to a nearby white board. "As Agent Littlejohn has noted, GPS coordinates usually have letters to help clarify if you're moving east or west, north or south." On the board, Tasha wrote out some numbers.

"As you know, the planet is round, and we can use the points on the circle to precisely indicate where you are on the globe. Latitude indicates whether you are north or south of the equator and is typically identified by a number followed by a capitol N or S. Longitude indicates how far east or west you are from the Prime Meridian, which is set in Greenwich, England."

"Why England?" Nic asked.

"Good question. Everyone can agree on where the equator is, but picking a primary longitudinal line was more challenging. Prior to picking Greenwich, there was no agreed-on prime meridian. Map makers in France had it running through Paris, in Russia, it was Moscow and so it was a bit confusing. Finally, in 1884, there was a conference in the United States, where twenty-five countries agreed to pick Greenwich, the home to the British Royal Observatory."

Pointing back to the white board, Tasha continued. "So, the two sets of numbers I've written here are GPS coordinates expressed in the DMS system."

Shelby interjected, "DMS?"

"Decimal-minutes-seconds, versus the decimal degrees system, which I'll address in just a moment." Tasha pointed to the first set, 21.3069° N, 157.8583° W. "These numbers are pronounced, twenty-one degrees, thirty minutes, sixty-nine seconds, north, followed by, one hundred fifty-seven degrees, eighty-five minutes, eighty-three seconds, west. The first number is latitude and refers to how far north of the equator the location is. The second number is longitude and refers to how far west of the Prime Meridian the location is. Now again, remember the planet is a circle, consisting of three hundred sixty degrees from the start at Greenwich all the way around the globe until you arrive back at Greenwich. To make things easier, you refer to longitude by how far east of Greenwich you are, up to one hundred eighty degrees," Tasha pointed to the globe on the desk. "Similarly you can refer to longitude by how far west of Greenwich you are, again up to one-hundred-eighty degrees."

Nic pointed to the board. "So, where is that?"

Tasha nodded. "The GPS coordinates I just read, are the coordinates for Honolulu, Hawaii." She pointed to the second set of numbers, 33.9249° S, 18.4241° E, using a marker to underline the S and the E. "The *S* refers to south of the equator and the *E* refers to east of Greenwich. These are the GPS coordinates for Cape Town, South Africa."

"So why are there no letters on our dead vic's tattoos?" Nic asked.

"Because there is another way to express GPS coordinates and that is simply using the decimal degrees without letters. With decimal degrees, latitudes south of the equator are expressed with a minus sign before the number. Likewise, with longitude, any location west of Greenwich is expressed with a negative before the number. While DMS, degrees, minutes, and seconds is more prevalent today, both methods are acceptable. Perhaps our victim had a preference for decimal degrees versus DMS."

Tasha turned to the globe on the table. Using a red-light laser pointer, Tasha pointed it at the orb while slowly turning the globe. "This red line is a possible latitudinal line from the Galaxy vic's chest tattoo."

She paused, repositioning the red laser line at the North Pole and moved it slowly down the globe to the South Pole. "Likewise, this red line is possible longitudinal line taken the numbers hidden in the string tattoo on the victim's neck."

Looking between the three, Tasha paused to let them catch up.

"So the GPS coordinates would be a latitude, taken from the treasure chest tats on the front of the victim's body, of 41.111078, reading as forty-one degrees, eleven minutes, ten point seventy-eight seconds and a longitude, taken from the string tat, of 74.026887, reading as seventy-four degrees, two minutes, sixty-eight point eighty-seven seconds. But without a negative before either number, you can surmise these coordinates refer to four different locations on the planet."

The Medical Examiner wrote out:

-41.111078, 74.026887

-41.111078, -74.026887

41.111078, 74.026887

41.111078, -74.026887

Tasha turned on the computer monitor next to the whiteboard. Going to the internet, Tasha pulled up a maps application and typed in the first set of numbers on the keyboard wirelessly linked to the monitor. A location dot appeared on screen, surrounded by all blue.

"As you can see on the monitor here, if I expand the view out, this first location is somewhere in the Indian Ocean." She typed in the second set of numbers. On the monitor appeared, a spot in water adjacent to land. "This second of coordinates is for a location just off the coast of Chile." Tasha entered the third coordinates. "This for a location in the Central Asian country of Kyrgyzstan."

Tasha punched in the last set of digits on her keyboard but paused to look at the others. "But it's this last location that I think is relevant to our situation, especially after what," Tasha nodded to the blue folder on the table, "you've shared with me."

"Where is it?" Shelby guardedly asked.

Tasha pushed ENTER on the keyboard and onscreen came what looked like a copse of trees.

The others squinted, but just shook their heads.

"What is this?" Nic asked.

Tasha expanded the map, bringing nearby landmarks into the image. "As best as I can tell, it's a family vault located in a Russian Orthodox Cemetery in Nanuet, just on the other side of the Hudson."

The letters CF from the victim's string tattoo loomed in Nic's mind. Bolting to his feet, he blurted, "How quickly can we get up there?"

"Maybe an hour. I have a van ready to go, Inspector."

"Need to go by my office first," Nic said, already sailing out the door.

CHAPTER 81

JANUARY
PALISADES INTERSTATE PARKWAY
ONE DAY TO INAUGURATION

Nic stared out the window, his thoughts off-kilter. Before leaving the city, he'd gone by his office where he'd picked up the book on orienteering that he'd recovered at the Galaxy murder scene. Not sure why, he eyed the book as they drove. As they motored across town in an unmarked, white police transport, Tasha had briefed Shelby and Olegina on the Galaxy murder scene, the tattoo discovery, and the weird blood scrawl on the wall next to the black-and-white photo of the bear. Crossing the Hudson and onto the Palisades Parkway, they'd settled into an uncomfortable silence.

Tasha took her eyes off the road for a moment, glancing at Nic.

"Inspector, you okay?" she asked.

Absently, Nic looked into the passing forest. "Yeah."

Shelby leaned in from the backseat. "Look, I don't want to be a backseat driver here."

"What?" Nic tersely replied.

The FBI woman defensively put her hands up. "Look, just hear me out for a second. Okay?" She paused before moving forward. "Grigor told us before he died that he told his killers Senator Ford can't be activated unless the trigger is in Russian, right?"

Nic nodded but said nothing.

"So, even if the killers call Senator Ford, they can't activate him, correct?"

"Yes—what's your point, Agent Littlejohn?"

"Even with Ms. O'riley's GPS tattoos, Russian cemeteries and all, I have to ask ... why are we making this trip? I mean, we all need to be back in Washington, right?"

Nic snapped. "Look. This may be nothing—or an old case, or Polar Strike or ... I don't know, but dead people don't have tattoos of a plot to assassinate the President of the United States on their body for *fun*. Let's just run this to ground and see what we find."

Shelby turned to Tasha. "How far is this again?"

"Almost there," Tasha quietly replied.

Shelby settled back into her seat. Crossing her arms, she stared out the window. "While Olegina and I were in the hall outside the office, when you were initially briefing Nic, I called my supervisor in Washington. I brought her up to speed on what we're doing. She's happy that we've defused the plot, but she's going to contact Secret Service. Tell them the FBI has credible evidence there might be an active assassination plot in play and ask them to be extra vigilant."

The van lapsed into silence as her words hung in the air.

Finally, Tasha broke the ice. Looking in the rearview at Shelby, Tasha said, "What's it like ... you know, to work forensics at the FBI?"

Meeting the ME's eyes in the mirror, Shelby tipped her head respectfully, "Well, when this is all over, maybe we should talk. Your work back at the precinct was really good. I think you have a great handle on your craft."

Trying hard not to smile, Tasha returned her attention to the icy road ahead. They drove on in silence for the next twenty minutes. Off the interstate, Tasha guided them past a number of strip malls and shopping centers before turning down a quiet, tree-shaded road. Almost reverently, Tasha slowed the vehicle, turning onto a narrow, private lane with a small sign in the stone wall. It read: CATHEDRAL AND MONASTERY OF SAINT GEORGE (ROCOR).

"What does ROCOR mean?" Shelby asked.

Almost in unison, the other three replied, "Russian Orthodox Church Outside Russia."

Momentarily surprised, Olegina's head swiveled between Tasha and Nic.

Nic turned to face her. "Both Tasha and I are Americans of Russian descent.

Letting her eyes drop to the blue folder beside her, Olegina nodded. "Of course, I remember now about your family Inspector—but Ms. O'Riley, your name is Irish, yes?"

"That's correct. Father is Irish, *my mother* was Russian. I can't read Russian as well as speak it."

"Was?"

Tasha nodded, silently. "Drug overdose twenty years ago."

Olegina lowered her eyes. "Sorry, I did—"

"No worries."

Shelby parked. A heavily bearded, robed man exited the main cathedral, and they disembarked as he arrived. Nic turned to grab something off the console before shutting the door.

"May I help you?" the prelate asked.

Nic took the lead, offering his hand. "Father—"

"*Reverend* Father," the man said.

"Yes, of course. Please forgive me." Nic removed his identification. "Reverend Father, I'm Nic Ford of the New York Police Department and we're running down a clue from a possible murder case. A lead we've received indicates a clue might be here. We were wondering—"

"Forgive me officer, but NYPD has no jurisdiction here. I'm going to have to ask you to leave."

With a haughty scowl, Shelby stepped next to Nic with her ID. "How about the United States Federal Bureau of Investigation?" She thrust her jaw out. "That good enough for you?"

"Officer—"

"Special Agent."

The cleric registered his disgust, having to deal with a woman in authority. "I'm still afraid you need a search warrant for coming onto our grounds."

Shelby smilingly replied, "Reverend Father, we mean no disrespect, but there are exemptions to the Fourth Amendment barring unreasonable search and seizure. One is under a condition of *exigent circumstances* when an officer," she paused to tilt her head, "is of the opinion that the time it would take to get a search warrant could jeopardize public safety. It is under this condition that I'm going to ask you again for permission to come onto your premises."

The cleric looked slowly between them before stepping aside. "How can I help you?"

Tasha pulled out a map of the area with the GPS coordinates marked on it. "We'd like to see this location."

A black cloud passed over the priest's face. "No, you cannot go there. This is the cemetery. I'm sorry, but you will need a warrant."

Olegina quietly stepped forward. In Russian, she softly said, "Reverend Father, you are from here or Rossiya?"

Caught off guard, the prelate muttered, "Rossiya. And you also?"

"Yes, Reverend Father, Moscow."

"I'm of Saint Petersburg. But it was still Leningrad when I was born." The man symbolically spit, "A pox upon communists."

A tiny smile creased Olegina's face. As the others watched in mild wonderment, Olegina said, "Reverend, you and I remember the thugs who held us under their fist in the days of the blatnoys, the communists." She gestured to Nic and Shelby, "We are here to stop people who would seek to restore evil—first in America, and then Rossiya—but we cannot be sure until we complete our investigation. There is a possible clue here that could help us immensely."

As her words died away, Nic, Shelby, and Tasha held their breath waiting for the cleric to order them off the property. Surprisingly, he took Olegina by the arm, escorting her through well-manicured, white-dusted grounds toward the back of the property.

Not wishing to jeopardize the moment, the three others drifted behind at a respectful distance. Slowly, the snow-covered paths, through copses of barren, leafless trees gave way to open space populated with tombstones standing sentinel over souls now departed.

Clearing her voice, Tasha drew even with Olegina and the prelate, pointing to a spot on her map. This time, rather than an objection, it appeared as though the holy man had been expecting this day. Nodding silently, he gestured.

In a small glade, beneath a majestic, American elm, stood a crypt that captured the essence of final repose—blended with expectation of the world to come. Obsidian marble leaned at a small angle up to an onion-domed roof, painted gold. Atop was perched a golden, Orthodox cross. Arches were carved into the walls, depicting icons of the Madonna and the saints. Next to it were two, snow-covered wooden benches. The door into the mausoleum was locked.

Shelby said to the priest, "Do you have a key?"

Shaking his head, he answered, "Only the family would have that."

Growing ever more irritated with the time this sojourn was taking, Shelby disgustedly looked at Nic. "I'm not shooting the lock off that. Any ideas?"

Lost in thought, Nic slowly reached into his pocket, removing something he kept safely in his closed fist. Gazing up at the cross, Nic glacially approached the door to the cemetery vault as the others drew near. With his empty hand, he gingerly brushed the solid marble door, his face a mask of sudden discernment.

"What is it?" Shelby asked.

Instead, Nic turned to Tasha. "Do you remember last month, when we were at the Galaxy, at the murder scene?"

Perplexed, Tasha uncertainly nodded. "Yes, but—"

Nic continued. "While you were attending to the bodies, Officer ... what was his name—Paddock—Officer Paddock and I searched the rest of the unit. It was like a hurricane had touched down, stuff on the floors everywhere."

"I remember."

"In the den, there were books all over. One of them didn't make any sense until just now with the tattoos you deciphered. The book was called *The Basics of Geocaching*."

Tasha looked momentarily stunned as if hit by a strike from the heavens. "Of course. The numbers, GPS coordinates, I remember." She gestured to the crypt, "And all this ... it ties in with that weird blood splatter we found on the wall next to the giant black-and-white photo of the bruin." Everyone looked at her. "There was this squiggly line next to the bruin picture. Initially, we thought it was an attempt at writing. But the dying vic probably didn't have time to spell out anything. Instead, it was a clue. A lightning bolt, striking the earth—

and don't you see, bruins are polar bears. Polar ... Strike. Pretty good attempt, don't you think?"

Heads nodded before Shelby huffily intruded. "I hate to break up this week's session of *Fun with Forensics*, but we're still out here. How are we going to get in *there*?"

Nic snipped, "I'm getting to that. As I was standing in the den, holding that book, I thought it odd that a mobster," he glanced at Shelby, "we think the Galaxy was owned by a criminal named Slaga Dmitirev.... Anyway, it didn't seem to make sense that Dmitriev would have a book on orienteering, but I assumed I would look at it further, down at the station after we logged it into evidence. I was going to leave it behind, when I noticed the back cover was slightly bulged. Inside, I found this."

Nic opened his fist to reveal the solid-gold key with a diamond-encrusted Russian Orthodox Cross on top that matched the cross atop the crypt. "This was taped inside the back cover. I had no idea what it was for ... until now."

Lifting the key, Nic approached the crypt. The key fit the lock perfectly and the door swung gently open. The vault was empty—save for a small table. On the opposite wall, was an icon of Mary and the baby Jesus. On the table sat a journal.

CHAPTER 82

JANUARY
WASHINGTON, DC
BLAIR HOUSE
ONE DAY TO INAUGURATION

"*When people gather again together in that distant time*—see, I still like *on that distant shore ...* " President-elect Robert Johansen looked up from his desk. "Chris, what do you think?"

In jeans and turtleneck, Chris studied his copy and relaxed on the sofa next to Cliff Kolfax, the president's incoming Chief of Staff. "You know, Governor, I do like *distant time.* I think it conveys perspective, instead of rhetoric."

Kolfax silently agreed.

Johansen nodded slowly. "I think you guys are right. Good. *Distant time* it is." Standing, Johansen stepped to the window. Gazing at the Executive Offices, he said, "Things will look different in the morning. How are the views from the Hay?"

"Not bad. Have to look across Lafayette Square, but okay."

The President-elect looked wistful. "Life changes tomorrow. And yet, does it ever change?"

"Robert?" Chris replied.

"Oh I mean, yeah—Presidents get their names in books ... and statues and even their own library and such ... but do you really ever change destiny? Is history an immutable force like a river that continues on ... regardless of what we do? Can one man ever alter the lives of others?"

Chris chuckled. "Well, Governor, if you ever get the answer to that question—we should quit politics, write a book, and retire."

Both men laughed. Johansen turned, moving to the door to his suite.

"Chris, thanks for the help. I have to leave now for the White House lunch with the President. Dinner tonight, right?"

"Yes sir. Look forward to seeing you and Helen."

"My best to Mallory."

With that, Chris stepped into the hallway, his detail coming around him. The agent in charge radioed, "Crystal Star is moving."

"Crystal Star has a headache," Chris thought. Election, information briefings, more fundraisers, Inauguration preparation ... once all this stress died down, he was sure he'd feel better. He breathed easier thinking it would be good to speak with Stephan soon.

CHAPTER 83

JANUARY
CATHEDRAL AND MONASTERY OF SAINT GEORGE ONE DAY TO INAUGURATION

After determining it was clear, Nic motioned the others inside. As they gathered about the table, Nic lifted the journal, hoping it would only confirm what they already knew. Instinctively, however, he knew there was one more corner to turn in the maze. Glancing at Shelby, who subtly nodded, Nic reluctantly opened the notebook.

Finding a blank page, he immediately moved to the next, then another, before leafing through the book like a rolodex. Expecting another bombshell, the others were surprised to see Nic audibly exhale. Suddenly, he couldn't breathe. Dropping the journal, he turned, exiting the tomb.

As Tasha went after him, Shelby peered at Olegina before spreading the notebook out. Blank pages greeted her.

"Empty," she said. "Damn, wild goose chase. C'mon. We have to get to Washington."

Emerging outside, she was still eyeing the blank journal book in her hands. "Nic we have to—"

Her words were cut short as she found Nic and Tasha with their hands up before the priest, a pistol in his right hand. Before she could react, the prelate said, "Phone and sidearm on the bench next to the others—left hand to remove it please. I would not want any accidents."

The cleric motioned them back into the crypt. "IDs on the table." As they complied, the prelate had a moment to study Nic. "Do I know you?"

Tsking sarcastically, Nic answered. "I don't know too many gun-toting priests. Who the hell are you?"

Motioning to Nic, he said, "Give me your ID." Quickly reviewing the credential, the holy man's countenance morphed to shocked surprise. Keeping his pistol trained on them, the prelate scanned the desolate cemetery. Satisfied they were alone, he shoved his weapon into his belt.

"Inspector Ford, we don't have much time," he said.

Struggling to contain his composure against time and circumstance, Nic bellowed, "Time? For what—who are you!"

But the stranger had stepped from the crypt. A moment later, he was back, distributing their phones and weapons. The three law-enforcement personnel rapidly directed their sidearms at the man. Nonplussed, the priest glacially removed the Kalimavkion from his head. Along with the head cover, came a wig, attached inside. The stranger reached across his face to his left ear, gently pulling off a false beard.

Nic and Tasha's faces went slack in recognition.

"You're dead!" Exclaimed Tasha.

Arms stretched wide, the man said, "Slaga Dmitriev, at your service."

"You died at the Galaxy. We have your body," said Tasha.

"You mean the one who looked like me?"

"Well ... I guess—yes."

"One of my men, Nikita, God rest his soul."

Tasha examined Slaga's exposed skin. "You have no tattoos."

"Correct."

"Why tat up ... Nikita you said?"

"Back-up. In case I ever truly had to destroy all paper records of what I hid here."

"What? What did you hide here?"

"Polar Strike. The entire file. It's in a vault behind the Madonna," Slaga pointed to the icon behind the table as he crossed himself.

"We already have that," Shelby sarcastically said.

Before Slaga could reply, Nic asked, "Have you been back to the Galaxy?"

Slaga nodded.

"How'd you get in? We had that secured immediately."

"There is a secret passageway from my master bathroom shower to the unit below, which I also own."

Nodding in admiration, Nic said, "Like a panic room, only bigger."

"It was you who created the blood-splatter clue on the wall, wasn't it?" Tasha softly remarked.

Turning an admiring eye to Tasha, the mobster said, "Yes."

For a moment, Nic looked distracted before removing the crypt key from his pocket. "Why leave this?"

Slaga took the key, pointing to the top. "I left it there to see who'd come and if they were a threat. There's a GPS chip in the cross. I saw the key moving this morning and have been waiting for your arrival."

"How did you know not to be at the Galaxy?" Nic probed, tiring of interviewing someone who offered little more than what he had.

"Inspector, I grew up in Russia, served in Afghanistan; I've been a global mercenary. You develop an intuition as to ... well let's just say, I put some protocols in place to alert me to the presence of my enemies."

Suppressing her sense of urgency, Shelby brusquely interjected. "Mr. Dmitriev, we need to get back to Washington and you need to come with us."

"Of course, but I have one request for the Inspector."

Instinctively, Nic knew. Angrily he shook his head. "No guarantees Slaga. The Specter left a broad trail of carnage. If that was you ... there's a lot to answer for."

"Against whom? Other criminals who stole and murdered civilians? Not once was a noncombatant injured."

"What about the things you stole?"

Slaga silently let this pass.

Exasperated, Nic tilted his head. "What *are* you asking for?"

"A head start. Once this all over, you give me twenty-four hours to disappear."

Shelby threw the journal onto the table. "For blank pages! This is BS. Nic don't let him con you. He's got nothing. We've foiled the assassination. This is just a cleanup operation."

The flinty hardness of Slaga's eyes told Nic the Russian was holding the last ace. "What?"

Wordlessly, the Specter brushed by them to the icon. He depressed a button at the base. Silently, an invisible drawer slid open. Sitting side by side, were a stack of documents and a journal book. Slaga removed a couple of documents.

"Polar Strike. Retrieved from Grupp's office," Slaga glanced at Olegina, "at Lubyanka." Brusquely, he tossed them onto the table. Next, he removed the journal. "My notes." It landed on the table next to the Polar Strike documents. He removed another page of paper which he proffered to the group. When Nic reached for it, Slaga shook his head, placing the document in the hands of the Russian archivist.

Reluctantly, Olegina took it. After a moment, she looked up blankly. "What is this? I mean it's in Cyrillic, but not something I recognize."

Slaga replied, "That's because while it *is* Cyrillic, it's not Russian."

Olegina reexamined the pages before it came to her, "German."

"That's correct."

"I don't read German. Sorry."

Reaching back into the drawer, Slaga removed another page. "I had it translated. It reads LAST WILL AND TESTAMENT OF ERICH VON GRUPP. Von Grupp ran Polar Strike for the KGB until he was hit and killed by a car in front of his office in 1992. Most of it is self-justifying nonsense—cause of the proletariat, the coming worldwide workers revolution, weakness of capitalism, and ongoing prattle ... but the last sentence, while a bit dramatic, seems to imply something hidden and ominous."

"What does it say?" asked Shelby.

Slaga covertly reached into his jacket pocket. When he looked up, he found the others guardedly examining him. He sniffed, "What?" while donning reading glasses. He read:

"*Glorious is the day the workers unite, before the world, in plain sight. From deep within Russia, across her pole, a gash to rip America's soul. No one will see it coming, not even the one you think. From out of the sun, the strike will come.*"

Slaga put his glasses away and commented, "Like I said, dramatic, but I don't think our work is done."

Shelby shook her head. "This is bullshit. Between the Lubyanka files *Olegina* brought and what we found at Grigor's, we have everything we need. End of story."

"Is it?" Slaga retorted. Looking at Olegina, he added, "Has anyone approached you about Polar Strike since you reported finding it?"

Olegina lowered her eyes. "I've not told anyone about it."

"Why?"

"My friend Anna worked at Lubyanka. She and some others were murdered by someone looking for something, probably the Polar Strike file. And ... " Pausing to refortify her resolve, she continued, "I was afraid they'd come for me. That's why I called Shelby."

Abruptly, Slaga tried to follow up. "But since you left, has anyone tried—"

Growing tired of the thug, Shelby butted in. "Yeah, Mr. Big-time Russian mobster guy. Right after she arrived, some pros tried to grease us outside of Andrews Air Base."

Slaga said nothing, but his raised eyebrows caused Shelby to blink. "Look, I don't know why. Okay?" She paused before motioning toward the Polar Strike files sitting on the table. "Has to have something to do with that. And you," Shelby caustically nodded at Slaga, "we wasted a drive up here for what!" With overdramatized embellishment, Shelby waved about the crypt. "All this skullduggery and you've given us nothing we don't already know. And besides, the killers are still missing a key data point. Senator Ford has been programmed but remains dormant unless he receives some bullshit phrase in Russian. So without that—"

"*Nyet*—no!" Everyone was shocked to find Slaga staring at them incredulously. "What are you speaking of? The trigger in Russian is meaningless. If delivered in English, it activates Senator Ford."

"What! How do you know that?" Shelby challenged Slaga. "We heard directly from Doctor Grigor—*as he was dying*, about the trigger and correct sequence; Russian activates the Senator, not English."

"Then he was lying."

Suddenly, from out of nowhere, Nic grabbed Slaga by the neck, shoving him up against the wall. Though a trained killer, Slaga was not a young man anymore and Nic's height, muscular build, and street-developed combat skills, caught him by surprise. Nic wedged his elbow into Slaga's windpipe before Shelby and Tasha pulled him back.

"Nic! Nic! Let him go!" Shelby yelled.

Tears pouring down his face, Nic finally relented giving Slaga a final push as he stepped off.

Shelby turned to the gasping Russian mobster. "How do you know he was lying?"

Slaga returned to the file drawer to remove one last piece of paper that he handed to Shelby. "I found this in Doctor Grigor's floor safe."

After a quick scan, she looked back at Slaga. "This was not in Grigor's safe when we opened it."

Rubbing his throat, Slaga rasped, "Why would I make this up? Perhaps he removed it." For a moment, he paused, lost in thought.

"What?" Shelby asked.

"Did you find anything else in the safe? Like a chart or a table or something?"

"No. Why?"

"When I was making copies of the papers in the safe, the last page came out all blurry. It looked like a table or something."

Shelby shook her head. "No. Nothing like that."

Tasha and Olegina had come up next to the FBI agent, both scanning the document in her hands.

"What does it say?" Olegina apprehensively asked.

"These read like patient instructions—which would make sense, given the relationship between Senator Ford and Doctor Grigor. Most of it seems to be medical jargon about supposed benefits the patient experiences when the trigger phrase is delivered: slowing of breath, destressing, and so forth. But it does not say when the trigger phrase should be delivered or why or—"

"What does it say Chris should do after hearing the phrase?" Nic softly asked.

Pinching her lips, Shelby tensely looked at him. "It doesn't. It does say the patient is to ignore his programming if he hears the phrase in Russian, but if in English, to immediately implement his instructions." Shelby slowly shook her head before lowering the page. "Why the two triggers—I mean why two ways of delivering it? This is like some twisted puzzle." Her eyes drifted to Olegina, then Tasha. "You guys?"

Tasha or Olegina shook their heads mutely and the room again descended into silence, all eyes subtly drifting to Nic. His head throbbing, Nic massaged his temples. At last he said, "Look, it's like Shelby said. If we know the details and what the trigger is—was supposed to be—can we assume the killers or whoever is coming after Olegina will stop now?"

Clasping Grupp's will in his hand, Slaga abruptly interrupted. "*Nyet.* The people who tried to kill you ... I mean no one goes to this much trouble to seize control of the Oval Office without having more than one backup in place. I know I wouldn't mount an operation of this magnitude without one. They know, or have, something we do not. These people who came after you," he said pointing to Shelby and Olegina, "and me, are trying to kill us to eliminate anyone who has knowledge of the plot." He paused to let this set in. "And they won't stop until we're all dead."

Nic had heard enough. "Okay. I need to get to Washington. I *am* an invited guest of my cousin, Senator—soon-to-be Vice President—Ford. I don't know how close my seat is, but I can try to assess things from there. You two," he gestured to Shelby and Olegina, "come with me back to Washington. Tasha, go back to Grigor's home and then the Clinic; see if we missed anything. Slaga, I could arrest you right now, but we need your help. Will you come with us?"

The mobster, confronted with the tension between an appeal to his vanity and a desire to ensure his freedom, squinted. "And?"

Nic flinched before grudgingly nodding.

* * * *

At the van, Nic removed his cellphone. Staring at the face for a moment, he stepped off. "Give me a minute."

The others settled into the van, watching Nic nodding solemnly as he finished his call. In the car, Nic stared out the window silently as Tasha took them back to the interstate.

"I called her."

"Who?" Shelby said.

"Mallory."

"*What* did you tell her?" Shelby tensely asked.

"Nothing. Just told her I was working an old case that Chris had prosecuted when he was still in the New York DA's office. Told her the perpetrator had been paroled but might have gotten Chris' cell phone number from an old record in his file and this guy might try to call Chris around the inauguration to harass or threaten him. So, I told Mallory not to let Chris answer his phone unless it was from me."

CHAPTER 84

JANUARY
HAY ADAMS HOTEL
FORD SUITE
INAUGURATION DAY

Standing next to the bed adjusting an earring, Mallory looked down as Chris's cellphone rang. Checking the caller ID: STEPHAN GRIGOR. Nic's instructions would not apply to family or close associates. She called to her husband in the bathroom, "It's Stephan, honey."

"Hey, Stephan."

After a moment, Chris pulled the phone from his ear, staring at it mutely. Noting this, Mallory's brow wrinkled.

"What did he—"

"He's not coming. Got the flu—he sounded awful. I could barely understand him."

"What?" Mallory questioned, genuinely concerned. "What did he say?"

Chris looked at his wife quizzically. "It was strange, actually. First he was speaking Russian, something about how he couldn't come in because of the flu."

"Yeah? What's so strange about that? What else did he say?"

Replaying the conversation, Chris tilted his head, "He said, 'There's an old Russian saying I think would be of interest today.' Then he switched to English and said, 'The long and brutal winter gives way to spring.'" Puzzled, Chris looked down, then at Mallory. "That's like really weird. What do you think it means?"

A strange look came over Mallory's face, but after a moment, she nodded. "Should we call him back?"

Chris shook his head. "Sounded like he was dying and going back to bed. Poor guy. I know he wanted to be here today. I'll call him later—see how he's doing."

Mallory grabbed her purse and jacket. "You about ready?"

Standing, Chris donned his overcoat as Mallory reached into her pocket. Removing her medical injector pen, she handed it to Chris. "Vest pocket, as usual. I'll take it back from you once we're seated at the ceremony."

Taking it, Chris absently asked, "By the way, have you heard from Nic?"

"Called a few minutes before Stephan. Something about an old case you worked. Guy you convicted is getting out and might have gained access to your phone number from his file and not to answer your phone unless it was Nic or anyone we know."

Absently, Chris nodded. "I hope he gets here on time."

"Honey, he's on his way. We'll see him shortly. Let's go."

CHAPTER 85

JANUARY
NEW YORK
INAUGURATION DAY

After the cemetery, Nic, Shelby, Olegina, and Slaga had departed for Washington, leaving Tasha in the City. Once Grigor's death had been reported, NYPD had established perimeter control about both Grigor's home and the Clinic for Right Being.

At the brownstone home, Tasha conducted another search of the darkened residence. Conditioned to, and working around death, she was mildly annoyed at her jumpiness. Dead people in a morgue—or brutal crime scenes—were routine stuff now, but death and ominous unseen shit like plots to overthrow her country ... shrouded in the mists of time ... was new territory.

In the den, where the body had just been removed, she slowly walked the room. It was very tastefully decorated—exquisite furniture, drapes, carpet, prints, and crown moulding. She examined a tiny obelisk, then a book, and a porcelain dish. The Zeus-Thetis painting, while not her style, aroused her in an odd way. Sitting at Grigor's desk, she swiveled slowly, surveying the room. Finally, her eyes landed on a solitary picture on a small reading-lamp table in the corner. The ivory and onyx matting blended in with the white curtains.

Closer examination revealed it was a black-and-white photo of a statue. At its base, it read DZERZHINSKY. A thought came to mind, "What had been his nickname?" But it flitted away before she could grasp it. After a moment, she shrugged and put it down. She took one more scan of the room before departing.

At the Clinic, she checked her watch, the sunlight attempting to creep around the edges of the dark curtains. Seven. There were a couple of hours until the swearing in. She flashed her badge at the police officer assigned to maintain the clinic, and she passed through the tape into the offices. Something about the officer seemed off, but she let it pass. With as little sleep as she'd had in the last day, her perceptions felt stuffy, like they had a cold.

Inside, she commenced a thorough inspection of Grigor's office: file cabinets, drawers, and credenza. She really wasn't sure what she was looking for. Grigor's clinic had already had a colonoscopy: it had been dusted for prints, files casually ransacked, and photographed. Really, what could she find now?

Finally, coming to a door that simply read LIGHT CHAMBER, she opened it, flipping the lights on. She jerked backward, totally unprepared for a room that looked like this. From what she'd learned from Nic and the others, she knew Grigor engaged in some mental shit like brainwashing or mind control, but this room crept under her fingernails. Descending from the ceiling, she saw a sinister, black metal tube with a crystalline wand extension, stretching menacingly outward.

Tasha approached the apparatus like it was a snake exhibit at the zoo. Sitting at the computer console, she pushed the power switch. Quietly, the machine hummed to life.

She smiled, thinking to herself, "Now, we're getting somewhere." But when the next screen requested a password Tasha groaned.

"What were you thinking?" She voiced to the empty room. Still, she took the mouse, scrolling to the password entry space. Gently, she tapped the mouse and suddenly stars populated the portal space. Adrenaline pumping, Tasha counted silently.

"Nine characters." She leaned back in the chair. "Crap." Slowly she swiveled, studying the room. She typed BLUEWALLS. Rejected.

A business card lay nearby. She read and typed DRSGRIGOR. Rejected.

DR.GRIGOR. Nope.

Rapidly, she revisited Grigor's office, searching for hints. There were posters of Moscow, Paris, and Venice. Books. Degrees on the wall. Art.

Back at the computer, she typed MINDTRICK. Nothing.

BRAINWASH. Denied.

KGBSCHEME. Likewise.

The picture from Grigor's house: *Dzerzhinsky*. "Too many letters. Damn. This is getting nowhere."

What if there were numbers or other characters? This would take all day. Her mind drifted back to the satisfaction she'd felt when deciphering the tattoo clues on the dead Galaxy victim and the impression she'd made on Nic—Inspector Ford. He was different than other cops. Quiet, very professional, and yet there seemed to be a sensitive side that he kept hidden. Equally, Tasha admired Nic's taste in clothing. Nothing too conservative, but very stylishly understated. Even his shoes and belts, new, not worn—

A sudden chill ran down her neck into her back causing her gut to tighten. That was it! That was what was wrong with the cop outside the Clinic.

When she'd first seen him, Nic's jacket had casually swept back as he reached for something and she'd seen his clean, polished belt. His badge was attached to it as plainclothes were wont to do. Earlier in the month, another NYPD office had died in the line of duty. As a sign of respect and honor, all NYPD and NYFD officers were wearing black mourning bands across their shields. Nic's badge had the same black band across it, even as the badge was out of sight on his belt.

The officer outside ... his badge was missing the dark stripe. It was a big deal to all officers. Something didn't feel right. Breath getting shorter, she took up her phone. Meaning to call the local precinct, to learn more about the officer outside, she slowly put the phone aside.

"Hell, maybe I'm just getting jumpy."

Putting her phone in her pocket, she checked that her sidearm was safely in its holster. But turning the swivel chair to stand up, a vicious blow to the back of her head knocked her unconscious.

Just before dropping into darkness, an image of the statue picture from Grigor's home again passed before her eyes.

CHAPTER 86

JANUARY
CAPITOL BUILDING ROTUNDA
INAUGURATION DAY

Located along the banks of the Potomac River—on land ceded by the states of Maryland and Virginia—Washington, DC, was brought forth on July 16, 1790. The original design of the city was the vision of a Parisian-born, US Army engineer, Pierre Charles L'Enfant. L'Enfant came to America with the French General, Marquis de Lafayette.

During his Revolutionary War service in the Corps of Engineers, L'Enfant made a favorable impression upon George Washington, who eventually appointed him to design the new federal city conceived by Congress to be the Capitol of the United States. L'Enfant envisioned incorporating many planning elements of European cities, sweeping boulevards, canals and fountains, monuments and green open spaces—all flanked by grand and epic buildings evoking images of Greek and Roman architecture.

This was to be the center of the world's new great empire. By its very existence, Washington, DC, would be engineered to dazzle and daunt, impress and intimidate, welcome and warn. Let our allies draw near. Let our enemies take caution.

And, at its center, would be a new acropolis, an august setting where the teachers, philosophers, scientists, planners, thinkers, shamans, doctors, leaders, and revered of this great nation would gather and chart its future: The House of the People.

As would befit a structure of this magnificence, its central feature would dominate the city's skyline, the Great Rotunda. Soaring to almost three hundred feet, the massive dome stands watch at the

East End of the National Mall and testifies to the bold ambition of the founders. To bring forth a new nation, committed to affording its citizens an opportunity to forge a better life—safeguarded through the creation of laws to nurture, guide, and protect it.

Across the ceiling, and through the oculus or eye of the massive dome, one can find the famous painting entitled *The Apotheosis of Washington*. Draped in purple, signifying royalty, Washington is being received into heaven and the pantheon of the greats. Below, on the circular floor of the great rotunda hall, are a host of statues dedicated to honored citizens such as Abraham Lincoln, Thomas Jefferson, Martin Luther King Jr., Ulysses Grant, Dwight Eisenhower, and Women's Suffragettes: Lucretia Mott, Elizabeth Cady Stanton, and Susan B. Anthony.

Surrounding them on the walls are various paintings from *the Dawn of America and the Republic, the Embarkation of the Pilgrims, Columbus, the Declaration of Independence*—and perhaps the best representation of one of America's most cherished of values: George Washington freely surrendering his military command and forces to the Continental Congress at the conclusion of the American Revolutionary War.

Every four years—at precisely noon on the twentieth of January—a second-term, or newly elected president, arrives at the Capitol to take the Oath of Office. It is a ceremony unlike any other in the world—both routine and irregular. Routine in that it is nothing more than words spoken. Irregular in that there is no coronation. No crown bestowed. No scepter received. No power imposed. The outgoing president departs freely and uncompelled, divesting themselves of all the trappings of office while the incoming chief of state arrives with no force other than the moral mandate that swept them into the White House.

It is one of the few days when the grand dame of American architecture gets dressed for a party. Thematically, it is understandably patriotic with overwhelming emphasis on red, white, and blue. On the exterior of the Capitol, massive tricolor banners descend from the roofs, creating an amphitheater of Americana—the backdrop before which one president will relieve the other and assume the watch for the next four years.

The interior of the Rotunda overflows with bunting and American flags. Important, and not-so-important, officials and invited guests gather here before being led to the platform outside where the swearing-in takes place. Champagne flows as useless small talk covers over insecurities, while social-political wannabes claw up the slippery pyramid of status.

It was upon such a day that two women—one born in poverty from Memphis, another born in similar circumstances from literally the middle of Siberia—entered the Great Rotunda of the Capitol Building of the United States.

While Shelby had been in Washington for years, the city still summoned goosebumps. The National Museum of African American History & Culture, the Martin Luther King Memorial, Howard University, and Frederick Douglas House all filled her with pride and a sense of recognition. Still, the common thread of being an American for her was the National Mall: at one end, Lincoln—at the other, the Capitol.

For an archivist from Moscow, Olegina had likewise been exposed to the timeline of Russia—blended into the urban landscape and daily existence of her countrymen. The Capitol Rotunda reminded her that history and culture wed to architecture, on a grand scale, could honor and inspire the people rather than serve as a bludgeon to suppress them.

Everywhere her eyes drifted, statues, paintings, building art, and the dome itself ... was as if the promise of America reigned eternal, riding atop massive columns of the rule of law, separating the country from the rest of the world. Understanding the urgency of what brought them there did nothing to diminish the soaring of her heart and tears welling in her eyes. Symbolic though it was, a deep breath was accompanied by a sense of, "This must be what freedom feels like."

Quietly, Shelby took her by the elbow. "This way."

The two women took up a position just across from the corridor leading to the inaugural platform. Shelby tapped her cellphone.

One ring later, Nic answered. "You in place?"

"Roger."

"I'll be in touch. Stay alert."

"Good luck with that," Shelby thought. Her mind drifted back over the last day. After a forced, late-night drive from New York to Washington, Shelby and Olegina rested for a couple of hours before cleaning up and getting fresh clothes. As they were leaving New York City, Nic had abruptly pulled their vehicle over to the curb in midtown and looked at Slaga.

"Go."

Mounting a protest, Slaga changed course, noting the animosity the Inspector still bore him. He opened the door, "Good luck," and stepped into the night.

In Washington, Nic had dropped the women off at Shelby's and departed for the Hay Adams to join his family. He and Shelby would stay in contact via cell until the ceremony was over.

Stopping first at FBI headquarters, Shelby had taken a deep breath before entering an office with a nameplate reading, SARAH BOXER, NATIONAL SECURITY SECTION. Her boss lit her up like a Roman candle.

"Littlejohn, where the hell have you been the last two days? I got Secret Service, NSA, CIA—shit even M&M's want to know what's going on."

Hands up defensively, Shelby paused in the doorway. "Chief, I'd like to introduce you to somebody." Reaching just outside the doorway, Shelby pulled Olegina reluctantly into the office. "Sarah Boxer, this is Olegina Bortsova. Olegina, Sarah Boxer, National Security Desk Chief."

Boxer stiffly came from behind her desk to shake Olegina's hand. "Ms. Bortsova, welcome to America. I hope you haven't been inconvenienced too much."

"No ma'am."

Turning to Shelby, Boxer said, "Seriously—"

Olegina awkwardly cut in. "Ma'am I just wondering if anyone in my country knows I'm gone."

Eyes squinting, Boxer looked between the two women, before returning to Shelby. "Did she enter the country with her passport?"

Shelby lowered her eyes. "No ma'am."

About to chew into her agent, Boxer abruptly caught herself. "Fine. We'll fix this later. Maybe we can return her the same way she came in. Bring me up to speed on your field trip to New York."

Shelby quickly detailed her investigation, finding Grigor, getting the triggering phrase, the trip to the Russian Cemetery, meeting Slaga Dmitriev, and learning that the phrase language was directly opposite of what the dying Doctor Grigor had told them. "Look, Sarah—Inspector Ford has ensured that his cousin won't get any phone calls prior to the Inauguration, but I don't think we're out of the woods yet."

Leaning on her desk, arms crossed, Boxer nodded. "Okay, okay. Let me pass this on, you get to the Capitol and assist Inspector Ford. Enter through the East Side entrance. There will be receptions taking place across Emancipation Hall. You can mingle there while surveying things. Do you know who or what you're looking for?"

Caught off guard, Shelby thought about the question as she shook her head. "Actually, that's the first time I've considered that. What would you look for?"

"Unknown, but I assume you're in contact with Inspector Ford?"

"Yes, ma'am."

"Good, just stay in the Hall near the exit to the parking garage in case the Secret Service needs to make an emergency evacuation."

"Ms. Bortsova was in close contact with a couple of the suspects, would it be okay to take her for possible ID?"

Her section head nodded. "I'll get things prepped with DC and Capitol police. They'll be blanketing the area for possible hostiles. Assassination attempts under your nose, even defused ones, are never well received—like finding a snake in the garden."

Nodding, Shelby smiled. "And I'll take care of getting Ms. Bortsova back to Moscow."

"Very good. Get going."

CHAPTER 87

JANUARY
CAPITOL BUILDING GARAGE
INAUGURATION DAY

"Does he know you are coming?" Vadik asked.

Phone to her ear, Sigrid replied, "No, General."

"Excellent. I want him distracted and thinking about ... other things when it happens."

"Yes, General."

The line went dead. Suddenly came a call from another number. Sigrid's eyes squinted. "Yes?"

A garbled voice said, "They know the correct sequence and language to activate. They still think the plan has been derailed, but they're on high alert."

"I'm sorry, you must be mistaken," Sigrid said before terminating the call.

Sigrid stared at the now-blank phone screen. Did this new wrinkle change their plans? She redialed the General.

"Yes?"

Sigrid relayed the new turn of events to Vadik.

"Do they know about our relationship with Byrnes?"

"No."

"Can your unit deal with these loose threads?"

"Yes, General."

"Then proceed.

Sigrid dialed another number.

"Sigrid?"

"Oh, I must have the wrong number. Sorry." She terminated the call. Opening the back, she removed and destroyed the SIM card as another phone beside her on the car seat vibrated.

"Hello?" she said.

"Sorry. I forgot, no names."

"Not to worry. I'm coming to visit."

"Now?" Came an anxious reply. "Today is not a good day."

"Of course it is. Think about what I'm going to do."

Urgent imagination suddenly replaced common sense as Adam Byrnes huskily croaked, "Where?"

"Basement. Members elevator."

"How are you going to get past security?"

"Let me worry about that. I'll call again." Sigrid ended the call before he could reply. She nodded to Viktor, behind the wheel of a black-and-white pack van with the words, IRON-LOCK SHREDDING SERVICE, on the side. Both were clad in service worker jumpsuits; he started the vehicle. In back sat two more similarly dressed men.

"Ivan, Kai, you ready?"

Silent acknowledgements as each returned to checking equipment and working kinks, real and imagined, from their necks and joints.

After a glance at a map, Sigrid examined a schematic of Washington's tunnel grid. "Viktor, Union Station please."

As Viktor drove, Sigrid donned a ball cap that read, IRON-LOCK SHREDDING SERVICE. In the parking garage, Viktor parked in a remote slot near a service elevator. The three men rapidly removed canvas bags and mid-size recycle containers. They loaded the bags while Sigrid summoned the lift. Descending to the basement, they wheeled the cannisters to a substation riser, upon which Sigrid spread the tunnel map. "Washington sits above a mass confluence of tunnels, old and new, that connect the city like a web. There are utility, sewer, transportation, and pedestrian tunnels, tubes, and passageways. Generally, most are service oriented, but a few are dedicated solely to maintaining the others. These are the ones that are least trafficked."

Opening her bag, Sigrid produced four swipe badges. "These allow unlimited access to all Capitol spaces. We're going to start with Union Station's main electrical tunnel running from here to the Capitol. About halfway, we'll encounter a large riser. Behind it is a door accessing the Capitol's primary maintenance corridor to another walkway. This walkway leads to a machinery shop utilized by the Capitol Architect's office. From the machine shop, we can move into the corridor near the Capitol Crypt, the lower Exhibition Hall, and from there we can access Rotunda Hall where the receptions are taking place. It also allows us to bypass the security scanners."

Receiving visual acknowledgement from each, Sigrid said, "Let's go." With practiced precision, the group moved into the tunnel, Viktor on point, Sigrid and Kai in the middle with Ivan on rear guard.

Reaching the machine shop, the men wheeled their cannisters in, removed their bags before stripping off the coveralls to reveal attire suitable for the inauguration. From the canvas duffel bags, each extracted a black cashmere top coat, a suppressor-equipped Sig Sauer P226 pistol and three capped fountain pens. Likewise, Sigrid withdrew the same items along with the Auto Bedlam switchblade and a small backpack-satchel that she donned before concealing them beneath an elegant, wool long coat. Donning black stiletto heels, Sigrid took out an ebony leather clutch that she lay on a nearby table.

Reaching into her bag one more time, Sigrid produced four communication systems, with ear pieces and wireless wrist mics connected via waist-mounted charging packs. Holding hers up, Sigrid said, "High sensitivity mics, speak softly. Viktor is Cap two, Kai, Cap three and Ivan, Cap four. I'm Cap one."

"Everything is in place, but we have some loose ends. The NYPD Medical Examiner has been dealt with. Officer Ford, the FBI agent, and the Russian woman are here. After we insert, move across the Rotunda. Viktor and Ivan will take Officer Ford while I deal with the two women. Kai you stay here as backup in case we need you. No firearms. Get close. With these crowds, it will be easy to use the poison needle-tip pens, preferably out of sight like a restroom or office. We want to cast as small a shadow as possible, but if you encounter security personnel, you know what to do."

Viktor, Ivan, and Kai each rolled their coveralls into the canvas bags before burying them in the garbage as Sigrid continued briefing them.

"In the chaos, there should be ample opportunity to blend in with the crowd. If need be, you can return this way, but it is not advisable as there will be swarming security afterwards and a higher likelihood of being caught in the tunnels. Rendezvous is at Union Station where we can take the train or recover the van and drive to New York."

From her clutch, Sigrid removed and applied some lipstick, stopping to check her appearance in the mirror above the shop's sink. For a moment, her mind slipped back to thoughts of a house on one of the small islands near Stockholm—she was clad in a heavy sweater and seated on the deck with a hot cup of coffee, her eyes lazily scanning the waves. Shaking her head clear, she thought "Steady." Putting her hair into a bun, she donned a short, black wig. After some final touches, she turned from the mirror finding the men in various stages of rest and preparation.

"Remember, this floor is empty for the day so we shouldn't be bothered until we're ready. I need to attend to Byrnes. When I'm finished, I'll return."

Taking her cellphone, she dialed the Speaker, let it ring once and hung up. Rapidly, a return call came.

"Are you here?" Byrnes said.

"In the basement, at your SUV."

"My wife is here in the outer office."

"Tell her you have a quick legislative meeting with a few other members before the ceremony and you'll be back in a short while."

Before he could respond, she hung up.

* * * *

In the Capitol Police Department, a phone rang on a desk surrounded by other desks amidst a cacophony of overactive uniforms and plainclothes.

"Duty Officer's desk," said a young female voice.

It was readily apparent the caller was attempting to mask their voice. "There is going to be an attempt on the President's life. Look for two women: one an African-American, the other a Russian."

The line went dead. Quickly, the officer jotted the pertinent facts of the call and then half-stumbled to a door marked SECTION CHIEF.

She rapped the door, disturbing the occupant who was eating a bagel and drinking coffee.

"Come!" came a grouchy, why-are-you-bothering-me response.

"Boss, I think we have a code red."

A thirty-year vet working his last Inauguration looked up annoyedly. But one glance at his junior officer's face and he dropped his bagel and coffee. Rapidly processing the details of the call, he removed a key from his desk, stepped to a painfully yellow, wall-mounted lock box. Using the key, he unlocked it to reveal a bright-crimson push button. "Thirty years," he thought as he hit the button.

In the outer office, an intrusive, highly charged sound similar to that made by submarines preparing to dive suddenly shocked the room. It was accompanied by a pulsing red light on the wall outside the Chief's office.

After fifteen seconds, the alarm turned off but the light continued its urgent journey. Stepping into the sudden chaos outside his office, the Chief put his hands into the air, calm descending across the room.

"Listen up."

* * * *

Making her way to the member's garage, Sigrid flashed a Homeland Security badge identifying her as a lowly GS Five working for the Congressional logistics and administration department; sent by the Speakers Office to double-check parking for the afternoon. Soon, Byrnes arrived. Without waiting, she pushed him against the massive SUV. "Open the back door."

Byrnes complied as Sigrid shoved him in and pulled the door shut behind her. Soon, Sigrid stepped out, turning to Byrnes, hurrying to reassemble himself.

"That was a taste. I want you thinking about what I'm going to do later. Wait here five minutes to let me get clear."

Shutting the door, the assassin glided to the elevator. Returning to the machine shop, she lost the wig, rearranged her hair, and donned a pair of glasses that made her look mousy before she and the others disappeared into the Capitol mix.

CHAPTER 88

JANUARY
HAY ADAMS HOTEL
INAUGURATION DAY

Nic pulled his room door shut behind him, even though he knew he didn't need to. The latest hotel-room door technology, if he could call it that, ensured that doors automatically shut themselves. But ... old habits.

In the hallway, he stopped for another moment to collect himself. While they'd luckily learned Grigor had duped his killers with the wrong trigger, things were still too raw—too close to home for him to relax. Who would have ever concocted a bizarre plot to eliminate the President of the United States ... by his own Vice President? It was just too ... *bizarre* was a great word. No one would believe him, but at some point, he was going to have to let his family know. Their doctor had sought to brainwash them ... and the Ford family matriarch: a Soviet spy her whole life. Bizarre.

Still, the puzzle was slotting into place now. On the drive back to New York, Slaga had explained that the programming Chris had received from Grigor was designed to suppress his natural tendencies to do the right thing. The trigger was to temporarily override this instinct long enough to allow the killing order to be processed and executed. Chris was a dupe, never knowing he'd been the subject of mind programming. Years of headaches, chronic nightmares, and fatigue proved his mind had been fighting back.

Once, when fishing, Chris had shared a weird dream that seemed to keep coming. Chris was in a classroom. A professor clad in white was at the chalkboard when a man in black clothes burst into the room. The intruder would come straight for Chris, grabbing him by the arm; he'd attempt to haul Chris away. The instructor fought valiantly against the black-attired man, but was ever-destined to lose the battle. Slowly, the nightmare assailant dragged Chris toward the door. Just as they were at the edge of the hallway beyond, Chris would awaken, sweaty, gasping, and crying.

Nic took a deep breath. Exhausted, he was a bit sullen and bitter about Elena. Did his grandfather know? His parents? Uncle John and Aunt Danielle? He was still functioning, but after today, he was going to spend a week somewhere in the Caribbean drinking himself to sleep every night.

On the elevator, he pushed a button and rode up to the top floor. As the door opened, four men in suits immediately greeted him. Putting his hands out, he allowed them to check him before escorting him down the hall to the Federal Suite where another four men fronted the door.

"Officer Ford," one said, "your credential please."

From his jacket, Nic removed his admission ticket and lanyard-strapped laminated credential.

The officer returned the credential. "Just the ticket for now." He made a note and then nodded to another agent. "The Vice President-elect is expecting you."

Nic stepped into the suite. Almost immediately, he was greeted by his mother.

"Where have you been? I tried calling you for the last two days. You missed the party last night."

Giving his mother a small peck on the cheek, Nic's hands assumed a defensive position. "Sorry ... massive case at work. Just could not be helped."

Chris bounded into the room, pulling Nic into a massive bear hug. "Bad guys don't stop do they? Glad you're here."

Nic forced a smile as he nodded. "Absolutely."

"Anything I was ever working on?" Chris asked.

Imagining what his cousin would say if he knew the Specter was still alive ... Nic shook his head. "Nah, just more mayhem and evil."

Chris furrowed his brow. "You sure? You seem tense."

"Just tired ... had expected to be here sooner."

"All right, but get something to eat or drink. We're leaving for the Capitol in about an hour. Glad you're here, cuz."

The Vice President-elect joined his wife as they glad-handed some other guests in the suite. Nic took a plate, helping himself to some food along with a glass of juice. He sat quietly in the corner, welcoming the solitude. As he watched Chris and Mallory, he could not quiet a thought: "What did I miss?"

CHAPTER 89

JANUARY
THE CAPITOL
INAUGURATION DAY

The Fords and their families were escorted to a special, cordoned-off part of the Rotunda, where official guests waited before being led to the inaugural platform. Nic took a glass from a passing waiter. Peripherally, he picked up Shelby, who had intermixed with a crowd of suits, more guests, and security. Subtly, she tilted her head. Unobtrusively standing behind a statue of James Garfield, Olegina nodded. The irony was not lost on Nic. Garfield had been the second of four American Presidents assassinated in office, the other three being Lincoln, McKinley, and Kennedy.

Nic leaned into his mother, "I'm going to the men's room."

"Now?" Sophia snipped before softening. "Hurry honey."

As he stepped off, he could not help but think "What an amazing country ... and how apropos we are from New York ... the home of the Statue of Liberty." Every school kid in New York had to memorize the words of Emma Lazarus' sonnet at some point:

... give me your tired, your poor,
Your huddled masses yearning to breathe free,
The wretched refuse of your teeming shore.
Send these, the homeless, tempest-tossed to me,
I lift my lamp beside the golden door!

Now, a third-generation immigrant was about to become the Vice President of the United States.

Nic grimaced as another thought intruded: things could have turned out worse. Much worse. He was glad that it was almost over. He'd need to brief Chris and Mallory—no need for any of the parents to know. Naturally, there'd be questions about Grigor's death, but he thought he should be able to finesse this.

He paused to admire the Garfield statue as Shelby joined him.

"Nothing from Tasha?" she asked.

Nic glanced at his cell. "No. How you two doing?"

"Nervous. Do you think whoever it was that attacked us will keep trying?"

"Unknown," he glanced at the spellbound Russian archivist. "How's she doing?"

"Good. I don't think she's too happy to be leaving. Diplomatic flight to Moscow tomorrow at nine."

A soft *gong* chimed throughout the Hall, just as Nic's phone buzzed in his hand. He glanced at it. "First call to seating. I have to run to the men's room. Text me if you need."

Nic faded into the crowd.

CHAPTER 90

JANUARY
THE CAPITOL
INAUGURATION DAY

Even though she was inside the Rotunda—literally feet from the actual ceremony—Shelby still accessed the news stream on her phone.

"Good morning, ladies and gentlemen. Along with Daniel Prestwick, I'm Shae Rogers and we're honored to be bringing you the Inauguration Ceremonies here on *AmeriNews*. As you can see, all about us, the preparations are in place for the installation of Robert Johansen and his Ideals of Tomorrow administration. Daniel, what do you make of this crowd?"

The other anchor nodded, "Astonishing. Unlike any Inaugural crowd I've ever seen. The atmosphere is buzzing; there's an energy and expectation about this administration. Since their election, Governor Johansen and Senator Ford have posited a new agenda for progress. Ideals of Tomorrow have captured the imagination of America, and the world. Jobs, infrastructure, technological breakthroughs in medicine, educational skillsets for a new century, and a rebirth of America's space program. I sense a new focus on the human spirit, bridging the gap between different and disparate groups of people. I don't know how they will accomplish it all, but there are high expectations across the land."

The first anchor echoed her compatriot's enthusiasm. "Just look at the pomp and circumstance on display here today. Just below the inaugural platform, the United States Marine Corps Band is injecting patriotic color into the festivities. And the crowds have filled the National Mall beyond the Washington Monument. People from all walks of life have made the trek here today to witness—"

With a grimace, Shelby muted the audio. They were getting a mite overhyped for her, and she needed to be alert. Her attention focused, she could see the outgoing President and First Lady joined by President-elect and Mrs. Johansen—being escorted to their seats. Just after them, the departing Vice President's entourage with the Fords and their families made their arrival.

Olegina came to join her.

"Where is the bathroom, please?" she asked.

Pointing at the stairs to the Emancipation Hall floor, Shelby said "It's ... oh just come with me."

In the deserted hall, they found a restroom. Once finished, they came to the sink. Olegina took out a cosmetics case. Satisfied with her lipstick, she gazed into the larger vanity mirror checking her appearance.

"In Moscow, the ladies's rooms are nicer," Olegina sniffed.

Shelby rubbed lip-gloss into place as her eyes found the Russian's in the mirror.

Shelby's youth was spent in Memphis, Tennessee. She had known racism and sexism from her earliest days. It was always a bitch being black and female. White people either thought she was invisible or treated her like she had the plague while the brothers were always looking to keep her down or get into her pants.

One day, in the third grade at Jefferson Davis Elementary School—another irony she seldom discussed—she'd been in the girl's room when the vice principal, Mrs. Taylor, emerged from a stall. At the mirror, she'd earnestly said, "Good morning, Ms. Littlejohn. Do you like the washroom?"

Not understanding, Shelby had replied, "Ma'am?"

"A clean bathroom must be something you look forward to coming to each day, I'm sure."

Not sure why, Shelby had been overcome with a great flood of shame. "Yes, ma'am."

Oppression and clean bathrooms—Shelby just smiled at Olegina and said, "I remember."

Olegina said, "I need some tissue." But finding none on the counter, stepped into a stall as the lavatory door opened. Shelby was mildly surprised to see Chief Boxer enter.

"Agent Littlejohn."

"Chief."

Something about Boxer's manner made Shelby's skin tingle.

"Where is Bortsova?"

From inside the bathroom stall, Olegina's antenna likewise picked up the tenseness. Suddenly she was back at Lubyanka. Her heart beat ratcheted up as she sat on the seat, lifting her feet out of sight.

Without waiting for a response, Boxer's sidearm, with silencer attached, was out of its holster. Quickly, she scanned beneath the stall partitions, seeing only open space. She gestured to the wall farthest from the door. "Over there."

Shelby squinted but said nothing. As she and Boxer moved toward the far partition, Shelby's eyes never broke contact with Boxer's, though she could see Olegina in the crack of the stall door just off Boxer's right shoulder.

"Left hand, remove your sidearm."

"Senior Agent Boxer, you know only Secret Service and CPD are allowed to have weapons inside the Capitol during an Inauguration. I'm not carrying."

"Open your jacket." Seeing Shelby's empty holster, Boxer kept her sidearm trained on Shelby. "Where is the Russian?"

"I should have known. The whole fucking time. You were tipping them—they knew my every move until we dropped off the grid in New York. Motherfuckin' traitor."

"Shut your fucking mouth, you overachieving little bitch. You were supposed to be dead already."

Shelby's murderous glare cut into Boxer.

"And don't look at me like that. I've been a good agent—the best."

"So why the Benedict Arnold? I don't remember them teaching treason at Quantico."

"And I don't remember them teaching *invest in the American dream and you'll get screwed.* If it hadn't been for that crash in 2008, I'd still have my rentals. Lost them all—lost everything."

"That's what this is all about. Greed? So, betray America because you made a financial mistake?"

"Nobody went to jail in 2008. None of those banks, investment guys, insurance companies. Nobody. Government just fucking bailed them out. Well, these guys at least pay cash for services rendered."

"Look you—"

"Shut the fuck up." Boxer raised the pistol at Shelby. "I've had enough of your sanctimonious—" Out of the blue, a shoe crashed into the side of Boxer's head.

Momentarily stunned, she fired off a couple of harmless rounds that nonetheless ricocheted off the marble walls, one shattering the bathroom mirror, the other falling to the floor. Desperately, Shelby grabbed her gun hand, thrusting it skyward as the two FBI agents came eye-to-eye. Boxer headbutted Shelby, causing her grip on Boxer's arm to loosen. Pulling free, Boxer took aim at Shelby's face when a burst of hairspray squirted into her eyes.

"Motherfucker!" Seeking to wipe her eyes, Boxer spun around leveling the weapon at Olegina retreating into the stall. But as she did, Shelby kicked up, knocking the weapon loose. Flying across the counter, it disappeared into the recessed space behind the shattered mirror.

Spinning to reengage with Shelby, Boxer executed a roundhouse kick hammering Shelby into the subway-tiled wall. Boxer followed, delivering a quick one-two punch combo that pushed Shelby to the edge of consciousness. About to finish the job, Boxer's eyes went from lasered focus on Shelby to dizziness then blackness, realizing she'd left Olegina alone too long to finish off Shelby.

Shelby's eyes cleared, coming to rest on Olegina still holding the garbage can she'd used to knock Boxer into tomorrow.

Rubbing her jaw, Shelby lurched to her feet still eying the Russian. "Damn girl, remind me never to piss you off." Shelby rolled Boxer over, reaching into her jacket to remove handcuffs that she used to secure Boxer to one of the bathroom door handles. Patting the unconscious woman's jacket, she removed and pocketed the keys to the manacles.

A quick check into the recess behind the broken bathroom mirror revealed Boxer's sidearm had fallen ten feet into the deep space, well beyond reach.

Shelby nodded toward the door. "Let's go. We'll return for her."

On the main floor, Shelby searched for another FBI agent as she checked her phone for any news from Nic. Nothing. But as she looked up, she found four men in government-looking suits across the hall eying the two women. Suspiciously, they consulted a tablet device in their hands before reengaging them. Satisfied, the G-men slowly inched toward them, through a throng of Inaugural guests, across the still-crowded Rotunda Hall.

Shelby jerked Olegina by the elbow.

"Oooh, you are hurting me," she yelped.

"Go."

The FBI woman shoved the still-clueless Muscovite onto an elevator that closed just as the agents arrived.

"What is going on?"

"Not sure, but those guys made us as suspects or something. The only type of alert that would prompt this type of response is a BOLO."

"BOLO?" Olegina said before adding, "Oh, from American police shows—*be on the lookout for*, yes?" After a moment, a puzzled look came over the Russian, "But why us?"

Shelby was only half-listening as she checked her phone for FBI alerts. "Son of a—that bitch Sarah, called CPD ... telling them there was an active assassination plot in motion and to look for two suspects who match our description. Now the entire law enforcement community is coming after us. Shit."

The car stopped, Shelby pushed Olegina to one side, while she huddled up against the other. Silently, she put a finger to her lips. Creakily, the doors parted. Sidearm drawn, she stepped onto the landing. Finding it empty, she motioned for Olegina to follow her.

"Give me your compact."

"What?" Questioned Olegina as she fished it out.

Taking it, Shelby opened it while cautiously sidling to the railing, tilting the mirror over the edge. Below, she could see a CPD officer motioning her way, while other officers quietly converged on the stairs. Behind them, the elevator door started closing.

Lurching back, Shelby blocked the opening with her foot. Shuffling in her coat, she yanked free a new, hard-shell, Ray Ban sunglasses case that she placed in the elevator door slide groove. The doors kept smashing into the case, preventing them from closing.

"Let's go."

Staying low, they slinked around the dome perimeter. Coming to a door, Shelby opened it, pushing Olegina in. As she did, Olegina happened to look below where her eyes met those of Sigrid's.

As Olegina gasped, Shelby stole a glance the same way. For a second, the two adversaries locked eyes—each taking in the full measure of the other, understanding they were the yin to the other's yang, knowing a final showdown was imminent.

"Go!" Shelby pushed Olegina into a circular stairwell. They moved speedily up the curved climb. As the door behind them re-opened, the two women managed to lay against the outer edge of the staircase, out of sight, as a torrent of blue poured into the space.

A flood of controlled frenzy—yelling and activity—came before a voice called out, "I don't see them. They must have taken another way! You two stay here and guard the door. Everyone else with me."

Diminishing sounds of rapid departure were followed by an incongruent eeriness as the stairway door softly closed.

"Where are we?" Olegina whispered.

"This is a stairway that I believe runs to the top of the Capitol Dome."

"How are we going to get out of here?"

Shelby looked at her phone. "Not sure. I have no reception in here so I can't call Nic."

Sitting in the silence, Olegina's mind wandered. She seemed to recall the Capitol was called the People's House. "This Dome is extraordinary," she thought, when she was startled by Shelby's hand on her arm. About to speak, she saw the urgency in Shelby's face—a finger to her lips while pointing below. While unintelligible, they could hear questioning voices followed by the unmistakable sound of two suppressed bullet shots and then thuds of things heavy, dropping to the floor.

Without being told, Shelby knew the officers posted at the doorway to the Dome stairwell were dead. A moment later, her ears picked up the sound of bodies being pulled out of sight behind the door. Then, as if in slow motion, they heard the sliding of the door closing. Carefully, Shelby looked over the edge of the stairwell, yanking back as a bullet flew past, burying into the plaster above her.

"Silencer," she whispered to Olegina. Pulling Olegina up, Shelby pushed the archivist ahead. "Stay to the outer part of the stairs; she can't see us." From behind, they heard the soft padding of someone climbing after them. "She's taken off her shoes," Shelby thought out loud.

The two women rapidly climbed the circular stairway exiting onto a landing outside of a massive sandstone drum. Nearby was a zigzag stairway that disappeared into the drum itself. Seeing no other options, Shelby and Olegina raced up the steps, reaching the top as Sigrid emerged onto the landing. Just as they disappeared into the sandstone wall, two more shots smashed into the stone, blasting fragments into the air.

Shelby muscled Olegina through the darkened passageway but fear was roughly shoved aside by surprise as they stepped into the bright-lit walkway of the First Visitor's Gallery extending three hundred-sixty degrees around the Dome. Massive windows sat on one side of the walkway, while on the other, a classic white balustrade overlooking Rotunda Hall below. As much as they might have wanted to gape at the Hall below, the painted Dome above and the DC cityscape outside, urgency prompted them to keep scaling the small stairway. On a hunch, Shelby checked, but to her dismay, there was no lock on any of the doors into or out of the Gallery.

Stumbling onward, the women hurried through the next door where they encountered yet another world; the stark Interstitial space. Constituting the area between the old building constructed in the early 1800s, and new dome built over the old one in mid-century, it was a honeycomb of massive girders, bolts, rods and beams resembling a ship's interior and hull. Upward they forged; the restricted space becoming both claustrophobic and hopeless. The air was tired and reeked of stillness. If they died up here, they wouldn't be found for months. Shelby battled to slow her breathing, self-talking her thoughts, "Focus. Forget the surroundings and Inauguration."

Soft, Marugo Ninja shoes smothered her footsteps as Sigrid tracked the American and Russian, thinking, "Strange allies these two; yet complementing each other: one insightful and patient—the other forceful and decisive." Seldom had the Swedish assassin felt even a hint of regard for an opponent.

Sigrid paused to reorient herself. She was higher than planned, but in retrospect, the farther from the ceremonies, the better ... less likely they'd gum things up. But, then came another, less expected emotion. She was actually enjoying the unusual environment she found herself hunting in. This location—the symbolism was right out of a movie, seemed perfect. This would be a trophy kill she'd savor.

Still, it would have been better if their original plan had stayed on track: quietly eliminate the two from the Rotunda, kill them in the garage, and dispose of the bodies on Maryland's remote Eastern Shore. Executing both atop the Dome was not ideal, but Sigrid could bring cleaners back the next night to sanitize and remove the corpses. Their missing status would raise some ripples, but that was easier to explain than dead bodies.

Ascending the steep stairs that continued to curve offered some safe harbor, out of their pursuer's direct line of sight. However, it was clear they were running out of real estate, their breathing was now very labored and no real places to hide. Arriving at the landing to the Second Visitor's Gallery, the women were spent. Opening the door, they were astonished by the vastness of the Rotunda Hall below and the majesty of *The Apotheosis of Washington*, the mural painted by Constantino Brumidi atop the Dome.

The sounds slithering up the stairwell below reminded them a grim appointment awaited if they tarried a moment longer. Passing back through the door, a fire extinguisher on the wall caught Shelby's eye. Squinting, Shelby seized the cannister.

Sigrid was certain she had the FBI woman and the Russian exactly where she wanted them: trapped and diverted farther away from safety. She was seemingly improving her position, and it appeared they were unarmed. As a snake uses its tongue to smell and track prey, Sigrid sought to listen for what the two women above her, were doing. But the acoustics inside the Dome were a bit sketchy. Outside wind swirled about the circular dome, rattling nearby windows and side walls.

She checked her watch; things would be going down very soon and she wanted to be clear of the Capitol. Time to finish this. Her thoughts briefly turned to her team. "I hope Viktor and the others are dealing with the Inspector."

At the landing for the Second Visitor's Gallery, Sigrid checked the slightly ajar door but passed it by, already knowing if they'd gone through, it would now be secured.

Counting on the fly, Shelby estimated that, unless their pursuer had a second clip, highly likely, the assassin would be down to her last rounds. Then a strange thought came to her. In these closed quarters, a marksman of this woman's readily apparent capability would have hit one or both of them by now. Why was she missing them?

Shelby knew they were running out of building space. Her mind sprinted through different developments, "Could the assassination still be carried out *without* Chris Ford—if he'd been deactivated? Or ... had they missed a backup plan ... something to be implemented in case something had altered the original plan? What if their hunter was driving them on, away from the Inauguration? Even if they overcame her, they'd never get back to Rotunda Hall to thwart whatever might be happening."

They were in the last passageway leading to the upper observatory deck, just below the Tholos. It was now. Shelby stopped. She rapidly gestured for Olegina to move behind a large, curving, white stanchion.

"We're out of space. We gotta suck her in. You wait here, but leave just a little bit of your leg out so that she can see you."

"What!"

"Just do it. Nothing's going to happen to you—I promise. Now here's what I want you to do."

Rapidly explaining her thoughts, Shelby then retreated five feet, scaling another metallic beam from where she could see Olegina's hiding space. She sensed, rather than heard, their predator sliding along the metallic flooring.

Up close, Shelby could not help but be impressed with the shorter, black-haired assassin. Everything about her reeked of a consummate professional, comfortable in the most demanding situations. Balanced. Focused. Careful. As she passed, Shelby instinctively knew to pull her head back just as Sigrid whirled to check behind her.

Sigrid was tiring of her pursuit; her senses were flagging, and the closed space summoned memories of a few months before at Lubyanka when she had barely made it out of the secret records room. Suddenly, she espied the tiniest piece of fabric protruding from behind the next bulkhead. Again, on high alert, she quickly verified clearance behind her. Finding nothing, she cautiously approached the stanchion.

"You can come out now," she cooed softly, but with a hint of finality in her voice.

The archivist appeared first. She stumbled onto the catwalk, spinning to face something unseen. Sigrid prepared to fire when Olegina hissed, "*You didn't have to push me!*"

Sigrid's brow wrinkled first in satisfaction and then suddenly recognition—she spun around, but too late. Shelby hammered the Swede's gun hand with the fire extinguisher, knocking the piece loose to clatter down the dome ... out of sight.

About to face the FBI agent, the svenskar killer suddenly pirouetted backward, surprising Olegina. Reaching into her coat, the assassin fluidly removed and snapped open the Auto Bedlam switchblade in her right hand—putting it to Olegina's throat.

"Back."

Shaking her head, Shelby took a step forward. "Bitch, I'm gonna—"

Sigrid applied pressure; a red droplet ran down Olegina's porcelain skin. Shelby abruptly halted.

As time stood still, the only sound that could detected was the low wailing of wind about the Dome. Death arrived to collect its due when, for reason's she did not understand, Olegina's mind glacially relaxed. She recalled a course from secondary school entitled, *Women's Safety Orientation*; it indoctrinated students in close-order self-defense. Of the varied methods of protection taught that semester, Olegina had struggled with most of them. Her upper-body strength never enough to deal with stronger, more determined opponents. Still, she excelled at *one*. The one she found herself in at this moment.

Something about Olegina's subtle change in body language caused Shelby to hesitate. As if she'd suddenly become a spectator, Shelby knew the next moments belonged to the Russian. Sigrid likewise detected, too late, the archivist's odd rebalancing. In a coordinated sequence of moves, Olegina first thrust her head back, smashing the Swede's nose while lifting her left shoe before driving it into the assassin's foot as hard as she could.

Momentarily caught off guard, Sigrid grunted before rebounding to slit Olegina's neck. But the Russian's surprise attack had bought just enough time for her slip Sigrid's grasp, the stiletto barely tagging the edge of Olegina's neck, drawing the smallest of cuts.

Olegina fell to the ground as Sigrid and Shelby faced each other. Out of the blue, Sigrid dashed away toward the last stairwell to the roof.

Shelby rapidly triaged Olegina. "Just a nick."

Olegina pushed Shelby off. "Please, go get her."

Shelby grimly smiled before carefully advancing to the circular staircase. Ascending the last mount, she found the observation-deck door open. Already impressed with Sigrid's abilities, Shelby was nonetheless shocked as she found both observation-deck police snipers on the ground with wicked neck slashes. One was dead, the other holding the wound tight.

"I'm okay; she went around that way," he rasped.

Shelby resolutely nodded as she prepared to call for backup but was dismayed to find both sniper rifles had been emptied. The police officer's sidearms were also gone—along with the shoulder-communication set of the dead officer. Only the living officer's set remained, but the cord to the mouthpiece had been cut.

"Shit!"

Realizing the hopelessness of the situation, Shelby grabbed the rifle, wielding it like a baseball bat, and started around the deck. She came to the north side in time to find Sigrid's black coat on the ground. Continuing around the deck, Shelby arrived to find, the assassin atop the railing in a skintight body-suit. Before Shelby could get to her, the Swedish woman leapt off.

Shelby could only stare in dumb shock as very quickly, from a satchel on the woman's back, a small base-jump chute deployed. Yelling at the top of her lungs, Shelby was unable to alert the police officers clustered at the bottom of the Capitol, far below. Helplessly, she watched as Sigrid landed atop the CSPAN building at the intersection of Louisiana and *D* Street, where she ditched the chute and disappeared into the building.

Turning, Shelby returned to the downed officer where Olegina was now containing the wound with a kerchief.

"Stay here. I'm going below."

"Be careful," Olegina needlessly offered.

CHAPTER 91

JANUARY
NEW YORK
INAUGURATION DAY

Tasha yielded to the jagged, sharp-edge stabbing in her head accompanying efforts to open her eyes. After a minute, she was more successful. Her eyes fluttered open, but the reward was hardly worth the excruciating pain.

She was lying on the sofa in the Light Chamber. Seated across from her was an older man. Attractive and well dressed, he reminded her of Nic Ford.

"Ah, you are awake. Very good," the man said with a Russian accent.

Sitting up brought another jab. It felt like her brain was the last ball bearing in a can being shaken by a five-year-old. "Who are you? Did you hit me?"

"I did."

Turning, Tasha saw the police officer with the badge lacking the black mourning stripe.

"Why?" She asked, already knowing, but trying to get acclimatized.

"Why are you here?" asked the older man.

Tasha silently rubbed the growing knot at the base of her skull. Across from her, the dapper man lifted up her ID card.

"Ms. O'Riley, one more time. Why are you here?"

"Fuck off, asshole."

Swiftly, the officer's nightstick flashed across the air like a cobra, smashing her in the arm. About to strike again, her assailant stopped as the older man raised a hand.

"Ms. O'Riley. We can do this all day if need be ... but I find that the threat of sexual violence—accompanied by escalating physical duress—often pries open the most unyielding of locks. It's up to you."

Just then, two more men entered the room. Along with the fake police officer, they all came at her. Before she could mount any defense, they were on her, muscling her onto her back. Holding her in place, one commenced pulling her trousers loose.

"Get off of me you—"

Out of the blue, came the unmistakable hiss of silencer-equipped pistol shots. The weight crushing Tasha into the divan went slack. One attacker collapsed to the ground next to her; the stone-cold look in his eyes was all she needed to see to know he was no longer a threat.

The older man screamed, "*Ostanovi yego*!"

Rapidly, bullets took down the second attacker. The last man masquerading as an officer was wearing a bulletproof vest, which deterred a couple of shots before the unseen assailant put one into the thug's forehead.

Slowly, Tasha rose up to see Slaga, pistol in hand, come to the sofa.

"You are okay?"

Modestly pulling her trousers up, she nodded, tears welling in her eyes. Angrily, she turned to the older man, still seated, but now not so comfortably.

"General Pyotr," Slaga said.

"How do you know ... " Vadik paused, nodding in slow recognition. "Bruno Shakli," a tiny smile creased his lips, "or whoever you are. At last, we meet."

"Why are *you* here?"

Expansively spreading his arms, Vadik replied, "In New York? Greatest city in the world."

Though they'd served in the same army—and in many of the same campaigns in Afghanistan—Vadik had resided in the penthouse, as officers enjoyed so many comforts that enlisted men did not. Slaga had slept in mud and eaten shit. He traveled by foot and endured frigid nights and blast-furnace days. All while the officers ate caviar, rode most places, and kept warm.

Years of riding in coach made a man hard—made him resent his betters, coating his skin with a layer of low self-esteem, and a knowledge he'd never be good enough for their ranks. It also instilled an ability to assess things more realistically, to read the lay of the land—understanding human nature, that people behave one way when worried and another when they enjoy the upper hand.

Despite the elimination of his goons, the General seemed quite relaxed.

"No *mudak*, what are you doing here in this Clinic?" Slaga roughly asked, gesturing with his pistol.

"Ah, the Clinic. I'd heard they were doing great work here and wanted to see for myself. Imagine my shock and sadness to find that Doctor Grigor had been murdered."

Slaga sneered at the response. "We've derailed your plans, you condescending prick. The Inauguration will proceed without a hitch. You have nothing ... " Out of the blue, the incomplete idea returned from the mist.

"Ford is still programmed."

A thin smile creasing his lips, the General's silence goaded the non-commissioned officer. "Tell me, or I'll hunt your family down and—"

"And what? Kill them? Torture them? You have to find them first."

Slaga smirked, "I broke into your office didn't I? Finding your family will be easy. I'll torture your sons—and your women, well ... I hear white-slavery is big business in Southeast Asia."

Vadik's eyes narrowed.

Most of the conversation had taken place in Russian, but finally Tasha cut in. "If you two are done comparing dick sizes, I need Grigor's password for the Clinic's computer." Turning to Slaga, she nodded at his pistol. "May I borrow that for a moment?"

Confusion registered on both men's faces, uncertain of this new direction. Gingerly, Slaga offered the sidearm to Tasha, "The action is a bit light so—"

Sweetly smiling, Tasha took the weapon. "No, I'm good. Thanks." Turning she shot Vadik in the foot.

Stunned, Vadik doubled over in agony. Unused to such insolence and violence on him, the oligarch howled in rage. "Both of you—*dead*!"

Tasha leveled her weapon at the General's crotch. "I find that the threat of sexual violence, accompanied by escalating physical duress, often pries open the most unyielding of locks, but in your case, I'm skipping some steps. It's up to you."

Warily, Slaga's eyes moved between them. "Tasha, allow me." He gestured to the computer, "Let's find out what he's not telling us."

After a moment, the ME nodded, returning the sidearm to Slaga. Moving to the computer, she sat at the keyboard. As she turned to ask for the password, her eyes widened. Vadik thrust his right arm forward, a sleeve-concealed, wrist-mounted pistol telescoped into his hand.

Enraged, he directed a shot at Slaga. Tasha leapt out, deflecting his arm. The shot passed over Slaga's head. Without thought, and on full reflex, Slaga responded with a single shot to the middle of the General's forehead. A small red hole materialized. Vadik Pyotr stared back in shock before slowly collapsing to the ground and dying with an astonished final breath.

"Shit!" Why did you shoot him? It was a single-shot weapon. Now we'll never get the code." Tasha examined her watch before looking up at Slaga. "Do you think he was bluffing?"

"Reflex. I'm sor ... " Slaga shook his head silently before nodding to the computer. "You sure you can't get in?"

"Nine characters. I've tried just about everything. Before you arrived, I was going through Grigor's things to find a—"

"What?" prompted Slaga.

She looked up before returning to the keyboard. "A clue ... a hint. I remembered there was a picture in Grigor's home of some old Russian dude."

"Lenin?"

"No."

"Stalin?"

"No."

"Did you recognize any surrounding landmarks?"

"He was wearing a full coat to his ankles, standing on a circular base—oh, and there was a yellow building in the background."

Slaga nodded in recognition.

"Dzerzhinsky."

"You know him?"

"Founder of the modern secret police in Russia. Lenin's pit bull."

Tasha looked at the keyboard, "But that's eleven characters. We need—"

"Iron Felix."

Mouth agape, Tasha stared back. "What?"

"Felix Dzerzhinsky. He was the architect of the Red Terror. Bloody and merciless, that's what they called him—and by extension, the statue of him came to be known as the same."

Tasha grunted. Hesitantly, afraid to be wrong, she typed in the letters. Suddenly the computer burst to life. Elated, she jumped up, giving the mobster a hug. "I've never broken into anything before in my life!" As the moment of victory ebbed, her demeanor returned. "Right. Well let's see what Doctor Dipshit had."

There were numerous files about Ford, Polar Strike, history of programming failures, minor successes, and past case studies. After a couple of minutes, Tasha sat back in the chair.

"There's dozens of files. Nothing that would suggest a new trigger or programming. I gotta think we're done here."

Slaga—who'd been dividing his attention between looking through Vadik's clothes for a clue and looking over Tasha's shoulder, nodded slowly before sitting on the sofa—closed his eyes in thought. He asked, "You opened them all?"

"Yeah. Well there was one ... I couldn't read it. Like some other language or something."

Slaga's eyes popped open. "Show me."

Tasha moved the mouse pointer around the console. “Where did you go?” A second later, she said, “Here it is. I don’t read Russian that well but even the characters look off.”

Coming to the console, Slaga saw the file’s name глубокое растение. The former special forces man’s eyes widened and a Siberian cold wave—straight from Oymyakon—crept down his spine. “It’s old Russian I think.”

Detecting the dread in Slaga’s voice, Tasha quietly asked, “What does it mean?”

“The rough translation is,” Slaga’s brow furrowed in thought, “Deep Plant.”

Tasha clicked the file. It held two documents: a birth certificate from 1923 and a family tree. “This is in Russian, but the other looks like a—”

Slaga glacially reached into her vision. It was clear to him now. The family tree was the blurred image, from the documents he’d copied that day in Grigor’s safe. The idea he’d first imagined after stealing Grigor’s files finally stepped from the mist. With his finger, he pointed at the last entry on the tree and then traced the lineage to the top.

Tasha gasped, focus shifting from the family tree to the birth certificate. “Oh my sweet Lord.”

CHAPTER 92

JANUARY
THE CAPITOL
INAUGURATION DAY

Nic's neck pain intensified on colder days. With the longer lines in the main Rotunda Hall, Nic had had to use the bathrooms on the next level down, in the corner of the Exhibition Hall, now cordoned off from visitors. Nic's badge had bought him a courtesy wave through by the CPD officer at the steps. The trip down the staircase had only exacerbated his neck. As he reached the men's room, another door in the shadows across the Exhibition Hall softly opened and closed.

Staying in the shadows, Viktor and Ivan came to the men's room. Listening from outside, Viktor said to Ivan, "What a stroke of luck. That's him in the stall. Use the pen. When he's gone, prop him up on the toilet, close the door. No one is on this floor, but I'll keep the door secure."

In the men's room stall, Nic adjusted his shirt and trousers. Finished, he removed his jacket from the metal hook and pushed the door open. Striding out, he'd planned to don his overcoat in front of the mirror for one last fashion check. But stepping from the stall, his foot caught the partition, causing him to trip. As he reached out to brace himself on the sink counter, he felt, rather than saw, an arm pass over his head. The soft *clang* of metal on metal broke from behind him. A flashback of his attack by the mobster in the alleyway from early in his career sent him into immediate combat mode.

Spinning to his right, he found a man dropping a broken pen as he removed a second from his vest pocket. The man made a stabbing effort at Nic, who grasped the man's wrist, slowing the pen's tip, which

Nic could see glisten in the soft bathroom light. Realizing he had but a single shot at disabling the man while avoiding what he was certain was a poisoned tip, Nic lashed his foot up into the attacker's groin.

Disciplined to resist injury, Ivan's grasp on the pen remained firm while he backed away to reformulate his attack. Flying at Nic, Ivan was shocked when Nic cast his overcoat over his head, while simultaneously using Ivan's momentum to run his head into the wall, knocking him unconscious. Rapidly, the policeman was on him, scavenging his clothes. No ID. Another pen and a Sig Sauer. Nic's street sense alerted him to soft noise from outside the door.

"Ivan? Ivan?"

Nic quietly chambered a round before turning off the lights. In the farthest stall from the door, he stood on the toilet. Using the flashlight on his cell phone, he ensured that he could be seen in the bathroom mirror from the doorway. Pocketing his cell, he waited in quiet rage.

Viktor put his ear to the door. Totally quiet. He opened the door, to darkness. Without thinking, he put on the light. Seeing Nic in the mirror, he took a shot before realizing he'd made a fatal error. Nic had popped off two shots across the stalls into the assailant's head. Viktor fell to the ground, dead.

Finally, the breath exited Nic's lungs. He continued to stare, crying in fear and outright shock. It took a minute before he could stop rasping. Lurching to the washbasin, he splashed ice-cold water on his face. He got control of his senses, and hesitantly conducted a more thorough search of both bodies. Nothing. Professionals. Grabbing his overcoat, he left the men's room.

In Rotunda Hall, Nic made his way toward the dais as the band concluded an opening hymn. The Oath of Office commenced. Suddenly, his cell phone buzzed. Glancing at it, he recognized it was from Tasha. Reading the text as he made his way toward the inaugural platform, he stopped.

Nic's head rose; his face was a mash-up of disbelief, anger, and betrayal. Putting the cell into his pocket, he stepped purposefully toward the dais.

CHAPTER 93

JANUARY
THE CAPITOL
INAUGURATION DAY

The Capitol security detail stopped Nic from reentering the seating area. He could only watch as President Robert Johansen shook hands with Chief Justice of the Supreme Court. The newly installed Commander-in-Chief took his seat as the noted opera diva, Miso Devanney, approached the lectern.

Composing herself, she began from deep within—a low gathering, as if the bellows from heaven had been loosed, sending forth a rising baritone of unstoppable power:

"*God bless America, Land that I love ...* "

Nic's thoughts drifted back to the day that Chris and Mallory graduated from college. While his newfound, deeply painful memories of Elena had changed, he still held fast to his belief that the Fords were a genuine American success story.

" *... stand beside her, And guide her, Through the night with the light from above. From the mountains, To the prairies, To the oceans, White with foam ...* "

Devanney's voice rose with a fervor reaching deep into the soul of America. Nic's eyes teared as he watched and listened, his heart begging, "Oh God, please let Tasha be wrong. Don't let this happen." Still, his doubts held him fast in place, unwilling to move.

The singer's arms, face, and voice joined with that of the crowd, many sobbing, sending the last words up as a prayer:

"God bless America, My home sweet home."
"God bless America, My home sweet home."

Abruptly, Chris stood and stumbled, clutching his throat. Off guard, the Capitol Police hesitantly moved forward, uncertain what was transpiring. Nic did not wait. Dashing down the steps, his eyes never wavered from his target as Chris fell to his knees unconscious; the dais was now in an uproar. Shouting and screams mixed with calls for medical attention.

Seemingly from thin air, three Secret Service agents materialized, tackling Nic before he could reach his cousin.

At their seats, Mallory reached into her pocket for her medical injector. Uncapping it, she moved to Chris. Her attention turned to Johansen. With a desperate lunge, she sought to push the tip in the new President's neck.

Kicking one agent in the head, Nic smashed his elbow into the second's jaw before dragging the last agent a few feet toward Chris and Mallory.

As the needle neared its target, a massive hand reached up to intercept Mallory's wrist, diverting her deadly missile from its mission. Eyes wild, she looked down to find Nic's gentle, but disconsolate gaze—a bonfire of their family's aspirations. Shrieking like a wounded animal in its final convulsions, Mallory fought to escape Nic's ever-tightening hold as an army of Secret Service agents with CPD officers, mistakenly thinking Nic was also an assassin, wrestled both him and Mallory to the ground.

Uneasily observing events spiral from their mental grasp, many on the dais poured into the aisles, seeking the safety of the Capitol Building. In the broader audience below, hundreds of thousands of spectators watched in horror.

Chris's eyes opened. Seeing, but not understanding, he also sought to dislodge Nic's hands from Mallory.

"Let her go!"

The Secret Service had simultaneously muscled Johansen away before finally subduing first Chris and then Nic. Briefly free, Mallory attempted to pursue Johansen. With the confined space constricting his options, a Secret Service agent stepped back, unholstered and fired a Taser dart at Mallory.

Mallory came to an abrupt stop before dropping, incapacitated to the ground. The medi-pen dropped from her hand, hitting the ground as she collapsed atop it. Shaking himself free, Chris crawled to his wife. Kneeling by her, Chris Ford slowly rolled her over.

"Mal?" he asked.

By then, the awful randomness of fate had completed its appointed rounds. Mallory's once-joyful eyes looked back, un-answering. Chris's frantic gaze moved from his wife's lifeless eyes to the injector-pen she'd landed on, still attached to her blouse. As it had hit the ground, the syringe had inverted upward, the needle driving into Mallory's heart as she'd collapsed on it. Poison—intended for a President—flooded Mallory's upper chest, killing her instantly.

Uncomprehendingly, Chris held his wife in his arms, weeping. Nic sat on the dais next to his cousin, his eyes drifting to red, white, and blue bunting draping the Capitol.

CHAPTER 94

ONE MONTH LATER
THE CAPITOL

Uncomfortably situated at a large table—like she'd seen others sitting at on TV, Shelby stared at the hostile faces of fifteen Senators and Congressmen who'd been appointed to the Stillwater Special Committee, charged with investigating all facts and circumstances surrounding the attempted assassination of President Johansen.

The hearings, with a heavy emphasis on sensitive information, analysis, and interpretation, were closed to the public, but there were numerous representatives from the various intelligence services in attendance. Already overcrowded, the Committee room reeked of body odor, sweat, lunch, and anticipation.

Immediately after the Inauguration, President Johansen had assumed office with no disruption, but with the assassination attempt casting pallor over the day, most of the Inaugural parties had been cancelled.

Russian President, Vasily Malenkov, disclaimed any involvement with Deep Plant, even denying its architect had been a Russian. As various pieces of the plot were revealed, it became increasingly evident that during the height of the Cold War, the Union of Soviet Socialist Republics had in place—without even knowing it—a scheme to decapitate the leadership of the United States.

Within days, any support for Vice President Christopher Ford remaining in office had evaporated. Resigning, he returned home to Manhattan, where after burying Mallory, he had gone into seclusion.

Nic Ford, Tasha O'Riley, and Shelby Littlejohn had received national praise for diligently uncovering and preventing the assassination. Olegina Bortsova was prepared to return to Russia, but after cursory debriefing by the CIA, it was determined her knowledge of FSB, SVR, and especially the secret room in Lubyanka was a goldmine. Olegina opted to accept asylum in America—despite the outrage from Malenkov and demands by the Russian media that she be immediately deported back to Moscow.

The chairperson of the committee, Senator Tennent Stillwater, gaveled the session to order.

"Special Agent Littlejohn, thank you again for being here today. Before breaking for lunch, you briefed us on Senator Ford's family history in America and that specifically his grandmother, Elena, was in the employ of the Soviet security apparatus—both before and after coming to the United States. When we adjourned, you were detailing for us how the Deep Plant programming worked. I'd like to continue there."

Nodding, Shelby reached for a file. "Senator, as best as we can tell ... it didn't." This produced an uproar that Shelby waited out.

Slowly, Stillwater gaveled the room back to a semblance of order.

Shelby continued. "What I mean, Senator, is that it didn't work on the vast majority of the KGB's test subjects. It did work on Senator Ford, but only to the extent that it produced a mild suspension of his normal constraints against socially awkward behavior.

For the most part, human beings have built-in guardrails that keep us from behaving in strange ways—preventing us from crossing boundaries and bringing unfavorable attention to us. It was these restraints that Doctor Stephan Grigor was able to overcome in his work with the Fords."

"Why?" Probed Stillwater.

"First, we believe Senator Ford's actions were designed to distract everyone—including the Secret Service and Capitol Police—to allow the assassination to take place."

After another outburst of cacophony, the chairperson continued, "—and why was Mrs. Ford interested in assassinating the president?"

"We're not entirely sure."

This elicited wounded outrage among the committee members. A female senator from North Dakota yelled, "She was a damn commie!"

More gaveling. "Order!" Stillwater was now using his gavel more like a croquet mallet. "Senator Briggs, you will refrain from another outburst, do you understand me?"

Melting under Stillwater's withering glare, Briggs demurred. "Yes, Mr. Chairman."

Stillwater resumed the questioning. "Why don't you think you understand her reasons?"

"Well for one: she's dead. Her psychiatrist, Doctor Grigor, the supposed brainwasher, is dead. The Russian oligarch, Vadik Pyotr, who stood to benefit the most from the assassination, is dead. But we do know one thing about Mrs. Ford, and it only came to light just before the assassination attempt."

"And what might that be? What could possibly motivate the wife of the incoming Vice President of the United States of America to attempt to kill the President?"

Shelby sat for a moment. Taking a deep breath, she answered. "Through birth, Mallory Ford, née Everhill, was a direct descendant of Vladimir Lenin, the founder of the Union of Soviet Socialist Republics."

At this point, the room exploded. It took Stillwater five minutes to restore order. "What are you talking about, Agent Littlejohn?"

Handing a stack of papers to an aide, who commenced distribution to the committee, Shelby held her copy up. "As you can see on this family tree, Mrs. Ford's great-grandmother was named Laia Ilyushin. In 1921, she came to work for Premier Lenin and his family at the Governor General's Palace in the locality just south of Moscow, known as Gorki."

Shelby shifted in her seat, "It was there that Lenin, at first governed the new USSR. Then, later, he spent more and more time dealing with health issues. Mrs. Ford's great-grandmother was serving primarily as a chambermaid to the Lenins. With Lenin's declining health, his wife often stepped in on his behalf, to deal with activities of state in Moscow. She was gone for long periods of time and it was during these interludes that Lenin and Laia began an affair."

The room rattled with hushed undertones as Shelby continued, "Once this situation came to light, Ms. Ilyushin was quietly dismissed from the staff. But after Lenin's death, his wife, Nadezhda, took pity on Laia and provided for her and her newborn daughter: Galina. Galina and her husband, Fyodor, left the USSR in 1950—first for London and then New York. Galina and Senator Ford's grandmother, Elena, were ... or became ... good friends after their arrival in New York."

"Agent Littlejohn, was Elena Ford aware of—" the chair looked at the family tree, "—aware of Galina Dement's parentage?"

Shelby nodded, "We believe so. After her arrival, Galina Dement gave birth to her daughter, Sara. Sara and Elena Ford's grandsons, Michael and John, were raised together. They often thought of each other as unrelated cousins. After graduating college, Sara Dement married Stephen Everhill. Their daughter, Mallory, was born a couple years later."

Murmuring around the chamber reminded everyone that while the hearings were closed-door, due to the national-security aspects of the case, Shelby's comments still underscored the lurid nature of the facts and proximity of assassination.

She continued, "Referring again to the genealogical record, Mallory Everhill and Christopher Ford were married soon after college and embarked on their respective careers."

A hand went up.

Senator Stillwater nodded, "The Chair acknowledges our esteemed colleague, Representative Nix of Baton Rouge, the Chairperson of the House Intelligence Committee and Co-Chair of this committee, Mr. Chairman."

"Thank you, Mr. Chairman. Agent Littlejohn, about when did Elena Ford and Stephan Grigor initiate the brainwashing of the Fords?"

Shelby took a file from an aide seated behind her. Glancing at it, she said, "Undetermined, Senator, but reviewing Doctor Grigor's files, we think soon after infancy."

"Why so early?"

"We think Doctor Grigor believed the children were more open to thought manipulation—"

"You mean ... brainwashing."

"Yes, Mr. Chairman."

Outrage was more contained this time, requiring less hammering by Stillwater. Finally, he nodded to another member of the panel, "Agent Littlejohn, I'm going to open things up to other members of the committee. The chair recognizes our esteemed colleague from New Jersey, Senator Abernathy."

Immediately a woman spoke, "Agent Littlejohn, I've known the Fords for years. I find this all too wild to fathom—a Hollywood scriptwriter could hardly imagine a more implausible scenario. How did Doctor Grigor overcome Mrs. Ford's natural mental defenses to induce her to such a horrific action?"

"Senator, thank you for your question. We believe that Doctor Grigor was using new blue-light therapies that may have allowed the implantation of thought conducive to these actions." Shelby took a breath before continuing. "We're still deconstructing Doctor Grigor's notes, but apparently a variant type of pulsating blue light—along with gentle electro-simulative charges—were able to transmit a type of photon information beam into the Ford's brains that implanted the assassination instructions. And with Mrs. Ford, she also was subjected to repeated exposure to images of her great-grandfather, as well as those flattering to the USSR and the propaganda of the proletariat—which allowed for the laying of programming that we think disrupted her prefrontal cortex and amygdala's ability to distinguish between the good of the proletariat and the evil of assassination."

Abernathy and her fellow senators stared in quiet confusion before Shelby continued.

"In other words, Senator, it's like coding on a semiconductor chip. Information and commands are processed like a decision tree. One plus one equals two, but one plus two equals three are examples of simple logic decisions. But complex decisions between good and evil, require more information to make a choice. Mrs. Ford's decision tree was corrupted, blurring between right and wrong inputs to making a correct choice or avoiding a bad one."

Questioning continued like this for the rest of the afternoon before the committee agreed that more research into the complexities of Grigor's programming would be necessary. Senator Stillwater resumed control of the meeting.

"Special Agent Littlejohn, thank you again for both your heroism and the copious amount of information you shared here with us today. While the committee recognizes there will likely be years of investigation ahead on this unfortunate moment, what are your immediate next steps?"

"Senator, we are still looking for former FBI National Security Section Chief, Sarah Boxer. We're still uncertain how, but she escaped from being handcuffed in the ladies's room where she sought to kill me." Shelby rolled her neck, as if removing a horrifying truth of the betrayal before continuing, "It appears that General Pyotr had his hooks in her. For how long, we're not sure. Clues found in her condo suggest she's fled abroad, possibly Cuba or Venezuela. Many of General Pyotr's thugs have been taken into custody and are being debriefed by the FBI and NSA." Shelby took a sip of water, gathering herself. "As most of you know, Speaker Adam Byrnes has also dropped off the grid. Prior to the Inauguration, he'd been under surveillance for passing information to the Russians, specifically General Pyotr. However, initial investigation into the Speaker suggests he was most likely ignorant of the assassination plot."

"What leads you to this conclusion?" challenged Stillwater.

"Interviews with his wife, family, and staff reveal nothing unordinary about his behavior or actions prior to the attempt on President Johansen's life. Analysis of video before and during the events on the Inaugural dais suggest the Speaker was just as surprised by events as everyone else. Since the Inauguration, Speaker Byrnes has gone to ground. The Russians claim to have no knowledge of his actions or current location.

"Lastly, there was a woman at the center of General Pyotr's operations who we've been unable to identify or determine her whereabouts. As you know, my encounters with this woman were brief and when last I saw her, she'd BASE jumped from the top of the Capitol, landing on top of the CSPAN building. We recovered her parachute, but it traced back to General Pyotr. Her skill set, with regard to close order combat, weapons, and comfort with high risk operations, were very developed; this suggests familiarity with intelligence gathering and possible affiliation with another country's security apparatus. We'll continue looking for her."

"Was the government of Russia involved in any of this?"

Shelby shook her head. "That's a question better intended for CIA or NSA, who I believe your committee is meeting with next. FBI does believe this was a one-off operation that fell through the cracks of history to land in the lap of a particularly brutal, but opportunistic, oligarch: General Vadik Pyotr." Shelby cleared her throat and continued. "It was his intent to assassinate the President and then after it became known that the assassin was Mallory Ford, Senator Ford would, most likely, not have been allowed to assume the Presidency. This would have elevated the Speaker of the House, Adam Byrnes to the Oval Office. Pyotr would have been able to sell influence the world over. As you know, he left the employ of the government of the Russian Federation years ago, but he was still close to President Malenkov—whether Malenkov was aware of Pyotr's actions is still ... unclear."

Stillwater put his gavel down, but it was clear he was not yet finished with his inquiry. "Agent Littlejohn, I only have one more question. Why make the attempt at the Inauguration? Why not wait sufficient time after the new administration had been in office for a time?"

Shelby leaned forward in her seat as imparting the wisdom of the ages. "You know Senator, I have no earthly idea. But, I have thought about it a little ... and I can only surmise that throughout its history—back to Peter the Great—Russia has felt a little disrespected by the West. This is a proud people, who *since* Peter the Great, have just had the bad luck of ... not decades, but centuries, of really *lousy* leadership. For General Pyotr this was just greed and he didn't care when it took place, the sooner the better. But maybe for Doctor Grigor, and possibly Mallory Ford, it was a way of making the big statement. Something like: 'We can strike you at your very core at any time. Never forget we are here. There is always a *reckoning*.'" She paused to look at her hands, "I'm not sure we'll ever know."

CHAPTER 95

ONE MONTH LATER
BUENOS AIRES

After killing Vadik Pyotr, Slaga had tipped his proverbial hat to Tasha and faded into the night. On the night of the murders at the Galaxy condos, Slaga had taken the liberty of transferring his accounts from Switzerland to his other bank in the Grand Cayman Islands. The next day, he'd moved some funds to an account in Argentina and arranged for the purchase of a unit atop a building near the Juan Segura Golf Course.

Olivia would soon be joining him. After getting sloppy with the Galaxy fiasco, he was very careful to launder her travel itinerary. He'd arranged for her to move to Madrid, then Paris, back to Madrid, then Miami, and finally Buenos Aires.

After Olivia had arrived, she began teaching Slaga about his new hometown. Awakening to sunrises over the Atlantic, they savored coffee on the balcony before breakfast at Pertutti or the El Faro Hotel. Never a big water man, Slaga found himself drawn to the shore overlooking the River Plate leading to the Atlantic. The shore seemingly swept his nightmares, fear, and pain away.

And beckoning was a world of night life, horse racing, and casinos.

As he stood on his balcony overlooking the Rio Platte, to the east, and the city to the south, Slaga allowed himself the pleasant thought that finally he could sleep again.

* * * *

NEW YORK

Nic rang the doorbell. After a moment, the door opened.

"Wow, you look—amazing."

"Why thank you, as do you."

They walked to the car where he opened her door before moving to the driver's side.

After normalcy returned to his world, Nic had been in his office staring out the window when there came a knock at his door.

"Come," he'd called. A smile came to his face when Tasha O'Riley entered.

"Inspector."

"Officer O'Riley."

"Please, call me Tasha."

Nodding, Nic smiled. "Tasha, how have you been?"

"Good but ...how are *you* doing?"

Pausing as a melancholy look—that lately had taken up residence on his face—threatened an outbreak, Nic fought it off, "...okay."

Awkward silence ensued before Tasha half mumbled, "Look, I was wondering—I mean, I have tickets for a martial-arts show at the Garden this weekend, and I was wondering if you'd like to go?"

Nic had almost forgotten what hope looked like, but in that moment, joy temporarily evicted depression. Smiling broadly, Nic said, "I'd love to."

* * * *

NEW YORK

Holding a picture from a trip to Tahiti last year, Chris gently traced Mallory's face with his index finger. She'd been so excited about the future. Their future. It was all possible. Within reach.

Putting it down, his eyes landed on a picture of Elena standing beside him on his first day of third grade. Another future. Another possibility.

Finally, he turned to the lamp stand where a pistol sat. Picking it up, he opened the cylinder—each chamber filled with death at the ready. His eyes drifted back to the picture of him and Mallory standing in the warm waters of the lagoons of Bora Bora. Slowly, he lowered the gun, removing each round. Taking the weapon and bullets to the kitchen, he depressed the pedal to his nickel-coated garbage can and dropped them into the waste.

* * * *

Costa del Sol

The porter put the bags down, collected a fair tip—one not likely to make an impression—and left the room. The woman stepped onto the patio. At the pool below, sun worshippers baked beneath an appreciative sun while others sought more vigorous pursuits at the beach beyond.

With her tablet, Sigrid found sanctuary in a cabana overlooking the nearby lagoon. Through a series of secure channels, she accessed her various accounts. Running a quick tab in her head, she figured she had a little over eleven million euros, approximately thirteen million plus dollars.

She'd been shocked and a tiny bit disappointed to learn of the General's death. It was a good gig while she had it ... exciting and allowed her to give vent to her ... needs.

In addition to her liquid assets, dumping her Stockholm and Manhattan properties would yield another couple million—more than enough to get a fresh start. Maybe Los Angeles—she just needed a large metropolitan area, preferably in Europe or America, with places given to ignoring what's right in front of them.

CHAPTER 96

INAUGURAL REMARKS OF PRESIDENT ROBERT K. JOHANSEN

"Mr. Chief Justice, President Lane, Vice President Andrews, members of Congress, the Inaugural Committee, members of the global community, and most importantly, my fellow citizens—thank you for joining me today.

"It is here today that we celebrate that most unique of traditions. The peaceful transfer of power from one American to another. No other country offers such a display of self-confidence and sacred trust as the Inauguration. At these times, we gather with both nostalgia and hope.

"In times of transition, we cherish our history, while conceiving of new horizons. Days past are examined and adorned with ornaments of our accomplishments, while failures are banished to history's dustbin. The future we offer is always better than the past that gave birth to it. This is our nature as Americans, and human beings, to be ever courageous, aspirational, and optimistic.

"What summons this spirit of hope? A dream of what America can, should, and ought to be. Liberty is the best architect for building a nation committed to the betterment of her citizens. It gives sustenance to our vision of how to improve the lives of our fellow countrymen. Our vision is forged in the crucible of our passion. And yet good government, the best government, is passion—tempered by common sense.

"America is led by this duality. A tension that exists between a noble desire to affect the lives of our citizens for the better and a prudent restraint on an intrusion upon the very right of people to live their lives as they see fit. This administration seeks to better meld this balance.

"What is this better way? New government is similar to a ship leaving port for the first time. Cautious, but desirous of knowing what her capabilities are. What can she accomplish? What are her limitations? Our administration will seek this knowledge in real time—with a focus on quickly advancing new ideas without overreaching the support and backing of our citizenry.

"Our initial focus should be on improving our economy. Enriching the lives of all Americans is not overreaching, but rather the first responsibility of government. To give Americans the skills to integrate into a twenty-first century marketplace, this administration will seek to create a new-jobs training program that ensures every worker who wants a job will be skilled for a job. Let the word go out that America is open for business and is ready with a modern workforce prepared for any challenge.

"As America looks to craft her future, she will look outward and upward. Our greatest aspirations are here on this planet—as well as outer space. Climate change demands a reengineered response. How do we best adjust to the new paradigms of living on Earth? These times expect a bold response. One that summons echoes of the New Deal and the creation of a new Works Program Administration that seeks to respond to rising tide and temperature through innovative solutions incorporating nature and human creativity. What jobs and economic enrichment could be created through the combating of forces that threaten to weaken our standards of living and way of life? America can, and America will, lead this revolution of imagining the American city, workplace, and home.

"But let us not forget the heavens where our imaginations take flight. Throughout its history, our space programs have not only pushed the horizons of exploration, they have also served as the accelerator of scientific accomplishment. They have divined unimagined insights into the cosmos while inventing a multitude of new technologies that demonstrably changed our lives. Artificial limbs, solar heating, pollution remediation, water purification, food safety, LED lighting, and a universe of healthcare innovations are all results of American's ascendancy into space. To the stars, we shall return with a focus on new knowledge as well as a better understanding of quantum mechanics and how it can shape a better, more efficient, and improved world for our citizens.

"Globally, America will remain engaged with all nations. We seek harmony with every country, but we live in a volatile world filled with ideologies antithetical to our own. From the dawn of the republic, America has always been counted on to provide support to our allies. Our foreign service is the best trained, best equipped, and best supported in the world. Every day, around the planet, they quietly go about the business of purveying, projecting, and protecting America's interests.

"However, there are always countries and cowards who—in their own selfish preservation—seek to oppose us and oppress their people. For them, we say '*not on our watch.*' If you won't seek to defend the basic human rights of your citizens, then we will use every tool available to us to oppose you. And where our citizens, interests, and property are threatened, we will not hesitate to unleash America's terrible swift sword to protect them.

"Lastly, but of paramount importance, our greatest national treasure: our children. We must commit to investing in young people. They are our lifeblood; the promise of tomorrow is unachievable without them. Our hopes and security rest on the generations to come. Equipping them to achieve their dreams, moves America forward, while simultaneously creating a critical mass of economic and inspirational energy vital to our Manifest Destiny. They are the bedrock of a prosperous, ambitious society, committed to equality, peace, and advancement for all.

"If we believe in the certainty of destiny and in freedom, then we believe in the wisdom of our citizens to make good choices that shape that destiny. Our elected leaders should seek to cast a framework for those ideas to succeed and yet not be intrusive in their design and implementation. Government should aspire to be the silent partner in the weaving of the great tapestry that is America.

"Today, we are challenged with great new demands from different corners of America—demands that cry for recognition and resolution—environment and education, rights and responsibility, health and budget, protection and freedom.

"So, my Fellow Americans, let us resolve to make this a monumental, epochal time of transformation. One that takes hold of each and every one of us, sweeping us away to a promised land—one of opportunity, change, and hope—to a time that leaves us breathless in its audacity, and yet grounded in the assurance that no American will be left behind.

"This will be a time of *can do*, where no dream is too bold or can't be achieved. Today is the dawn of the American Ascension from the wisdom of our past into the promise of our collective abilities.

When people gather in that distant time and look back on these days, they will surely say *this* was the Age of Triumph."

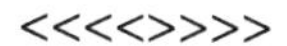

Made in the USA
San Bernardino, CA
09 July 2020

75196937R00206